just stop me

escape to new zealand, book nine

rosalind james

synopsis
♡

Sometimes you have to run away to find yourself.

Lots of young women dream of being a princess. Nina Jones isn't one of them. After escaping from her palace/prison in the back of a gardener's van, she ends up in a beach cottage on New Zealand's South Island. She's meant to be looking after a cantankerous widower. Too bad she doesn't know how to boil an egg.

Iain McCormick may be an All Black, a member of New Zealand's elite rugby team, and a bona fide celebrity. During the offseason, though, he's meant to be a regular Kiwi bloke. A good son, a good neighbor, and a good citizen. But civility comes harder when you've been dumped at the altar. He doesn't need anybody he has to look out for. He definitely doesn't need to fall in love.

Yeah, right.

author's note
♡

table of contents

♡

acknowledgments

♡

Many people aided in the research for this book. Any errors or omissions, however, are my own.

My sincere thanks to the following: the wonderful people at Kaiteriteri Kayak for telling a probably-insane novelist how to put a kayaker into mortal danger and get her out again; Sharron Hickman of Exclusive Tours for my unofficial-but-amazing Waiheke tour; Ed Coutts of Waiheke Unlimited for the luxury homes tour; Christine Hafermelz-Wheeler, goldsmith and specialist jewelry maker, for the tour and the explanation of her craft; and Robyn Langwell for letting me live in Nina's cottage. And thanks to Anne Forell and Victor Romero for watching so much rugby with me!

Thank you to the All Blacks for winning the Rugby World Cup for the second consecutive time in 2015, and for continuing to inspire me by their example on and off the field.

As always, thanks to my awesome critique team: Barbara Buchanan, Carol Chappell, Anne Forell, Mary Guidry, Kathy Harward, and Bob Pryor, for helping make the book better.

Finally, a special thank-you to my husband, Rick Nolting, for his support in this crazy journey.

Generally, by the time you are Real, most of your hair has been loved off, and your eyes drop out and you get loose in the joints and very shabby. But these things don't matter at all, because once you are Real you can't be ugly, except to people who don't understand.

- From *The Velveteen Rabbit,* by Margery Williams

the swan princess
♡

Nina Jones lay sleepless in the Swan Bed and thought about Marie Antoinette. And not in a frivolous-queen kind of way. More in a head-chopped-off kind of way.

Marie had slept in this bed, too. It hadn't worked out all that well for her.

You are not getting your head chopped off. You're getting married. Get a grip.

She stared up at the underside of the bed's canopy in the light cast by the ornate antique lamp set on the rococo side table. The gilt carvings gleamed, and the cream silk draperies, shot with gold thread and embroidered with flowers, cascaded down on either side of the bed. A huge gilt-framed mirror on the opposite wall reflected the room, from the wedding-cake icing of wreaths and ribbons in the heavily plastered white ceiling to the golden curtains pulled across the expanse of multi-paned windows, sealing in the warmth against the January chill. And, of course, there were the priceless paintings, part of one of the world's great collections, making their own statement. Paintings that would have been beautiful if they hadn't looked so... gloomy. Still lifes and portraits of bewigged ancestors, almost all with black backgrounds.

Why did still lifes always have to include rabbits, anyway? Who wanted to look at a dead bunny?

She closed her eyes and imagined a bedroom in a tiny cottage at the beach. Wide plank floors with a little sand sifting, unremarked and disregarded, between the cracks. A white iron bed piled high with pillows, with a cream-colored throw tossed across at the foot just in case you wanted to snuggle in. The windows open to the soft sea air, the tang of salt nearly palpable, bringing in all those mood-altering ions. Plain white curtains hanging to the floor, drifting a little with the night breeze. The sound of wind in the trees—palm trees? Yes, definitely. Maybe wind chimes, too. Bamboo ones, off in the distance, their faint music lulling you to sleep, stealing into your dreams.

No. She opened her eyes again. That wasn't real life. She had to quit daydreaming.

She'd never played Truth or Dare—she hadn't had that kind of adolescence—but it was time for it now. Call it Truth *and* Dare.

She pushed the down comforter aside, swung her bare feet onto the exquisite, antique Chinese silk rug, and prepared to get real.

truth and dare
♡

Nina headed out her bedroom door and down a hallway lined with carved wainscoting, passing the marble busts of severe-looking ancestors set on pedestals in semicircular niches. All the way down the broad corridor and around to Matthias's suite, situated in a corner of the seventeenth-century building overlooking the lake. The best view, for the most important person.

Matthias hadn't gone to bed yet. She found him working at his laptop, sitting in his private study wearing a dark paisley dressing gown over his pajamas, his blond hair gleaming in the light of a desk lamp.

As always, he closed the lid when she entered the room. "Sabrina," he said. "We discussed this. We are not spending the night together this week. Not until the wedding."

"That's what I want to talk about. The wedding. I've had some…thoughts."

He sighed; a faint, patient sound. "There's nothing to talk about, or to think about, either. The arrangements are all made, and you have nothing to do but attend. You have your schedule. If there's any difficulty, you can consult Raoul."

She wasn't getting fobbed off on his scary chief of staff, though, not this time. She sat down on a silk-upholstered

3

chair in a masculine pattern of rust and brown. "I do have a difficulty, and I'm not going to consult Raoul. I'd like some... time."

"Some time," he repeated. "What sort of time? I'm not understanding you."

He still looked handsome; a fairy-tale prince from a fairy-tale romance. He still looked coolly good-natured. It had taken her a while—too long, but then, his whirlwind courtship hadn't allowed much time for thought—to realize that he always got his way. If he didn't have to raise his voice, that didn't make him any less determined, or any more willing to compromise. It just meant he made assumptions other men couldn't afford. Assumptions that he would be able to get exactly what he wanted.

"It's all gone too fast," she said. "We've hardly been together in the past two weeks, ever since I arrived in Neuenstein. I know this is any woman's dream come true, but I'm not... I'm not sure."

His brows shot up. "Have you discussed this with your mother?"

Everything in Nina tightened. "No. And that's another thing. My *mother?* I'm twenty-five. I've been earning my living since I was four." She saw the faintly derisive twist of his handsome mouth and said, the force of her fury shocking her, "And, yes, that's exactly what it's been. *Earning.* Hard work."

"Modeling."

"Yes. Modeling."

Be a good girl. Do what the man says. And she'd done it, no matter what. When she'd been scared, when she'd been sad, when she'd been sick, for more than twenty years. She'd been reliable, and she'd been professional. Always on time, always prepared, always in shape. And always prepared to do what the man said, because it hadn't been only her future, it had been her mother's, too. She'd known that from the time she'd known anything. But it had become harder and harder to shut down the feeling of "wrong," and now, it was impossible.

4

There was an alarm shrieking in her head, and she couldn't turn it off.

She'd always told herself that eventually, she'd be done with modeling, and then she'd be in charge of her own life and could choose her own path. Well, the rest of her life was here, and it was now.

Matthias must have noticed her stiffen. "Well, that's all over, isn't it? And a girl's best friend is her mother, they say. Cold feet are natural, but there's nothing to worry about. Go to bed, Sabrina."

She wasn't just stiff now. She was rigid. "I'm not ready to marry you," she said, and saw his head jerk back at last. "I want to wait until I'm sure."

His expression wasn't quite as amiable, although his faint smile didn't alter. "Not possible. The guests have already begun to arrive. The wedding is in five days."

"I know it's inconvenient," she said, hating the pleading note in her voice. "I know it's embarrassing. But how inconvenient and embarrassing will it be if we find out afterwards that we've made a mistake? And you can do this. You're the prince."

"I'm aware of that."

"So you can do what you like. You know you can. Give me a month. We can always do it quietly later on. I feel rushed, and I don't think that's right."

"We don't have a month, and there's no such thing as 'quiet.' Not in my world. So here's what we're going to do," he went on, overriding her protest. "Tomorrow, you and your mother will go to the hunting lodge for a few days. Take some quiet time in the mountains. I know this has been an adjustment, a strain, and the last thing I want is an unhappy bride. Once you get some rest, you'll feel better. I'm afraid you'll have to do the appearance at the children's hospital first, but after that, you can have some time in the fresh air, far away from the cameras and the public. Restore your equilibrium."

"No," she said, and saw his blue eyes widen, his mouth

harden, just for a moment. "A few days aren't going to do it," she continued. *Strong,* she told herself desperately. *Determined.* "I need an announcement. That we're putting it off."

"But you must see, my darling Sabrina," Matthias said, his tone gentle, "that that's impossible. We *are* going to be married."

"Would you rather I say it in the cathedral? Because that's how I feel." She forced herself to continue despite his change of expression. "I *can't* say 'I will.' I can't say it and mean it. I try to see myself saying it, and I... I..." She groped for the words. "I can't," she said again. "I know this hurts you," she added desperately, "and I'm sorry. I'm so sorry. I know your mother—"

She broke off, then. His face had taken on a grim look she'd never seen. She'd never dared to bring that up, and she'd been right.

For a moment, she felt a disquieting shudder that was nearly fear, and then he spoke. "It'll be all right on the night," he said, and he was back to looking calm again. So self-assured, so self-controlled. The things she'd always admired in him, and the things that had always intimidated her, if she were honest. "Stay at the hunting lodge until the day before the wedding, in fact. It'll add to the mystique. The bride unveiled. You and your mother can relax in the meantime, and you'll see, it'll be everything you've dreamed. You wouldn't want to let her down, or me either, because of a whim or a childish fear, would you? And if you'll excuse me," he said, getting to his feet, "it's time for both of us to be in bed, especially you. You have a busy day tomorrow, and you're feeling overwhelmed right now. I understand that. It's enough to make anyone hysterical, isn't it, being a princess? You'll see, though, how you settle in once the deed is done. Meanwhile, you can take some time, restore your nerves, and prepare yourself to make me proud."

In the hunting lodge. The hunting *fortress*, more like. Remote. Isolated. Guarded.

She looked into his calmly smiling face, and she knew that he meant it. He wasn't going to let her go.

no surprises

♡

Iain McCormick's mother was late. Again.

He signed autographs for a couple of eager young boys, then stepped back, pulled his hoodie a little farther down over his face, and slouched against the wall of the International Arrivals Hall in the Auckland airport, attempting to conceal his 6'6" frame as best he could.

It wasn't that he minded signing, exactly. It was more that he wasn't fit for public consumption. He wasn't shaved, he wasn't rested, he wasn't happy... and he wasn't under any illusion that any of that mattered.

Harden up.

He'd been up at five to meet his mother off the London flight and accompany her south to Nelson. Which wasn't bad—she was his mum, after all—but she should have come out the doors first. That was what you paid the extra money for. Passengers kept straggling out, though, without her appearing amongst them, and he was getting a bad feeling.

Then she turned up, and the bad feeling got worse.

It wasn't that she looked bad. She didn't. Slim and fit as always, her brown eyes sparkling with vitality, her dark hair cut sleek and shorter than usual. She'd clearly had a glam cut in London.

But she wasn't alone. Oh, no. Of course she wasn't. She was carrying a bald, chubby baby and chatting nineteen to the dozen to a frazzled-looking woman pushing a luggage cart piled with two suitcases, a stroller, and an infant seat. The three of them were trailed by a teenage kid in baggy black track pants, a bright red flat-billed cap with "SF" on it, and an orange fleece jumper. Iain noticed the kid because he was pulling the big flowered suitcase that could always and only belong to Iain's mother.

He'd offered to buy his mum a new suitcase last year. She'd said, "But why, love? I've had this one for yonks, and it still suits me. Besides, I can always find it on the carousel." Which made sense. Anything louder than that hot pink, bright yellow, and fluorescent green would have been banned on humanitarian grounds. Add in the orange fleece and the cap, and the kid pulling the case was a screaming neon sign.

Iain waited another moment while the woman with the cart was greeted by a big fella in shorts and jandals. The bloke was kissing his missus and taking the baby now, though, so Iain grabbed his duffel and ambled forward at last, shoving his hood back along the way.

His mother saw him coming, of course. Most people did. But most people didn't have the same reaction she did to the sight. She called out, "Iain!", grabbed him close, and squeezed him tight, then pulled back, laughing, and reached up to hold his face between her hands, her eyes searching his. "How are you, my darling?"

Embarrassing, maybe. But it was nice to know your mum was always happy to see you.

"Not too bad," he said, which wasn't quite true, but close enough.

She smiled, gave him an affectionate pat on the cheek as if he'd been two, and said, "But where are my manners? This is Angela... and Tom, isn't it? Feel as if I know you already. I'm Carmella. I met your wife and the wee fella on the journey. This is my son Iain, here to meet me."

Iain shook hands with the bloke, who looked up at him

and said, "Iain McCormick, that right?"

"Yeh," Iain said. "Pleasure."

The woman said, "Well, there's another surprise," and laughed. Keyed up, still. Fatigue could take you that way, after twenty-five hours or so. "Your mum's been so kind, trading seats with me and all, just because Oliver was fussing. Traveling in style, that was us," she told her partner. "First class all the way from London, can you imagine?"

Iain glanced at his mother, she looked straight back at him with a challenging glint in her brown eyes, and the couple moved off after a few more words of good-bye.

"Every time," Iain told his mother once the little family was out of earshot. "Every single time. I don't know why I bother."

"It's not every time," she said. "It's occasional. Consider it your charity work, via me. Anyway, how ever could I relax up there in my comfy bed after meeting Angela? The baby was fussing, poor wee thing."

"I do my own charity work. And everybody in Business Select must've loved that."

"Rubbish. Babies cry. It's their job. If anybody minded, they could just get over it." She looked searchingly at him again. "Still narky, I see. Iain, you've—"

"Nah, I'm fine," he said, cutting her off. "How's Vanessa?" He'd much prefer to talk about his sister, the reason for his mum's UK visit.

She paused a moment as if deciding whether to push it, but finally said, "Going on well. Sad for me to leave, she said, but I imagine Henry was keen to have me gone. Three weeks with a mother-in-law in the house is about as much as flesh and blood can bear, new baby or no."

That one got a smile out of him, one of the rare few these past months. He didn't go on, though, because the kid was still there, hovering one step behind Iain's mum.

He wasn't a boy, though, Iain suddenly realized. He—she—was a girl. Tall, and more than thin. Fine-boned and narrow through the shoulders and hips, which was why she'd looked like a boy to him. Well, that and the height. And the clothes. She'd been standing there staring at the five-meter-tall statue from *The Hobbit* set as if it were supremely fascinating. Finally, though, she quit studying the Dwarf King and looked at him.

He saw dark eyes partly concealed by heavy, angular black spectacles, a square face, some serious cheekbones, and a whole lot of mouth, her full lips turning up at the outer corners as if she were smiling. Some trick of her features, that was all. She definitely wasn't smiling. Her face was pale, completely bare of makeup, and the cap hid all of her hair, so it must have been short. He couldn't imagine how he'd thought she was a boy, but all the same, it wasn't a great look, and the baggy fleece jumper and oversized track pants weren't doing her any favors either.

She was still holding the handle of his mother's suitcase, so he reached out and put a hand on it. The girl let it go so fast he nearly dropped it, then stepped back.

"I'm sorry, darling," Carmella told the girl. "I almost forgot you. You're so quiet, but that's no excuse. That's what that journey will do to you, isn't it? Iain, this is Nina."

"Morning," he said, and *didn't* shake hands. Was he going to have to meet the whole bloody plane? Had his mum organized a jolly sing-song back there in Economy? He wouldn't have put *that* past her either.

"Nina's coming home with us," his mum said.

Iain turned from where he'd been preparing to leave—*finally*—and stared at his mum, then glanced at the orange girl, but she was looking down again. "Maybe we could have a chat," he told his mother.

"Or maybe we could have a coffee." The tone of his mum's voice brooked no argument. "It was a long flight, and more to come."

"I'll be right back," the girl said. Her accent was... American, probably, but with a tinge of something else. And her voice was something else, low and dark and husky. A whisky voice, the kind you sipped and savored. Or maybe she just had laryngitis.

"We'll be over there," Carmella said, indicating the Long White Café in one corner of the echoing Arrivals hall. "Iain will order you a coffee. What would you like?"

"I'm just… just a minute," the girl said. And she was off.

Iain breathed a bit easier when she was gone. "Mum. No."

His mother wasn't headed toward the coffee counter. Instead, she was looking after the girl, an unaccustomed frown appearing on her face.

Iain walked on, willing her to follow him. "What is that," he asked, "her prison uniform?"

"Are we judging by appearances now?" his mother said tartly. "I'd have thought you'd have learnt a bit better by now."

"Cheers for that."

"Well, honestly, darling, what's it to you? She was my seatmate, and she was lovely. And what's more, I've found somebody to keep Dad company, since heaven knows that's not going to be me."

It was one of the odd facts of life that his gregarious mother didn't always get on with her own dad. But then, Iain's granddad was more than cantankerous, especially since his wife's death the previous year.

"He thinks you boss him," Iain said. "And I won't say he's wrong. But wait. *What?* No."

"Nonsense," his mother said. "Is that really what Dad says? Men. They want you to baby them, and then when you do, they say you don't respect them."

"This girl." Iain persisted doggedly, moving up one spot in the short queue for the coffee. They wouldn't have needed to queue if his mum had been in Air New Zealand's comfy Business Select, in the seat he'd taken care to secure for her. She'd have been filled with all the coffees she could've drunk. She wouldn't have met the girl, either. *'That's* who you've found to help Granddad? What do you know about her? And no, I'm not talking about how she's dressed. I'm saying that she won't look me in the eye, and she doesn't have any luggage. You *can't* keep picking up strays. It's not safe. She could be a criminal, for all you know."

His mother snorted. "A criminal, right. That sweet thing? And not *safe?* I'm not a good judge of people now? I don't think that's me, love."

Iain stepped to the front of the queue and suppressed a stab of... call it annoyance. Call it that.

"Sorry, darling," his mother said with a sigh. "I know. But I don't think you'd like any girl just now, do you? She may be in trouble—in fact, I'm sure she is—but there are all kinds of trouble. Trouble isn't always your own fault. I'm willing to bet hers isn't."

He didn't bother to answer that. The girl was going to come back, and he was going to have to be polite. He was a New Zealander, he was an All Black, and he'd been raised by this woman, all of which meant that there was no other option but "polite."

But no more than polite. It was going to be a coffee, a shake of the hand, and goodbye.

No lame ducks. No strays. No surprises. He'd make that clear to his mother.

Yeh, right.

dream come true
♡

Nina washed her hands, then took off the glasses that had been doing their best to give her a headache, set them on the counter beside the sink, and wished she could leave them there. She hadn't realized how much even the lowest-strength reading glasses would blur her vision.

She didn't take off her hat, though, and definitely didn't check her no-doubt-matted hair. She didn't want to look at what she'd done. She didn't remove the elastic bandage binding her breasts, either, even though it was feeling like a medieval torture device, or maybe the world's longest mammogram. She needed to wait until she was well clear of the airport for that, and she needed to *get* clear fast.

On the thought, she was once again checking the ziplock sandwich bag that contained her stash of cash and her passport, driver's license, and bank cards, wishing she'd thought to pin the bag inside her clothes. Finally, she pulled out the little travel toothbrush and tiny tube of toothpaste that were almost her only possessions.

At the moment. Just at the moment. Just for now.

Carmella and her aged, widowed father had seemed like the perfect solution to her dilemma, falling into her lap like magic. A place to hide far from the city and the media, and

14

someplace to live that wouldn't cost her anything and might even pay a bit. A chance to relax, maybe, with... normal people. *Nice* people.

It had seemed too good to be true. And it *was* too good to be true, because she'd finally accepted, she hoped, that there was no such thing as magic, and definitely no such thing as rescue.

And because of Iain. She hadn't been expecting Iain. He hadn't seemed enthralled by the prospect of her working for his family, and he'd looked about as easy to move as a mountain.

He was the size of one, that was for sure, all solid arms and legs, massive shoulders, and deep chest. She'd put him at close to 250 pounds, and he was never going to win any modeling contracts. A ferocious face, maybe even a little scary, with dark stubble covering his slab of jaw, a crooked nose, and a white line of scar tissue bisecting one devilishly slanted black eyebrow. Mostly, though, it was the look in those shockingly blue eyes. That stare of his could pierce right through a person, and that was what it had done to her.

He wasn't excited about his mother picking her up, it was clear. And she doubted he'd be subtle about expressing his opinion.

The woman beside her finished washing her hands and headed over to the hand dryer, a toilet flushed behind her, and Nina put her toothbrush down and rinsed her mouth, postponing the moment when she'd head out there again.

The white, strained face in the mirror didn't look much like the woman who'd confronted Matthias two—three—however many days—earlier. But it was the face of the woman who'd run away from him.

She'd gone from his suite back to her own bedroom that night, had dressed in jeans and a sweater, and *hadn't* packed a bag. Instead, she'd sat on the bed and waited until six, when the palace doors would be unlocked.

Maybe she would have been allowed to do it. To simply have walked out of the huge front doors and through the iron gates, past both sets of guards. To have refused the men's protection and insisted on walking alone in the dark to the village. From there, she might have found a way out, somehow, and maybe nobody would have stopped her. But if they *had* stopped her... what then? Would it have been the hunting lodge at once? Or was that a stupid thing to fear? She didn't even know.

She could have gone to her mother, too. But her mother was so excited for her to marry Matthias, so sure, so... insistent. She had been from the start. And as gutless as Nina knew it was, she hadn't felt able to stand up against both of them. She couldn't have withstood her mother's stricken eyes, the knowledge of all her mother had done for her, her happy belief that this was the culmination of her life's ceaseless effort to get Nina to the top.

She'd reached the top. Now all she wanted was to find a way down.

She'd written a note to her mum on the stationery she hadn't been meant to use until after the wedding. It was all she'd had, though, so she'd pulled out a heavy cream sheet with its embossed deep-blue crown and, beneath it, the stylized logo of a forward and backward *S* that had been especially designed for her.

S for Sabrina, because she wouldn't be Nina anymore. And *S* because it would be her only initial. She wouldn't have a last name, either. She would be Sabrina of Neuenstein, and that was all. Visible to the entire world. And... erased.

She'd looked at that crown, at those intertwined initials, and had felt nothing but panic.

Dear Mum, she'd written,

I had to leave. I'm sorry. I love you.

Nina

She'd left the note on the desk together with her huge sapphire engagement ring, just one piece from the Crown Jewels she'd been shown in the vault the week before. The jewels that would have been hers, the ones she was leaving behind without a single regret.

At six, with the palace just beginning to stir with liveried servants who'd pressed themselves against the corridor walls when she'd passed, she'd gone downstairs and taken her usual walk through the grounds. A walk that didn't have to be monitored, because the heavy black iron gates were.

She'd forced herself not to run through the silent, dark gardens to the former stable block that housed the outdoor staff, where she'd risked a quiet tap on Axel and Gisele's front door, then done her halting best to explain the situation to one of the palace's many gardeners and his comfortable wife.

"I don't want to put you in a bad position," she'd said when she'd been sitting on the couch in their tiny living room, holding a cup of tea she wasn't managing to drink, "and I'm sorry. Just… if you had any ideas."

It had been too much to ask of people who didn't owe her a thing, just because one of them was a kind-eyed man with gentle hands who'd talked to her about roses, and his wife had a nice smile. But she hadn't known what else to do, so she'd asked anyway.

"You were right to come," Axel had said. "I will take you to Gisele's uncle Fritz, and he will see you on from there. Now, while things are still quiet, but there are delivery trucks beginning to come and go. I will say it is for supplies. I will *make* it be for supplies. And Fritz will do the rest."

"But… it's the prince," Nina had said.

"Ah," Axel had said, and smiled. "But you see, we do not all love the prince. Fritz is a republican. And he has a daughter in Switzerland."

Nina hadn't left the palace in a gold coach after all. Instead, she'd left in the back of a gardener's van, buried under sacks of fertilizer, fighting nausea at the stench. And when she'd heard Axel's quiet voice saying, "We are through the gates," she'd begun to shake with relief, had had to stifle tears.

Overdramatic? Probably. Hysterical? Maybe. What was the worst that could have happened?

She'd thought about it as Fritz's daughter had cut her hair and combed the color through it, as she'd rummaged in her husband's closet and come out with the clothes Nina was wearing now. What would actually have happened if she'd made a fuss in the entry hall that would have forced the guards to let her go alone, or even if she'd had the courage to wait and say "No" in the cathedral?

Nothing, surely. It would have been over. This wasn't the eighteenth century, and nobody could have made her marry Matthias. Nobody would actually have thrown her into the dungeons. Even though the palace *did* have them. Matthias had given her a tour of them the week before, saying, "My ancestors could be ruthless, as I've mentioned."

He *had* mentioned it. And she'd seen the family motto, too. Part of the coat of arms carved into the paneling of the Great Hall, etched into the mantelpiece of the huge hearth in the library.

Teneo quod meum est.

"I hold what is mine," Matthias had translated in his perfect Oxford English. "Or 'I hold my own,' if you like. Or both."

He'd looked at her, smiling gently, and she'd been able to tell that nothing had changed. The motto still fit.

And, overdramatic as it might seem in hindsight, she'd done it. She'd made the choice. She'd walked out. Now, she settled the canvas shopping bag over her shoulder, walked out of the toilet, and prepared to take on New Zealand.

a little backbone
♡

Iain was close to the head of the queue, watching a single hard-working barista alternate between taking orders and making coffees. In the only coffee shop in the international terminal of New Zealand's largest airport. The scale of it told you pretty much all you needed to know about the country, and was the reason why, as often as he left, he always came back.

His mother called out "Nina!" and Iain looked around to see her walking straight past them, a traffic-cone flash of orange and red. She turned her head, checked her step, and came over to join them.

The fella in front stepped to one side, and Iain was finally able to approach the coffee counter. "One long black and one trim flat white, please," he told the barista. "What can I get you?" he asked Nina.

"Skinny latte, please." She didn't say it to him. She told the barista, then dug in the depths of her tote, pulled out a twenty-dollar bill, and handed it over.

"I've got it," Iain said.

She turned and leveled those dark spectacles at him. "No, thank you," she said, taking her change. "I do. I'll be right back." And she was off again.

"Still think she's a criminal?" Iain's mother asked, heading over to a long counter under a giant green mural of a sheep-dotted One Tree Hill to wait for their coffees. "Confidence artist, you reckon? Not too flash at ingratiating herself, is she?"

Iain set the suitcase in place beside him. "Well, could be she's training." He smiled at the snort from his mum, then caught a glimpse of the newspaper left at one end of the counter.

Runaway Bride? screamed the bold black headline. His smile died, and he reached out a long arm and flipped the paper over, but not before his mother noticed.

"Are they still going on about it, then?" she asked.

"Dunno. I don't look."

"Well, that's wise," she said. "How's your dad? Have you been chatting with him at all?"

He glanced more sharply at her. "A bit. I'd say he's missed you."

"Did... did he say that?"

The barista called out their orders just then, and Carmella began to jump to her feet, but Iain put out a hand. "I'll get it." And when he came back with the coffees, she began to talk about something else. About anything else.

$\heartsuit\heartsuit\heartsuit$

Nina turned her back on the sparse crowds trickling through Arrivals and tried to ignore the prickling at the back of her neck.

Nobody is watching you, she told herself, but after weeks of being followed everywhere she went, the feeling was hard to shake.

What was the difference between being guarded and being monitored?

Reporting. She answered her own question. A kindly question from Matthias about the money she'd withdrawn from the bank—*her* money. About the dresses she'd bought.

Asking to see them.

Or maybe the right word was *Control.*

Two tries, and she hadn't yet managed to enter the correct fourteen-digit code from the phone card she'd just bought in the airport shop. She fought back tears of frustration. *Try again. It's pressing a few numbers, that's all.* If she couldn't handle this, how would she ever manage everything else she had to do?

Finally, the phone was ringing. And ringing. Three times. Four.

"Hello?" The voice was elderly. Irascible. Five AM, Melbourne time.

"Granddad?" Her own voice quavered despite herself, and she had to shut her eyes for a moment.

"Nina-Girl?"

That brought the tears closer, and it took her a moment to answer. "Yes. It's me."

She heard a kerfuffle at the other end of the line, and then it was her gran talking. "Nina? We're just on our way today. Tell me you're ringing us because you've had second thoughts."

Nina had to hold the phone away from her ear for a moment. "I... how do you know?"

"I've heard it in your voice anytime these past two weeks," her grandmother said impatiently. "I've tried to tell your mum, but she wouldn't listen. I hope she's listening now."

"I didn't tell her. Gran, I've... I've run away."

The words were barely a whisper, but her gran heard them. "Good on you," she said. "Where are you?"

"I can't tell you. And I know that sounds crazy," Nina hastened to add. "Maybe it is. I can't tell that either. But please—tell Mum I'm safe. Tell her I'm sorry." She gripped the hard plastic receiver tight and had to reach out with the other hand to steady herself against the phone console. "I won't call again, not for a while. I just... I had to do it. I'm sorry."

"Darling," her gran said. "Listen to me."

It was her no-nonsense voice, and Nina thought, *Please don't tell me I'm wrong. I can't stand another person telling me I'm wrong, telling me what to think.* She stood, numb, and waited to be told.

But that wasn't what she heard.

"You don't have to do anything you don't want to do," her gran said, and Nina was having to prop herself up again, but from relief this time, and gratitude. "You're an adult woman. You can choose what you do, and you should be doing exactly that. If you ran away, you had a reason. If you don't want to tell us, you don't have to. You don't owe that Matthias a thing, and I don't give a toss if he's a prince. You do what you need to do and never mind the rest."

A rumble in the background, and her granddad must have grabbed the receiver. He was barking, "Too right," in a voice that had Nina holding the receiver away from her ear again, to wince this time. "You tell that bugger to go jump in his lake," her granddad continued with no diminution of volume. "I'll tell him so myself, if he rings up. I'd say you need to come to us, though. Come now."

"No," Nina said. "I can't. Honestly. It's better if I don't. And, please, Granddad. Don't tell Mum where I am, all right? Just for now. Just for a little while." She didn't want to drag anyone else into this, and she didn't want to be where Matthias could find her. Her mother would tell him, Nina knew it. Her mother was no more capable of standing up to Matthias than Nina was herself. And then they'd *both* come, maybe, and... the dread rose at the thought. She couldn't handle it, weak as that was. She needed to disappear where nobody knew her, to be anonymous until she knew she could be with people without being... without being erased.

She heard more muffled, spirited conversation, if you could call it that, at the other end, and then it was her gran again. "You do what you want," she said. "I'll sort your mum, and I won't tell her anything, either. At least I won't tell her *that*. I'll put a flea in her ear about the rest of it, though, no worries. I've been telling her for twenty years to stop pushing you, and this is how it ends up. No surprise to either your granddad or me. She's your mum, and she loves you, but she never could tell the difference between her dreams and yours. You go on, now. But if you need us, you come. Or call. If you need anything at all, you tell us."

"I love you, Gran. Both of you." Nina choked up a little, but that was all right, surely it was. Just for a moment.

"And we love you, my darling. Now go on and get started on that life of yours."

It took her two tries to get the receiver back into its cradle, but she was finally tucking her phone card into her plastic bag and heading back to the café.

Would Carmella and Mr. Scary still be there? Maybe so, and maybe not. She wasn't sure which outcome she was hoping for. Right this minute, all she wanted was to leave, to take a bus into the city and find a spot at a backpacker's hostel, and then a job in some far-flung spot. A farm, or a café in some inland town where people cared more about... about the lambing, maybe, than they did about minor European royalty and its latest scandal. At least that was what she assumed. She'd never been to New Zealand, but she knew that sheep figured into it.

The thought of going back out there to somebody who knew her—even somebody who'd just met her—made her nervous, as foolish as that was. But she'd seen the stack of newspapers when she'd bought her phone card.

First the headline, big and black. *Runaway Bride?*

And beneath it, just visible above the fold, a head of shining dark hair crowned by a borrowed diamond tiara, the radiant smile pasted onto her face as she'd learned to do so many years ago.

Her absence had been noted, clearly. She didn't want to know any more. She needed to disappear. *Just for a few weeks,* she told herself. *Just until I can think straight. Just until I figure out what to do.* Her life was out of control—out of *her* control—but there had to be an answer. She just hadn't thought of it yet.

Right now, she was as far away from Matthias as it had been possible to get without actually heading to Antarctica, and that was Step One. That was what had made her walk to the Air New Zealand counter instead of United or Qantas. Her first thoughts had been LA or Melbourne, but those were the first places Matthias—or her mother—would look. She'd wanted "remote," and she'd got it. The country's South Island would be even more so, which was a terrific reason to go there. So she ignored the throbbing in her head from the horrible glasses, the ache in her breasts from the cruel elastic bandage, and the dragging fatigue that made her want to sit in a corner and weep, and went back to the coffee stand instead of finding that bus.

They were still there. Iain's broad back faced the room, but his mother looked up and waved, and Nina straightened her shoulders and headed toward them, sliding quickly onto a stool next to Carmella and ducking her head over her coffee.

"All sorted, dear?" Carmella asked.

"Yes. Well, I don't have my ticket to..." She blanked on the name. ". . . onward yet." She took a sip of lukewarm milky coffee. "But the plane doesn't leave for two hours, right?"

"To Nelson? We can take care of that," Carmella said, and Nina didn't miss the way Iain's head shot up at the words.

"No," Nina said. "I'll buy my own ticket." *And then what?* the cruel inner voice mocked, and she shoved it back down.

"Good," Iain muttered, not quite under his breath.

"I can see you have reservations about me," Nina said, hardly able to believe her nerve. "Can I ask you what the problem is?"

His eyes, which had been narrowed, flickered a fraction. "Are you saying I'm being rude?"

No front of amiability or softness with *this* man. The hardness was right there to see.

"Maybe I am." She didn't dare look at his mother. This was her new leaf, and she was starting out right, no matter how hard that was. Iain wasn't a prince, he wasn't a celebrity, and he didn't have any kind of power over her. If she couldn't stand up to a normal man, what hope was there? "Or maybe you're just being honest," she told him. "Maybe you could tell me what your issue with me is, and we'd have something to work with." She stopped, then, and tried to keep looking at him.

"Right," he said. "Right." He paused, his black brows drawn down over his nose, and she waited.

When the questions came, he fired them out like bullets, and they tore into her in exactly the same way. "Why are you here with no luggage? Where are you from? You don't sound English. Why would you want a boring job like this, looking after a stroppy old man out in the wop-wops for what I doubt is going to be much pay? You're not very glamorous, it's true, but you could probably do better."

Carmella made a faint noise of protest, and he looked at her and said, "She asked for honesty. She's *not* glamorous. It's obvious."

"It's all right," Nina told Carmella. If she'd wanted confirmation that her disguise was working, she had it. And if she'd ever wondered how men treated women they didn't find attractive, she knew that now, too. "I'm not glamorous, no," she told Iain. "I hadn't realized that was a requirement for this job. And I'll point out that you're not exactly glamorous yourself."

It seemed she had a little backbone after all. Who knew?

But, really. The man was wearing blue nylon gym shorts, a hoodie, and flip-flops. Plus, he had that face. He'd only have to walk into a bar to have every bouncer in the vicinity standing up and moving into position. And he was criticizing *her* appearance?

His eyes were trying to smile, and his grim mouth wasn't having any. "You could be right about that."

Get it over with. "I want the job because it sounds like a quiet spot, and that's what I'm looking for. I've got no luggage because I was in a hurry, but that'll be remedied as soon as I buy some clothes. I have an Australian passport, which makes me eligible to work here. And I like older people. I like them better than younger people, to be honest again." *I certainly like them better than you.* "If you hire me, I'll do my best. I don't take anything on unless I'm prepared to do my best."

He blinked at that, and that was all. "You don't have an Aussie accent."

"I've been living in the States for years, and in the UK a bit too. But I'm true-blue dinky-di all the same." She put her hand into her carrier bag, which she'd been clutching in her lap, pulled out the little blue booklet, flashed the kangaroo and emu at him, then shoved it back inside before he could ask to look at it more closely.

"Not always a selling point on this side of the Ditch," he pointed out.

The Ditch. The Tasman Sea that separated New Zealand and Australia. "Maybe not, but it's true, so…" She shrugged with a nonchalance she didn't feel. "Anyway, I'm here to work, so either take me on or tell me to bugger off so I can get a bus into the city and find somebody who wants me."

It sounded brave. Pity it wasn't real, that she'd had to channel her granddad for the "bugger off." She needed this job. Anyplace else would ask even harder questions. She had no work experience that would count for anything, and she didn't want to let anybody study her passport and put two and two together.

To get the job, though, she had to pretend she didn't need it. *Fake it till you make it.* She kept her chin up and willed it not to tremble. She didn't think she was succeeding, but his hard eyes had softened a little.

"You're tired, eh," he said, and just like that, she felt the tears welling up.

"Yes," she said, forcing them back. "I am."

"Sorry about that." He did look sorry, at least a little bit. And he kept asking questions all the same. "You said you left in a hurry, though. Why? What job did you do before? Are you wanted by the police? Have you committed any crimes?"

"If I had, I surely wouldn't tell you, would I? And I'm not going to tell you what job I did before." She hurried on even as his eyes widened and his mouth opened to speak. "But I've always worked, and I know how to do it. And crimes against fashion, maybe, but that's all." She skirted the issue of the police. She wasn't "wanted" in the way he meant, anyway. "Am I qualified to look after your grandfather? Probably not. Am I willing to do it? Yes, I am. So whatever you decide, say it and let's get on."

He produced an actual smile at that. "You really *are* Aussie, eh."

"Are you done, darling?" Carmella asked him a bit waspishly. "Honestly. Dad just needs somebody to cook and clean for him a bit, somebody tough enough to stand up to him, hopefully interesting enough that he quits moping, and not desperate enough to steal his bits and bobs, none of which are worth anything anyway. And you know he'd be driven mad by some jolly-hockey-sticks middle-aged lady. Seems to me that Nina fits the bill on all counts."

Except the "not desperate" part, but at least she didn't steal. And she wasn't too sure about "interesting" or "tough" at this point, either. She wasn't jolly, so that was one out of four, maybe.

Iain raised hands the size of oven mitts in a gesture of surrender, then dropped them to the table. "Yeh. I'm done. I still can't see why she'd want the job, but if she does, I reckon it's her funeral. But if Granddad tells us they're getting married, don't say I didn't warn you."

Nina had been feeling a bit more charitable toward him. The "sorry" had helped, and so had the smile. His final remark, though, had her spine stiffening again.

"Trust me," she said, "I'm not going to be marrying anybody. That's a promise."

a biddable girl
♡

Eleven thousand miles away, another conversation was taking place.

"Enter," Matthias called out when he heard the quiet knock on his study door. He didn't look up from his computer, though, until he'd finished studying the financial statements he was perusing. And even then, he didn't invite Raoul to sit down.

He hadn't raised his voice since he'd been a teenager. There were more effective ways to communicate one's displeasure.

"Yes?" he asked when he finally closed the laptop and lifted his head.

"Some news," the chief of staff said, and if he were anxious or upset at being in his prince's disfavor, he didn't show it. The hawklike eyes under their hooded lids were as inscrutable, his posture as erect as ever.

Matthias doubted the news would make him happy. If Raoul had had anything important to report, he wouldn't be here at the routine time Matthias had scheduled for this daily report—nine o'clock at night.

Raoul went on. "I have Gerhard"—Matthias's chief of security—"working on the task from all angles. Sabrina's

28

checking account shows activity. She withdrew three thousand Euros from the branch of her bank in Geneva. After that, nothing on any of her accounts or cards."

They'd got the account numbers and access from Sabrina's mother, Trudi, right at the start, when she was at the stage of hand-wringing anxiety for her daughter. Whether she were anxious that Sabrina was losing her chance to make her own and her mother's fortune, or truly worried about her daughter's safety—that, Matthias couldn't tell, although he had his suspicions.

Matthias's gaze sharpened. "So little? And nothing since? She's not gone far, then."

"Three thousand was the maximum the branch allows in one day."

Matthias dismissed that with a wave of his hand. "Silly girl. All she'd have had to do was make a bit of fuss."

But then, Sabrina *didn't* make a fuss.

A biddable girl, they'd used to call it. The phrase was out of fashion these days, and the idea as well, but not with him. Not with most men, if they were honest. A beautiful, obedient wife, a wife other men envied him and lusted over—that had been his goal. A princess who would appear gracious, ladylike, and elegant in public, who would be popular with his people and a soft face for the monarchy, and who would bear his children and not give him any trouble in private.

A hard thing to find, but he'd found her. Better if she'd been a virgin, of course, but there you were, you couldn't have everything. She'd told him she'd only been with a few other men, but it probably wasn't true. Women lied; it was their nature. She *was* sexually tentative, though; quick to doubt herself. That suited him as well. Raw material was always the best; the easiest to mold into the shape you preferred. The last thing he wanted was a woman who issued orders in bed, the sort who was always telling you what she wanted, intent on her own pleasure. Another modern development he could do without.

She was the best candidate he'd ever found, in fact, and he'd acted fast to secure her. He was thirty-five, without an heir, and his pursuits were dangerous. He liked fast cars, fast planes, and fast ski slopes. He craved danger and action in the same way timid Sabrina craved security. And he hated his younger brother. He needed sons, two for preference, and as quickly as possible. He'd gone to all this trouble to woo and win Sabrina so she could give them to him, and he wasn't letting her go now just because she'd had a whim and succumbed to her fears.

They'd had a word for that, too, back then. "A fit of the vapors." He should have soothed her more the other night, perhaps have taken her to bed after all, have tied her to him more tightly. She'd felt alone, and that had frightened her, as so many things did. He should have kept her close by his side until the wedding. In his bed. In his room. He'd take care to do it, once she came back.

Her leaving for good wasn't an option. It would make him look ridiculous, and he never looked ridiculous. And besides, she was the best one, and he always got the best one.

"And from there?" he asked Raoul. "What else?"

The other man didn't shrug. Raoul was too controlled for that. But Matthias could hear the shrug in his voice. "From there, we have her on the British Airways flight to Heathrow. A ticket agent recognized her. But nothing since."

Matthias picked up the gold pen on his desk and rolled it between his fingers. "Did you check passport control out of the UK, in case she moved on?"

"On an Australian passport? Not possible to get into that system."

"You said anything was possible for Gerhard."

"Not that."

Matthias accepted it with ill grace. "It doesn't matter anyway. With only three thousand Euros, and nothing withdrawn since, it's unlikely. She doesn't know how to do anything but model, and if she goes to her agency, I'm sure Gerhard can at least trace *that*."

The UK made sense. It was nearby, inexpensive to fly to, and she was familiar with the country. He'd have expected her to run to the States, back to LA, but who knew what foolish idea Sabrina would have come up with?

"And Trudi's accounts? What of those?" he asked Raoul. He'd questioned Sabrina's mother as thoroughly and impressively as he could, but she truly seemed to know nothing. After that, Matthias's first impulse had been to suggest that Trudi would be more comfortable back in her own home. But it was always unwise to give into impulse or emotion. Better to keep her here, where he could monitor her more easily. Sabrina would be back soon enough, one way or another. Better to have all going on as normal until then. He'd told the guests and the press that she was at the hunting lodge, and nobody knew anything different. There was gossip, yes, but there was always gossip. As long as he got her back by the wedding day, everything would be fine.

He'd asked Trudi to inform him, of course, if she heard from her daughter. She'd sworn—with tears—that she hadn't. He knew Raoul would keep a close watch on her activities all the same. Just in case she *did* care more for her daughter's whims than for her future.

"Nothing on Trudi," Raoul said. "We have her phone monitored, of course, and her email as well, but she's had no communication with Sabrina. Not with anybody in the family, in fact, but her own parents."

"In Australia," Matthias remembered.

"Melbourne," Raoul agreed.

Matthias frowned down at his desk. "Check on them as well," he decided. "Sabrina's close to them." So eager for somebody to love, which was another thing that made her perfect. She'd never leave him once the first baby came. He'd make it clear that he'd never let his heirs go, and she wouldn't leave without them. Not like his own mother. She'd been happy enough to run off with her sons' swimming teacher in a scandal that had titillated the world. That would never be Nina. He'd been convinced of it.

Damn it. Where *was* she? The rage rose, and he shoved it coldly away. Rage wouldn't get the job done.

"Expensive," Raoul said. "Unless we hire somebody in-country to get into the phones. They're calling Trudi from a landline."

"Nobody in-country," Matthias said immediately. "And the expense doesn't matter. As to how she got out—what do you have there?"

The heavy eyelids drooped. "Nothing. The cameras show her leaving the palace, walking on the path toward the gardens, as always. We've checked and re-checked the footage at the gates, around the perimeter, and found nothing. The staff all swear they didn't see her. She disguised herself and climbed into the back of a tradesman's van, perhaps, and left that way, although they say not. Over two dozen vehicles left the grounds that morning. We've checked them all, and we have nothing."

Matthias hissed through his teeth. "It *cannot* be nothing."

"Everyone has been asked."

"Then ask them again. If you and Gerhard can't do this— find somebody who can."

farewell spit
♡

Iain stretched out his legs in the bulkhead seat on the right-hand side of the 50-seater Air New Zealand turboprop and stared resolutely out the window. He'd looked around once to check on the girl behind him and seen her squashed into the window by the big Samoan bloke in the aisle seat. She'd been fast asleep with her head resting uncomfortably against the glass, the ugly black specs askew, the ball cap sticking out to the side. If anybody had ever looked at the end of her rope, it was her. Which didn't fill him with confidence that she could handle his irascible grandfather.

Do not feel sorry for her, he told himself. *You are not responsible for whatever's going on. She isn't your problem.*

If she hadn't bought her own coffee, maybe, and her own ticket. If she hadn't pulled the cash for it out of that pathetic carrier bag, hesitated a moment, then handed it over with what he could tell was resolution screwed out of her depths. If she hadn't had dark circles under her eyes, and hadn't forced her chin up and met his eyes with what had looked like the very last of her courage. And if what she'd said hadn't resonated with him the way it had, a punch straight to his gut in that husky little voice.

I don't take anything on unless I'm prepared to do my best.

Now, though, he wasn't looking at her, and he certainly wasn't looking at his mum, seated beside him. He hadn't been back to his family's place for nearly three months. Not since the fifteenth of October. And he didn't want to go now, which was why it was time to harden up and do it. It was only for a week.

They'd crossed Cook Strait, and the South Island was appearing beneath him, impossible to ignore. Starting with the sweeping arc of Farewell Spit stretching out a full thirty-five kilometers, a thin, curved crescent of white against the crystalline blue of sea and sky. And all of it was right there again, the whole disastrous weekend crowding in close. No shoving it away, not anymore.

His mum must have seen the tension in his back, because her hand came to rest on his shoulder. "All right?" she asked quietly.

"Yeh." He didn't look at her. "Course." And after a moment, when he didn't turn, she dropped her hand.

The green valleys and undulating hills were coming into view beneath him now, with the mountains rising behind them, the deep blues and forest greens a dark background to the shining golds and emerald greens of the coast. The flight attendant told them to raise their seat backs for landing, but Iain didn't need telling. He'd been sitting bolt upright for the entire hour. And he truly thought, for one craven moment, that he couldn't stand it. That he was going to land in Nelson, buy another ticket, and turn straight around and leave again.

He'd been sitting in this exact spot that day. Maybe on this exact plane. Chalk it up to bloody-mindedness that he'd chosen the same seat today. And it hadn't been his mum next to him then. It had been Sienna, with most of the rows behind them filled with friends and family coming to see them married on what was sure to be a beautiful day, because almost every day was beautiful in this sun-kissed northern section of New Zealand's South Island.

If any place were truly "Godzone," surely it was the sheltered spot where his grandparents had spent their entire lives, and where his parents had moved to join them four years ago. The site of Iain's happiest childhood holidays, and, he'd thought, the perfect setting for his transition into this latest stage of what had been a pretty bloody good run so far. And Sienna had been amenable, hadn't wanted to be married from her own parents' home in Hamilton. Because she'd been embarrassed by its modesty, he realized now. A warning sign if he'd ever seen one, and one that he'd ignored.

His niggles hadn't had a chance to settle, only two days out from eight straight months of professional rugby. He'd still had a black eye, in fact; relic of the final Bledisloe Cup match against Australia. And he'd had another month of test rugby to go with the All Blacks, some of the toughest of the year. But Sienna had had sporting commitments of her own with the Silver Ferns in December, just when Iain's season ended. As always, they'd been two ships passing in the night, grabbing their chance to be together. Even for their wedding, their brief honeymoon. They'd take a longer break in January, they'd promised each other, when they could take it together. And Iain would go on tour a married man, which had suited him most of all. It wasn't the wedding he'd cared about anyway. It was the marriage.

He hadn't felt any of the aches that day. Not that he ever paid them much notice. They were as much a part of a rugby player's life as the ever-present gym and the white lines marking the pitch, as sweat and tape and hard collisions and bursting lungs, as creeping doubt and fierce resolve and the overwhelming desire not to let your mates down. He'd played every match of his career prepared to leave his heart and soul, not to mention his sweat and blood, on the field in support of his teammates. He'd counted himself lucky to do it, and had known they'd do exactly the same for him.

He'd known all about commitment, and he'd been ready to give it. He'd held Sienna's hand, looked out at that same graceful curve of white sand down below, and felt... blessed.

Until it had all turned to custard, that is.

♡♡♡

She'd done it at the altar.

She'd walked all the way down the aisle of the Anglican church in Motueka on a glorious spring day, preceded by a tiny flower girl who was some sort of cousin of hers, then by her teammate and best friend, Hailey Roberts. Hailey had looked petite, pretty, and glossily brunette in scarlet satin, but Iain hadn't looked at her, much less at Hugh Latimer, his best man. He hadn't looked at anybody. The congregation had oohed and aahed over the flower girl's progress, but Iain had barely noticed. His eyes had all been for the tall, slim ivory figure drifting down the aisle on her dad's arm, her face concealed by her veil, her steps slow, nearly faltering, her dainty heels treading the pink rose petals into the carpet. He'd watched her and thought, *It's happening.*

It was tempting to think, now, that he'd known, that there'd been a moment of disquiet, of premonition. But in truth, whatever he'd seen, he'd chalked up to pre-wedding jitters and their lack of time together. Anyway, he had enough steadiness for both of them. She loved that about him. She'd always said so.

Pity that it took two after all.

So, no. He hadn't known. He hadn't guessed. That she'd get to the altar, accept her father's squeeze of the hand before he left her to sit in the front pew, then turn to him, and still—*still*—not have told him. That as he lifted her veil, his heart pounding as if he'd been playing in the toughest match of his life, she'd look at him, her blue eyes stricken, her breasts in the low-cut gown rising and falling with her rapid breath, and say, "Iain. I... We have to talk."

♡♡♡

Nina's body jerked up against her seatbelt with a heart-stopping jolt. Her eyes flew open, and she threw up a hand and let out a cry. A roar filled her ears, and her body was still trying to hurtle forward.

Oh. The plane had landed. Never mind.

"All right there?" the big man beside her asked. He was tattooed and huge, taking up more than his allotted seat space, but then, she took up less, so that worked out all right. And his face was kind. She was noticing that these days.

She squinted at him, felt for her glasses, and pushed them back into place, which blurred his features considerably. "Fine," she told him. "I'm fine." She looked out the window to avoid any more questions, and saw that the little plane was taxiing toward a small building that must be the terminal. It was less than a minute before the plane had pulled to a stop. Another announcement, and the man beside her was standing up, moving into the aisle, and reaching into the overhead bin.

Nina didn't stand. She didn't have anything to reach for. Besides, they were going to be exiting down the stairs at the rear of the tiny jet, and she was at the front. It was going to take a while to empty a plane full of holidaymakers, almost all families and couples. Of course that was what it would be, on a weekend just after the New Year. Vacation time. Family time. For other people.

She noticed that Iain didn't stand either. He was too tall to make that anything but awkward. He'd taken off his hoodie, though, leaving him in a slightly wrinkled gray T-shirt with the Adidas logo on the front. Another fabulous fashion choice.

She waited until he'd passed her, then followed him down the narrow aisle. He had some truly spectacular arm muscles, with forearms much bigger than her own upper arms, and an expanse of shoulder that had to be seen to be believed. The man was *huge*, in fact. Even his neck was about twice as thick as a normal man's. How did you get your *neck* that muscular? He was like some kind of mutant new species of superhuman.

Wonderful. She'd been going for "easy." Instead, she'd ended up with The Incredible Hulk.

Meanwhile, her head was throbbing mercilessly, and she wasn't sure her aching breasts would ever be the same again, despite the painkillers she'd taken back in Auckland. And she needed something to wear that wasn't orange. That would be good.

She was on the metal steps now, the last one out of the plane. A light breeze pulled at the thin fabric of her athletic pants, but the air was soft and warm, the sun not quite hot. She saw mountains in the distance, and got a momentary flash of disquiet. But this was nothing like Neuenstein. The mountains weren't high enough, except for a few peaks glimpsed far to the south, through gaps in the nearer hills. What it was, was overwhelmingly... green. Houses climbed the slopes, but not far. Beyond that, it was just gentle folds, trees and grass and ridgeline, and then the bowl of serene blue sky.

Space. Peace, maybe.

With The Hulk, though? Maybe not.

She followed Iain's broad back across the tarmac and into a high-ceilinged room that seemed to be all there was of Nelson Airport besides an outdoor patio where travellers were relaxing with coffees and beers. Iain didn't linger, though, just headed out the front door. Most of the passengers from her flight were already there, standing around waiting for something, but she couldn't think what.

"Bag claim," Iain said.

On the *sidewalk?* Not too much of a surprise, though. The whole thing was amazingly casual. She hadn't had to go through any security to get on the plane in Auckland, and there didn't appear to be any at all here. She hadn't realized there were still places in the world where you didn't have to be screened.

She expected Carmella to say something, but Iain's mother wasn't paying attention. Instead, her eyes were sweeping the curb, her body rigid with what looked like tension. But nothing happened, other than a tractor coming around the corner pulling a metal cart piled with bags, then the driver hopping out and detaching it even as passengers yanked their suitcases off and headed for curb or parking lot.

Two quick toots of a horn, and a green older-model RAV4 was pulling up to the rapidly emptying curb. Iain moved toward it with his mother following, and Nina lagged behind, unsure of herself. Were they changing their minds about her? Was she going to be stuck in this airport, miles from a totally unfamiliar town in a foreign country?

The hysteria tried to rise at the thought, and she forced it back. *You were just thinking a few hours ago that you wanted to take a bus into the city,* she told herself. *You have some money. You'll be fine.* It would be this job, or it would be another job. All she needed was *some* job. And never mind that she'd only ever had one kind of job, and didn't know how to do anything else. She could learn, surely. Other people did it all the time.

Iain was opening the door and standing back for her, and she slid into the car before any of them could change their minds and leave her there. Iain slid in after her, his knees pushed up high in the rear seat, and she tried not to look at him as she fastened her seatbelt.

"Morning," his mother was saying to the man behind the wheel, leaning over to peck him on the cheek. "Thanks for coming."

He grunted and pulled out into traffic, and Carmella half-turned in her seat and said, "This is my husband Graeme. Graeme, this is Nina. She's coming to help with Dad."

Nina saw sharp blue eyes under craggy brows in the rearview mirror, and hair as black as sin, as black as his son's. He looked to be as tall as Iain, too. Somehow, she'd stumbled on the Mutant Superhero family.

"Morning," Graeme said. Then he glanced back at his wife and said, "Flight OK? Vanessa all right, then?"

"Yes," she said. "Fine. All fine. And wee Calum's got so big and strong already, looking around like he's taking it all in."

She didn't get much reaction to that, and everybody sat in silence as Graeme drove.

"Um…" Nina said after another minute passed. Iain was looking out his window, and neither of his parents was saying anything. This was the strangest family reunion she'd ever seen, the unspoken thoughts all but bouncing off the hard surfaces of the car.

Or maybe that was just her.

"Yes, dear?" Carmella asked.

"Um," she said again, "I'm wondering if there's a place I can buy some clothes. Before we get to the town, I mean. Since you said it was small."

Iain had turned his head, at least, but he was frowning, and Iain's frown was... she'd call that "volcanic." As in, "about to erupt." Or about to transform. Any minute now, he'd probably be bursting out of his clothes.

Oh, right. Clothes. "Because I don't have any," she said. "Clothes, I mean. So if there's a cheap place…"

She had plenty of money. In accounts she didn't want to access. Last-minute tickets across the world hadn't come cheap, and she didn't want to use her cards here. She was almost certainly being overcautious, but she couldn't help feeling like a rabbit bolting for its burrow.

Anyway, she didn't want to care about how she looked. Call it a vacation. A beauty vacation. Except for the orange. There were limits.

"We'll go to Shopwise in Nelson," Carmella said decisively. "On Quarantine Street," she told her husband.

He glanced at her and said, "We will, eh. Out of the way."

Nina couldn't help wincing at his tone. Iain was looking at her again, and he said, "Take her to get some clothes, Dad. Reckon that's a crisis."

"Oh, thanks," she said, and to her surprise, it came out sarcastic.

He smiled, lightening the thunderous expression. "Or could be that's the new look, eh. Nobody's ever accused me of being up on the trends."

"Well, I was going to say." She cast a quick but obvious glance at his baggy athletic shorts. "That I could borrow from you and look even… more so."

That got a quick huff of laughter out of him. "Go from

bad to worse, you mean. Too right."

Iain's father was taking a left at a roundabout, which must have been the correct direction, because Carmella's stiff shoulders relaxed a fraction. The little group inside the car stayed silent, though, for the next ten minutes, and Nina's unease crept back again until Graeme pulled to a stop outside a two-story building on a commercial street.

"I'll come with you, love," Carmella said. "We'll text when we're done," she told her husband, and Nina picked up her carrier bag and climbed out of the car. She had to make a grab for the roof along the way as the movement brought a wave of dizziness.

Hang on, she told herself fiercely. *Last thing.*

Well, no, it wasn't the last thing. But it was the next thing. It was the thing she had to do right now.

Carmella walked into the store as briskly as she did everything else, making no reference to the scene in the car, and it was hardly Nina's place to ask.

The interior was air-conditioned, and it felt good. "All secondhand," Carmella said. "Biggest op shop around, and nothing much over a few dollars in here, so we can go wild. What fun for me, dressing a young girl. Like playing Barbies, eh. Very nearly as much fun as buying all those baby things for my first grandchild." She was already flinging hangers around on racks, considering and rejecting. "What d'you reckon? I'd say shorts, a couple skirts, some pretty tops, and some togs as well. Got to have togs if you're going to be at the beach, and you don't look too hard to fit."

Togs? What were togs? And fitting her would be harder than Carmella realized. Nina plucked at the elastic bandage with a grimace. *Dressing room,* she thought. *In two minutes.*

Carmella was still talking, though. "We're not too flash in Kaiteriteri, and it'll be warm for months yet, so you can keep it simple. A dress or two, maybe, if we find something pretty. And we'll go round the corner for undies and shoes. Nothing more horrible to contemplate than the idea of wearing used undies. If you need some help with that, I'll see you right.

We'll call it an advance on salary. The pharmacy as well, I'm thinking. We'll get you looking pretty, and you'll feel better."

"I told myself that I wasn't going to be taken over again."

The second the words were out of Nina's mouth, she wished she could recall them. Carmella stopped in the act of flinging a yellow skirt over her arm and stared at her.

"Have I been too managing?" Carmella actually looked distressed, and that wasn't right. She'd been nothing but kind. "Are you running from your marriage, darling? Is that the reason for the specs and the hat?"

Nina's hand went up to the glasses. "You can tell?"

"Well, yes, love. It's the way you squint."

"Oh."

"You know—it's Nelson," Carmella said. "Whoever he is, he's not going to find you in Nelson, much less in Kaiteriteri, out in the wop-wops. If you look up 'backwater' in the dictionary, you'll probably see us. I think you could lose the disguise now."

Nina drew the glasses off slowly, then held her breath and removed the hat.

She knew what reaction she'd feared, and she didn't get it.

"Oh, that was unfortunate, darling." Carmella's voice was so sorrowful that Nina let out a surprised laugh. "You can't have meant to do that."

"I sort of... sent somebody out for 'blonde,' Nina tried to explain. "And this was what came back. At least how it turned out on my hair."

Her hair had been her trademark. Part of her identity. Not any more. Now, it was chopped short, all the soft wave cut out of it, and colored a hideous yellow-orange. She guessed "brassy" would describe it, although even that word didn't do justice to the color of her shorn head.

"Not quite right with your skin, was it, dear?" Carmella said kindly. "But not necessary to hide under a hat all the same. I'll get used to it, I'm sure."

"But you can't..." Nina didn't know how to ask. "I don't remind you of anybody?"

"Hmm." Carmella put her head on one side. "Can't say you do. Did you think you did? I'm sorry, but I can't think of a celebrity with hair exactly like that, if that's what you mean. No doubt there's some pop star I don't know about who's done up that way, though. People do all sorts of mad things, don't they?"

"Like you say—it was unfortunate." Nina felt, suddenly, immeasurably more cheerful. She'd steer clear of makeup. A bare face and the horrible hair—that would be enough disguise to keep her anonymous all the way down here. She shoved the glasses and the hat into her plastic bag and said, "Let's shop. I could hardly look worse."

done with women

♡

Iain climbed out of the cramped back seat and into the front, stretching his legs with relief.

"Bloody hell," his dad said, pulling away from the curb. "Half the morning gone already, and now they're *shopping?* How long will *that* take?" He shook his head. "Let's get a coffee." He looked more closely at his son for the first time. "All right, mate?"

"Yeh. Fine."

His dad nodded, and that was it for their heart-to-heart. Iain wanted to ask what was going on between his parents, but the set of his dad's jaw told him it would be fruitless. His dad was never demonstrative, but he hadn't even kissed his wife after three weeks apart? No wonder Iain hadn't been able to make a fist of his own relationship.

Well, no. His parents probably hadn't had the same... issues. Still, though. Something was wrong, and he didn't know what it was. Something to do with his own botched wedding? With his granddad? With his mum leaving, being gone over Christmas? He didn't know, and he didn't want to. He'd be a no-hoper as a wise counselor, and anyway... no. But the drive had been bloody awkward even beyond his own thoughts, and he was already regretting going along with his mum's assumption that he'd spend a week of his holiday with the family—and help out around the place as well, because that was what he always did when he came.

Business as usual. He wasn't a newlywed, he was single, he was available to help, and that was the way it went. And he hadn't been home for three months. He'd rung, but that was all. Maybe that hadn't been enough, but he hadn't felt like he'd had a choice.

He'd turned around and flown straight back to Auckland on that bleary-eyed morning after his non–wedding night, and he hadn't looked out the window. After that, he'd crawled straight back into the familiar routine of training and gym and match day like he was pulling a blanket over his head. You worked your hardest during the week, you put yourself to the test on the day, and if the team was good enough, you won. Simple.

He'd headed off for the Northern Hemisphere with nothing but relief, and had welcomed the four matches against Scotland, Ireland, Wales, and England, each more brutal than the last. The All Blacks had won them all, because that was what they did, and that was the world in its proper place again. The rest of it, he'd promised himself, he'd think about later, when he could handle it.

And then he'd flown home to Auckland again, and he'd *gone* home. Alone. To a house from which a considerable amount of the furnishings and all the warmth had vanished, and everything he'd pushed out of his mind for all those weeks had hit him like a ton of bricks.

He hadn't been able to stay much more than a week, so he'd run away once again, and for the past month, he'd traveled. No place he'd intended to go with Sienna—no Pacific island beaches, and definitely no secluded honeymoon resorts. Instead, he'd done what he always did to feel better and work things through—he'd pushed his body. At first, he'd taken a backpack and headed to Canada, had skied the steepest slopes he could find in British Columbia before heading south to tramp through California's Death Valley, where the bleakness of the landscape had been a perfect match for his mood. Then it was a drop down into Mexico and Costa Rica for the diving.

He'd gone where nobody had heard of him, where they might have known that rugby was a sport but couldn't have cared less about the men who played it. He'd let his size and his fearsome looks scare away conversation, and been glad of it. The only attention he'd attracted had been from cops and security guards, and the occasional woman looking for a bad boy, daring his grim expression.

He hadn't even been able to face going to his own would-be best man's wedding. Three weeks ago, when Hugh Latimer had been married to one of the most beautiful women in New Zealand, he'd done it without Iain's support.

Iain had meant to come back in time. He'd even bought a ticket. And he hadn't used it. Instead, he'd sat alone on a beach in Baja on that December night, drunk his way steadily through another six-pack, tried not to feel disgusted with himself and ten years older than his twenty-seven years, and failed miserably. With the emphasis on 'miserable.'

You could only wallow for so long, though, and he was getting bloody sick of it. Besides, it was past time to start getting serious about his rugby fitness. He'd be reporting for training with the Blues in a couple weeks. He'd be turning up for the new season as a single man, and he needed that not to matter. The only way to work yourself back to normal was to start, and going for a coffee with his dad was about as normal as it got.

He ducked his head out of habit through the café's doorway, ordered at the counter, then took the chair facing the window in a corner to avoid autograph-seekers and waited as patiently as he could manage as his dad stared at the same page of the newspaper for much too long.

As an exercise in male bonding, it was a dead loss.

It must have been nearly an hour before his dad's phone finally dinged with a text. Graeme glanced at it, stood up without a word, left the café for the car, and within a couple minutes, was pulling up to the curb outside the op shop again. "About bloody time," he said. "They'll want lunch now, mark my words."

Iain wasn't listening. He'd got out to give his mum the front seat, and Nina was standing there on the pavement. Her hat was off at last, and her hair was... he guessed "odd" would be the best word. A bit like Big Bird, all sticking-up feathers, and so yellow it was nearly orange.

Maybe "horrible" was a better word.

She still wore no makeup, and she still looked dead tired. But without the hat and specs, he could see her face. Her eyes were probably too big, too wide-set; dark smudges against her pale ivory skin, with more smudges beneath. *Haunted,* he thought in a flight of unaccustomed fancy. Her nose was a straight, perfectly carved line, and maybe too long, and her eyebrows were full and nearly straight as well until they winged up near the outer corners. Her mouth, on the other hand, curved in a lush, full, purely feminine shape, providing soft punctuation to the severe, square lines of her cheekbones, nose, and jawline.

She wasn't pretty, not exactly, not in the way he was used to thinking of it. It was too arresting a face for that, the features too pronounced. But it was a strong face. One you'd notice, and not one you'd forget. And the rest of her...

She was holding three or four plastic shopping bags, but that wasn't what he was looking at. He was looking at a little rose-patterned skirt that stopped north of her knees, a red T-shirt, and a simple pair of flat brown sandals with skinny straps.

Well, no, he wasn't looking at the clothes. Not so much.

She still looked slim, her arms and throat almost painfully so. But how had she hidden those full breasts, the sweet curve of her hips? How could he have missed them, even under the hideous orange jumper? He couldn't have guessed at the tiny waist in the baggy track pants she'd worn, or imagined her legs. They were too thin, like her arms, but... shapely, that was the word, tapering down to impossibly fragile ankles and pretty little feet.

All of her, from her slender toes to the long, graceful neck, looked carved from warm ivory, making you wonder what it would be like to see her naked, if it could possibly all be that good, and knowing that it had to be.

"Put Nina's bags in the boot, please, darling," his mother said, and he realized he was staring.

"Course," he managed, and reached for them. Her hand brushed his, and she jerked hers away, dropping two of the bags, causing one of them to spill a scatter of bright-colored undies onto the pavement. Pink and purple ones trimmed with lace, another one that was white with colored dots on. And a yellow pair with a happy face over the crotch. That one was... interesting. And sliding out behind them, the shine and lace of bras, the top one all delicate pink-and-cream striping. Maybe matching some pair of undies he hadn't seen.

Get it together, boy. Was he fifteen, getting this kind of hard rush from seeing a girl's underwear? It had clearly been too long.

He was dropping onto his haunches on the thought, aiming to rescue her things. Unfortunately, she dropped down at the same moment on the same errand, and his head banged sharply into hers, causing her to cry out and fall back on her heels, groping for the pavement behind her. He lunged for her with the reflexes that were his bread and butter, got an arm around her waist before she hit the ground, and pulled her in.

They crouched together there for a moment as he heard her panting breath, saw the gold-flecked brown eyes widen, felt an indentation of waistline beneath his hand as strongly curved as Farewell Spit, and couldn't move. Couldn't look away.

"Sorry," she said. It was barely a whisper, and he looked at the softness of that mouth and thought, *bloody hell.*

"All right?" he asked. "Your head."

She was scooting backwards out of his grasp, though, and he looked down and saw endless centimeters of toned thigh, her skirt having ridden up when she'd fallen. And then she was kneeling, bare knees on hard concrete, gathering the undies into the bag again, and he was taking her shopping from her and standing up, doing his best to regain his composure.

He suddenly realized he hadn't apologized. "Sorry. I thought you—I mean, I—"

"What?" she asked, standing up herself.

He laughed, and her head jerked at the sound. "Sorry," he said hastily again. "I thought—in the airport. I thought you were a boy. You made me... you took me by surprise, eh."

"No," she said. "Not a boy."

He didn't look down at the slim-fitting red T-shirt, but it was one hell of an effort. "No. I see that."

She reached for her bags again, saying, "Wait a second, please." She dug around in them, then pulled out the ugly red-and-black hat and a pair of huge sunglasses before handing them over again.

"Is that necessary?" he asked.

"Yes."

She put on the hat and sunnies, and he sighed and said, "Bugger." The hat didn't go with the shirt, and that was the least of it. He wanted to see her face.

His mum said, "Darling. Language."

He'd forgotten she was there. He crooked an eyebrow at the girl and said, "My language bother you? Sorry."

"No." She was heading for the car, and he went around the back, bunged her bags into the boot, and gave himself a stern talking-to.

This was nothing but a bad idea. He should probably have given in to his more discreditable impulses on his holidays, have gone on and been Bad-Boy Dangerous with the pretty climber in Yosemite or one of the schoolteachers on their holidays on the Baja beach. Or with both of them. They'd been up for an adventure, and more than willing to help him work out the demons. But to his shame, he hadn't trusted himself not to scare them.

Sienna had never seemed to want his tenderness in bed. She'd been excited by the ferocity he showed on the rugby pitch, and she'd told him so. But frightening a woman had never felt anything but wrong, especially once he'd grown and trained himself into his full size and strength.

At any rate, the tenderness seemed gone for good now, and all he had left was the ferocity. Which made it a good idea to steer well clear of fragile-looking women with delicate ankles who weren't sending out any signals at all, other than the flashing yellow "Caution" kind.

The last thing he needed in his life was a woman with such obvious baggage. He had enough baggage for two, and he was done with women.

Yeh, right.

on my sheep farm
♡

Nina was going to ignore him. Another guy who only paid attention to her body? *No.* Another guy, period? *Double* no. Her finger had barely lost the groove from the heavy engagement band.

Yeah. She'd call that a big, fat 'no.'

She pulled the car door open, bent to climb inside, and felt herself going sideways. Her vision blurred, then began to fade, and her legs somehow wouldn't hold her. She made a grab for the top of the door, missed, and fell, pain blooming in her hip along the way.

Car door, she thought dimly. Her knee hit next, and her shoulder, the impacts felt only hazily. *Sidewalk.*

Voices over her. Talking. She had to open her eyes, but it was so hard. She needed to lie here a minute more. Just a minute.

"Nina." It was Carmella's voice, and it was urgent, so Nina had to open her eyes, even though she didn't want to.

The three of them surrounded her, Carmella crouching, a hand on Nina's cheek, Graeme looming overhead. Iain was… she squinted. At her feet, lifting her legs into the air. She grabbed frantically for her skirt.

"Stay there." His voice was rough, and much too

commanding. "We're getting the blood to your head."

She struggled to her elbows despite his words, feeling desperately embarrassed. "I'm fine. I don't know what happened."

"Dehydrated," he said, letting go of her legs, "at a guess. Hungry, probably. Tired."

"I'm fine," she said again, still tugging at her skirt. She swung onto her feet, then had to stay crouching a minute, head down, until the blackness and dizziness cleared.

"Right," Iain said. "We're going for lunch. A cold drink, a sit-down, something to eat. Come on." His arm was beneath her, supporting her to her feet, and she let herself lean into him. Just for a moment. Just because it helped.

"Lunch," she heard Graeme mutter. "I knew it."

"Don't say it, Dad," Iain snapped. Carmella's eyes opened wide, and Nina found it in her to wonder whether Iain normally rebuked his father, and to guess that he didn't. And then Iain was setting her onto the seat of the car and shutting the door, then coming around himself and climbing in.

"Soon be there," Iain told her. "Switch the air con on, Dad."

"I'm fine," Nina said for probably the third time. "I can..." She couldn't stop the tremble in her voice. "I can do the job. Honestly."

"Course you can, darling." That was Carmella from the front seat. "Tomorrow."

Nina was going to be tough. She was going to be strong. But it didn't seem to be happening today.

Graeme was silently obeying his wife's directions, they were pulling up and parking, and Iain was out of the car and had his arm around her again, was escorting her into a little café lined with hanging flower baskets and depositing her in a window seat. He set a glass of water in front of her, said, "Drink this. I'll be back with something to eat," and went up to the counter with his parents.

They ate lunch, and nobody said much, but Nina couldn't bring herself to care. She forced herself to work her way through some of the quiche and half of the pumpkin soup the server put in front of her, grateful that nothing required cutting or chewing. Both of those things felt beyond her. It seemed her rope had an end, and she was at it. Iain glanced at her from time to time, but not like a man with a desperate passion. More like a man dreading involvement.

She was finishing one last bite of quiche and feeling a little better when he confirmed it.

"Tell me you're not pregnant," he said.

The sudden silence at the table was broken by the clatter of Nina's fork hitting her plate. *"What?"* she managed to ask.

He made an impatient gesture. "The specs you didn't need. The ugly hat you're still wearing. The no-luggage. The fainting. Tell me you didn't run here for the medical care, or to have a baby who'll be a New Zealand citizen. Or worse— you're running away from some bloke who's going to be turning up here. Tell me you didn't take his baby from him, because that's not on."

If she'd had any softer feelings toward him, they were gone. *"His* baby? *HIS* baby?" She couldn't even continue. She was spluttering.

"Well, yeh." His blue eyes were ice-cold now. "Babies tend to belong to both parents. Least that's how I've heard it, specially when the boot's on the other foot. When men are the ones trying to run away. Women are quick enough to point that out then."

"You know nothing about it," Nina said. "Absolutely nothing."

"Darling," Carmella told her son. "No. Stop. Back up."

Iain turned those flintlike eyes on his mother. "You're too soft, Mum. How many questions have you asked her? None, I reckon. I've asked her a few, and how many has she answered? Just about none. A few hours in En Zed, she's already fainting, and you want to make her our responsibility? Why? Haven't we got enough problems of our own?"

Both Carmella and Nina were talking now.

"I don't have any problems," Carmella said. "And you

don't have any compassion. No room at the inn, indeed."

"Now she's the Virgin Mary?" Iain said. "I don't think so. And you don't have any problems? Not how it looks to me."

Nina's own stuttered exclamation had gone unnoticed amongst the voices. Now, she shoved her chair back and brought her palm down hard on the wooden table, rattling her dishes and startling the others into silence.

She was trembling again, but this time, it was with anger. "First," she told Iain, "I am not pregnant, not that that is one single bit—one little, tiny, *infinitesimal* bit—your business. Secondly, if I *were* pregnant, and I were running away from the father? That would be my business too. It sure wouldn't be yours. If you did wonder about it, why wouldn't you figure I might have a good reason? It sounds like you think all women do is take advantage of men. Guess you're single yourself, huh? I can't imagine why."

She couldn't believe the words that were coming out of her mouth. She *never* talked to anybody like this. But the whole thing was, suddenly, too much.

He'd opened his mouth to reply, but she put a hand up and went on. "And I told you. I'm Aussie. If I need medical care, I'll go to Australia. It's bound to be better than I'd get on your sheep farm, or whatever it is. But I *didn't* ask for it. I didn't ask for anything. Your mum offered me a job, and I took the job. It was between your mum and me, and you can just... just..."

"Bugger off," Carmella offered helpfully.

"*Thank* you," Nina said, just as Iain said, "Whose side are you on? And what about language?"

"It's only bad language when you say it," Carmella said. "When *I* say it, it's putting you right. I'm the mum. It's my job. You were out of line, Iain. Face it. Nina doesn't owe you any explanations. I don't know what you're on about anyway."

"You don't, eh," he shot back. "Then why's she wearing that hat?"

"You don't like my hat?" There was a mist over Nina's

vision again, but it was red this time, and it was burning hot. "Too bad. Tough luck. Kiss my…" She couldn't say that, not in front of his parents. ". . . *hat*. Because I'm *wearing* it. I'm wearing it to… to *bed* from now on. I'm wearing it in the *shower*. And you can just *live* with it!"

"On my sheep farm."

He was *mocking* her, and the mist rose higher. She needed to be where he was not. She rose out of her seat and held out her hand to his father. "Keys, please."

He sat still and looked at her, his blue eyes, twins of his son's, sharp and assessing, and she said, "I'm not going to steal your car. I want my clothes. And yes," she told Iain, "*I* bought them. Not your mother. Me. Have I asked you for anything, including your opinion of my looks? No, I have not. And yet you've told me. You told me I looked bad, and then you let me know I looked good. Except, guess what? You had no right to tell me either thing. Just like I haven't given you *my* opinion of *your* looks, and I'm not going to, because you didn't ask me. If you want to know, though, please do ask. I'd be happy to tell you."

She yanked at her tote, fumbled inside for her plastic bag, pulled out another twenty, and slapped it on the table. "This is for my lunch. And thank you very much," she told his parents belatedly. "For the ride. For the shopping. But I'm leaving now."

Graeme pulled the keys out of his pocket without another word and handed them to her, and she took them and said, "Thank you" again with as much dignity as she could muster, then turned and headed for the door.

She still felt sick. She still felt lousy, and scared, and way too tired. But mad, she was discovering, overrode almost everything. Mad kicked *butt*. From now on, she was going to work a whole lot harder on mad.

♡♡♡

Iain sat there a minute, not looking at his parents. He didn't need to hear it. Then he rose and followed the girl out.

Well, bugger. That hadn't gone well.

He had a bad feeling that he was going to have to apologize to her. Why else was he going out there?

He'd been sure that he was going to hate this day. He hadn't known the half of it.

She'd got to the car now, but she wasn't opening it. Instead, she was standing there, looking at the boot in a blank sort of way.

"Here," he said, reaching out to take the key from her hand.

She wouldn't let it go, though. His hand was around hers, but she was clutching his dad's key fob and struggling against him. "You can't stop me," she said. "You *can't.*"

What did she think he was going to do? He released her hand and stepped back a pace for good measure. "Not trying to stop you, am I. But if you want to give me the key, I'll open the boot for you."

"Oh." She held out the key, and he took it, shoved back the keyhole cover, and opened the back of the car.

She collected her bags and stood looking at him warily, and he gazed at her morosely and sighed. "I'm going to have to say it, aren't I?"

"Say what?" She was clutching her shopping bags tightly to her, looking as poised for flight as a hummingbird, as if she were afraid he would grab them from her, or grab *her.* "I don't want you to say anything, except maybe 'goodbye.'"

He might as well get it over. "That I was… that I… wasn't right." *Weasel.* "To say it, I mean. I didn't mean to. The 'pregnant' thing. It occurred to me, and then I said it. It slipped out, you could say."

"You might want to talk to somebody about your impulse control issues," she said, and he let out a surprised huff of laughter.

"Not usually my problem," he said. "More of a recent development. And since I'm doing this, I may as well go in boots and all and say that I shouldn't have criticized your ugly hat."

She looked at him sideways from under its brim. "You realize you just did it again."

"Whoops." He *did* smile this time, and she smiled back. Reluctantly, but she smiled. "You could take your revenge," he suggested. "Could make me feel a bit better for picking on a girl, specially such a tired one. Go on and tell me what's wrong with me. I'm a big target, and an easy one." He gestured to the T-shirt and shorts he'd rolled out of bed into. They didn't look any better now than they had all those hours ago, he had a feeling. "And we haven't even got started on my unfortunate face. The nose and all."

"Hmm," she said. "Yes. You are. A big, easy target, I mean. But I don't imagine you'd really care what I think, and that would make it so much less satisfying for me to tell you. So never mind. I don't go around getting mad too much anyway. It's a hard thing for me to keep up, it turns out. Pathetic, I know, but there you go."

"Well, yeh," he said with a grin he couldn't help one bit, "it is. You didn't even make me say 'sorry.' You're meant to do that. Though I'll probably get chucked out of the Man Club for telling you the secrets."

Her own smile was faint, but it was definitely there. "Is that really so hard? I say it all the time."

"Hard for a bloke to come face-to-face with the fact that a woman doesn't admire him, maybe, and worse if he's got to admit she's got a good reason. And to say it out loud? Yeh, that's even harder. Exposing the soft underbelly and all. But I was. Wrong. See, I'm doing it. I'm saying I'm sorry." *Ha. Not such a weasel after all.*

She eyed him. "So how tough was that?"

"Surprisingly, not too bad. Maybe because you didn't try to make me do it. And because you look a bit fragile, maybe. I don't kick puppies much, either."

Her eyes had lost some of the dull fatigue. "Is that what I am? A puppy? Huh. That's a new one."

"More of a kitten, I'd say," he found himself answering, to

his astonishment. A *kitten?* Pretty soon, he was going to be crooning love poems in her ear. Never happening. And yet he went on anyway. "Not enough claws, though. You may want to work on that."

"That was my attempt back there. Claws, I mean. I thought it was pretty good. No? Not?"

"Nah, It was pretty good. Got me out here, didn't it? Apologizing, even. That's... you could say it's rare."

"Well, then, good for me, I guess. Say goodbye to your mother for me, will you? Tell her I'm sorry it didn't work out. I'll just go and..." She lifted the bags in the vague direction of the town center. "Look for a place to stay or whatever. Find a job. There's bound to be something. It's a busy time."

Right. And there he'd be, kicking the puppy again. There was no hope for it, so he said, "She'll have my hide if you run off. And it probably *isn't* my business who looks after Granddad, as long as she isn't actually a criminal type. I won't be around that much, or that long, either. You won't have to worry about me."

"Kittens can probably be criminals too. It's probably a known variety. Besides, you don't know anything about me, and I *am* running." She was facing him straight on, and there was no smile on her face now. "And I'm not going to tell you why."

He opened his mouth, then shut it again. "Bloody hell," he muttered. "I'm going to be begging you to come back, I can tell. That wasn't my plan at all."

"Well, decide," she said, looking much less like a kitten. "I need to make a plan myself."

He heaved a sigh and gave it up. "Right, then. Come back."

homecoming. or not.

♡

She'd won. *Ha.* She'd *won.* She *never* won.

The exhilaration drained away, though, within minutes, leaving her shaking with adrenaline in its aftermath.

It probably hadn't been the right choice. She probably should have gone for a backpacker's hostel and a job serving up... ice cream, maybe. Scooping gelato, that was the ticket. Something easy, something she could handle. It had been defiance more than anything that had had her accepting Iain's apology, then his invitation, and defiance wasn't the soundest basis for decision-making.

She sat pressed against the door in the back of the car, trying to shake off the feeling of gloom, and stared out the window at neat and tidy but fairly unremarkable commercial streets, and then, after another roundabout, at the beginnings of countryside. Rolling green hills glowing in the sunlight, vineyards, and what must be orchards. Rows of trees, anyway. On and on, the car swaying around the curves in a hypnotic rhythm. She put her head against the glass and closed her eyes. Just for a minute.

A touch on her arm. "Nina."

"Hmm?" She blinked, disoriented.

"We're here," Iain said.

"Oh." Iain's parents were out of the car, she realized, and Iain was waiting for her. She stumbled out and stood, staring blearily at black pavement, nothing but a parking space beside a road that wove up a hill with houses climbing the uphill slopes.

There was a noise from the other side. She turned and saw green; trees and bushes. And blue. Blue sky, and blue water that stretched in both directions. A faint, rhythmic sound filled her ears. The sound of waves, lapping up against the shore. Not crashing waves, though. Gentle ones. The sea.

Iain and his father were pulling luggage from the back of the SUV, and Nina reached for her bags, but Iain said, "Nah. We've got it." So it was with only her canvas tote that Nina followed Carmella down a gravel track through palm trees and giant ferns, with sidewalks leading down to barely glimpsed backs of houses.

Carmella stopped at the last house before the track ended, said, "This is us," and led the way. Twenty feet along a concrete path, they came out from the greenery into a little courtyard paved with bricks, with three buildings around it. Some sort of shed at the back, a two-story house to the right that must look out onto the water and that sported a square tower sticking smack up in the middle. That was nice. And to the left, perpendicular to the big house, a little one-story cottage. All of them built of white-painted wood, a tidy contrast to the riot of greenery surrounding them.

A man was coming around from between the two houses, walking fairly quickly, but with the aid of a stick. His hair was white, his bristling eyebrows were, too, and his face was furrowed in a way that reminded Nina of Iain and his father. Were all New Zealand men grumpy?

"About time," he barked. "I was thinking you'd had a smash."

Carmella stood a little straighter. "Hi, Dad." She went forward and kissed his leathery cheek. "It's good to be home. How are you?"

He ignored that. "You couldn't have rung and told me you

wouldn't be here for lunch?"

"Sorry," Carmella said. "Haven't switched out my SIM card yet."

"Huh," the old man grunted. "Should've told Graeme to text, then."

Nina could almost see Carmella bite her lip, but the two men were coming up behind them now.

"Well, good news, Dad," Carmella said. "I've brought you somebody to stay with you and give you a hand. This is Nina. Nina, this is my dad, Arthur Carmichael."

Nina got a penetrating stare from brown eyes this time. "How ya goin'," the old man said. "But I don't need a minder. You can turn around again and take her back to Nelson."

"No, I can't," Carmella said, her voice losing the edge of uncertainty. "She's well and truly knackered. Got on the flight with me, what was that? Close to thirty-six hours ago, and she looked out on her feet then. She needs to have a good long lie-down, and a few good meals as well. Look at her."

"Doesn't sound like somebody who's going to be taking care of me, then, does she?" the old man said. "No disrespect intended," he told Nina. "Nothing wrong with you, I'm sure. But I don't need you."

"None taken," she said. "Mr. Carmichael."

"Arthur," he snapped. "I'm not a Pom."

She blinked. Oh. Not British. Right. Proud to be from the Antipodes, and fiercely egalitarian. She got it. He was so much like her own granddad, she had to smile a little.

"Oh," he said, "I see how it is. She told you"—he jerked his head at his daughter—"that I'm lovably grumpy. I'm not. I'm a bloody-minded, bad-tempered, sour old man. It'd be an awful job. I'd run you off within days."

"Got it," Nina said. "Probably true. I don't know much about looking after people, to be honest. So it won't be a shock if that happens."

"Huh," he said. "Not as soft as you look, are you?"

She wasn't sure what to answer, so she didn't say anything.

She *was* as soft as she looked, she was pretty sure, however soft that was. Anyway, her brain wasn't exactly operating at full speed, and witty repartee was beyond her.

"Well, you'd better come in," Arthur said grudgingly. "Carmella's right about that, anyway. You're dead on your feet. I'll give you a bed for the night, and then? Mark my words. You'll be out of here fast enough."

"Fine," she said. "Just show me where."

He turned without another word, and none of the other three had said anything, so Nina followed him through the door of the little cottage.

She'd want to see the beach. Tomorrow. Right now, she was passing through a tiny porch with a stacked washer and dryer, then through a modest eat-in kitchen, its walls painted white, with blue curtains moving softly in the breeze coming through an open window above the sink. An arched opening on one side of a cozily furnished living room brought her to a choice of three closed doors, one at each end of a little hallway and one in the middle.

Arthur flung the left-hand one open. "Bedroom," he said. "Bath's in the middle. I'll put a towel and facecloth out for you. My room's the other door. Don't come in there. I don't need company. Reckon you may as well have a wash and a rest, though. Don't expect me to cook your tea, because I'm not going to. You can help yourself to whatever's in the kitchen, but mind you clean up after yourself."

"Thanks." Nina barely heard him. She was eyeing the tidy double bed longingly. There wasn't much furniture in the room—just the wooden bed with its white duvet, a nightstand, a little rectangular table and chair in one corner, and a small dresser against the far wall. A row of four pretty white hooks on the only other available space sported wooden hangers, and she guessed that counted as the closet. But the yellow wallpaper was printed with tiny purple flowers, a soft purple throw lay at the foot of the white bed, and the floor was made up of wide planks, with a thin rug of printed fabric beside the bed the only floor covering. Filmy white curtains swayed against the soft puff of summer air coming through the open windows, and a few birds added their song to the sound of the wind in the trees. There was a murmur beyond it all, too, that surely must be the sea.

Arthur said, "Goodbye, then," and stumped out of the room, closing the door behind him. Nina set her tote bag down on the little table, slipped off her sandals, and lay down on the white bed. She pulled the purple throw up over her, snuggled into its softness, turned onto her side, and closed her eyes.

She'd take a rest. Then she'd get up, take a long-overdue shower, and have a talk with Carmella. In a minute.

off the rails
♡

There wasn't much to eat in the house, Carmella found. Two hours after they'd arrived, and after Graeme had headed straight back to the office, she was showered, changed, unpacked, and feeling marginally more human. Now, she was holding open the door to the fridge and blinking through blurry eyes at the contents.

Iain came to stand beside her, and she put out a hand absent-mindedly and rubbed it over his broad back. He was still her baby, no matter how big he'd grown, and the pain she'd seen in his eyes today had hurt her as if it had been her own.

"Not too flash," he said, nodding at the nearly empty shelves. "I'll go get groceries tomorrow, eh."

"Thanks," she said.

"Right now, though, I'll pop over to the pub for a takeaway. Chicken pie do you?"

"Anything." She shut the door to the fridge with relief. "Almost too tired to eat, tell you the truth. And I know, it's my own fault, giving away my seat. Made me feel better to do it. I guess that's why I did. But your dad will be home from work any minute." She shut her mouth on the words. Of course Iain knew that. It was her own nerves talking.

Iain looked at her, his gaze fierce and inscrutable, then, to her surprise, bent and kissed her on the cheek. "She'll be right, Mum," he said gently.

The tears filled her eyes, hot and unbidden, and her hand came up for a second to clutch at his heavy shoulder. "Thanks, darling," she said, her voice wobbling despite her best efforts, and tried not to think about what it meant when your husband didn't seem to care that you'd come home after almost a month, and neither did your dad.

Graeme took his time getting home himself that evening, not returning until after Iain had returned with their takeaways.

"Oh," her husband said, sitting at the kitchen table after washing his hands. "Still on the takeaways, I guess."

"Well, yes," she said, unable to control the edge in her voice. "As there was nothing to eat in the house."

"Had to do the work of two, didn't I," he said, starting in on the chicken pie. "That Malcolm fella you hired just before you left was useless, by the way. Had to let him go after a week and start over. I'll fill you in tomorrow. Glad you're back at last, anyway."

Conversation ground to a halt at that, until Iain finally leaped into the breach and asked about his sister and the baby. And after dinner, he got to his feet and said, "I'll do the washing-up, Mum. Go on to bed."

She nodded and looked at Graeme. He said, "You're knackered, eh. Go on. I'll be up later."

She turned and dragged herself upstairs to the bed she and Graeme had shared for thirty years with the tears pricking behind her eyelids, and wondered what had gone wrong with her marriage, and why she hadn't noticed sooner. Or had there been anything to notice? She couldn't tell. She couldn't even remember. She hadn't paid enough attention, maybe, or it had been too gradual. Or both. In any case, the wagon had gone straight off the rails now, and there was no missing it.

How was she meant to fix that? Especially if she were the only one who cared enough to try?

funny face

♡

The birds woke Nina.

She drifted up through layers of sleep into dim, pale-gray light. *New Zealand,* she remembered. She'd been taking a nap. But it was getting dark, and it was summer here, so that would be late. How long had she slept?

The birds, surely trees full of them, were singing their hearts out, some of them melodiously, some of them monotonously, but all of them incredibly loudly, and she couldn't hear any other sound. Nothing in the house, for sure. She sat up and realized she was still wearing her clothes, but somehow, she had not just the violet throw over her, but a heavier cream-colored one as well.

Oh. Carmella must have covered her up. Nina's plastic bags of new-to-you clothes were in the corner of the room, too. She hadn't brought those in herself, had she? She could barely remember. It was all pretty hazy.

She had no phone, no watch, no way of knowing what time it was. But birds didn't start singing at night. It had to be morning—just before dawn—and she must have slept the clock around. That must be it, even though her internal clock was more than confused. New Zealand was exactly backwards from most of Europe time-wise. Dawn here, sunset there. Or not sunset—full dark. It was winter up there. She shook her head. Too hard to figure out while she was still groggy.

Time to set that right. First day of her new life, and all that.

Out in the little hallway, she looked at the two closed doors, remembered, *Bath in the middle,* and paid it a visit.

It wasn't exactly clean, she discovered. The mirror was speckled, and the sink was a little grubby. Arthur not having somebody to look after him, she guessed.

She washed her hands afterwards, looked into a tiny mirror on an old-fashioned wooden medicine cabinet hung above a sink set into a white Formica counter, and winced. Her ugly hair was standing up worse than ever, the shadows under her eyes were dark and deep, and she felt sticky and grimy after days of travel.

The wedding is in five days. It would be more like three days away now. Was Matthias looking for her? *No,* she told herself sternly. Surely not for long, anyway. He'd smooth the whole thing over and move on. He'd probably blame it on her— well, she *was* the one who had run—but that was all right. He might think she was immature and flighty, but what was he? He hadn't been willing to let her go. What did that make *him?*

Her panicked flight seemed a little extreme now, and more than a little embarrassing, but she'd only run because he hadn't let her walk. She wasn't used to blaming other people, but maybe just this once, she'd give it a try. Anyway, why should she care what Matthias thought of her? Or what the royals and jet-setters of Europe thought, for that matter? It wasn't like they were *her* friends. They'd write their own script for this, she was sure.

Runaway Bride.

Well, there was the rest of the world, too. She'd been on the front page of the newspaper in New *Zealand,* for heaven's sake. But once the wedding date had passed without trace of her, it would all begin to die down, and the world would move on to the next scandal. She'd lie low until then, and after that? Nobody would even remember her name. She'd go back to what she'd always been: a face and a body.

For the past few years, she'd mainly been known as a lingerie and swimsuit model, in a certain famous catalog that was "read" by men as often as women. This would do anything but hurt her career. Now, if anybody did recognize her, she'd be that sweet girl with a bad-girl secret.

Ha. *That* was heartening. She'd never had a bad-girl anything.

What was her mother thinking, though? Where would she be? Still at the palace, hoping Nina would come back, or… or turned out instantly? Would Matthias have blamed her?

She had a pretty good idea of how her mother would be feeling, whether she were in the palace or back in LA. Angry, confused, and… hurt. Nina never disappointed people, and now she'd disappointed everyone.

The guilt twisted in her stomach, trying to pull her down into gloom again, but she yanked herself back up with a ferocious effort. Her mother would know what Nina had done, because *her* mother would tell her. And whose life was it, anyway? If you ran away from your wedding and all you felt was relief, surely it was the right decision. Maybe somebody else could have done it differently, but she wasn't somebody else, and she'd done it the best she could. She'd *done* it, at least, instead of going through with it because it was what was expected of her, the path that other people had chosen for her, the one they'd said was best for her. And it was the right choice. She knew it. She could have made everybody happy, and it would have made her miserable.

Time to focus on the here and now. She was dirty, and she needed to get clean. Job One. So she went back into the bedroom, collected the few items she'd bought at the pharmacy the day before, took a long, hot shower, and felt better.

She hadn't bought any makeup. "Imperfect" was her best disguise, and off camera and without makeup, she was definitely imperfect. Her features were too big for what she always thought of as the "walking world," the world off the screen and the page. On film, her uncompromisingly square face with its pronounced bone structure, its too-large eyes and overfull lips, became haunting; sexy and sweet and a little bit sad. And heaven knew that thinness was what the camera wanted as well. Her bones were so small that her ribs never showed, even under her worst stress-induced weight loss. One thing was certain: no client had ever complained that she was too thin. She was, in fact, that rare creature prized by all modeling agencies: a tall, thin, slightly-built young woman with thick, shiny hair, a freakishly low waist-to-hip ratio, full breasts, no drug habit, and no attitude.

Off-camera and without makeup, though, she was a quiet, skinny girl with a funny face, big boobs, and, now, a bright-yellow shock of hair that hadn't felt the touch of any product today and was showing it. Nobody's idea of a princess. More like the sulphur-crested cockatoos she'd used to see when her granddad had taken her for a bushwalk. And it didn't matter how she looked anyway. This job didn't depend on it. She was going to lose it based on her performance, beg a ride back into Nelson, and go for the ice-cream scooping.

That was a cheering thought too, oddly enough. She'd fallen down from that pinnacle, and now, she had nothing to lose. Plus, she was in a house on the beach, at least for today. She might as well enjoy it. So she went back into her room, pulled on shorts and T-shirt, put away her new wardrobe in the little dresser, shoved her ugly red hat onto her head, and let herself out of the room, then out of the house the way she'd come the night before.

She was supposed to be taking care of Arthur. That wasn't going to go well when it happened, but she wasn't going to worry about that yet. He wasn't even awake, and right now, it was time to explore.

♡♡♡

Iain pulled the pillow over his head. Bloody birds.

He tried his best to go back to sleep, but they were just so... loud. And he'd gone to bed too early the night before, the discipline of a lifetime kicking back in after his so-called "holiday."

Right. Two weeks to finish getting to full fitness, and they started today. He threw the duvet back, rolled out of bed, and pulled on a pair of running shorts and a T-shirt, then made the bed and sat on it to pull on socks and running shoes.

Five minutes later, he was out the door, down through the break in the line of trees at the back of the garden, and onto the crescent of beach that edged the little bay. He saw pink striping the sky, a broad swath of golden sand beginning to glow in the reflected light, a calm turquoise sea, and endless sky.

And the girl. Nina.

His feet were carrying him straight over to her instead of around the little bay and onto the rocks he had to cross in order to get to the much longer expanse of Kaiteriteri Beach. He needed to run in the sand, so good for his strength and his ankles both, then do the winding road to Marahau and back before the holidaymakers arrived to run him off it and put a premature end to his career. A good, fast, hilly fifteen kilometers to kick his day off. Good as gold.

Except that he wasn't doing it.

Nina was facing into the pink streaks of sunrise in some sort of upside-down frog pose. Her hands were clasped, planted along with her elbows on the flat ledge of sand; her knees tucked onto her biceps; her toes touching. As he watched, her legs rose slowly into the air. Her knees drew together as her legs straightened and her toes pointed, and he suspected that if he knew anything about yoga, he'd be impressed.

She must be feeling better, then. He'd knocked softly at her not-quite closed door the day before, not five minutes after she'd gone inside. When she hadn't answered a second knock, he'd pushed the door open and looked in. She'd been fast asleep on top of the bed, curled up in the fetal position, one thin arm flung up over her head. Her red cap had been off for once, and her shocking yellow hair had been sticking up onto the pillow. She'd looked about fifteen years old, and completely vulnerable. He'd set her bags down, then been unable to resist getting another blanket from his granddad's couch to cover her better than the light throw that seemed to have been all she'd managed to grab before she'd collapsed.

But that had been yesterday. She didn't look vulnerable today. She looked fit, and surprisingly strong considering her thinness. Her turquoise T-shirt had slipped down, exposing more than a few centimeters of her back, the same ivory as her bare arms.

She wasn't tanned at all, he realized. She seemed to be the same color all over.

The same color all over. And it was a bloody nice color, too.

He was close to her now, but he didn't say anything. He'd made her fall the day before. Probably best not to do it again. So he waited, and after a minute, she kicked down gracefully, landing on first one foot, then the other, and pressed back into a pose he actually recognized. Not from doing it, of course. From seeing some of the backs doing it in the gym as a warmdown, while the forwards were pushing a little more tin. Though if the forwards had a teacher like this, they'd probably be keener.

"Downward-Facing Dog," he said, and she lost the perfect alignment. She hesitated a second, then she jumped her feet forward to her hands and rose to stand. She had some color in her cheeks at last, he noticed.

"Sorry," he said. "That's probably like coming up to a bloke who's painting a picture and asking him about his technique."

She smiled, and it was a wide thing, a sunny thing. His heart may actually have stuttered a bit, because her smile was… it was glorious. So sweet and joyful, it sliced straight into him.

"No," she said, and laughed. Her laugh was husky, like her voice. Purely incongruous, coming from that fragile body.

"I'm no artist. But you know the pose. Somehow, I hadn't pegged you as the yoga type. Want to join me? It's such a beautiful spot, it's almost criminal *not* to do yoga here." She raised her arms over her head with total unselfconsciousness, grasped one wrist with the opposite hand, and stretched, her back arching like a bow.

She was... something special. Baggy shorts, blue T-shirt, bare feet. But mostly... Nina. Mouth too wide, eyes too far apart, all brown and gold and ivory and pink. Glowing.

"Are you always this happy?" he asked, unable to resist smiling himself. "Yesterday a bit out of the ordinary, then?"

"Yes. No. Maybe." She heaved a satisfied sigh, then turned around and looked out to sea, out to the dawn, and he missed seeing all of her face. "But how could you be anything else here, no matter what was going on?"

"Oh, I don't know. Seems people can find a way to be unhappy, no matter what."

"Yes." She still wasn't looking at him. "Perspective. It's a thing. Maybe it's good to escape here sometimes and be reminded. But you always live here, I guess. Maybe you don't see it."

She didn't know what he did. He didn't know why it should come as a surprise. *On your sheep farm,* she'd said.

He didn't enlighten her. "Nah, I don't live here. Never have. Just a brief visit. But En Zed's not too bad, eh. None of it."

"That's right. You told me you wouldn't be here for long." She stretched again, one arm reaching high overhead, her head bending on her long, graceful neck until it almost touched her shoulder. "So where do you live?"

"Auckland. The North Shore. Close to the beach there, too."

She came upright again, turned her head, and smiled at him. "That sounds nice."

"I thought it was when I bought it."

Her eyes changed, shifted, and she lost some of the sunniness. "But now you don't?"

He shrugged. He didn't want to ruin her mood. "Call it a glitch."

She let it go, to his relief. "So are you going to do yoga with me?"

"Nah," he said. "I'm going to run. I need to run."

She nodded, not seeming to need more explanation than that. "Whatever gets you there," she said, confirming his impression that she, somehow, had understood him, that it was more than training. "See you later, then." She stepped one foot back behind her, raised her arms to the sky, and arched her back, then moved smoothly into another stretched-out standing pose, and he left her to it and started down the beach. Striding out, long and loose, letting the salt and the morning and the air fill his lungs.

And Nina. Long limbs, smile wide as the sky, as bright as the sun that was rising now against the horizon to his left. His heart lifted with the exercise, with the day. And, maybe, with the memory of her.

can't boil water
♡

Nina didn't keep watching him, even though she wanted to.

He'd taken *off*. Who would have guessed that somebody that big and muscular could run that fast? Now, she focused on her breathing, timing it to the sound of the gentle waves lapping against the sandy shore, and flowed through the familiar, long-practiced motions of her practice, and soon she was past him, and past her fears and guilt, too.

Yoga on the beach. That would be "paradise" no matter what the rest of it was. But the rest of it was good, too.

By the time she'd worked the kinks out of her body and stilled her mind, the sun was fully up, the day beginning to warm. She looked at the turquoise water longingly. It just *asked* you to swim. It was so clear, she could see the golden, sandy bottom and glimpse the occasional white shell. The scoop of bay that had formed this beach was only about three hundred feet long, and there only seemed to be five or six other houses back in the trees that lined the hillside below the road. Best of all, the way the beach curved out just here, beneath Iain's family's house, she thought it might be cut off from the others at high tide. But she hadn't seen a soul out here anyway, except for Iain. She could go back to the cottage, get her swimsuit…

But she'd slept here last night, and she had to pay that back somehow. Do one day of… whatever she could manage to do for Arthur, anyway. At least offer, before she got kicked out.

If he wasn't awake, she'd go ahead and swim. If he was, she'd swim later. The ocean would still be here, and the ocean was free.

She walked back up the golden sand and up onto grass, through the break in the vegetation that edged the house's front garden, and was in the midst of the birdsong and greenery once more. A wooden table and chairs stood near the house, on a stone patio sheltered by a pergola covered with climbing vines. Wisteria, and roses. What a place to eat your breakfast. Short palms and giant ferns that were more like trees were planted around the edges of the property, with flowers running riot at their base. She recognized birds of paradise and calla lilies, but there were so many more, purple and blue and yellow and pink, an explosion of color and scent. And in the middle, a rectangular patch of thick grass— and a huge hammock slung between two palm trunks at one side. Offering another invitation that she'd love to accept after her swim, if nobody else was using it.

Or not, if she were already gone. Strangely, the thought still didn't panic her the way it had yesterday. Maybe sea air really *did* carry those negative ions that made you happy. Or maybe she'd just accepted the inevitability that this was short-term. *Very* short-term, and then she'd find a ride into whatever larger town was closest, a backpacker's hostel, and a job she could actually do.

She'd make it. She didn't eat much.

She skirted the big house and let herself back into the cottage, going on through the porch and into the kitchen.

Arthur was sitting at the table, his metal cane beside him. "Shoes," he barked.

Nina looked at him. "Uh…"

"Take off your shoes in the house."

"Oh." She went back out to the porch, where she'd seen a

shelf holding a line of shoes. Arthur's own, and some that had to be a woman's, flattened and worn down at the sides. Shoes that had belonged to an older woman, possibly a heavier one. A woman who hadn't needed new shoes as much as she'd needed flowers, maybe. Shoes that were still on the shelf, as if the owner would be right back.

Nina set her own sandals beside those heartbreaking others and came back in, the grit on the kitchen floor scritch-scritching under her soles.

Maybe the sand in her beach-house daydream wasn't such a great thing after all. Ever since she could remember, her mother had had somebody to clean, and lately, Nina had seemed to spend half her time in hotels. She'd never really experienced anything but 'clean,' and was ashamed to think she'd never paid enough attention to how things got that way, or appreciated it nearly enough.

She smiled at Arthur. "Sorry. I didn't know. Good morning."

He grunted and said, "You could have a cup of tea, anyway. As you're here. Make me one as well."

"Thank you." She found the electric kettle and filled it at an old-fashioned stainless-steel sink, then pushed the button. She followed Arthur's directions for tea and mugs.

"Milk in the fridge," Arthur said.

"I don't take milk, thanks."

"Well, I do."

"Oh. Sure." She opened the fridge, then rocked back. Something had spoiled in here. She found the milk and sniffed at it cautiously, then shut the door again fast, fixed the tea, and brought his over to him.

"You had a good sleep, eh," he said.

"Yes. I did. And I was out on the beach for a while. I'm sorry. I didn't know when you woke up."

He nodded. "Well, as you're still here, you can fix breakfast. But that doesn't mean you're staying. I meant what I said. I don't need a minder."

"Oh. Sure. Umm…" She looked around a little wildly. "So

do you have... what? Toast? What do you eat?"

He stared at her from under the beetling brows. "Same as everyone. Eggs on toast. Sausages. Fried tomatoes."

She swallowed. "Right. Umm... I'll just..." She got up and went over to the stove. It, too, wasn't entirely clean. Greasy, in fact.

"Pans are to the left," Arthur said.

She found a frying pan in a cupboard, pulled it out, and set it on the stove, then went to the refrigerator again, braved the smell, and found a carton of eggs. She searched until she found a packet of sausages. Not the precooked things she'd been hoping for, but pale and... gummy-looking.

As she brought them out, her nose wrinkled.

"I don't think these are good," she told Arthur.

"Rubbish. I had them yesterday."

"Well, they smell bad to me."

"Bring them over." She did, and he lifted the packet to his nose, grimaced, and handed them back. "Right, then. Chuck them in the bin."

One down. Good, because she had no idea how you cooked sausages. "Scrambled eggs good?" she asked brightly.

"Nah. Poached, of course."

Poached? "I don't know... how to do poached. I can do scrambled, though."

He stared at her as if she'd sprouted something nasty. "You don't know how to boil an egg?"

"No. I don't."

"That a hole in your general knowledge, or about the size of it? You telling me Carmella's found me a minder who can't boil water?"

Gelato scooping, here I come. "I'm afraid that's about it. I eat a lot of nonfat yoghurt, and I can make salad. I'm good at salad. Lots of greens and vegetables, and sometimes I put slices of chicken on it. Lemon juice, too. That's very... tasty." Well, by her standards. Boneless, skinless breasts, bought precooked. "And veggie smoothies," she went on. "You could call that my signature. With kale and beets and chia seeds, and a few blueberries or a carrot, you know, for sugar, and…" Her voice trailed off. Arthur was looking at her with nothing less than horror now. "They're very healthy," she added lamely.

"Why on *earth*," he said, "would Carmella hire you to look after me? Could be she doesn't like me much, but I didn't think she was actually trying to *kill* me."

The real question was, why had *she* thought it sounded like a good idea? Because she'd heard "house on the beach," and pictured herself… well, she'd glossed over the details, to be honest.

"If she'd wanted to kill you," she pointed out, "I would've cooked the sausages."

He grunted out what could possibly have been a laugh. In somebody else. "Could be your nerve failed you."

"Well," Nina admitted, "I didn't exactly tell her I didn't know how to cook. I thought maybe I could figure it out. Somehow. If the smoothies and salads aren't an option. No," she went on at another glare, stifling a giggle of her own. "I see not. But if you tell me what to do, I'll do my best."

"Reckon bacon-and-egg pie's not on, then. Or even bangers and mash. Roast lamb, either." He sighed. "Can you at least make a toastie? And in *this* house, veggies are cooked. If I ate all that, what you said? I'd be on the toilet for days."

A little snort might have escaped her. "Well, I'm willing to learn. The toastie and all. I could start with that, maybe."

He snorted himself, and there was nothing little about it. "Willing to *burn*, more like. I already had a young bride. Don't need to go through that again."

This time, she didn't succeed in keeping the laughter back. Out it came, like a bubble rising to the surface.

"You can probably clean, anyway, let's hope," he said. "You could do that before you go, if you like."

"Um… sure. If…"

"Let me guess," he said with an almighty sigh. "If I tell you how."

"If you knew how," she was somehow bold enough to say,

"you might be doing it."

"Huh," he said with his usual glower. "I have a bad hip. Didn't you notice?"

"Anything wrong with your arms?" His eyebrows lowered, and she realized she was talking herself out of a job. "I mean, I can vacuum," she added quickly. "And... wipe things, you know. I just don't know about... products."

Rosa, their maid, had always sprayed, though. Stuff out of cans, and bottles with squirt tops. And she'd had rags. "Do you have rags?" she asked hopefully. "I know there are rags involved. Sponges, too."

A smile was cracking his seamed face at last. "Sweet little thing like you, butter wouldn't melt in her mouth. You fooled Carmella into thinking you could do this."

"Well, I may have... embellished a little," she admitted.

"What *do* you know how to do?"

Stand in front of a camera and look sexy. Yoga. She didn't think either of those was on his list. "I can drive. I'm a very good driver."

"Well, when I need a chauffeur to take me two streets over to the shop, that'll be good to know." He shook his head. "We could sit here and have a yarn about all the things you don't know how to do, but I'd probably drop dead of starvation and old age before we got to the end of it. So I guess I'd better teach you to boil an egg."

He did teach her. The results weren't perfect, but she did it. And somehow, by the time she'd gently taken each of the four poached eggs out of the pot with a slotted spoon and laid them carefully on a paper towel, she was actually hungry. Of course, the eggs were a bit too done, and she *had* managed to break one of them, so it looked a little... raggedy.

"That's yours," Arthur said. "See you slip it into the water more carefully next time."

She laughed again. "Yes, sir." And then she tipped the eggs onto the thick slices of buttered toast—even though she *never* ate buttered toast—arranged slices of kiwifruit in a neat fan on each plate, set the plates on the table, and felt like she'd managed a five-course dinner.

"I cooked," she said. "How about that?"

Arthur grunted, of course. "We won't tell Carmella what."

"Well," she said, "I'd appreciate it." She grinned at him, and she could swear there was a twinkle in his eye.

She didn't start eating, even though she was suddenly starving. Instead, she jumped up again. "You know what? If I cooked, we should have placemats, don't you think?" The table wasn't bad, just a little sticky. But it felt like an occasion, and she wanted to celebrate it.

Arthur told her where to find them, and she searched out some pretty yellow flowered ones of quilted cotton.

"Those were Madeline's favorites," he said. "Don't use those."

"Really?" She looked down at the cheerfully patterned things. "If they were her favorites, maybe you *should* use them. Wouldn't they remind you of her?"

"No." The twinkle was gone, his tone all the way back to gruff. "Use something else."

She brought over a pair of blue ones, and they ate their breakfast in silence until Nina said, "When did your wife pass away?"

He shoved away from the table. "Too much chat. If you're going to be here, do something. Don't chat at me." He picked up his plate and his cane, stumped over to the sink, and put the plate inside. "Maybe you know how to do the washing up."

"I can do that. And vacuum, too." And she'd figure out how to get everything else cleaner, too. Somehow.

"Good. Make yourself useful, then."

He left the room, and Nina took another bite of eggs and toast, then looked at her plate in surprise. Normally, when the atmosphere got tense, especially when somebody was angry with her, her breath instantly grew shallow, her body froze, and her throat closed. She'd always had trouble eating after somebody had been harsh with her. But today, she was still hungry.

Because he wasn't really angry with *her*. He was old, and he was lonely, and he was sad. And from the way he moved, he hurt. It wasn't about her. It was about him. But she *had* made him almost smile. And she'd cooked him breakfast, too. So she finished her eggs, drank the last of her tea, and stood up to do the dishes.

First, though, she'd clean out the sink. There was always something in the cabinet underneath to scrub with. She'd noticed that.

the couple that bins together
♡

Iain was about to walk into the cottage, but he checked himself and knocked first. It wasn't just his granddad anymore.

He heard something from inside, a muffled sound that might have been "Come in," so he opened the door cautiously and stepped inside, kicking off his jandals before heading into the kitchen.

The smell nearly knocked him back on his heels, and Nina had turned from where she was squatting on her haunches in front of the open fridge. Now, she got to her feet—and hit her head on the freezer door, recoiling with a yelp.

"Ow ow *ow.*" She was doing a little dance, her hand clamped to the spot.

"Bloody hell," he said, coming across the room fast and reaching for her, trying to check out her head. "Are you all right?"

"Ow," she said again, then dropped her hand, pulled away from him, and laughed. "Yes. *That* was dumb. Add it to the list today. I had no idea housework was so hazardous."

"Something die in here?" he asked, checking out the overflowing kitchen tidy and the additional orange rubbish bag she'd pressed into service.

"*Yes,*" she said, shutting the freezer door and crouching in front of the fridge again, beginning to take jars out of the door shelves and turn them over. Checking the expiry dates, he realized, because half of them were going into the rubbish. "Or something's alive, more like. Like about twelve billion bacteria colonies. They're staging an uprising. Can't you smell it?"

He grinned. "Yeh. I can. Quite the pong in here. You *are* tougher than you look."

"Nope. I'm sure not." She was hauling out produce now, tossing limp celery and green potatoes with abandon. "But your granddad is. He was telling me that if he ate like I did, he'd be on the toilet for days. *Ha.* If he's been eating this and surviving, not to mention using that bathroom? He's got a stomach made of cast iron."

He had to laugh at that. "Need a hand?"

"Well, you could show me where to dump it." She shut the fridge door and rose to her feet.

"I'll do better than that," he said. "I'll do it for you."

"Nope," she said. "It's not even ten A.M., and I've already made poached eggs today, and vacuumed, and scrubbed things you don't want to hear about. I've cleaned out a fridge, too. And now I'm going to empty the trash. Those may not seem like big accomplishments to you, but they work for me."

He was already dumping the contents of the tidy into the larger rubbish bag and twisting the top of the bag, shutting out the stink. Now, he tied a knot in it and hefted it. "Nah," he said, "I'll take it out for you. But I'll show you where, how's that?"

"This isn't going to get you anywhere, you know," she said. "Carrying my garbage for me."

"You mean you're not going to shag me for it? Well, bugger that, then." He let the bag drop and headed for the door. When he heard her gasp, though, he turned back again. "You know, you could just say, 'Thanks.'"

She had her hands on her hips. "You are the most—"

"Yeh? Well, so are you." She was glaring, and he wasn't, quite. He was... curious, maybe. Waiting for what would come next.

What came next was a minor explosion, apparently. "Just because I want to make sure there aren't strings attached? And do you have to be such a... a..."

"A what? You can say it. Go on."

She cast a glance behind her.

"Yeh," he said. "Granddad knows the word too."

"Asshole," she whispered. "At times," she hurried to add.

"Now, see," he said, "bet that hardly hurt at all. You look like you've never said it before."

"Well, I haven't, all right?" She was glaring worse than ever. "Not out loud where anybody could hear me."

"Lucky it was just me, then. And yeh, reckon I do. Have to be one, that is. Can't you tell I'm not a very nice person? I would've said it was obvious."

She snorted. "It is *not.*" And when he just looked at her, she added in clear exasperation, "You look out for your mum and your granddad. You looked out for *me* when I fainted. You *apologized.* You've got a lot to learn about not being a nice person. It's just at *times.*"

"Are you going to be outing me? On the nice bit? Heaps of people out there who could give you an argument."

"They must not know you very well, then." And, yes, she was picking up the rubbish bag, even though it was heavy enough that she'd probably have to drag it. "Since you're so nice and everything, show me where it goes. *Please.* I've got a lot to learn here. And I need all the instruction I can get."

She muttered the last bit in that husky little voice, and he glanced at her, startled.

She looked up at him, not seeming one bit intimidated by his size, sighed, and said, "What? You think that was sexy? Trust me. It wasn't sexy. Everything I'm wearing is going to need fumigation, and I'm in serious need of some eye bleach, because I've seen more disgusting things this morning than I have in my entire life. I couldn't pretend to be sexy right now if you *paid* me. And if you knew me, you'd know that's a revelation."

What? She had his head spinning all the way around. What was she telling him? But she jerked her head at the door and said, "Show me," so he headed for the door and over to the rubbish bins, stored to one side of the shed.

And, no. It wasn't sexy. Except that she heaved it up and dropped it in there, brushed her hands together as he shut the lid, said, "Phew!" and laughed up at him with the sunlight sparkling on those golden flecks in her eyes.

And, before he could stop himself, he was grinning back and saying, "Yeh. The couple that bins together, sins together."

"What?"

"It sounded good when I thought it up just now. What d'you reckon?"

"Never going to catch on. So did you want something?"

Yeh. I want you. "Uh…"

She sighed. "Never mind, I got it. You're not interested, I'm imagining things, and I don't need to worry. Even though you shaved and all."

Well, no, that hadn't been the impression he'd meant to convey. "Well, yeh," he said. "I tend to do that. I look too rough otherwise, people seem to think."

"Oh. Well, you hadn't yesterday, so I thought…"

Was it better if he said he'd thought about her when he'd shaved and dressed, or that he hadn't? He didn't know. The truth was, he *had* thought about her. He was wearing a collared shirt as well, a dark blue knit one, over less disreputable shorts, and he felt, suddenly, as self-conscious about it as if he'd turned up in a dinner jacket. It seemed she could tell what he'd been thinking, and she didn't want any.

He was still working it out when she asked, "Did you come over to see your granddad, or to check whether he'd fired me yet? He hasn't, but it's only a matter of time, so you can relax. My Phantom Baby and I will be out of here any minute now."

"Oi. I *said* I was sorry about that. Not fair to bring it up again."

"No? I didn't think there was a statute of limitations."

"The rule book was written by a woman, then. Men get it out there and move on."

"Yep," she said, "we can hold a grudge, all right. Especially us puppies."

"I said 'kitten,'" he protested. "I didn't say 'puppy.'"

"You *definitely* said 'puppy.' You said both."

He sighed. "Next time, I'm recording it and playing it back. And what I came over to ask was whether you or Granddad needed anything from the store. Groceries and that, as I'm making a run into Motueka for Mum. And now that I've seen the state of Granddad's fridge, I'm thinking the answer is 'yes.'"

"Do you…" She hesitated. "Do you think I could come with you? I'm not going to be able to write down the right things. I'm not a very experienced grocery shopper. I have another errand I'd like to do as well, if that would be OK."

"No worries. Company's good. Besides, puppies like to ride in the car."

She laughed and gave him a backhand swipe to the arm, and he caught her hand, said, "Long as you don't bite too hard," and smiled at her.

Her eyes widened for a second, and then she tugged her hand free, started back to the cottage, and said over her shoulder, "Well, good, then. Thanks. I need to make a… a list of my own, I guess. And take another shower, too. I am *not* going anywhere like this. Can you wait?"

"Course."

"Wait," it was clear, was the operative word. It seemed that his sex drive, as well as his sense of humor, was kicking back into full gear again. It also seemed that he was going to have to look elsewhere to gratify at least one of those. He was only here for a week, and he had the feeling that a week wasn't going to do it.

♡♡♡

He found his granddad on the couch, watching the cricket on the telly.

"Good thing, too," Arthur said once Iain had explained his errand and Arthur had headed into the kitchen and lowered himself painfully into a chair. He watched with his usual scowl as Nina hunted out a battered little spiral notebook and pen from the overflowing junk drawer. "She's determined to starve me to death," he complained, pointing at the fridge with his cane and fixing Nina with an accusing stare. "She's binned most of my good food already, did she tell you? Chutney, tomato sauce, and all. Left me with a few biscuits and kiwifruit, a loaf of bread, and her threatening to make me drink some sort of sewery sludge instead of good Kiwi tucker. I've said she can stay one more day, seeing as she's still tired and all, but if she fixes me anything like that? Make no mistake, she gets the chuck, and no beg pardons." He glared at Nina. "You hear?"

"Yes, sir," she said meekly, but Iain could see her eyes dancing again. "I promise to cook your vegetables into submission."

"Ha," he muttered darkly. "More like I'll have to."

"Not if you show me," she said. "I'm not the best cook," she explained to Iain. "So I may need some help from both of you with this list. What are easy things that you make with... heat?"

With *heat*? "Uh..." Iain tried to think. "Steaks, maybe. Burgers. Fish fillets. Those would be the easiest. Fastest, too."

"And then you do... vegetable-y things to go with them?" she asked hopefully. "In a pan?"

Arthur shook his head in disgust. "'You need some help, Dad,' Carmella told me. 'If you don't want to move in with Graeme and me, or at least eat with us, let me find you somebody to come in and fix your meals. You're losing weight, Dad.' And *this* is what she finds for me. I'm going to be skin and bones."

"I *said* I'd learn," Nina said. "When I come back, I'll make you lunch. I'll make you a... a sandwich or something. Ham." She wrote it down. "Men like ham, right?"

"And cheese," Iain added helpfully.

She paused with her pen above the paper. "Cheese isn't good for you."

"Bite your tongue," Arthur said. "That kind of talk will get you tossed out of En Zed even before I can manage it. Cheese goes on that list, and you take care that it comes home with you as well, or it's the chop for you. And I can make my own lunch, thank you. I can make my own dinner, too, come to that. Looks to me like I'm going to have to."

"Well," she said, "then what's your problem?"

"Got a mouth on her," Arthur warned his grandson. "You take care."

"No worries," he said. "Already sussed that out, haven't I."

Nina didn't look upset, though, not the way she had when *he'd* said things. She looked... *pleased.* And that was odd, because if *Iain* was narky these days, his granddad surely won the trophy. But she just said, "Well, tell me things to write down. Vegetable-type things. *Simple* things. And Arthur can show me how to make them. Or it's the kale smoothies. I'm making vegetable *something* with this steak, and that's that."

"Fish," Iain said automatically. "If you buy fish," he explained at her inquiring glance, "you have to use it today. The rest will keep a bit, though you'll need to use the mince within a couple days as well."

"She won't be *here* in a couple days," his granddad said. "I'll have given her the sack."

Nina ignored him, wrote it all down painstakingly in her notebook, and said, "What else?"

"Everything you chucked out," Arthur growled. "Every single thing. I'll be checking, mind. You miss something, and I'll know."

semi-famous
♡

When Nina got out of the shower, Iain was on the couch with his grandfather, watching cricket. He'd changed his clothes yet again, she saw, and was back to gym shorts, T-shirt, and running shoes.

He stood up when she came in. And to his credit, he looked at her face, even though she'd changed, too, and was wearing a raspberry-colored V-necked T-shirt that came close to showing cleavage. She'd worn shorts with it, though, instead of a skirt. She hadn't missed the way he'd looked at her yesterday, and if he did that, other people would, too.

She pulled the hat and sunglasses on, and he sighed and said, "Notice how I'm not saying anything."

"Except that you are."

He grinned. "Did you wear it in the shower?"

"None of your business," she said loftily.

Arthur said, "Quiet. I can't hear."

"He can't hear," Iain said. "Reckon we'd better get on. We may not be back in time for Granddad's ham sandwich as it is."

"Ham and *cheese* sandwich," Arthur muttered.

"You might have to go on over to the big house and make it, Granddad," Iain said. "We're a bit less decimated over there. Nina hasn't taken it over yet. I'll text if it looks like we won't be back by one."

"You think I'm helpless?" The old man glared at him.

"Oh. Money," Nina said. "Groceries."

"I've got it," Iain said.

Arthur said, "I'll settle up with you later, though I should take it out of Nina's wages. There was nothing wrong with that tomato sauce."

Nina walked to the car with Iain, then, and they drove a bare few blocks through a tiny commercial district and were on the road to Motueka. An incredibly *winding* road that Iain handled with ease, taking the sharp curves with one hand on the wheel and the fingers of the other one barely grazing it, negligently helping out. Taking the road fast, but not too fast, not scaring her the way Matthias always had. Iain clearly knew what he was doing, and he also clearly wasn't showing off. He just drove that way, like he *felt* the car, and was perfectly in tune with it. He was a physical animal for sure.

After a few minutes, he said, "You said you had another errand. Short errand, or long one? If it's long, we should do it before the supermarket. You may not know this, what with your stunted development in the food department, but those things you make with heat? They require refrigeration."

"I'm not an actual idiot," she said. "I just don't *cook*. And I don't know about short or long. I wanted to go to the library. Is there a library?"

"Yeh. Motueka's got quite a big one. So do I have time to go to the gym while you're there, or not?"

"Well, whatever you want, surely. But wait. You're going to the gym? I thought you already went running today. Somehow, I thought it was a long run."

"It was, reasonably. That's just cardio, though, so now I'm going to the gym. Well, now or later. Soon as you tell me how long you want to spend at the library, because I'll be a good hour and a half."

When she kept looking at him, he sighed and said, "Just tell me, all right? I'm on holiday. Doesn't matter to me if I do the shopping and then drop you back here, or if I do them the other way round."

Well, *this* was disorienting. She was used to fitting into other people's plans. *New leaf,* she reminded herself. She was a runaway bride now. Everybody would think she was selfish anyway. Nothing to lose. "Library first, then, please," she decided. "I'll be glad to take my time. I'm sort of on holiday too."

"Not much of a holiday so far, seems to me."

"Well, it's the change that matters, right? And I wouldn't call yours much better." When he glanced sharply at her, she said, "Running, the gym, and grocery shopping for your family? I don't know about New Zealand, but where I come from, that's not exactly, 'Peel me a grape, Alfonse.'"

He shook his head, then slowed as the town appeared up ahead. "You could be right," he said. "Just keeping up with your conversation is a full-time job."

He dropped her at the library, which was down a seemingly endless single street that appeared to be about all there was to commercial Motueka. It was busy for all of that, with most of the population seeming to have decided that their day would best be spent sitting at a café's sidewalk tables under the shade of an umbrella. It might be busy, but it couldn't be called bustling, and neither could the library.

Nina found her books—nothing she'd ever have imagined checking out before—and then decided to go for some novels as well. Swimming in the ocean, then lying in a hammock reading a mystery? That sounded to her like an even better choice than a sidewalk café.

She had to admit that she glanced a few times at the row of Internet-connected computers, too, but fortunately the terminals were all occupied by young people—backpackers, presumably.

There was nothing she had to check anyway. The outside world could go on without her. Another liberating thought. Instead, she found a comfy beanbag in a sunny corner by the window where she could watch Motueka passing by outside, all sundresses and shorts and sandals, then opened her book and settled down with a sigh. People came and went around her, and some held low conversations, their heads bent over wooden library tables. It was all very... peaceful.

"Nina." A voice was saying it from far away, then saying it again from closer up, or she was floating toward it. Something was brushing her arm, too.

"Oh." She blinked into Iain's blue eyes. "Huh. I must have fallen asleep. I keep doing that."

"You do, yeh." He was on one big knee beside her, close enough that she could see that his hair was wet, and that a shadow was already beginning to show on that square jawline.

His beard must be heavy. What a surprise. The Hulk genes, probably.

"Was the gym nice?" she asked, stretching an arm overhead and taking a deep, audible breath. She was still so... sleepy.

"Very nice," he said solemnly. His eyes were warm, and there was a smile playing around the corners of his mouth. He looked good, smiling like that.

"Mm. They must have nice soap."

His smile grew a little more. "Why would that be?"

"Smells good."

He *did* smell good. Clean, and faintly pine-scented. She could have closed her eyes and known that it was a man beside her, and an attractive one, too. Why was that?

"You smell pretty good yourself, if we're confessing," he said. "What I'd call sweet. Like baking, eh. Can't be that, though, as baking takes heat, and you don't do that."

"Mm. Also calories." She couldn't stop looking at him, somehow. He was just so... *big*. And solid. If he held you, you'd be so... *held*. You could lean right up against him, and if he had those arms around you? That would be so completely, so deliciously secure.

Moving right along. "Honey-almond body butter," she said. "I bought it yesterday. With your mum."

"Buzz kill," he said, and she stifled a giggle.

A severe-looking lady sitting alone at a table with a huge pile of books beside her looked up and frowned, and Nina whispered, "Whoops. Shhh. We're loud and bad."

"Well, *I* am, anyway," he said, his voice low, and deep enough to send a few very nice tingles up her arms—and right down her body. "Not so sure about you."

What was she *doing?* She was lying sprawled in a beanbag chair, that was what, flirting with a menacing mutant who was looming over her and looking ready to pounce. Two days before she was supposed to be married to somebody else.

Bad, bad idea. She never did this kind of thing. She behaved herself. She was *cautious.* It was too relaxing here, that was the problem.

"Right," she whispered. "We should go. I forgot to ask— do you have a library card?"

He blinked. "Uh... no." He didn't whisper, though. She'd bet he couldn't do anything that soft.

"Shoot." She looked at the pile of books on the floor beside her with regret. "You have to have proof of residency to get one, probably. I guess you wouldn't."

"No worries," Iain said. The severe-looking lady frowned at them again, but he ignored her. "We've got this." He stood, gestured at the books, and asked, "All these?" and at her nod, picked them up and tucked them into one big arm, then held out a hand to her and pulled her to her feet. "Come on, bad thing. Let's go get a library card."

♡♡♡

There was desire, Iain thought. And then there was this. The need to lean over Nina as she lay in that beanbag, looking so sleepy and sexy. To give in and take that hat off her, then move over her, plant one elbow on either side of her head, and take her head in his hands. To thread his fingers through her hair and give her the kisses that mouth deserved, long and slow and sweet, until he'd begun to learn the secrets of her, had found out how she liked it. He was guessing she'd like it slow and tender. That was good, because that was how he wanted to do it. And then he could find out if her lips could possibly taste as honey-sweet as the rest of her smelled.

The way she'd look under him, too, the way her eyes would drift shut, the way she'd sigh...

In the library. Maybe not.

He had to wait in the queue for a woman to finish checking out her books, and he cast a glance at Nina, standing beside him. She was settling her hat more firmly over her hair, her expression serious now, not sleepy anymore.

Well, bugger.

He stepped to the front when it was his turn, set the books down, pulled out his wallet, and began to remove his driving license. "I'd like to get a library card, please," he said. "I'm here on holiday, but my family lives here."

"I'm afraid you do have to be a resident," the woman behind the desk said, and Nina said, "I *told* you."

The young bloke scanning returned books, though, was staring at Iain. He edged closer, sneaked a peek at Iain's license, and said, "You're actually him." He was looking quite excited, too, which was more hopeful.

"Well, yeh," Iain said. "I don't have an electric bill or whatever you need," he told the lady. "But if this fella here's of reputable character, maybe he could vet me. I'm in the area quite often."

The bloke was reaching under the table, then bringing out a memo pad together with a pen. "Could I have your autograph?"

Iain signed, but the lady behind the desk was still looking at him with suspicion, and Iain wondered what he'd been thinking. How would he look if he *couldn't* get a card and check out Nina's books for her?

Like a bloody fool, that was how.

"He's an All Black," the young fella, Iain's new best friend, was telling the woman. "Plays for the Blues as well. He's a lock, plays at 4. And his mum and dad *do* live here."

"Oh," the woman said, her expression clearing, a smile finally appearing on her middle-aged face. "Are you Finn Douglas? I'm sorry; I'm new to the area." She was patting her ample chest now. "How exciting. I saw pictures of your wee baby, and your wife expecting again, too. So sweet, after the tragedy and all."

Her gaze went to Nina, then, and she lost the smile. "Oh," she said again, her tone entirely different.

What, she thought that Finn Douglas, famous family man, he of the three kids and pregnant wife, was having a secret tryst in his hometown library? Probably not happening.

However funny it was, Iain might be better off preserving Finn's reputation, for his own sake as much as Finn's. There was nobody more fearsome than the Blues' new strength and conditioning coach in a temper. Which was why Iain had always been glad to be playing his rugby with Finn and not against him.

"Finn's not playing anymore, unfortunately for us," he told the woman. "I'm afraid I'm not him. Just another big unit packing down in the scrum."

"Oh." She *did* look disappointed, and he almost laughed. "Well, if your parents *do* live here, I suppose we can make an exception." She handed him a form. "Fill this out and bring it back, please."

"All right," Nina said when he moved aside to fill in his details. "Explain."

She was glaring at him worse than the librarian, and he got a little confused. "What?" he said. "Nothing too exciting. I'm a sportsman, that's all. And apparently, I got above myself. Got cut down like the tall poppy I was, too."

"You're *famous*." She was still glaring. Not quite the reaction he was used to.

"Well, not *that* famous, apparently," he pointed out. "As you heard. A lock's not exactly a glamour position. Not as bad as a prop, but not too far off. My ears aren't as shocking, though, if you notice."

"You realize that I have no idea what you're talking

about."

"About which part of it?"

"About *any* part. Start at the beginning and explain very slowly."

"Right, then," he said. "Seems this is my day not to impress. I'm a rugby player. A forward, not one of the flash boys at the back, meaning I do the hard yards. More tackling," he explained when she still looked blank. "I bash people for a living, you could say. I play for the Auckland Blues, and I play for the All Blacks. Which is En Zed's national team," he added with a sigh. "World champions for the past ten years or so, as it happens. We like to think we're known a bit outside the country. Apparently not."

"Sorry," she said. "I'm not what you'd call a sports fan."

"Despite the hat."

That one took her a moment. "Oh. Right. That's a team too, I guess. I never really looked at it."

He groaned. "If you live in the States and you don't even know gridiron—football, I mean—there's probably no hope."

"Well, football's boring," she said. "Sorry, but it is. Is rugby more exciting?"

"We like to think so. Faster, anyway, if that appeals."

"And you play it."

"I do."

"The reason for the scars. And you're... semi-famous."

He couldn't help it. He laughed. Which got him a disapproving glance from the librarian. "Semi. Though I'm apparently no Finn Douglas."

"Well, I'm not happy," Nina said, "but all right. So are you going to get a library card, or what?"

"Yeh," he said. "I'm going to get a library card. So I can get you your..." He glanced at the stack of books, then took a more careful look. "Cookery books. *Thirty Dinners in Thirty Minutes,* eh. *Kiwi Classics the Easy Way. Cookery for Kids.*"

He raised an eyebrow at her for that one, and she said, "Sounded like my speed."

He was still exploring. "Not to mention *Senior Yoga*. Hmm. You get Granddad doing Senior Yoga, and we're going to have to alert the media."

"I'll never do it if I don't get the *book*," she said.

So he applied himself to the serious business of obtaining a library card. If he wasn't going to impress her, he'd have to settle for making her happy.

one emotion. or more.
♡

Once Iain finally had his card, he insisted on carrying her stack of books to the car, which made Nina smile.

"You know what your dirty secret is?" she asked when he opened the car door for her, then set her books in the back seat before heading around to his side.

He gave her a quick, startled look and said, "What?"

"You're a gentleman."

"Oh. Well, no. But we'll let that go."

Wow. All righty, then. Probably best. It wasn't a good idea to flirt with a *regular* guy. It was a much worse one to flirt with a star athlete, no matter what Iain had said about his lack of fame. A teenage girl had come up to him while he'd been getting that library card and asked him to pose for a selfie with her, which had inspired a few more shy autograph requests before Iain had cut it short and made their escape. He might not be this Finn guy, but he wasn't nearly as anonymous as he'd pretended. And Nina was done with celebrities. She was done with *all* men, for a good long while. She had enough problems. She'd make an exception for Arthur, but that was it.

"Actually," Iain said, his hand on the key but still not starting up the car, "we should go for lunch before the shopping."

"Oh, no," she said. "I'm fine. Besides... Arthur's lunch."

"*You* may be fine, but I've just done my second workout, and if I don't eat soon, *I'll* be the one passing out. And I wouldn't put money on your being able to hold me up. If I hit the floor in the supermarket, I'll probably take the whole rack of eggs down with me. Imagine your embarrassment."

"I'm very strong," she assured him.

"Enough to hold up a hundred thirteen kg's of dead weight? You're not *that* strong. And Arthur," he added, forestalling her next objection, "can go over to my parents' place and make himself a sandwich, since you've binned all his green meat and moldy cheese. He told you, he knows how. I'll text him straight away and tell him he's on his own."

"He'll whine," she said, and Iain laughed.

"Yeh. He will. Come on." He was climbing out of the car again. "Lunch."

Which was why they were sitting, twenty minutes later, at one of those sidewalk tables under their very own umbrella, drinking coffee and eating flattened, grilled sandwiches filled with chicken, vegetables, and, yes, cheese. Toasties, in fact.

She'd tried to order hers without cheese, and Iain had said, "Doesn't taste nearly as good without it."

"I never eat cheese," she'd explained. "Fattening."

He'd wrapped one of those giant hands around her wrist and lifted her arm for inspection, which would have bothered her, except that he'd had a teasing glint in his eye. "Not a problem, I'd have said."

She'd tried to ignore the touch of that hand, the feel of his strong fingers wrapping around her wrist, and hadn't succeeded one bit. She'd looked at him, her eyes widening, and something in his own eyes had changed, the warmth kindling in them the same way it was spreading through her body, making her knees tremble.

His voice had been lower than ever, and a little husky, too, when he'd said, "I'd say you could eat a bit more. If you wanted to, of course. I'd say you could indulge. Sin a little."

She'd pulled her hand away, even though a treacherous part of her had wanted him to keep holding her, and had told the young man waiting patiently behind the counter, "A little cheese, then, please. Just a bit." Not because Iain had said it. She wasn't doing everything everyone told her anymore. But she'd lost nearly four pounds during her two weeks in Neuenstein, and she was on vacation. Other people ate and drank on vacation, right? Other people did all sorts of crazy things on vacation.

So, yes. She was eating cheese. And bread. And it tasted *good*. The tangy white cheddar was trying to ooze out the sides between the toasted, flavorful slices of flat Turkish bread; the chicken breast—the real thing, not pressed—was warm, too, and a little smoky; and the red peppers, onions, and whatever else was stuffed inside this thing didn't hurt one bit either. She could tell they'd used butter, or something equally fat-intensive. There was oil in the dressing on the salad of mixed baby greens piled beside the sandwich, too, and she didn't even care.

She held up the messy concoction and studied it. "I could manage this, maybe," she told Iain. "Making it, I mean. Your granddad said 'toasties.' It's just a sandwich that you smash. How do you smash it, though?"

"Full directions?"

"Yes, please."

"Right, then. Put it in a frying pan, one you've heated up, with a bit of butter melted in it. Not too hot, or you'll burn it. You want it to cook slowly, so the cheese melts. Press on it with a spatula as it cooks. A bit gently, like, so you don't squash all the filling out. Slice everything else thin, the veggies and all. And ham's the best in these, from a man's point of view. Or if you do use chicken, put some bacon in there as well. The way to a man's heart is through pork products, eh."

"Wait a second." She reached for the little notebook and pen in her purse, turned to the latest page, and wrote it all down.

"I can't believe you're writing down a recipe for toasties,"

Iain said.

"There's a lot to remember. And your grandfather specifically mentioned not burning things. I'll make a salad for him too, though. I'm guessing he's not getting enough vitamins in his diet." She put the notebook and pen away, picked up her sandwich again, but didn't take a bite yet. "When did your grandmother die?"

He lost his smile. "Over a year ago. Just after Christmas. Cancer. She went fast. Over eighty, and she was never much of a one for going to the doctor, or complaining, either."

"Oh." Nina remembered those shoes still on the shelf in the back porch, as if the owner would be back at any moment to step into them. Or as if Arthur couldn't bear to clear away the evidence of her presence in his house. In his life. "Poor man. The holidays this year must have been so rough, then. No wonder he's grumpy. What a tough Christmas for him."

"I reckon," Iain said. "I wasn't here."

"You weren't? And your mum and sister were in the UK? So it was just your dad and granddad here alone?"

He shifted a little in his chair, not meeting her eyes. "Yeh. I was overseas until a few days ago."

"Oh. Playing rugby?"

"Nah. On holiday."

"Oh," she said again.

"Trust me," he said, "it wouldn't have been better if I'd been here. Just three of us being that narky together instead of two."

"Not my business anyway," she said. "What you do. So what's—" She stopped, hesitated.

He sighed. "I can't wait. What?"

"Well… your parents. Is that what's wrong between your mum and dad? Is it that your mum left? Or are they always like that?"

"I don't know that either," he said. "What's wrong, I mean. The atmosphere's a bit fraught, eh. And you weren't at their house last night. It wasn't what you'd call relaxed."

"So are they retired?"

101

"Not even close. They run a kayak hire and sea shuttle business here in town. My grandparents started it yonks ago, and it's still in the family. Maybe Dad wasn't happy that Mum left just as business got busy. I don't know. But I can't believe he'd begrudge her going to help Vanessa. He's got a soft spot for her."

Nina blinked. "But—no wife, no kids at Christmas, and not seeing his grandchild, either? How many other siblings do you have?"

"None. Just the two of us."

"Iain." She couldn't help an exasperated sigh. "You don't get that he might have been lonely, just like your granddad?"

"My dad's not what you'd call the sentimental type."

"Right," she said. "No emotions. Just like you."

"You don't know whether I have emotions."

"Sure I do. Everybody's got emotions. You can show them or not, but that doesn't mean you don't have them."

"Well, what do you call all the narkiness? Ha. Hate to tell you, but anger's an emotion. Least it is the way I do it."

"Well, congratulations. *One.* There are a whole bunch of others, you know."

"I wouldn't know. Being emotionally stunted and all."

She sighed. "I didn't say that."

"If you'll eat that sandwich," he said, "we'll go grocery shopping, and I'll see if I can manage a sobbing meltdown amongst the fruit and veg, if you like. I'll work up some tears while you finish up, how's that? Looks like I'll have heaps of time. Anybody ever tell you that you eat slowly?"

"I savor my food," she said with dignity. "Rather than inhaling it. It's a concept you might want to study. It makes it last longer, too. I have to watch my weight."

His smile made the skin around his eyes crinkle again amongst the faint white lines of his various scars. He'd been cut around the eyes and chin a *lot.* There were marks on both cheekbones, too, she'd noticed. She didn't think she wanted to watch rugby.

"I watch my weight, too," he said. "Watch that it stays up

where it's meant to be, that is. I eat five thousand calories a day while I'm training. If I savored, I'd never have time to do anything else. But when it's special? When I'm really enjoying it? I take my time. I savor, no worries. "

His voice had dropped, got that husky note in it again, and his eyes were... she'd call that look "intense." She took a deliberately tiny bite of her sandwich. He could just wait, that was all. "I've got some more news for you," she told him once she'd swallowed it down. "You think you're being subtle, but you're not."

"Nah." He was smiling again, watching her eat, obviously knowing she was dragging it out just to tease him. "I never said I was subtle. I'm trying to chat you up. Could be I'm out of practice, though. If I'm not doing it right, I'm open to suggestion."

"Then I suggest," she said, "that we go grocery shopping. And if it's entertaining you, go for it. But don't imagine that you'll get anywhere. I'm not much of one for sinning."

"This just practice for me, then, you reckon?"

"That's it," she said, setting the remnants of her sandwich down and wiping her hands on her napkin. She hadn't finished, but for once, she was stopping because she was full, not because she had to. "You practice your chatting-up technique, and I'll practice my cool, witty rejections. I'd say we could both use the practice. How's that? Win-win?"

He sighed and got to his feet along with her. "Well, not so much. But I'll keep practicing anyway, probably, now and then. Can't seem to help it."

wolf eyes
♡

Nina cooked fish that night. It only took a few minutes, to her surprise.

Iain had steered her toward thin fillets of snapper. "It's the best, and the easiest," he'd said. "If it's fresh enough, you just fry it up in a bit of olive oil. Salt, pepper, and lemon, and you're all good. Easy as."

She'd asked him exactly what to do and what to cook with it, and had taken notes. He'd been amused, as usual, but he'd told her. So she'd roasted little potatoes in the oven, following his directions, had put together a simple salad of baby mixed greens, cucumber, and avocado all by herself, and had even made her own salad dressing out of olive oil and lemon juice, following a recipe in one of her new cookbooks. The whole thing really *had* only taken thirty minutes, including the potatoes. She hadn't realized cooking could be that simple.

Of course, all the good smells had made her hungry again, but she *was* on vacation. And the only forbidden items had been two very small potatoes and a tiny bit of olive oil, not chocolate cake. Or cheese.

Arthur even ate the salad. "It's not cooked," he said grudgingly, "but not too bad."

"So am I fired?"

"Reckon I'll keep you one more day, anyway. What are we having tomorrow?"

"Steak, remember?" And she was going to eat it, too. "And green beans, and more salad."

"Also not cooked."

"Elder abuse," she agreed, and got a huff out of him that might have been a laugh.

"You watch yourself, missy," he said. "You get too saucy, I *will* send you packing."

"Well, wait until I wash your sheets, all right? I'm going to tackle the washing machine tomorrow. Good times. And Iain said he'd take me kayaking, once he finishes scraping the shed so he can repaint it. I have to say, you people really don't know how to take a vacation."

"What, lying on the beach, boring yourself to tears, and giving yourself skin cancer into the bargain? Nah. A man likes to stay busy. May go give him a hand myself."

"Do that," she said. "I'm sure he'll appreciate the help. Plus give him more time for that kayaking. I want to try it." And it would be good for Arthur to feel useful, too, she thought privately and *didn't* say.

"Tell him to trail a line if he's going to go out on the boat, see if he can bring me back something," Arthur said. "I don't trust you with those hamburgers. At least I know you know how to cook fish. Or we could freeze it for when you burn something. Sure to happen soon."

"You could tell him yourself," she suggested, "if you're going to be working with him and all. I know you don't like to talk, but you might be able to bring yourself to open your mouth enough to impart that suggestion."

"Careful, Miss Sauce."

She had to smile at that. "He'll agree with you about the necessity of a backup plan to my dinner preparations, I'm sure. And about the sauciness, for that matter. He's well aware of all my limitations. But I was wondering," she went on while she was on a roll, "why all of them are right next door, and yet we're… here? If Carmella was worried about you eating, why weren't you eating with them? Before I arrived to save you from your desperate straits, of course, with my extreme skills."

Carmella had stopped by tonight to check on Nina and Arthur, had been her usual brisk self, but with an undertone of sadness and fatigue that seemed like more than jet lag to Nina. As if Iain's mum were lonely, too.

Arthur was glaring again, but Nina pressed a little more. "I mean, I'm sure she'd have wanted you to, from what she told me. She's worried about you."

"Well, she doesn't have to be. I'm not helpless. And I told her and Graeme when they moved down here that I wouldn't get in their way. Got her own life, hasn't she, and I've got mine. I'm no hanger-on."

"Well, no, but you're her *dad*. And it would be company for you." *And for her. For all of you.*

"I don't need company."

"No? You liked watching cricket with Iain today, though, I'll bet."

It was true. Iain had sat with his granddad some more after they'd come back from the store, even after Nina had announced that she was going for a swim, when she'd finally succumbed to the irresistible temptation of that turquoise water. Which was maybe the *tiniest* bit disappointing, selfish as that was of her. His granddad needed his company more. But he'd seemed today like he'd have jumped at the chance to go swimming with her.

Well, she'd been wrong, obviously. He probably *had* just been practicing, with the flirting and all. Teasing her, because it was fun. At least *she'd* thought it was. But she'd seen the double takes and secret looks he'd inspired from the women in the grocery store, and she didn't think they were all rugby fans. There'd been a couple of Scandinavian girls in the checkout line who'd done a whole lot of unnecessary hair touching, lip biting, and sidelong-glancing. Nina would've been willing to bet that they didn't know rugby from a hole in the ground, but they'd recognized a sexy beast when they'd seen one, and they'd wanted him.

If Iain had noticed any of it, he hadn't let on, but surely he had. Nina always knew when men were staring at *her*. She didn't like it when they did, but Iain would just be flattered, surely.

If he wanted company on his holiday, she didn't think he'd have to work very hard to find a woman who'd jump at the chance. That was probably what he was doing tonight. She'd heard him tell Arthur that he was going "out." He'd practiced his chatting up, and now he was putting it to use on somebody who wanted it. Which was just fine with her. She wasn't looking for a man. She hadn't even wanted the one she'd had.

"Course I didn't mind Iain. He doesn't chat at me, that's why," Arthur said now, and Nina had to work to remember what they'd been talking about. "Knows how to sit still and shut up, doesn't he. Unlike some people." He stood up awkwardly, his face twisting with what Nina knew was pain, and grabbed for his cane. Nina thought about the Senior Yoga book, and decided that tomorrow might be better. One step at a time.

"Not as bad on the dinner as the breakfast," Arthur said, reaching for his plate and carrying it to the sink as he had that morning.

"Is that a 'Thank you?'"

He didn't smile, but it was a close-run thing. "Could be."

"Careful," she said. "Your shell could be cracking a little bit there. Better back off fast."

"Told you I was a grumpy old bugger. Told you I wasn't lovable."

"I'll bet Madeline thought you were. That's why you always put your plate in the sink, isn't it? You helped her. I'll bet you did a lot of things for her."

The curtain came right down again. "I'm going for my walk," he said, turning for the door. "And no, I don't want company. I don't like company. You want company so badly, go down to the pub."

"Maybe I will." Was that where Iain had gone? Probably. And also none of her business.

"Mind you're careful if you're coming back in the dark, though," Arthur said. "City girl like you, used to streetlights, eh. You sprain an ankle out there, don't think I'm nursing you."

♡♡♡

She didn't go to the pub, of course. Walking into places alone wasn't her favorite thing anyway, especially not places where men came over to buy her drinks, their eyes too hungry, their smiles too avid, their hands brushing hers. It wasn't fun. It made her feel like prey, and she hated being prey.

She wasn't wearing makeup, and she *did* have a funny face, and the goofy hair now, too. But it would happen anyway. It always happened. She gave off some sort of vulnerable, sweet "tender morsel" vibe no matter what she wore. It was her livelihood, but it also attracted all the wrong people.

She didn't particularly want to see Iain using his newly refurbished skills on somebody else, either, and never mind why.

Besides, she was tired again. Too many weeks of waking in the night, the thoughts she'd suppressed during the day coming back to haunt her dreams and her thoughts.

So, no, she didn't go anywhere. She went to bed early with her mystery novel instead.

She'd only intended to read for a few minutes, but that wasn't how it turned out. She turned page after page, her hands clutching the book for dear life.

Eunice left the train station and climbed the hill toward the village. She was glad she'd written to him and asked his advice. He'd tell her, surely, what was best to do.

The path was lonely here, dark and cool even under the summer sun. She hurried along a little faster. She was jumpy these days, ever since she'd read the first article. She'd be glad to get to the café and ask him what he thought. Whether she should go to the police with what she knew, or not. Whether they'd even believe her.

A twig snapped behind her, and she whirled. Then she smiled in relief. "Oh. It's you. Did you come on the train, too? I didn't see you."

He was smiling, still, but his eyes weren't. His eyes were... fixed, somehow. Staring. Wrong. He kept walking toward her, raising both hands toward her.

Why? Why was he... what was he doing? She took a step back, opened her mouth and tried to ask.

And then she tried to scream.

Nina shut the book with a snap, her hands trembling. The sea still murmured outside, more loudly than the night before. She lay rigid, and heard a creak from outside. From the lounge, or the kitchen. Or the door.

Old house, she told herself. *Creaking. It's a story. Just a story.* She should have borrowed a romance, but she hadn't wanted to read about True Love, about Prince Charming. It would only have made her sad. But a mystery had been the wrong choice.

She forced herself out of bed and over to the table by the window, searched through the stack of books with trembling fingers, and found one of her cookbooks. She shut and fastened the window despite the warmth of the night, pulled the curtains tight across it, climbed back into bed, and opened it up at random.

Pear Crumble With Ginger and Vanilla Custard, she read, making herself focus. She could do that, probably. It said *Cookery for Kids* right on the cover.

They grew pears here, too. The area was famous for it, Iain had told her. In fact, that Finn person—his family had pear orchards, Iain had said. She concentrated on the ingredients list with all her determination.

Six pears, peeled, cored, and chopped. And 115 grams of butter. That sounded like a lot. There was cream in the custard, too. Maybe she could leave those things out. She sighed. Probably wouldn't work. She didn't think you could leave things out in cooking. She could just eat the pear part, maybe.

When the book fell from her hands and into her lap, she jolted awake, startled again. *Oh. Book. Sleep.* She reached for the lamp, switched it off, turned onto her side and fluffed her pillow, and wondered how you cored pears. She rarely ate fruit. Too much sugar.

She'd ask Arthur. He'd probably know. He'd say something caustic about her question. It would be something everybody else knew. But she'd bet he'd eat the crumble.

♡♡♡

She woke with a jolt. Something was tapping. Scraping at the door.

Darkness surrounded her. The silence was nearly complete. All she could hear was the sea, louder tonight, or maybe it just seemed like it. And that scraping.

She sat up.

Scraaaaape. Knock. Scrape.

Somebody was trying to break in.

Matthias. Coming to find her. Or worse. Raoul. Raoul of the narrow, shaved, tanned skull, the immobile face, and the cold, unblinking stare from his hooded yellow-brown eyes.

She'd never known what Raoul was thinking. She'd never wanted to know.

Scrape.

We are going to be married.

She was sitting rigid, her eyes wide open in the dark, a fistful of the duvet clutched tight in one hand.

Finally, she dared to move, groping with one hand for the light on the nightstand. Her fingers found it at last, but there was no switch. She couldn't remember where the switch was. She was fumbling frantically now with both hands, reaching, feeling.

At last she traced the cord, found the button, and turned it on.

Nothing.

The closed bedroom door. The yellow wallpaper with its

110

printed flowers. Her two dresses hanging from the hooks on the wall.

The scraping had stopped, but now she heard a new noise. *Knock. Knock.*

It was coming—surely it was coming—from above. It had to be a tree branch, scraping against the roof after a shift in the wind. That was all. Nobody was trying to break in. Nobody had found her. Nobody could have, because she hadn't told anyone where she was. And nobody would be breaking in, because the door wasn't even *locked*. It was Kaiteriteri, not LA.

She forced herself to lie down again, but she didn't turn off the light. Her eyes stayed open.

When she'd been little, she'd been afraid of wolves. She'd lain in bed just like this and imagined them padding silently after her. Stalking her, their yellow eyes gleaming in the darkness.

There were no wolves in New Zealand. Well, maybe in some zoo. And she didn't think kiwis were big killers. They were small flightless birds. They had long bills, yes, but what would they do, come running after her to give her a good pecking?

It was a nice, jokey pep talk, but it didn't work. She flung back the bedding in a convulsive movement and slid out of bed. A few steps to the dresser, and she was pulling on the first thing her hand landed on, which was the rose-printed skirt. She hadn't thought of buying a nightgown, so she'd been sleeping in a turquoise tank and a pair of underwear, which had proved perfectly adequate for the warm summer nights. She grabbed the duvet off the bed and wrapped it around her shoulders, though, because she didn't have a jacket or even a warm sweater, and she didn't turn the light out. She didn't want to come back to the room in the dark.

It might be shameful to be so scared over nothing more than a mystery novel and noises in the night. Her fears in Neuenstein seemed sillier and more unfounded with every day that passed, and so did this. But at least she didn't have to lie in the dark and feel them. She could go outside.

It was cool out there, making her glad of the duvet, but it wasn't entirely dark, to her relief. The moon was half-full, hanging low in the sky, its pale light competing with hundreds of winking stars, some of them obscured by scraps of fast-moving clouds. She used its illumination to find her way along the path between the cottage and the silent, dark house next door, until the sidewalk ended and her bare feet sank into chilly, damp, lush grass. The noise of the sea was much louder out here, the repeated crash and hiss of waves filling the night air. That would be due to the wind, too, or for the same reason. A shift in the weather.

She searched for the track to the beach. It wasn't as easy to find in the dark, though, and she walked along the edge of the lawn beside the half-seen bulk of trees and bushes, groping her way from one trunk to the next, peering into the darkness for the gap.

Her hand touched the wrinkly-smooth trunk of a palm and found a protrusion. A rope, tied around it. She could feel the knot.

Ah. The hammock. Even better than the beach, maybe. She climbed into the welcoming cocoon of fabric, draped her blanket over herself, and experimented with swinging the hammock from side to side. It worked. With a little movement of shoulder and hip, she could rock herself. She kept the gentle motion going as she looked through palm fronds at the moon and the faint wisps of cloud trailing across it. At the constellations, at once familiar and unfamiliar, although she'd never seen the stars this bright, not in big, busy Melbourne. She swayed, and looked, and let herself be lulled by the breeze rustling in the palms, so much less menacing out here, where she could identify the sound. Somehow, even though she wasn't under a sheltering roof, she felt safe. Alone. Unwatched.

At some point, she stopped rocking the hammock, and after another little while, her eyes drifted shut.

She slept.

mistaken identity

♡

Iain didn't know what had woken him, but as he lay in the dark, he recognized it. A shift in the wind. It had swung around while he'd slept, was coming from the east now. The dangerous direction, the one that kept kayaks on the beach, or put them there. If you were lucky. That wind blew straight across the Pacific and into Tasman Bay, producing swells that could reach well over a meter high, and could swamp a kayak before you even knew what was happening.

The east wind always made him restless. Or maybe it was more than that. Maybe it was his unsatisfactory evening, starting with the dinner he'd cooked for his parents. His mum had looked so knackered this morning, insisting on heading straight into the office despite her jet lag, that Iain had decided that the least he could do was take the food prep off her.

He'd made the same easy dinner he'd suggested to Nina, and his mum had said, "Thanks, love. That was very thoughtful of you," but the meal had been an uncomfortable ordeal all the same. His mum had been drooping, his dad even more taciturn than the day before, and Iain hadn't had a clue what to do about it.

"I'll do the washing up," Carmella had said, finally giving

up poking at the remnants of her fish and laying down her fork. She'd hauled herself to her feet, and Iain hadn't liked what he'd seen on her face.

"Nah, Mum," he'd said. "I will. You go on."

She'd nodded, and he'd cleaned up, and then he'd gone to the pub. The alternative had been sitting with his dad and watching telly, and Iain hadn't known if he could manage that without saying something. He didn't know what the hell was going on, but he was more than regretting coming down for this visit.

He'd thought about inviting Nina to the pub as well. But she'd run so hot and cold all day, he'd thought it might've spooked her, made her feel rushed. Lunch had been one thing, but he'd seen her almost visibly draw away from him once they'd started shopping. It had been the way other blokes had perved at her, maybe, which had been so much more obvious in the narrow aisles of a crowded supermarket. Like they all had the right to look, and to let her see them looking. As if she'd be glad of it, when he knew she wasn't. She'd had the hat on again, but there was no disguise for that body, not unless she wore the baggy jumper and track pants, and why should she have to do that? He'd frowned them down when he'd caught them at it, of course, but that had only accounted for the ones he'd noticed. It may have given her second thoughts about him, too, though, as skittish as she was. Not like he hadn't done some looking himself, and he knew it.

Later, when she'd announced that she was going swimming, he'd seen the same hesitation in her, and had sensed that she was afraid he'd invite himself along. So he'd let her go without suggesting it, and had gone to the pub by himself, too. He'd leaned against the bar, said his hellos to the locals, drunk a single pint, and talked a bit of fishing when he could and more than a bit of rugby when he couldn't avoid it. He'd also had to field a few jocular questions about the whereabouts of his wife from the more clueless sorts who hadn't got the memo, but that had to happen sometime, so it might as well be now.

It hadn't exactly been a piss-up for the books, but he was back in training now anyway, and it had helped the time go by. He hadn't practiced his chatting-up skills much, though. When the opportunities had presented themselves, in forms both blonde and brunette, he'd found he hadn't cared enough. Just like his time in the Americas.

When he'd come home, both houses had been dark and quiet, and he'd climbed the stairs to his room and gone to bed. The exercise he'd done, the beer, and a lifetime spent training himself to fall asleep in whatever airplane or hotel room he found himself—they'd all sent him off quickly enough.

But now, he was awake again. The wind was blowing, the palms were rustling wildly, and the sea had a bit of a roar to it. Those swells, coming in as advertised.

He rolled to one side of the bed and checked his phone. Two forty-five.

Sleep. He tried, and the wind blew, and at last, he gave up. He'd take a walk by the sea, he decided, would surrender to the wind and the roar of the waves. He'd let both of them fill him until they drowned out the noise inside.

He'd been sleeping in his briefs, so he grabbed a pair of skimpy athletic shorts and a T-shirt. If he got cold, so much the better. That would do the business quicker.

He crossed the lawn, his feet knowing the way even in the dark to the track that led to the beach.

He wasn't quite there when he saw it.

Bloody *hell.* Not again. Every summer, his parents got this. A backpacker looking to kip on the beach, taking advantage of the Kiwi dislike of "private property" signs and fences to wander straight into his parents' garden, and then their hammock. Iain had sent off a few in the early morning hours himself during his visits, and that was nothing to the number his dad had turfed out.

Enough was enough. His mum didn't need to come out in the morning and find some greasy backpacker weeing in her flowerbeds—something else that had happened more than once.

His frustration had found an outlet at last, and he was across the remaining meters of grass in a flash. It was simple enough. He grabbed one edge of the hammock in both hands, gave it a heave, and tumbled the bugger out. The fella landed hard, with an *oof!* of surprise, but Iain wasn't done. He was going to toss him onto the beach, and he was going to let him know that he'd better stay there.

He didn't get the chance. The man was already gone, squirting out from under the other side of the hammock, dancing around the palm and dodging down the track to the beach.

Good riddance.

A long second passed before the image registered in Iain's brain. The slim shape of that running figure. The swirl of a white skirt in the darkness.

Oh, shit.

He started to run.

♡♡♡

Nina was sprinting faster than she ever had in her life. He was here. He'd found her. Somehow, he'd found her. He was *here.*

She was halfway down the tiny beach within a few seconds. She cast a wild glance behind her and saw him, an image from a nightmare, or from her novel, but he wasn't in a dream or a book. He was real. He was back there in the dark. Running with his hands outstretched. And gaining on her.

Wolf eyes.

He was going to catch her. He was going to take her.

It was because of Matthias that she ran into the sea. Because Matthias hated to swim. His lessons had ended when he'd been eight, when his swimming teacher had eloped with his mother. He'd refused to get into the water ever since.

But Raoul could probably swim.

She was already in the water on the thought, though, heading out with big, running strides. Too late now. She was committed.

These weren't the gentle, lapping waves of the afternoon. They were breakers.

The first one caught her before she saw it and rolled her under. The salt water invaded her nostrils, burned her nose, but she held her breath and let the wave take her. When it had done its worst, she stumbled to her feet again and ran with the undertow to catch the next one. This time, she dove under, stroked hard, came up on the other side, and kept going, aiming to get well beyond the breakers, beyond the danger.

Another look back, but she was in the trough of a swell, and she couldn't see. She rode the heaving sea up again, and there he was. Dark shape against dark water. Coming toward her. It was the nightmare, and there was no escape.

Yes. There was. There had to be.

The point. You could swim around the point to the main expanse of Kaiteriteri Beach. Or run the rocks when the tide was out, the way Iain had this morning. What would the tide be now? She didn't know. She couldn't think. But the moon was out from behind its concealing cloud now, and she located the jutting black point with its wave-carved rocks and aimed for a spot beyond it.

Beyond it, because Raoul wouldn't know about the other beach. She could lose him there. Lose him in the water.

She was the one who was getting lost, though. Every time she put her head up, she had to reorient herself again in the swell, had to find the rocks again, and the panic was trying to take her. The waves were too high. Too rough.

It's not far. You're so close. So close.

Finally, she saw it. Light. The scattered few points that had to be the security lighting of a tiny town at night. She was on the other side. All she had to do was get to shore.

She swam. She had no other choice. The tide carried her with it, carried her toward the light. *Tide's coming in,* she realized somewhere in the back of her brain. Coming in, and carrying her. Helping her escape.

It was a big wave, a rogue, that knocked her for a loop. It picked her up as she got close to shore, flung her landward with enough force to rattle her, pulled her under so she hit the bottom a jarring blow with the bridge of her nose, hard enough to stun her. The wave was sucking her out again now, dragging her under with its force. She couldn't move. She couldn't get her head to the surface.

She came up at last, dragged in a huge, whooping breath, pushed off with her arms, and stumbled to her feet. And then she was being picked up again. Not by the wave this time. Being grabbed under her arms and dragged toward shore. Which was when he lifted her right up off her feet.

She tried to struggle, tried to fight. She was gasping, kicking, lashing out. Being taken all the same up the sand, up out of the water, as if she weren't fighting at all.

She had to get back into the water. She *had* to. It was her only chance.

"Nina," the voice was saying. "Nina. No. Let me help you."

He didn't want to help her. He wanted to *take* her. And she wasn't going to let herself be taken.

Three more steps, four, and they were on dry land. She was in his arms, on shore, and she couldn't get away.

"*No!*" The word exploded from her, and she was still trying to twist away. "Let me *go!*" He was too strong. She couldn't get loose. Her strength was almost gone, and his wasn't, and he was going to win.

"Nina," he said, but the voice was too deep for Matthias. Too deep for Raoul. He was setting her on the sand, on her feet, and she stumbled, but he put a hand out. "Bloody *hell*," he said. "I'm sorry." And that was when she realized.

"*You.*" She couldn't even remember his name. Her body was drained, limp, like somebody had removed all her muscles, her face ached from where she'd hit it, and if he hadn't been holding her up, she would have fallen. "You...

you... *asshole!*"

He wasn't even listening. "What the hell were you *thinking*, though, running into that kind of sea at night? You could've been drowned, especially if the tide had been going out!"

"What was *I* thinking?" She was shivering, shaking with cold and fear. And rage, too. "I was thinking I was being attacked! I was thinking about saving my *life!* What is *wrong* with you? Are you *insane?*"

His jaw dropped. His chest was rising and falling with effort, but he wasn't shaking, not the way she was. "Me? *Me*, insane? I'm not the one who ran! All I did was dump a backpacker out of my parents' hammock. I never imagined she'd—you'd—go mad and do a runner into an unfamiliar sea with one hell of a swell. How was I meant to know you'd do something that stupid?"

"You were *chasing* me!"

"Of course I wasn't chasing you." He sounded nothing but... *exasperated*. "I was just coming after you! Of course I was coming after you! I was trying to tell you, at first. And then I was trying to *save* you."

"I was saved! I was out! And to *tell* me? To tell me *what?*"

"That I was *sorry*, all right?" He was glaring at her, looking absolutely fearsome, and absolutely ridiculous. "I was apologizing!"

She gaped at him. "That's... that's your apology?" She couldn't help it one bit. She was laughing, and if it was hysterical, who could blame her? "That's your *apology?* Running a woman down like you're going to *kill* her? Buddy, you are going to be single a long, *long* time."

He wasn't laughing, though. He was still staring at her. "You thought you had to run into the sea to get away from me? Why?"

And just like that, she was back to being mad again. "Because I didn't know it was you! And if you can ask that, I'd say you've been living under a rock your entire adult life. Do you ever read the news? Why don't you ask, oh, let's think. How about any woman in the *world?* Ask her what she thinks when a huge man starts chasing her at night. Does she think, 'Oh, how fun, we're going to have a race? I hope I win?' Not exactly. Not *ever*. You *bet* she's going to run into the ocean. What did you expect?"

He'd lost his outrage, finally. "But I... I only chased you because I saw it *was* you. I didn't want you to hurt yourself. I didn't want you to be... scared."

"You didn't want me to be scared," she repeated in wonder. "And that was your solution. Anybody ever tell you that you've got lousy judgment?"

"Recently? I reckon just about everybody has, or they could have. Including myself." He reached cautious hands out for her. "Bloody hell, Nina, I'm sorry. And you're shaking. Are you all right? Hurt anywhere?"

It was true, she realized dimly. She *was* shaking. It was all catching up, and she was trembling violently, the world going black around the edges, even blacker than the night. Her nose hurt, and her head was swimming. "I think..." she said faintly, "I might..."

A soft curse, and he was picking her up again, the same way he'd carried her out of the surf. One hand under her knees, the other around her back, holding her tight against him. Except that this time, it wasn't scary. "Put your arm around my neck," he told her. "Let's get you home so I can warm you up."

"You're... dreaming," she managed to say. "If you think I'm going to let you warm me up." His T-shirt was wet and cold, but the chest underneath it was as solid as she'd imagined it. She'd rest her head against it for a minute. Just for a minute. And then she'd tell him to put her down. In a minute.

guilty
♡

Iain was swearing at himself. *Bloody idiot. Stupid. Clumsy bugger.*

Nina was all right, he told himself, clutching her more tightly to him as he took the footpath up over the hill in huge strides. She just needed to get warmed up, and she'd be all right.

"I'm too heavy for you to keep carrying," she said as he crested the hill and started down the other side. "Put me down."

"I've carried *bags* heavier than you. And you're cold."

"Well, so are *you.*"

Ah. If she were back to giving him stick, she must be feeling better.

"Nah," he said. "I'm good." If he'd felt the cold, the warmth of her body against him was taking care of it. It had been the last thing on his mind when he'd first picked her up. But now that she was talking again and he wasn't worried she'd pass out, he was noticing the smoothness of her skin, not to mention the softness of the breast pressed into his chest. She was all natural, it seemed. Well, he could hardly help but notice, could he?

Maybe she could tell, because she was struggling to get down, so he set her gently on her feet. "All right?" he asked.

"Here we are."

They'd reached the top of the hill and the start of the track of crushed stone that led down to the houses, and she started along it gingerly.

"Ow." She was doing some hopping. "This is your fault, too, so you know. I'm holding you responsible for the fact that I'm hurting my feet right now."

He sighed. "I'm going to ask you. May I please pick you up again?"

She was glaring, and despite himself, he was smiling. "Yes," she muttered. "But don't get turned on."

"Nah," he said, lifting her easily and starting down the track. "Never happen."

She was still shivering, so he tucked her up a little more closely against his body. "Shower," he said. "That's what you need." He ducked down the narrow side track to the house, maneuvering her around the greenery, and set her down in the courtyard. "Go on in there and get warmed up."

"Oh. My blanket." He must have looked blank, because she said, "It's still in the hammock."

"I've got it. Go get in the shower."

She nodded jerkily and went inside, her thin frame shaking with cold, and he went in search of her duvet. It had fallen under the hammock when he'd tipped her out and had blown against the trees. He carried it into the cottage, where the sound of running water told him Nina had made it into the shower. Good.

He stood in the kitchen and inspected the white duvet. A bit damp, but not too bad. Maybe not enough to keep her warm now that she'd got so chilled, though. He tossed it onto the bed in Nina's room and went to his nan's linen cupboard in the hallway in search of another blanket, stripping off his sodden T-shirt along the way and instantly feeling warmer. A towel for himself wouldn't come amiss, either.

The moment he opened the cupboard door, the smell of lavender brought his nan back to him so strongly, he blinked. Her house had always smelled like flowers, because she'd loved them. His granddad had helped her with the weeding as they'd grown older, even with his hip, had barrowed mulch for her and dug the beds. Who was doing all that now? His mum, he guessed.

He remembered other homecomings, other years. His nan bursting from the house on hearing their voices, her arms stretched wide in welcome, a smile blooming on her round face. His granddad following behind, more reserved, but happy, too, you could tell. And the way it had felt when Nan gathered you into those soft arms. Like home. Like... love.

Even that last time he'd come, when she hadn't been able to run out at all, but had still raised her arms from the bed to him, pulled him close, and held him tight. And had been so glad to see him.

He swallowed around the lump in his throat and grabbed a pink towel from the top of the stack, scrubbed it over his head and chest, then dropped it on the floor. He'd be fairly rapt to get into a shower himself. That sea had been rough. He'd had some bad moments out there, when a trough had hidden Nina from him and he'd feared he wouldn't find her again. When he'd seen her face-down in the surf, there at the end... that hadn't been the best, either.

She was fine, though. And the water had stopped running in the bath, he realized. He shook his head as if that would clear all the uncomfortable thoughts and searched out a warm woolen blanket, then shut the door on the cupboard and the memories. He went into her bedroom, pulled the top sheet into place, and spread blanket and duvet over it. There. That would do.

Which was why he was in there when she walked into the room, dressed in nothing but a pale-blue towel wrapped around her body, one hand holding it closed.

The moment she saw him, she rocked to a stop and gasped, "Get *out* of my bedroom!"

He had both hands up, was backing away. "No worries. Just putting another blanket on for you."

"Oh." Her towel slipped, and she made a grab for it.

"Good. Fine. Sorry. But…"

"Yeh." He edged around her, trying not to look at anything. "Going. See you in the morning." And then he stopped and examined her more closely. "What's wrong with your nose?"

Her hand flew to its bridge, and she winced. "Nothing. I whacked it on the sand, that's all."

He put a hand out, felt gently around it, and she said, "*Ow!*" in outrage and stepped back.

"Sorry. Just checking to see if it's broken. It's not, I don't think. Just bruised. A bit swollen, though. Does it hurt?"

"Well, *yes*, it hurts. You have to *know* it hurts, the way your face looks."

He shrugged. "You get used to it. Right. Get in bed. I'll be back."

She was gaping at him. "*What?*"

He sighed. "I'm not going to attack you. Please. Get… dressed, or whatever." He deliberately didn't look down her body at the slipping towel, her slim shoulders, or the ivory swells of her upper breasts. Well, he couldn't help but *see* them, but he didn't *look*. "Get in bed. And I'll bring you something for your nose."

When he came back from the other house, though, he took care to knock, even though her door was ajar. At her "come in," he brought over the Nurofen tablets, water glass, and icepack, setting all of them on her bedside table. He pressed out two tablets from the packaging and handed them to her with the water. "Here. Anti-inflammatory, and it'll help with the pain."

"Now he's drugging me," she said, making him smile, but she sat up and swallowed them down. And he did his best not to notice the clear outline of her breasts under another of those thin ribbed singlets.

"Keep the ice on for ten minutes or so," he told her. "I've put two more packs in Granddad's freezer. You can ice it on and off for the next day or so, and it'll help. Take two more of the Nurofen when you wake up. And now get some rest."

"It's probably three in the morning," she muttered from beneath the blue icepack, lying down and yanking at the covers.

He pulled the duvet up over her and settled it into place. "Three-thirty, actually."

"Your granddad gets up at six-thirty."

"I'll come over and cook his breakfast. My penance, eh. Sleep as long as you like."

She took the icepack away so she could talk more easily. "He likes this whole fancy thing. I hope you know how to do it."

"Huh? He likes chipolatas and eggs on toast." He put the icepack back over her nose. "Keep that on."

"Chip-o-*what?* Great. Another thing I don't know how to cook."

"Sausages. Quit being so stroppy and go to sleep. Otherwise I'm going to feel too guilty."

"You should already feel guilty." The words were murmured, though, and her eyes were closing. "I'll yell at you some more tomorrow for trying to kill me. I'm too tired now. Would you go away, please?"

He smiled, brushed his hand along her cheek for just a moment, enjoying the silky softness of it, and said, "Yeh. Going." And then turned out her light, shut her door gently behind him, and left her.

the y-word
♡

Nina did sleep in the next morning. She only woke once, when she heard voices. The rumble that was Iain, and the grumble that was Arthur. She smiled despite the dull ache from her nose and rolled over in bed. Iain had remembered, then. The next thing she heard was the rattle that must be him pulling pans out of the cupboard. The voices continued, low and comforting, and she slept.

She woke again, sometime when the birds were quieter, which meant it was a lot later. She made it out to the kitchen after a bathroom stop where she'd looked once at the red swelling at the bridge of her nose, the bruising under both eyes, and hadn't looked again.

Arthur was still at the table. Or there again, maybe. His hair was standing on end, as if he'd been out in the wind that was still rattling the palms outside, and he was reading a newspaper.

Her stomach lurched at the sight. She wouldn't still be in there, though. It would all be over. The wedding day was tomorrow—well, almost tonight. Four o'clock tomorrow morning, New Zealand time. It would surely be obvious by now that she wasn't coming back. So she put it out of her mind, said, "Morning," and went over to make herself a cup of tea.

Arthur looked up sharply. "What are you doing up? Thought you were meant to stay in bed."

"Oh." She turned on the jug and reached for the box of teabags. "Iain told you. And not all *day.*" She waited for the water to boil, then poured it into her mug and turned around to face Arthur.

He was gaping at her. "Bloody— What happened? Iain didn't tell me it was that bad. You're never telling me *he* did that."

"Of course not. It was an accident. I fell and hit my face." This morning, her dash into the sea seemed as melodramatic as the rest of her New Zealand odyssey. She hoped Iain hadn't shared the details.

"And fainted," Arthur said. "He said it wasn't the first time, either. You need to see a doctor, missy. I told Iain so, and I'll tell him again, now I've seen you."

"I didn't *faint.* I just got a little tired. I was doing some... running. I do not need to go to the doctor." She was reaching into the fridge for eggs and the spinach she'd bought the day before. She'd scramble a couple of egg whites with plenty of vegetables, she decided. Despite the potato last night, she was hungry again. Probably *because* of the potato last night.

"Sit down," Arthur said, heaving himself to his feet and coming over to open the freezer and pull out another icepack. "Iain said ice, and he was right. Put this on, and I'll make you something to eat. I'm not having you passing out in my kitchen, causing me all that agro."

"I told you. I'm not going to pass out. I'm fine." Well, not quite. She *was* a little shaky. She just needed some protein, though, and *then* she'd be fine.

"Who's the employer here?" Arthur was glaring, thrusting a bony finger toward the table. "Means you do what I say. Sit down and put that thing on your face." He was pulling out a pot as he spoke, setting it on the stove, and filling it with boiling water from the jug. "Sausages, or just eggs?"

"Um... just eggs." She was capitulating, it seemed. "And

no toast," she added hastily, when he'd begun cracking eggs into a little bowl. She had to get a handle on this eating thing.

"Rubbish. Of course you need toast. If you ate more, maybe you wouldn't be fainting left, right, and center."

"I *can't*. I have to be thin."

He turned to study her. "You have one of those diseases where you won't eat? If you do, it's the doctor for you, and straight away, too. I'll drive you there myself if I have to, since nobody else in this family seems to know how to look after a woman."

She was tearing up, but that was the ice hurting her nose. "No," she said. "It's my job. Part of the... the requirements."

"Any job where you have to starve yourself isn't a job worth having." He was dropping bread into the toaster, and she wanted to tell him not to, but she remembered how good it had tasted yesterday. She didn't have to eat all of it. Just a bite.

"It pays a lot, though," she said.

"Make you happy, does it?" he asked, scooping the eggs out of the pot. *He* didn't break the yolks, she noticed.

"Well, no," she forced herself to admit. "Not so much." It never had. But then, most jobs didn't, she knew. People did them because they had to, just like her. She was lucky that hers paid so much better than most.

"Ha," Arthur said. "Need the money, then?"

"Well... not really. I have some saved." *Some* would be one way to put it. Even after she'd paid her mum and agent each their fifteen-percent management fee, not to mention the mortgage on the big house in the Hollywood Hills, she'd been able to invest six figures most months for the past five or six years.

It was more than a cushion by anybody's standards, except that it had never felt like it. The bills were so high, for one thing. That was one reason her mother had always urged her to accept every assignment. No matter how much Nina made, how much she had in the bank, it always felt like they were hovering on the brink of disaster, the way they had been when Nina was little. Those years when she hadn't been able to get that many bookings, no matter how hard she'd worked at being pretty, no matter how quiet and good she'd been at every assignment, so they'd ask her again.

Weeks had sometimes gone by between shoots in those early years, when Nina had been six, eight, ten. Her mum had muttered to herself and gone through the bills over and over, had been on the phone to the agency, saying, "If it's something Sabrina's done, just tell me, and we'll get it sorted." And Nina would creep off to her bedroom, get out her homework, and try to concentrate on it, would try not to go over and over how she'd stood, how she'd acted. Wondering if she shouldn't have talked when the photographer's assistant had come over and chatted with her during the break. If she shouldn't have drunk the juice the lady had offered, because maybe they'd thought that meant Nina wasn't committed. You had to be committed, and juice made you fat. But she'd been thirsty, and she'd forgotten.

And it had continued like that, no matter how successful she became. "A break? No," her mum had said just a few months earlier, before Matthias. "We can't afford to take a break. We've got too many expenses, and we don't know how much longer you've got in the business. We have to make hay while the sun shines. You're at the top until the minute you step aside and give up that spot. And that's if it doesn't happen sooner. All the client has to do is find a prettier face or a better body, and you're out. If we take a break, we may as well have quit entirely. Everybody will forget about you just that fast. There are new girls coming up all the time. If you aren't willing to give it your all, there are a hundred of them waiting to take your place. Never forget that."

Well, so what? The way she felt right now, she'd *give* them her place.

That was stupid, though. You didn't turn your back on that kind of opportunity, and she wouldn't, not for long. She'd tell the agency that she was available again. She'd call her mother. Sometime. Soon. But not right now. She *was* going to take her break first. It wasn't about Matthias, and it wasn't about her mother. It was about her. People took vacations, and this was hers.

Right now, Arthur was giving her *his* opinion even as he energetically and extravagantly buttered her toast. "Then what good's the money, if you don't need it and don't like the work? You could find something else to do. You're not stupid. Not too bad to have around, either. For people who want other people around, that is. Somebody'd have you, anyway. Not me, of course." He limped across to put the plate in front of her, along with a knife and fork. "But somebody who doesn't mind your chatter. Here. Get that down you, and could be you'll start to look less peaky."

She didn't pick up her fork, though, even though her mouth was watering at the buttery, yeasty smell of the wholegrain toast. She didn't normally eat bread, of course, but surely it wasn't always as flavorful as it was here.

"I'll eat it on one condition," she said, setting her icepack gratefully aside.

"I take it back." Arthur sat down opposite her. "Nobody's going to have you. Too stroppy."

"I am known," she said with dignity, "as an especially cooperative... worker."

Arthur snorted. "Yeh, right. Pull the other one. I'd like to see the rest of them, then. *Eat.*"

"I'll eat it. *If* you let me show you a couple exercises afterwards."

"I get my exercise. Walk every day, don't I. Walked down to the shop while you were still lying about in bed. Walked last night after dinner. I had to, if I wanted a moment alone."

"I think you could get a little more freedom of movement," she said. "Fifteen minutes," she added, since he looked on the verge of erupting again. "Or I don't eat. I'm perfectly capable of throwing this away."

"Little witch, that's what you are," he grumbled. "Ten minutes, then. Long as it's not something naff. You have me sweating to the oldies, and I'm giving you the sack, nose or no."

"Sweating to the *oldies?* Um... no." She was laughing now. "Although I'd pay money to see you doing that. I never heard of it."

"Madeline liked it. God knows why. Excitable little fella shrieking up in front like he'd just won the Lotto, and her dancing about the lounge with the rest of them up there on the screen. Said it kept her fit for gardening, kept her looking pretty for me, so if I cared about that, I could just keep my mouth shut." He stopped and cleared his throat, then went on. "Yeh. Well. It seemed to make her happy enough, but you won't catch me poncing about like that. Ten minutes, then. Long as it isn't that. And if I do it and I don't like it," he added, "I'm not doing it again, so don't bother asking."

"Done." She smiled sweetly at him, picked up her knife and fork, and cut herself a slice of egg and, yes, bread. The yolk oozed out over the hot buttered toast, and she was awfully glad she hadn't had to put her threat to the test.

♡♡♡

Iain opened the door when nobody answered his knock, walked through the kitchen, and stopped dead.

Nina and his granddad were sitting in facing kitchen chairs in the lounge. Both of their arms were stretched high over their heads, and Nina was exhorting, *"Deep* inhale. And... *exhale* as you *sweep* your arms all the way down to your thighs. *Inhale,* and hands slide down your calves toward your ankles. And... *exhale* as you roll up one vertebra at a time, and bring those hands back to rest on your thighs."

His granddad got upright again, saw Iain, and stopped.

"Not ten minutes yet," Nina said. "Come on. Just three more."

"Nah." Arthur was reaching for his cane, rising to his feet. "We're done."

Iain may have had his mouth open. He may have. "Uh, don't mind me. I can come back after you're done with your—" He stopped at an emphatic shake of the head from Nina, and changed it to, "Stretches. Uh... good on ya, Granddad."

"Nah," Arthur said. "Blackmail, more like. And all right, I did it," he told Nina. "But only because I gave my word."

"And you did great," she said, standing up herself and grabbing her chair by its back, then reaching for Arthur's. "I'll bet Iain does a whole lot of stretching. What do you think, Iain? Is it worth it?"

"Oh, yeh. If you don't want an injury." He kept the smile from his face with an effort. *Bloody hell.* He'd never have credited it. And then he got a better look at Nina as she turned with the chairs, and he didn't want to smile anymore. "How's that feeling?"

She shrugged. "Fine."

He took the chairs from her. "I've got them."

She sighed. "I'm not weak, and I'm not fragile. I'm fine. What is *wrong* with you two?"

"Maybe it's that dirty secret. Gentlemen, eh. And you can't look at me with that face and tell me you're not fragile. Why aren't you sitting down with ice on your nose?" He carried the chairs into the kitchen and shoved them under the table again.

"I told her she should go to the doctor," Arthur said, following him. "Maybe you should tell her again as well."

"*And* it starts again," Nina said. "Tell me you came over here to set up our kayaking date."

"Can't," Iain said. "Wind's still out of the east. It's dying down, though. I'll take you tomorrow." *And you're not fit for it anyway,* he *didn't* say. He wasn't completely clueless. "I actually came over to ask Granddad if he wanted to go into Motueka with me. I need to go to the gym," he told his grandfather, "and I was thinking maybe you'd be willing to go to Mitre 10 while I'm working out. You could pick up the supplies to paint that shed. Get us started faster, eh."

"I could," Arthur said grudgingly. "If you like."

"I thought you'd know the best brands," Iain said. "I had

my own place all done up by the tradies, hardly got involved myself, so it's been a wee while since I did my own paint shopping."

Arthur snorted. "Nobody'll ever do as good a job as you will yourself. How many times have I told you that? Reckon I'd better come help you, then."

"Heaps," Iain said. "How often you've told me, that is. I listened, too, if you'll notice. Whenever you're ready to go, then. We could have lunch as well, take our time." He looked at Nina. "And *you* could have a lie-down with that icepack."

"You were doing just fine," she informed him, "until you revealed your hidden agenda. I am doing laundry today, thank you very much."

Arthur said, "Let's get on, then," and walked out of the house, and Iain bent and whispered in Nina's ear, "I could call the media while I'm out, too. Wouldn't have said you could do it."

"Don't you *dare* say the Y-word to him," she hissed. "Or I'll never get him to do it again, and it's *good* for him. But it was a good thought. The hardware store, I mean," she added, switching tacks in the way that always turned his head around. "Making him feel useful. That was thoughtful. And sweet."

His granddad called out, "We going or not? Rattle your dags."

"One sec," Iain called back, then looked at Nina. "Take it easy," he said. "I mean it. I think you took a good head knock there. Ice and rest would be the best. Let Granddad cook the steak tonight, and we could combine our efforts tomorrow, maybe. Do those burgers together, since I bought the same things you did. Easy as."

He got his reward. Her eyes lit up. "Family time. What a good idea. Just what *I* thought."

"Barbecue," he agreed. "What d'you reckon? Out on the patio?"

"Oh, yes. Perfect." She smiled at him with that sweetness of hers, and his heart may have squeezed a little. Just a little.

"Right, then," he said. "I'll make it happen."

He walked out the door to join his granddad and wondered how she could do that. Could do nothing but smile at him, and make him feel like her hero. And why that should feel so good.

getting real

Nina was still smiling when Iain walked out. Somehow, he kept sneaking his way into her heart.

It was the way he'd seemed to care so much about her safety the night before, maybe. He'd helped put her into the danger in the first place, but her foolish heart seemed determined to overlook that and to remember him lifting her into his arms and cradling her so close to him, holding her so carefully. And then his gentleness in setting her down, the way he'd pulled the blankets up over her and touched her cheek. His sweetness to his granddad, too, even proposing the dinner for tomorrow that was exactly what Arthur seemed to need. The thought that he was willing to cook it with her, despite all her limitations.

And when he'd bent and murmured into her ear, stirring all those treacherous currents. . . that had been sneaky in a whole different way. She'd had to fight a rush of desire that had tried to turn her knees liquid, and she wasn't sure it was wise to focus on exactly where the tingles had gone.

It was probably just because she'd seen him too close to naked the night before, and that he was so... big. That would overwhelm any woman's defenses, surely.

She'd been alarmed when she'd first seen him in her

bedroom, and flustered when she'd been trying to talk to him while she held her towel up, and had seen how hard he seemed to be working to keep his eyes on her face. Despite her aching head, despite her fatigue, she'd felt the intensity of his focus as surely as if his pheromones had been meeting hers in midair and reeling them in, and the rest of her right along with them.

And when she'd been in bed, and he'd been standing over her wearing only a pair of shorts. . . she hadn't been able to look away. It hadn't just been his chest, or his shoulders, though those were impressive enough. It had been the trail of dark hair leading down from his navel and into the waistband of the wet, low-slung athletic shorts. Those shorts hadn't left much to the imagination. Not that she'd tried to look, of course. Just the opposite. But it had all been at her eye level, and he'd been standing so close.

Size doesn't matter.

Well, maybe. She couldn't help wondering. She had a feeling it might matter a lot.

She shook herself, then regretted it as the motion set up an answering echo in her face. Tomorrow was supposed to be her wedding day in a royal palace, and instead, she was standing in a shabby New Zealand kitchen with two black eyes, imagining another man's... attributes. And how they would feel inside her, how much they might... stretch her.

Stop it. That is nasty. *Laundry.*

She went into Arthur's bedroom, as bold as brass. Of course, it made it easier that he wasn't home. She'd gone in to vacuum the day before, and had noticed that it was a little musty. Now, she opened the windows to let in that east wind and began to strip the bed. Something else she'd never done before.

And it broke her heart. The right side was completely neat, untouched, the sheet folded perfectly over the blanket on top, tucked into the mattress on the side, the pillow fluffed, the pillowcase uncreased. On the left side, things were different. It was as if the bed had a line running straight down the middle. As if Arthur couldn't bear to take up the whole space, because the right side was still, and would always be, Madeline's.

Nina blinked back the tears, collected the sheets along with Arthur's towel and washcloth from the bathroom, and went to the back porch to put them into the washing machine. She added some more laundry from a basket next to the machine. She couldn't fit all of it in, but she'd do the other things next.

She did get a little stuck at that point. *Soap*. You needed soap. And there were all sorts of choices about fabrics and temperatures and things. Fortunately, there was a box of detergent on a shelf next to the machines, and it had directions. So she did her best, pushed buttons, and mentally crossed her fingers. What was the worst that could happen? Clothes, soap, water, machine. She had this.

She found the linen closet in the hall beside the bathroom, after a little hunting around. It smelled good in there, like flowers. There were lavender sachets on each shelf, that was why. Homemade, it looked like, probably taken from the bushes growing on the edge of the lawn. Madeline had liked flowers, she'd bet.

She found clean sheets and went to fix the bed. The fitted sheet took her a while to figure out, but she got it. She made it as neat as she could, then put fresh towels in the bathroom.

There was a stack of tablecloths in the closet, too. A pretty green one printed with colorful spring flowers and garlands caught her eye, so she went into the kitchen and spread it over the table.

There. It was more cheerful in here already. Arthur might complain, but she thought he'd secretly like it. It would remind him of Madeline, but was that really a bad thing? How could it be?

She hesitated over the next part. Would Carmella be upset? Surely not. Another reminder of Madeline, at least if the number of vases in the cabinet were any indication. It would make *her* happy, anyway, and how could flowers ever be bad? So she hunted out scissors and picked up a basket she'd seen on the back porch, then went boldly around to the front of the main house.

White calla lilies and orange birds of paradise fell to her scissors, and then she ranged farther afield. A spectacular show of orange that was another kind of lily. Some sort of purple flower that was almost like a lilac. The climbing pink roses, and others. She took some, but she left plenty more. There were so many.

The wind was still gusting, but more mildly now. A few white clouds scudded across the sky, and the sea and the birds both lent their songs to the day. Suddenly, Nina needed to join them. She hadn't felt like singing in a while, not since she'd gone to Neuenstein. But she felt like it now.

She hummed at first, as she set flowers gently into her basket. The songs she'd always sung: the American country classics her grandparents loved to play back in Aussie. The songs that felt like comfort and happiness, even when they were sad. There was nobody here to hear her, so she went ahead and let the music come, and something else came with it.

Joy. That was what it was. Joy that she was here, and it was beautiful, and she was free.

When she came back into the house with her heaping basket of flowers, the washing machine had stopped.

She'd hang the laundry on the line. That was what you did here, just like in Melbourne. She'd seen the strings of the clothesline hung off the side of the shed, and she knew how to do that. She'd helped her grandmother do it, and the breeze would dry everything fast.

She'd hang everything up, then come back and fix her flowers. And then she'd make a salad for lunch, if she weren't too tired, and lie down with her icepack. It felt like more than time for a rest, but she was almost done. So she went out to the back porch again, still singing, opened the washer door…

The song died in her throat.

Surely everything hadn't been that color before.

She grabbed a laundry basket and started pulling out the wet clothes, her hands shaking. The dark olive pants seemed all right, and the khaki shorts, too. Not too bad, anyway. The towel and washcloth were the same color as before. Red. But the undershirts and boxer shorts, and Arthur's white sheets? There was no question, and it wasn't a trick of the light. They were pink. They were all pink.

Her face gave an almighty throb, and she swallowed hard. She thought for one wild moment about stuffing all of it into a rubbish bag, taking it out to the bin, and hoping Arthur wouldn't notice.

No. She wasn't hiding anymore. She'd hang these things up on the line and take the consequences. Yesterday, she'd planned to be scooping gelato. What had changed?

That you want to stay.

All at once, the brave thoughts deserted her. She leaned against the washing machine, wrapped her arms around herself, dropped her head, and tried to breathe. The position made her aching face hurt worse. Once again, the tears came to her eyes, and this time, she couldn't hold them in.

She hadn't cried when she'd made it through the palace gates. Not when Mathilde had cut off her beautiful hair. Not when the plane had lifted off for Heathrow, when she'd come through Customs in New Zealand, when she'd come out of the sea the night before and realized she was safe. Even when she'd talked to her grandparents, she hadn't cried. And now, her shoulders were heaving, the painful sobs were working their way up through her chest, and everything was escaping despite all her efforts to hold it back.

It was too much. She'd tried so hard for so long. And now she was here, and this should be *easy*. Everybody else could do this, and she couldn't. She couldn't even be *normal*. She didn't know how to do any of it.

She'd thought she could make a new life. Who was she kidding? She only knew how to do one thing. She was going to have to go home and do it again, without her best asset, her hair. She had no choice. And she was tired. She was so tired.

Tired of being hungry every single day. Tired of being easy to work with. Tired of doing what everybody said, of smiling, smiling, smiling. Tired of living where she didn't want to live. Tired of feeling ungrateful for not wanting what she had, for not wanting to help her mother anymore, when she knew how much she'd been given, and how much of it had come through her mum's tireless efforts.

She had no right to feel sorry for herself. Nobody had ever had less right. She had it all, and knowing it didn't help one bit. She stood there with a basket full of soggy pink laundry beside her and cried out the disappointment and loss and, most of all, the dragging fear. Fear that this was all she could be, and that it wasn't enough. That *she* wasn't enough, and she never would be.

She cried until it hurt, until she had no more tears, until she was drained and empty. And then she forced herself to push off from the washing machine, stumbled into the bathroom, looked at her horrible face, and watched the tears well up some more.

"Low point," she said aloud to the swollen, blotchy thing in the mirror, her voice coming out in a hoarse croak. "Low point."

She didn't want to be perfect? She didn't want to be beautiful? Well, congratulations. She'd made it.

And if she didn't want to be erased? Then she had to be real. And real wasn't always good, was it? Real was this. Real was doing it wrong. Real was mistakes. Real was the Velveteen Rabbit, the story her gran had read her every Christmas instead of any of the others, because the old story by Margery Williams was Nina's favorite.

Generally, by the time you are Real, most of your hair has been loved off, and your eyes drop out and you get loose in the joints and very shabby. But these things don't matter at all, because once you are Real you can't be ugly, except to people who don't understand.

Real wasn't always pretty. It certainly wasn't always perfect. She'd spent her whole life trying to be perfect, and she'd almost lost herself.

She wasn't perfect, so she had to live with it. She was a woman who had only learned how to boil an egg the day before, a woman with two black eyes and a swollen nose who'd run out on the most desirable man in Europe by hiding under a load of manure. And who'd dyed an old man's possessions pink and was probably going to lose her job.

She had a choice. She could lie down and pull the covers over her head because she was too ugly even to see herself, and she didn't want to know herself. She could go home and pick up her old life again. Or she could stay here and do her best to become Real.

a big unit
♡

The second Iain walked into the courtyard, he saw them.

"Uh…" He stopped dead with his gym bag over one shoulder, a grocery bag over the other, and the heavy box of paint and supplies in his arms. "Something you haven't mentioned to me, Granddad?"

It was all right there in front of him, gaily flapping in the breeze. Line after line of… pink. Pink sheets, which were possible. Pink socks and undershirts, which weren't. But it was the pink old-man boxers that were doing him in.

"What the—" his granddad said, "How—"

"Red towels," Iain said wonderingly, catching sight of one as a sheet billowed out in the wind. He was laughing now. How could you not? "It's so obvious that it's almost… well, it is. It's epic. It's… it's bloody spectacular."

He sobered, though, at the thought of Nina with her notebook and her painstaking lists. "Don't go off on her," he warned his granddad.

Arthur was scowling at him, then stumping his way to the cottage carrying the other grocery bag. "I was married for fifty-nine years. You think I don't know how to treat a woman who's made a mistake?"

Iain opened his mouth, shut it again, went to put his

supplies into the shed, and headed into the cottage himself. It seemed the old man was never going to stop surprising him.

As soon as he was inside and setting his bag down in the kitchen, he saw her in the lounge, swinging her legs around to sit up. She'd been lying on the couch, then.

She didn't look right at all, though, and he was in there in a few strides. "How is it you seem even worse?" he asked.

Arthur was talking at the same time. "Who said you could bring flowers in?"

Her face was working, and Iain thought, *Oh, geez. She's going to cry.* But instead she said, "Wait. Wait. I'm—" She put a hand up to her head, and he could tell it hurt, and he was furious. At her, or at himself, he couldn't have said.

"OK, first," she told his grandfather, "*I* said I could bring flowers in, I guess. But if you want grounds for dismissal, go look outside, because I wrecked your sheets."

"That wasn't all," Arthur said. "Didn't do my underwear any favors, either."

"Oh," she said in a small voice, and swallowed. "You already saw. Of course you did. Well, I'm sorry. I made a mistake. I'm sure it was a dumb one, but I didn't know. I'll... well, I'm not sure if I can pay for all of it right now, but I will as soon as I can. You can tell me it was stupid, and you can fire me, if you have to." She straightened up some. "But you're not allowed to yell at me about the flowers. I was trying to make your house look better. When I came, it was dirty, and now it's clean and has flowers in it, and I don't see why you should yell at me for that."

"It does look better," Iain found himself saying. "It looks good." There was a big vase of pink roses and some other purple and white flowers on the coffee table. He was noticing it now. And, his sluggish brain finally registered, there'd been an arrangement of huge orange lilies on the kitchen table as well.

"D'you mind?" his grandfather asked, glaring at Iain. "Was I yelling at you about my sheets?" he demanded of Nina. "Did I say anything?"

"Well, yes," she said. "You did."

"But did I spit the dummy? No, because it doesn't matter. Who's going to see my underwear? Nobody, that's who. You made a mistake, and you learned."

He was scowling truly ferociously as he said it, and *now,* for some reason, Nina was tearing up. Iain hadn't seen her cry yet, not even the night before, but there was moisture pooling on her lower lids, and as he watched, a heavy silver drop spilled over and made its way over one of those exquisitely carved cheekbones.

Her face was paler than ever, the red bruising around her eyes standing out vividly, the top of her nose swollen, and he couldn't, he *couldn't* stand it. He said, "You need to be in bed. Why the hell aren't you there? Why did you do all this? I told you to rest!"

She wasn't crying now. She looked narkier than he'd ever seen her, in fact. "Do *not,*" she said, her voice trembling, "*bully* me! I've had *enough* of that!"

"*Bully* you? I'm not bullying you! I'm trying to help you!"

"Maybe you could say, 'Nina, how are you feeling? And then, you know, *suggest.* Instead of ordering me around as if I'm a child."

It rocked him straight back on his heels. He started to speak, then stopped. "Right." He ran a hand over his hair, then glanced at his grandfather. Arthur raised his eyebrows at him, but didn't say anything. Not exactly helpful. "Right. How's your head?"

"It hurts some," she said, still looking wary. "Is that what you want to hear?"

"You take some more Nurofen?"

"No. I just lay down a few minutes ago."

"Then I *suggest,*" he said, "that you may want to take two of those, and then lie down on your bed for the afternoon and rest that head. If you want to go do that, I'll bring you an icepack."

"Thank you," she said with dignity, pushing herself to her feet. "I believe I will."

He stood there as she left, and when he heard her door close, he looked at his grandfather. "What?"

Arthur shrugged. "Did I say anything?"

"But you thought it."

The old man snorted. "I think heaps of things. Doesn't mean I have to natter on about them. Thought you were going to take her an icepack. Reckon you'd better do it. Talk's cheap."

♡♡♡

Nina heard the knock on her door and said, "Come in." And once again, Iain was standing over her and handing her an icepack.

She didn't put it on right away, though. She smiled ruefully at him and said, "Déjà vu."

"Well, yeh."

"I suppose you think that was pretty ungrateful of me back there."

"Nah. Not really. I can come on a little strong. It's been mentioned. Comes with the job, maybe."

"Bashing people for a living," she remembered.

"Something like that. Could make you not so subtle in your interpersonal relationships."

She smiled, then winced. It really did hurt. All the crying hadn't helped at all.

"You take those tablets?" he asked.

"Yes. I did. Um..." She bit her lip. "Sit down, if you want." She scooted over and fluffed up her pillows behind her so she was half-sitting. "You're looming a little."

He perched on the edge of the bed, but he didn't seem to be misinterpreting her gesture. Well, she wasn't exactly tempting right now. In any case, all he said was, "That one comes with the territory as well. The looming."

"A big unit."

"So they say."

"It sounded dirty," she found herself admitting, "but it

145

couldn't be, not if you said it to the librarian."

A low, surprised chuckle at that, and so much warmth in those eyes. "Guess you could take it a couple ways, but at the time, no, that wasn't the idea."

He'd backed off when she'd asked him to. Time to give him some honesty in return. "I don't think I did that too perfectly myself in there," she said. "I'm working on my own interpersonal relationships, I guess you could say. Coming at it from the opposite end, maybe. Trying to be a little more... assertive. Sort of a work in progress, though. I might have a hard time hitting the mark exactly right. It's all a little new."

"Uh—" He scratched his crooked nose. "Yeh. Well, if it helps, I thought you did all right."

"Thanks. And thanks for your... concern, I guess I'll say. Everything go OK, with your granddad and everything?"

"Yeh. And before you ask, yes, the gym was nice. I thought about you when I used my soap."

"Mm. Smells good."

"You mentioned that. I bought a few more things for dinner tomorrow as well. Wine and that. I'll let Mum and Dad know tonight."

"Great."

"Right, then." He lifted the icepack and set it gently over her nose. "I'll let you rest. Get you fit for that kayaking tomorrow, I hope. We can take it easy. And by the way."

"Hmm?"

She couldn't see him from under the ice, but his voice was low, deep, and full of amusement. "Granddad's pink undies gave me one hell of a laugh. Cheers for that."

She was still smiling when she heard the door close.

barbarian 1. or more.

♡

Iain didn't need to head down to the beach the next morning. The tide wasn't out far enough for him to use the rocks to get between the bays, which meant his run would be starting from the road. But he went down there anyway because he'd looked out his bedroom window and seen Nina, and she hadn't been alone.

He may have thrown on his running gear more quickly than usual. In fact, he was still tugging his T-shirt down over his chest and his hat onto his head when he got to the beach.

He could barely see Nina from here, because there were two fellas between him and her, both standing with their backs to him.

As he advanced toward the group, he had second thoughts. This could turn out exactly like the hammock thing. He probably wasn't meant to wade straight into her chat with his game face on.

He kept forgetting she wasn't his. Some primitive part of him stubbornly insisted that she was, and his civilized mind kept dropping the reins. But he stopped walking all the same and waited to check it out.

Civilized Mind 1, Barbarian 0.

"Come on," one of the blokes was saying. "You'll like it, I

promise. We've got a sweet place over there. We're about to go cook breakfast. You should come."

"Thank you, no," Nina said, and Iain found that he was letting out his breath. He wasn't going to have to find out what he'd have done if she'd agreed to go, what, *home?* With *two* blokes who'd picked her up on the beach?

Yeh. He had a pretty good idea of what he'd have done.

"Aw, come on," the other man was saying. "You know you want to say yes. We'll take good care of you."

"I don't want to say yes," Nina said in a tone he hadn't heard from her before. "That's why I said no. Please go away." At least she was starting to say that last bit, but the men still weren't moving, so she got drowned out. By Iain.

"Lady's said no," he said. "Twice. Bugger off."

He had a lot of voice, and they both heard it. *Now,* they were moving. They swung around, in fact. T-shirts, shorts, jandals. Young, big, Kiwi, and would-be cool.

Guy Number Two took a step back, but Number One said, "It was just an invitation. Nobody has to get all pissy about it."

"Ah," Iain said. His voice hadn't got any louder. Just deeper. "I might do anyway, though. I've got this wee issue with impulse control, you see."

They took one more look and made the highly prudent decision to take themselves off. Unfortunately, Number One muttered, "Arsehole," as he went.

That was it. Iain thrust a hand out as fast as a striking snake, grabbed the neckline of Number One's T-shirt, and had hauled him in by it before he had time to do so much as blink.

It was full-on game face now. Most men couldn't stand up to it, and this bloke wasn't the rare exception. "You need to learn some manners," Iain said. "Like what 'no' means. Get out before I decide that I'm the one to teach you." He let go of the shirt with a shove that sent the other man stumbling, and then watched to make sure they were going. Which, of course, they were.

They hadn't recognized him, but it hadn't mattered. They'd recognized the important part.

He still didn't turn to look at Nina. Not until he'd got the adrenaline sorted.

Civilized Mind 1, Barbarian 1. And he knew how the tiebreaker would've turned out.

When he finally decided it was safe to look at her, she had the big sunglasses on, and her hair seemed brighter yellow than ever and was sticking straight up, as if she'd slept on it funny. But she was wearing little black shorts that sat low on her hips, not to mention a deep crimson bikini top. Yeh. Not to mention that. It was all perfectly normal, not a bit extreme, but there was nothing "normal" about Nina. The contrast of the red top and her ivory skin, of the full curve of breast and the deep indentation of waistline... it was all fairly eye-catching. She was too thin, but she was so beautiful.

"Thanks," she said. "But sorry. Annoying, I know. Yoga on the lawn is clearly a better option. Which stinks. I like it out here. I think they saw me all the way from the road, though."

"Guess you get that a lot," he said. She was surprising him again. He'd have expected her to be shaken by the encounter, or upset that he'd got physical, or both. She was such a confusing mixture of vulnerable and saucy, shy and straightforward. That must be why she kept him so off-balance.

"Well," she said, going straight into another of those standing poses, a deep lunge with one arm outstretched in front and the other in back, "it must happen to you just as much as it does to me, based on what I've seen."

"Difference is, all I have to do is look at them, and they go away."

She gave a little huff of laughter and shifted position, one of her hands going to the sand by her front foot, the other stretching overhead. Which gave him a view straight down her bikini top at all that creamy flesh, and he couldn't pretend not to be looking.

"Wish that worked for me," she said. "When *I* look at them, it has the opposite effect."

"Because you have a prettier smile," he managed to say.

"True." She tipped forward and raised a leg and arm high into the air, then lifted off a bit with her front fingertips so she was balanced on a single foot. She made it look easy, though he'd bet it wasn't. "Also a prettier ass. At least that's what my friend there says."

Iain's head whipped around. The two blokes weren't in sight anymore. Unfortunately. "He said that? You should've told me."

She came back up slowly and steadily, then dropped back into the stretched-out pose again. "Why do you think I didn't? But I wish somebody would inform men that telling a total stranger who's indicated zero interest in you and is just trying to do her workout, "Baby, you are *rockin'* that. I'll bet your body's been banned by the government as a health hazard, because it's just too sweet," is right up there with dick pics, attractiveness-wise."

"You know," Iain said, one part of him wanting to smile while the other part wanted to smash something, "I used to think you were naïve. When was that? Oh, yeh. Yesterday."

"Nope." She jumped her legs and switched feet, then started over on the other side. "And if you've sent dick pics, by the way," she told him over her shoulder, "please don't tell me. I'd like to preserve my own illusions about *you,* at least."

"No worries," he said to her back. Which was, yes, pretty sweet, though he wasn't going to tell her so. "Nobody's ever mistaken me for a classy fella, but my knuckles don't drag quite that low."

"So did you come out here to tell me we were going kayaking today?" she asked, dropping down into the second pose.

"Yeh," he said, even though he hadn't. He'd come out here because she'd been standing with other men, and he hadn't wanted her to be. He wasn't sharing *that,* either. "About three o'clock. That suit you? I'm guessing you're feeling better, but we'll take it easy all the same."

"Sure," she said, back to the balancing.

"And dinner," he reminded her. "Our family party. Another cookery adventure for you."

She came up and turned to face him, then raised her hands overhead, clutched one wrist with the opposite hand, and stretched to the side. Once she was vertical again, she said, "I'm getting direction for that one, though. From the master, I'm hoping."

Was she doing this on purpose? If she'd set out to light him on fire this morning, she could hardly have done a better job. "Uh... yeh," he managed to say. "Seven o'clock for dinner, I thought. As it's Friday night."

And then he forgot whatever else he'd been going to say, because she was unsnapping her black shorts, undoing the zip, and then, yes, she was wriggling her hips and sliding the shorts down her legs. She stepped out, dropped them onto the sand, pulled her sunglasses off to reveal her still-bruised eyes, tossed the glasses on top of the shorts, and said, "Good. I'm going swimming. So I guess you'll want to do that thing you said. Bugger off."

She smiled sweetly at him, turned, and ran into the clear turquoise water. And no matter what else he saw that day, there wasn't going to be anything prettier than that.

♡♡♡

Nina didn't go out to check on the progress of the shed-painting, even after Arthur had headed out there, still grumbling after the round of "stretching" she'd subjected him to after breakfast. She may have been a little extra-pathetic to get him to do it, have even made her lip tremble a tiny bit, and she wasn't one bit sorry. Whatever it took to get him in the habit.

Now, though, she headed outside herself, waved at the two of them, then went out front to the hammock carrying her book. It was much better suited to daytime reading, she'd decided.

Truth be told, she'd probably been a little overenthusiastic with the yoga and the swimming this morning, considering her still-tender face, but it had been such a relief to wake up feeling better—not to mention feeling unmarried—and she hadn't wanted to waste any of her precious time in this beautiful place. There hadn't been an end date attached to this job, and she could probably stay a while, but... it wasn't wise. Iain had said he'd be here a week, and it was already half over. However attached to anything here she was becoming, the last thing she wanted to do was hang around, hoping Iain would come back for a visit. It was all very... complicated.

She was supposed to be reading, but her finger stayed in the book as she thought about the men turning on the beach this morning to reveal Iain looking like Moses parting the Red Sea. And when he'd reached out and *grabbed* that one, the same one who'd made the comment about her ass, with that look on his face... that had sent a message to some primitive part of her own brain. And all the primitive parts of her body, too. Which was probably why she'd stripped down and gone into the water. So he'd watch.

She sighed and opened the book. She'd read. Much safer. It was her wedding day. You could hardly blame her for being a little irrational.

The hammock swayed, the birds sang, the palm fronds rustled, the sea whispered and sighed, and the words blurred. When the book fell to her lap, she didn't try to resist.

She woke up in time to make toasties for lunch, which took her about half an hour to get right, but turned out not too bad. And when Iain came in at three, she was ready.

She wasn't going to flirt, and she certainly wasn't going to do anything more. You wouldn't have to be a psychologist to know that she was on the rebound. She was going to enjoy kayaking, and that was all.

And then he wrecked it, just by walking through the door. He came in carrying a plastic bag and asked her, "Ready? Got your sunscreen on? I meant to remind you this morning of how strong the Southern Hemisphere sun can be, with your skin and all. I noticed you didn't seem to be tanned anywhere." He cleared his throat. "I mean, I didn't see any tan lines."

She might be smiling, and she might be leaning a hip against the kitchen counter and looking up at him from beneath her lashes. And seeing him respond to it, bruising and all.

"You're right," she said. "I protect my skin. I put sunscreen all over me. Always."

His voice came out a little strangled. "Good."

She picked up her sunglasses and shoved them onto her nose, then grabbed her hat. Enough was enough.

"Yeh," Iain said. "About that." He hefted the plastic bag. "I've got something else, too. I saw this in a shop window today. Impulse buy, you could call it. But I'm not sure how you'll take it."

"Oh, boy," she said. "Something for me, you mean?"

He reached into the bag and pulled it out. A baseball-style hat with a curved bill in a deep raspberry pink, printed with a curving fern design on the front. "I thought you could trade off, maybe. Since you've decided to wear the other one to bed and all. I thought it could be a—" He waved it through the air. "A peace offering, I suppose you'd call it, for the other night."

She didn't take it. She wasn't sure what he meant by the gift, and she needed to know. "Are you a—"

"Am I what?"

"Never mind." It didn't matter anyway. It wasn't of any concern to her, surely.

"Nah, I have to know now. A secretly great shopper? A pirate? What?"

"Right." She plowed ahead. "Are you one of those guys who tells his girlfriend what to wear?"

"*Me?*" He gestured at his usual T-shirt and shorts with one big hand. "Do I look like that guy?"

"I'm not talking about what *you* wear. I'm talking about what you want *her* to wear."

"Ah. How much I want to control what she wears. Hypothetically, because I haven't got one. A girlfriend, that is. That the basic idea, though?"

"Well, yes. I've been noticing that you've got a… an in-charge aspect to your personality, let's call it. A little alpha male in you." She was doing it again. She had to *stop*.

"Aw," he complained. "Just a little?" He was smiling, but his eyes were burning her up. "Yeh, nah. You can set your mind at rest. Clothes-wise? No. I'm generally just rapt that she's turned up. Well, occasionally I may have a suggestion, if I'm honest. Not for going out, though."

"Uh-*huh.*" It was hard not to laugh, even as the tingles moved down her body and set in to do their wicked work. "We'll let that go, shall we?"

"If we have to. But you're still blaming me for mentioning the hat." They were moving on, then. Probably best. "I didn't say anything about the orange jumper or the track pants, though, did I?"

"No." She fought the smile. "You didn't. Attractive, huh?"

"Well, not so much. But this—" He waved the hat again. "I just…" He shrugged. "I saw it, and I thought you'd look cute in it, and that you might like it. If you don't, though, no worries."

He was shoving it back into the bag. She could tell he was embarrassed by her refusal, and she put out an impulsive hand to stop him. Somehow, it landed on the extremely solid bulk of his forearm, her fingertips touching all those ridges of muscle, and his entire body stilled. He was staring at her, and she took her hand off his arm, tried to forget the feel of him, and said, "No. I want it. Please."

His body relaxed, but he didn't say anything. He just pulled the hat out of the bag and handed it to her. And he smiled.

She put it on and settled it into place. "What do you think?"

His eyes, which had seemed so cold on the day she'd met him, hadn't been cold since, she realized. Not when he'd looked at her. "Brilliant," he said. "Better, if you ask me. But maybe you want to look in the mirror and say. As this is meant to be about what *you* like, and as it's your body and all that."

"You got that?"

"Yeh. I did. I know I seem like a clueless sort of fella, but I can usually grasp the plot once somebody spells it out in simple enough words."

"Well, *I* didn't know. I mean, you don't look—"

He lifted one eyebrow at her, which she'd already noticed he could do. The one bisected by the white scar. "Careful. Sounds like you're judging me based on my appearance." He sighed. "And here I've not even *mentioned* your hair, and not got one bit of credit for it."

"You just did," she pointed out.

"Bugger," he said with a grin.

"Language," she retorted, and he laughed, the sound filling the little room.

"Go look at it in the mirror," he urged. "As I seem to be falling further behind by the moment."

She went to the oval mirror hanging in the lounge, feeling ridiculously lighter and happier just from that little bit of teasing and fun.

The hat *was* better, she saw. The curved brim framed her face, and the deep raspberry color was a warm contrast against her skin. He'd chosen surprisingly well.

She turned to find him still standing behind her. "You were right," she told him. "It's pretty. Thank you. Plus, it hides my hair."

"You see?" he said, his smile all for her. "You set me up for that, and I'm not even taking it. I'd say this round goes to me."

so disappointing

♡

Matthias had the announcement made on his wedding morning.

Made to the media and the lesser sorts who'd been invited only to the cathedral, that is. He told his houseguests himself. He, unlike Sabrina, didn't run away.

He went to the sideboard as usual and selected the same breakfast as always, the one instilled in him by his English nanny, and then by his English boarding school. The place where he'd learned that you could be in control, or you could be bullied. There were no other options. He'd been bullied at first, until he'd learned how to be in control. After that, he'd exacted his revenge and had settled the score.

When he sat, conversation quieted, even more than usual. They were all wondering, he knew, so he told them, dropping the announcement into the silence like a stone falling into a pond.

"I'm sorry to tell you all," he said, unfolding his white linen napkin and placing it carefully in his lap as the footman poured coffee from a silver pot, "that the wedding has been canceled. You will feel free, of course, to stay another night, until you can make your travel arrangements. Tonight's ball will not, alas, take place."

A moment of stunned silence greeted his words, and he took the opportunity for his first sip of coffee. His hand was perfectly steady; his face, he was sure, perfectly composed.

All eyes, he saw with inward satisfaction, had gone to Trudi, who had never learned the value of self-control. A dusky flush had spread up her carefully made-up cheeks.

"That's a bit rich, I must say." That was the Duke of Carlton, a cousin to the Queen and no genius. He let loose, right on cue, with the hearty, braying laugh Matthias despised. "Left at the altar, are you? Hard luck, old boy. That brother of yours is going to be pipping you at the post after all."

"Indeed," Matthias said, turning a bland gaze on him. "But we can't all have your good fortune, of course."

Everyone froze. The Duke's wife had been famously photographed years earlier having her breasts fondled in a Paris garden by an American millionaire, leading to the highest-profile of royal divorces.

"But what has happened?" demanded an elderly Marchioness, a relation of Matthias's father whom the late Prince had cordially detested, and about whom Matthias had never seen a reason to change his opinion. She turned to Trudi and demanded, "Has that silly girl of yours run after all, then? I never believed the hunting lodge story for an instant. Or was it somebody else? Off with one of the guards, maybe? American girls and their democratic ideas. As if being poor were romantic. Pfah."

"Rubbish," Trudi snapped, her vulgar Australian accent in strong showing. Matthias loosened his involuntarily tight grip on his coffee cup, forced his face to relax, and reminded himself that at least he'd been spared a most unsuitable mother-in-law. "She's taking some time, that's all," Trudi went on. "She hasn't been well, and this was all too much for her. I'm going back to Los Angeles today to speak to her, and we'll get it sorted."

Blessing Number Two, Matthias thought. Trudi was no use to him, and if he hadn't been sure that Sabrina would return, he'd have rid himself of her days ago.

"Ah. Got cold feet, has she?" the Marchioness said. "You're too much like your papa, Matti. I always said it. Cold feet for a cold fish. Your parents all over again."

Now, it wasn't just an intake of breath. It was shock, rolling over the enormous table like a wave.

"I'm afraid I wasn't entirely clear," Matthias said, his tone silky-smooth. "The wedding is not postponed. It is canceled. I trust all of you not to discuss this outside our inner circle, but Sabrina was not everything she... Well." He touched his napkin to his lips. "We have discovered that we don't suit, let us say." He continued into the silence, "I do, of course, rely on your discretion in not revealing even this much of my reasons."

Breathless responses of, "Of course," and "Naturally" greeted that, while Trudi's mouth opened and closed like a fish's. Matthias allowed himself the tiniest smile. It would be all over Europe by lunch, and the rest of the world by afternoon tea. The rumors would fly, and he wouldn't be a jilted groom. He'd be a man who'd had a lucky escape.

"Now," he said, "please do continue eating, everyone. A cold breakfast is so disappointing, isn't it?"

No, it hadn't gone over badly at all, and at three o'clock in the afternoon, he stood beside the royal family's pew in the nave of the cathedral, his bodyguards hovering at a discreet distance, and contemplated his future.

The cathedral was still closed to the public, those unlucky or unaware guests who hadn't received their notice being turned away at the gates. Matthias was alone but for the bodyguards, who didn't count, in the vast, echoing stillness of the stone palace built for the glory of the Church and the State. Or, more accurately, for the ancestor who had made the choice to build it, and had made it happen.

Any young woman of sense would have done anything, given up everything, for the chance to marry into all this. The public duties were laughable in this tiny but supremely wealthy principality, the rewards immense. Sabrina had left, and therefore she *wasn't* a young woman of sense, whatever

Matthias had thought. She was unstable, and unsuitable. Which meant another candidate, and fast.

His brother Andreas hadn't been at breakfast, of course. He would only have appeared for the ceremony, grinding his teeth at being that much further from the throne. Matthias had deliberately omitted him from the list to be informed of the cancellation, hoping he and his fat *hausfrau* of a wife would be turning up at the gates, foolish, excited, and unsuitable as Sabrina.

Andreas would be raising a glass with his duchess tonight, no doubt. Celebrating, as if Matthias wouldn't be able to breed an heir on a better candidate before another year had passed. And then a second one, as originally planned. As many as it took, until there was a boy.

She'd be younger this time. Sabrina had been too old anyway. What if the first three or four were daughters? He hadn't thought it through well enough. He'd been impulsive, in fact, and impulsivity was always dangerous. Sabrina had seemed perfect, but it had all been a deception. And anyway, twenty-one was better than twenty-five—nearly twenty-six, actually—in all ways. More malleable, and with more years of potential childbearing in front of her.

This time, she wouldn't have her own career, either. A member of the British minor nobility, perhaps. Bred to value a title, most of her family money long gone in taxes, death duties, and poor investments, and without illusions about marital bliss. Britain was full of them, still. Girls brought up to marry well and not much else. A choice between a stockbroker in the City, or the handsome Prince of Neuenstein? It would be no contest. She wouldn't be a lingerie model, but that was the tradeoff you made. That was the indulgence that had cost him this time.

He didn't have to love her, after all. He didn't even have to particularly desire her. She only needed to be tolerable enough and thin enough for him to be able to work up the enthusiasm to get her pregnant. He'd make it clear that getting fat wasn't acceptable, would have the doctor watch her weight during the pregnancies, when women let themselves go, and who would ensure that she was back to normal as quickly as possible afterwards, ready for the next one.

That was a plan, then. The details, he'd leave to Raoul. A shortlist of suitable candidates, a few trips to the UK, and it would be done.

He set it aside. Consider, decide, and act. That was his way. He'd decided. The action, he could delegate for now. He was done.

He clasped his hands lightly behind his back and stared up at the stained-glass window above the pew, at the motto inscribed on a ribbon below the image of a crowned figure.

Teneo quod meum est.

I hold what is mine.

Sabrina had done her best to humiliate him, yes. But with a few easy moves, he could still win. A rumor or two, a new bride, and he would be nearly there. But there was still the matter of evening the score. She hadn't paid the price for her deception and betrayal, and that wasn't acceptable.

He turned around and walked down the long aisle that Sabrina wouldn't be treading, his steps echoing hollowly against the stone. Out to his car and back to the palace, taking the corners fast, pushing the limits of the car and the road, because it was *his* car, and *his* road.

Because it was his right.

real and then some
♡

"First thing you do," Iain told Nina when they were out on the lawn, beside the two single kayaks lining one corner of the garden, "is listen."

Nina sighed, and he tried to ignore how good she looked in her new hat, or how pleased she'd looked to get it. *Focus. Friends. That's what she wants.*

"This," he said, holding up a stretchy black Neoprene mass, "is your spray skirt. Step into it like a... well, like a skirt."

He went through all the steps, had her in her PFD—her personal flotation device—next, pulling the straps tight, and he *didn't* reach for her to tighten them himself, no matter how much he wanted to.

"Hot, though," she said, plucking disconsolately at the foam vest. "It's shallow out there. At least near the shore. Is it really necessary?"

"You never know," he said. "You'll never need it, until you do. Besides, it's the law. Try going out there without a PFD, and next thing you know, a water taxi will be stopping beside you and some bloke even narkier than me will be telling you to put it on or go home. And if you don't? He'll be putting you on the boat and taking you out of the park."

"Got it," she said. "And by the way—remember that in-charge thing I said?"

"My unfortunate nature. And you forget. It's the family business. I used to do this during the school holidays—take people out on boats and give them this talk."

"But you aren't doing it now."

"Nah. If they're Kiwis, they tend to get personal. Gets boring."

"The rugby star deal."

"That'd be it. It's a small country, and a rugby nation, you could say. I do some maintenance on the boats, though, normally, when I'm here. Help out where I can."

"Or paint the shed. You know, in my experience, star athletes tend to spend the off-season doing something a little more glamorous. Cruising the Mediterranean. Shopping in Paris with their supermodel girlfriends."

"Known a lot of star athletes, have you?"

Her face went tight, but all she did was shrug. "I've heard."

"Well, those wouldn't be Kiwis, I'm guessing." *Huh.* Maybe she *had* known a star athlete, and hadn't liked him. Could explain her reserve with him, maybe, though it seemed like more than that. "Grab the bow of your boat. We'll take them down to the beach one at a time."

She was stronger than she looked, and she wasn't a princess, either. She carried the boat without complaint, even though he took as much of the weight as possible. She paid attention to his instructions, too, and when it was time to launch the boats, she got herself into hers with a grace that he envied.

"I'm surprised you fit in there," she said, when he'd pushed her out to launch her, and then gone back to hop into his own boat, splashing out far enough from the beach to get himself off the sand.

"It's all in the technique. Fitting, that is." He laughed out loud when she rolled her eyes. "Sorry. Couldn't resist that one. How'm I going?"

"Good, if you were sixteen," she said, making him laugh again.

"Well, most blokes probably *are* about sixteen inside," he said. "To tell you a secret you probably already know. Juvenile, you could say. Or just preoccupied with the same things, always."

"You astonish me," she said. "Like I haven't noticed you sneaking those peeks at my chest."

"And yet I still made you wear your PFD." He did his best not to grin like an idiot. "Depriving myself like that. If I *had* been sixteen, that might've been too much of a sacrifice, laws or no."

Now, *she* was the one laughing. "Right, Mr. Smooth Mover. I think I'm getting why you came home from the pub alone the other night despite your animal magnetism. Tell me what to do here." She plucked at the loose black fabric around her waist. "I suspect that if you'd been a kayak guide, you'd have been fired. I'm sure you were supposed to tell me by now. You're distracted."

He sighed. "I am. It's true. Right. You fasten that skirt around the cockpit like this. And next you'll get a paddling lesson. This is me focusing, now that you're covered up and all. You may want to take note, admire my mental strength."

She smiled again, and he did his best to get his mind out of the gutter and take her through the rest of it. She frowned lightly, focused, and did it all, then followed him through the water, skirting the green coast, the endless series of scooped-out bays, each with its own beach, that made up Abel Tasman National Park.

"Must be the yoga," he said, pulling up a bit to her right, keeping her between himself and the beach, where she'd be safest.

"What?" she asked.

"You're going well," he said, and she smiled at him, so sweet and so happy, and he may have had to swallow at the naked joy on her face.

What would it be like, he wondered, to be the one to

inspire that kind of joy in her? To have her face light up like that when she saw you? To have all of her light up for you, and then to slide inside all that warmth?

Good, that was what. It would be good.

He didn't take her far, not for this first time. Just over to Fisherman's Island to see the baby fur seals.

"Oh," she said, paddling up beside him, and there was that joy again. "That's pretty much adorable. But are they all right? They seem so lonesome. It sounds like they're crying."

"No worries. They're all good." He smiled at the wriggling little dark-brown shapes against the huge, tumbled black boulders at the shoreline of the island. "Just pups, doing their job. My mum said that after that flight, remember? 'Babies cry. It's their job.' They're yipping like that because they're missing their mums, want to remind her they're still here. But the mum has to fish. She has to eat, or she can't make her milk. She'll be back, though, no worries. She never leaves for long. You won't find many bad mums amongst seals."

"No dads, though, I'm guessing," she said.

He glanced over at her. No smile on her face now. "No," he said. "The males come around during the breeding season, do their bit, and then they're off again. This is the only time in the year the female's not pregnant, in fact. Within a few weeks, she'll be back in season again, and the males will be back as well. Male seals don't progress very far either in terms of their priorities. Then it all starts again. Seals don't get much choice in the matter."

♡♡♡

Not necessarily so different, she thought, and didn't say. *For some people.* Pretty much how her own father, a tall, dark, spectacularly handsome and even more spectacularly unreliable Russian choreographer doing a guest stint with the Melbourne Ballet, had viewed his role in the deal, from what her mother had told her. A visiting seal for sure.

Iain turned back with her and took her paddling around

Split Apple Rock, a huge granite boulder that sat offshore, split in two as if by a mighty hammer. He told her a Maori story that mothers had told their children, about the rock being a taniwha egg laid at the edge of the sea monster's domain. A story told in order to keep children safely close to shore, to protect them, just like the seal mothers did, like mothers were supposed to do.

He talked to her as if he really were a tour guide. No more cheesy banter at all, and she tried not to miss it. Then he took her back to the house. They dragged the kayaks up from the beach, and he said, "Come over in an hour or so, and we'll make dinner together."

He'd been nothing but normal, really, and she had to fight the disappointment. But then, however down-to-earth he seemed, he *was* a star, on a brief vacation before his life started up again, and she'd made it clear she wasn't going to be his holiday fling. She wasn't irresistible right now anyway, and that was fine. She wasn't trying to be. She was trying to be normal, and a friendly kayak tour was a whole lot more normal than getting the full-court press on a playboy prince's yacht. It was a whole lot less likely to end with you hiding under manure sacks, too. So she showered, changed into a green sundress, went over to the big house for the first time, and didn't get farther than a sunny kitchen, where Iain cooked with her, instructed her, smiled at her efforts, but didn't laugh at her. A subtle difference, but an important one.

Wedding day. It was her wedding day. To somebody else. Of course it felt strange.

When Iain had the burgers ready to go onto the barbecue, Nina ran back to the cottage for another of Madeline's cotton tablecloths, a yellow one printed with flowers, and picked up the huge vase of lilies she'd arranged earlier in the day for the occasion.

"Ready?" she asked Arthur, who was already waiting by the back door. "For my first-ever home-cooked dinner party?"

"Wouldn't be standing here if I wasn't." He glanced down

at the tablecloth, and she held her breath for a moment, but he didn't say anything.

She tucked one hand through his arm, smiled at him, and said, "Then how about walking me over there?"

"Huh," he said. "I could." And she squeezed his arm, slowed her pace to match his, and thought that, as a non–wedding day, it hadn't been too bad so far.

Iain helped her with the tablecloth, they set the table, and Carmella appeared with a smile and said, "How lovely."

And it was. The flower-bedecked table, its wooden chairs softened by colorful cushions, set on the stone patio under the wisteria and rose arbor, the sweet scent of roses mingling with the savory aroma of cooking on the soft evening breeze.

Everyone was fairly quiet at first, focusing on their food, nobody more so than Nina. The Moroccan spice mix she'd mixed with the ground lamb at Iain's direction provided a tangy contrast to the velvety, tender meat; the kumara wedges were crisp and flavorful; and the coleslaw gave just the right cool bite. Plus, there was wine. Nina almost never drank wine, but she made an exception tonight for the light Pinot Noir. One glass wouldn't hurt. She was eating ground lamb and bread anyway. She might as well succumb entirely.

Once Nina finished answering Carmella's questions about her first kayaking trip with Iain, though, with a few amused interjections from the man himself, the conversation lagged, and Nina couldn't think how to get it going again.

Finally, Carmella said, "Oh, I nearly forgot. Dad, why didn't you tell me that they're planning a birthday do for you down at the pub?"

He shrugged a bony shoulder. "Maybe I wasn't keen."

"Really?" Nina asked. "It's going to be your birthday? When?"

"Sunday," Arthur said. "Just before Iain goes back to Auckland. That's timing, eh."

"Actually," Iain said, "I'm thinking of staying on for a couple days. The workouts are going well, and I could give you a bit more help in the shop, Dad."

"Wouldn't come amiss," his father said, as his mother shot Iain a sharp glance. "Too much to do, and not enough people to do it. As usual."

"Good timing, then," Arthur said, "for the party, I mean. Even though I'm too old to care about birthdays. Nonsense at my age anyway. Nobody should be celebrating eighty-five."

"That's ridiculous," Nina said. "How could you ever be too old to celebrate? Considering the alternative, right?"

Nobody said anything, and she realized with horror why that was. *Madeline.* "I'm sorry," she said. "I didn't think. But... isn't it true anyway, surely?"

"Yeh," Iain said. "It's true. You're still kicking, after all, Granddad. Too mean for the devil to want you, and Nan must not have talked God into changing His mind yet about letting you in, because you're still here. Give her a little more time, though. You know she'll manage it. Meanwhile, we're stuck with you, so we may as well go down to the pub and drown our sorrows."

Arthur barked out a laugh and said, "Too right."

"I'll never understand the things men can say," Nina said. "If I'd said that, I'd be... just *horrified* afterwards. I'd *think* it, maybe, but I could never *say* it."

Both Iain and Arthur were smiling now, and Arthur said, "That's why women were made a bit softer, maybe. Otherwise, all the men would've clubbed each other to death long since, and the whole human race would've died out."

Nina laughed and said, "So what do we do for your birthday night? I mean, what special?"

"What d'you mean, what do you do?" Arthur said. "You either decide to take yourself to Motueka, thanking your lucky stars that you've got a night off at last, or you come to the pub and suffer through it with me. Going to have a country band and all, they say. You'll like that, missy. All your favorites."

Iain looked at her in surprise, and Arthur said, "Been singing all over the shop, hasn't she. All day long. Can barely hear myself think."

"If it's bothering you," Nina said, "you could tell me to shut up. I know you know how."

She got his huff of almost-laughter for that. "Did I say it was bothering me? Just said you did it, that's all. Better than chatting at me."

"Well, a party sounds lovely," Carmella said. "And of course we'll all go. Won't we, Graeme?"

He shrugged. "Since I haven't heard about it before, and you're telling me I am, reckon I'm going, yeh."

Carmella's lips tightened, and Nina could have sworn she winced a little. "Come on, darling," she said with a brittle laugh. "That isn't what Dad needs to hear."

"I'll try again, then," Graeme said. "I'll be there, obviously. You've just told me so. And I'm also sure you'll tell me on the night how I'm meant to go on, if I get it wrong."

Carmella looked down at her plate, and silence fell for a long moment, until the scrape of Iain's chair on the stone patio broke it.

"Right," he said. "That's enough. What the hell is wrong with you, Dad?"

Now, it wasn't just silence. It was shock that held everyone still, and then Graeme turned a grim face to his son. "You don't tell me what's enough," he said.

"Yeh," Iain said. "I do. Mum deserves better than that from you."

His father held his gaze, the old bull facing off to the young one, and then Graeme stood up abruptly from the table, tossed his napkin onto his chair, and said, "Thanks for dinner, Nina. Good tucker. But I have to work tomorrow. Somebody has to keep this business going." And he headed back into the house.

Carmella took a long, shaky breath. "Well," she said quietly, "that's told me."

"Told me, too," Arthur said. "I'll go have a word." He grabbed his cane and heaved himself to his feet.

"Dad," Carmella said, putting a hand out and rising herself. "No. Not your business." She looked at Iain. "Nor yours, either, darling, but thank you for trying. Time for me to face this. Time for me to take care of it." And she followed her husband into the house.

"Well," Nina said in a small voice into the silence, "that was terrible."

"Yeh," Iain said. "I guess this family party wasn't our best idea ever."

"Rubbish," Arthur said. "Got it out in the open. Things are better in the open than rotting away underneath. Give them a chance to work it out. You don't throw away all those years, unless you're an even bigger fool than Graeme." His tortoise eyes blinked, and he swung around to look at Nina. "I'm going back home." He shook his head at her offer to accompany him and took himself off.

Which left Nina and Iain looking at each other. "Um..." she said. "Great burgers?"

That surprised a laugh out of him. "Welcome to my family. Hell of a relaxing spot, Kaiteriteri." He began to gather dishes, and she stood hastily and started to stack plates.

"I'll do it," he said.

"No," she said. "I'll help."

She cleared the table with him and loaded the dishwasher, trying not to listen to the faint sounds of voices coming from the other room, even after Iain had shut the door from the kitchen. After that, though, Iain looked at her and said quietly, "Best that you go on back, probably," and she nodded and took herself across to the cottage.

It wasn't anything close to how she might have imagined this evening ending, in her unruly imagination. But it was what was happening.

Living in paradise, she thought as she let herself quietly into the little house, apparently couldn't solve all your problems after all. And "real" wasn't always everything it was cracked up to be.

tipping point
♡

Carmella followed the sound of the television to the lounge, where Graeme was sitting on the couch, his arms folded across his chest, his feet planted on the carpet.

She reached for the remote on the coffee table and clicked the set off.

"Oi!" He turned his head and glared at her. "I was watching that."

"And now you're not. We need to talk."

He stood to his full height and turned to face her, his expression giving nothing away. Still as upright as ever, still the tall, strapping man she'd married, but... blank, somehow, the way he'd been so often since she'd come home. And maybe before. To her shame, she couldn't remember.

"No," he said. "We don't have to talk. I already know what you're going to say. I ruined your dinner. I didn't behave well. I'm a grumpy bugger."

"Graeme." It wasn't easy to go on. "I know something's wrong. I've been thinking it's something that'll pass, but I don't think it will. I'm afraid to hear, but I need you to tell me. You don't..." She had to stop again. "Is it just... was it Christmas? Are you angry that I left you alone? Or is it more? Do you... do you not want to be married to me anymore? If

170

that's it—tell me. Please. I can't stand this."

She had to hold onto the back of the couch after she said it. Otherwise, she was going to float away. Her head didn't seem to be anchored to her body. Her mind wanted to be somewhere else. Anywhere else.

His face was still giving nothing away. "I never said that. I never said anything like that. Maybe I just don't appreciate being told where I'm to go, what I'm to do. Maybe I've got an opinion."

"All right," she said. "What is it? Tell me."

He shrugged. "No point. You don't listen anyway."

The hurt was still there, but she was getting angry now, too. "I can't read your mind. You have to tell me."

He shook his head like a frustrated bull. "I'll go to Arthur's party. You could've told me sooner, but never mind. Anyway, I've got the accounts to go over before I go to bed, and they aren't going to do themselves."

"No," she said. "No. This matters more. We need to talk about this."

"There's nothing to say. We already said it. I'll be going to Arthur's party, and I'll be…" He sighed. "I'll make an effort, all right? Meanwhile, I'm doing the accounts, and you're going to bed. That's it."

"Then…" She said it. "If that's it, I can't stay."

"You don't have to stay. Go on to bed. I'll do it."

"I can't…" Something was ripping inside her. Tearing loose. "I can't live like this. I can't do this. I need you to love me, or to tell me that you don't, and let me…" It hurt so much, too much, but she said it anyway. "Let me go."

"Of course I love you." He said it, but it didn't sound like it. It didn't sound like it at all. "When have I said anything else? And this is what I'm talking about. You leave for a month, leave me alone to do it all without even talking it over, then you throw a wobbly because I'm not saying the right things. I can't do it right, I can't say it right, and I know it. If you don't want that, you don't want me."

She raised a hand, dropped it again "All right," she

whispered. "All right." Then she turned and left the room.

$$\heartsuit\heartsuit\heartsuit$$

He almost went after her, but what was the use? Instead, he went to the desk in the corner of the room, switched the computer on, pulled up the spreadsheet, and started on the next round of the endless bookkeeping that was part of running a small business. He could hear her moving around overhead. Probably changing her clothes to go to book club, since it wasn't an exercise class night, or Garden Club, or any of the other endless things she found to do.

He wouldn't say anything next time. She said she wanted him to talk, but only if he was saying what she wanted to hear. During those brief times when she was in the same room as he was, that is.

He heard a heavy tread on the stairs, and then she was in the doorway again, the handle of her flowered suitcase in one hand, and he'd stood up without realizing it. "You going somewhere?" he asked.

There were tearstains on her cheeks, and he felt a low dragging in his gut. Shame, trying once again to take him down.

She raised her chin with the strength he'd always admired in her, and her voice was nearly steady when she said, "I'm going to stay at Dad's tonight."

"Because we had a few words?" he said. "No."

"Yes, Graeme," she said, her brown eyes steady, and so sad, and he wanted to hit something.

He had to do something, but what?

"I can…" He cast about for something to say. "I can sleep on the couch. If you don't want to…" Now he was the one who had to stop. "If you don't want to sleep with me."

"No," she said. "I don't want you to sleep on the couch. I don't want to punish you. It's the last thing I want. But I feel like you're punishing *me*, and I don't even know what I've done wrong. I don't know how to fix it, and I don't feel like you want to try. So I'm going to sleep at Dad's. I'll figure something else out tomorrow, I guess. Someplace to go. And when you want to get this sorted with me— I mean..." She swallowed. "If you do. Guess that's the issue, isn't it? That's what you think I'm doing to you. Telling you what you think, what you should feel, what you should do. So I'm not going to tell you what you should do. I'm just going to tell you what I'm doing." She held out her hand, and he realized for the first time that she was holding a piece of paper.

He reached for it, dreading what he'd see. *A lawyer,* he thought numbly. *No. Not that.* He'd stuffed it up for good. This was it.

It wasn't a lawyer. It was a simply printed black-and-white flyer.

Melvin Anderson, M.F.T.
Individual Therapy
Couples and Relationship Therapy
Family Therapy

"No," he said, trying to hand it back. "No. I can't."

She swallowed again. He could see it. "Right, then," she said. "Then I'm going. But I hope you'll change your mind. I love you, Graeme. I've loved you since I was twenty-one, and I can't stop. I just... I can't. But it hurts too much. I can't stay here and feel like you..." A sound like a sob broke loose, but that couldn't be it. Carmella didn't cry. She got on with things. She coped. "And feel like you hate me," she whispered. "I can't lie beside you and know that you... that you don't want me. It hurts too much. If you can stand to lose me, then..." She stopped, heaved in a breath, and went on. "Then you already have. And I have to go."

"No," he said again.

"Yes." She turned and left the room, and he heard her saying something to Iain in the kitchen, then the sound of the door opening.

He stood there like a big, dumb block of wood, looked at

the paper in his hand, and crumpled it in his fist. He wanted to move. He needed to do something. But there was nothing. For once, there was nothing. No place to go, and nothing to do.

He'd have died for her without a second's hesitation. Always. Still. Forever. He'd given up his own business and moved here four years ago to be with her parents, to take over the kayaks, because she'd wanted it. He'd worked his entire life for her, and for the kids, too. But mostly for her.

All he'd wanted was to be the one who stood between her and danger, between her and want. And somehow, he'd done it wrong. More and more wrong. Something was in his way, and he couldn't see what. Everything he said came out wrong, and he didn't understand it. He didn't know how to stop it. He didn't have a clue. When he'd go to touch her, she'd jump, so he'd stopped touching her. He couldn't stand it, but he knew that trying to spill his guts to some weedy fella with a soft voice and softer hands, somebody who wouldn't understand that a man who wasn't good at talking couldn't just... start—that wasn't going to change anything, and it wasn't going to help.

His deepest fear had always been losing her. Now, it was happening, and he knew it was his fault, and he couldn't see how to fix it. It was his job to take care of her, and he hadn't done it.

He sat down again and stared at the accounts, tried to focus, as he always had, on the work, because providing was what he did. And for the first time ever, he couldn't do it.

your favorite shoes
♡

Nina was in bed with her mystery again, which she still somehow hadn't finished, and wasn't going to tonight, either. She could feel her eyelids drooping, because way too much had happened today. And then she heard the door opening and closing. Some thumping sounds, and more doors.

Iain. He'd come to find her.

She didn't think. She was out of bed, not bothering to pull anything on over her underwear, and opening her door.

Carmella whirled, two feet away at the linen closet, her hand at her chest. "Oh," she said. "You startled me. Sorry. I'm just looking for a bit of bedding."

Her face didn't look right, somehow. "What is it?" Nina asked. "What's wrong?"

"Oh, you know," Carmella said, her voice sounding high and tight, "Nothing much. Just a woman who's left her husband, that's all."

"Oh, no," Nina said. "Oh, I'm sorry."

Carmella's striking face worked, and Nina could see the tears she was trying to hold back. She knew exactly how that felt, and exactly how impossible it was to do it.

"Can I..." she asked hesitantly. "Can I help?"

Carmella shook her head violently once, twice. Her arms

175

came around herself, and she was bent a little at the waist now.

This, Nina knew. She knew for sure. Carmella needed other arms, and the arms she needed weren't there. So she did the only thing she could think of. She took two steps forward and put her own arms around Carmella, and the older woman gasped. And then she lost the battle, and she cried. Nearly silently, the sobs racking her slim, strong body, while Nina held on, rocked back and forth, uttered a few inadequate sounds of comfort, and did her best to offer back some of the support Carmella had given her.

At last, Carmella straightened up, wiped her hands over her cheeks, said, "Goodness," and tried to laugh, but it didn't work too well. "I'll just… clean up," she said. "I'm sorry. What you must think."

"No," Nina said. "No, of course not. What I think is…" She had to choke back her own tears. "That I'm so sorry. So desperately sorry."

That started the tears again, and Carmella ducked into the bathroom and shut the door. Nina looked at the pink-and-yellow-flowered suitcase standing by the linen closet, and her chest ached. She wheeled it into the bedroom and thought about how little you could see into somebody else's life from the outside. About the struggles you never knew about, all the pain they hid beneath the surface. The kind, cheerful, competent woman she'd met on that flight—this wasn't the same person, and yet she was exactly that person.

It didn't take long for Carmella to come out, and of course she had herself under control again.

"Oh," she said when she saw her suitcase lifted onto the little table in the corner of the room. "No. I'll just take it into the lounge. I'll get some sheets and sleep on the couch. No worries. And tomorrow, I'll…" Her face twisted again. "Make a plan," she said helplessly. "Some plan."

"No," Nina said. Of this, she was sure. "You'll sleep here. I hardly have any clothes. You know that; you helped me buy them. As long as you don't mind sharing the hooks and the dresser with me, I'll sleep in the hammock, and you take the bedroom. You need it, and I don't. I'd rather be outside anyway." *Now that I know that your son won't dump me out and try to drown me,* she didn't say.

"I couldn't," Carmella said.

Nina was already yanking on her shorts, though, and had gone out to the linen closet and pulled down another duvet and pillow. "Nope," she said. "It's done. I'm gone." But she came back anyway, because Carmella had sat on the bed with a thump. Nina sat beside her, put her arm around the older woman, and said, "I'm sure he loves you. I'm sure he does. How could he not?"

Carmella gave a watery laugh and swiped at her eyes with the heel of one hand. "I'm... too managing. I'm bossy."

"No," Nina said. "You're wonderful. You're kind, and loving, and helpful, and so competent. You're the woman I want to be."

Carmella had lost the battle with the tears, and they were staining her cheeks again. "Oh, darling," she said. "I wish that were true."

"It's true," Nina said. "Iain couldn't be as wonderful as he is if you weren't." And then she was the one pulling back. "I mean," she stammered, "he's a good man, and good men usually have good parents."

"What d'you reckon?" Carmella said with another trembling smile. "Think we've both said too much tonight?"

Nina gave her one last hug and said, "Probably so. I'll see you in the morning, OK? Maybe things will feel more hopeful then."

♡♡♡

Iain had finished the washing up, then lingered in the kitchen. When he saw his mum push open the swinging door, pulling her suitcase before him, his heart sank.

"Uh... going somewhere?" he asked her. "Need help?"

She shook her head once. "No. Sorry, darling. I can't talk.

Look after your dad, will you?"

"Mum…" he said helplessly. "No."

She dropped the handle, and the suitcase banged to the floor. "Everyone wants to tell me no." Her voice was shaking. "I get to say no, too. And I'm saying it. No. No more."

Iain had already started forward, but she shook him off, picked up her suitcase, and said, "No. No. I'm going." Then she was out the door, and gone, and he was left wondering what had just happened.

"Right," he said aloud. "Right. Harden up." He went through that swinging door himself, saw his dad sitting at the computer in the corner of the lounge, as usual in the evening.

"Dad?" he asked. "How you goin'?"

His father didn't even turn around. "No," he said. "Not tonight."

That was two for two, then. Iain hesitated another moment, feeling like the most useless lump on the planet, then headed out to the beach.

He'd go for a walk. And if that didn't work, he'd go to the pub. A pint was better than nothing.

The tide was halfway to full, making it still possible to walk around the rocks to the longer beach, if you didn't mind wading a bit. He never minded wet, so he walked down the tiny Honeymoon Bay beach, and then started to jog, life settling a bit, as always, with the movement. He splashed around the point, ran on firmer sand the entire long length of Kaiteriteri Beach, then back and around again. The water was deeper this time, but no matter.

By the time he was walking back, he was calmer, at least. He couldn't fix his parents. He wouldn't have a clue how. He was here, and he'd… well, he was here. That was about all he had.

He almost missed Nina. She was sitting on the low branch of the gnarled pohutukawa that grew at the edge of his parents' property, just at the point where bush met beach. The tide was nearly high enough to cut their end section of beach off from the rest, and he was glad of it. He hoped he was as friendly a Kiwi as any other, but he enjoyed those brief moments of high-tide privacy.

He caught a flash of white—her duvet, wrapped around her shoulders. The setting sun was beginning to tint the clouds overhead with glorious shades of pink and brilliant blue, their soft light reflected in the rippling waters of the sea. And still, there was enough light to recognize Nina. Or maybe he'd found her some other way. Maybe he'd felt her here.

"Hi," she said when he approached. She scooted over a little on her branch and dipped her head toward it, inviting him to sit. "Clearing your head?"

He dropped down beside her, stretched his bare feet out in the sand, and sighed. "Sounds like you know."

"Your mum's in my bed," she said. "I mean, in the guest bed."

"You know more than I do, then. My dad wasn't talking."

"Is that unusual?" she asked quietly.

He let out a long breath. "No. Probably not. Don't think she's ever walked out, though. Never that I know. And it's never felt like this. Like tonight."

"Mm." She was quiet for a minute, and he was, too. Then she asked, "What was it like with your grandparents? I mean, what were they like together? The same as this?"

"You mean my mum's parents? No, they weren't. My dad's dad... well, he was a hard man and no mistake. Granddad's a softy in comparison. I realize you wouldn't see it, not the way he is now, but he was different when my nan was alive. He was so mad about her, you could see it. When she was in the room, he'd be looking at her. Or looking over from time to time, like he needed to. Always looking out for her. I don't think she ever..."

"Doubted," Nina said quietly. "Not like your mother is right now."

"But it's mad," he said. "He—Dad—he feels that same way about Mum, I'd swear it. So what's he doing? Damned if

I know. Why would you throw it away?"

"I don't know."

More silence, then, while the gentle waves lapped onto the golden sands, whispering their message of timelessness, and of time passing, all at once.

"Granddad said something to me once," Iain said, almost reluctantly.

Nina looked at him from under her duvet, but didn't say anything, and he went on. "It was when I was thinking about making a commitment of my own. And I asked him, how could you be sure it was right? And he said—"

He stopped, and she didn't ask him, "what commitment?" in the way he'd half-expected. She just asked, "What did he say?"

"He said it was like a pair of shoes. Not what you were expecting, eh. Me neither. He said something like, 'When you have those shoes that you've broken in, and they're just right, fit you perfectly. Could be that they don't look as flash as they once did, but you don't care about that. They're comfortable, like, and when you put them on, you can walk anywhere. They'll carry you forever. It's like that, but they never wear out. They change, of course. They'll have some scuffs, even a hole or two, maybe, but they still work. And the thing about shoes is, there's a right one, and there's a left. They're not exactly alike, but they're a pair. They only work together. You lose one of them, and the other's useless. Best shoes you ever had, and one's useless without the other. That's what it's like.'"

It was a minute before Iain could continue, and still, she didn't say anything. He looked at the puffs of pink and blue cloud overhead. He listened to the murmur of the sea, and finally, he said, "Nan was sick already when he said that. He knew he was about to lose his other shoe. And he couldn't stand it."

"Oh, Iain." She was crying, he realized. Silently, the tears silver streams on her pale cheeks. "It's so beautiful, and so sad. It breaks my heart."

"Yeh. Broke mine." He cleared his throat. "She was like Granddad's light, my nan. A bit of a light for all of us, you could say, but for him? She was like his sun, and when she went, it was like night came."

"But she'd have been so sad to know that," Nina said. Her voice was trembling, but it was sure. "If that was how she really was, she'd never have wanted him to feel like that. She'd have wanted him to live. She'd have wanted him to be warm again. Surely, any woman who truly loved a man would want that."

"You think love is so selfless? Not so sure. Not always, anyway."

"Not always, maybe. But if it's right? Then I think so. If it's real."

She was there next to him, so sweet and strong herself. So real. He put a hand out, because he couldn't have done anything else, and touched her cheek, the silkiness of her skin a revelation against the rough pads of his fingers, and watched her huge eyes in the soft light of evening. Not so much a sun as an evening star, Nina. Or a moon, maybe. Glowing soft, but glowing all the same. Or not a moon. Moons were cool, and Nina wasn't cool.

He gave up thinking about it. That wasn't what he wanted to do. His hand was under her chin, tipping it up, and he was leaning down, brushing his lips over hers, and if her cheek had been soft? Her mouth was in some other dimension. Soft, and rich, and full, and he was kissing her more. How could he have resisted that? His arm had gone around her, was pulling her closer, and that was surely her own hand, he realized dimly, on his shoulder, holding him to her, holding him tight. Her mouth opened under his, and he was tasting her, and that was nothing but rich, warm sweetness, too.

She was the one who broke it off. Of course she was. There was no way that would ever have been him.

"Iain," she said, and he realized that she wasn't holding his shoulder anymore. She was pushing against it. "Stop."

"Oh." He sat up and blinked. There she was, though, eyes

wide, lips parted, and... bloody *hell.*

"I can't," she said. "Not now. It's... I can't now."

"Oh. Right."

"You're just on vacation," she said. "I mean holiday."

"Yeh," he said. "I am."

"And I'm... yeah." She laughed, a short, uneven, husky sound, that voice of hers trying to drag him down into her sweet depths again. "It's not the right time for me, either. So, no. But can I say..." She had her hand on his shoulder as if she couldn't help it either, then was touching his face, nothing but gentle. "You are the nicest man."

His head jerked back. "Me?"

She laughed, just that edge of roughness to it. "Yes. You. I'm sorry if it ruins your self-image. When I met you, I thought, The Incredible Hulk. And now?" She smiled, her face luminous. "Now more than ever. So much toughness. So much strength. And so much else. So much more."

"And yet," he said, even as her words warmed him, "still no."

"Maybe because of that," she said. "You'd be too easy to love. And I can't afford to fall in love."

The word hit him hard, a dose of cold water. She smiled sadly and said, "Yeah, right? You can't either. And I already knew that." She got up, adjusted her duvet over her shoulders, and said, "So I'm going to bed. Or to hammock, I guess. But I hope you'll still take me kayaking. I have to admit—I still hope that."

"I'll take you," he said. "You have to know I will."

"Then I'll look forward to that." She turned and headed up the track to her hammock, and he let her go, and sat on the branch, and wondered if his grandfather was the only man in his family who was ever going to get it right.

no princess
♡

Iain fixed his dad's breakfast the next morning, and heard him say not much at all. Then he went for his workout as usual, stopping afterwards at Toad Hall in Motueka for a smoothie. He ordered, sat at a long wooden table in one corner of the garden near the fountain, and grabbed a nearby copy of the Christchurch *Press*.

He didn't start reading straight away, though. He should bring Nina here, he thought. For the pizza. Ha. Probably not. Or the real-fruit ice cream. Even less likely. He couldn't see Nina selecting her fruits, then watching them being blended together with the rich vanilla ice cream and squeezed out into a cone.

She'd be shocked at the idea of such decadence. Just like when she'd eaten melted cheese on her sandwich, or a lamb burger, and he'd seen her eyes nearly glaze over with pleasure at the rich tastes and silky textures. She wouldn't order an ice cream, but he'd bet he could tempt her into taking a lick or two off his. That wouldn't be bad to watch, either. Watching her eyes close, seeing her lick up that treat... no, that wouldn't be bad at all.

He needed to see if there were a way, somehow, that would work for them. He needed to take her kayaking again today, and then for ice cream. And maybe, tonight, to the back garden of the pub. He needed to tease her and smile at her and look into her eyes. He needed to drive her home and take her for a walk on the beach, to hold her hand. And to kiss her. He needed to kiss her so badly.

He was still smiling as he picked up his smoothie, sipped at it, and finally looked at the newspaper. *This afternoon,* he promised himself. Kayaking first, and then—they'd see. His granddad's party was tomorrow night, and it was true. Iain had a few more days before he absolutely had to be back in Auckland. He could spend them here. He could spend them with Nina. No matter how frustrating it might be, it would be better than being at home alone and thinking he should have tried harder.

No princess. No bride, said the headline, and he glanced at it incuriously. Not exactly local news. And then he stopped with the straw in his mouth. There was a picture beneath that headline. A beautiful girl in a tiara, her smile radiant as the sun.

Nina.

It couldn't be. It wasn't possible.

He scanned the lines of newsprint, reading faster and faster.

It was billed as the complete fairy-tale wedding, complete with golden coach, snow-white horses, and a guest list studded with European royalty and Eurotrash. Instead, Prince Matthias of Neuenstein announced today via a spokesperson that his wedding to top Milady's Boudoir model Sabrina Jones has been canceled.

The rumors have circulated furiously for a week, and been just as furiously denied. Today, there was no more denial possible. Sabrina Jones is officially a Runaway Bride, a no-show at what was to have been the royal wedding of the decade.

Insiders have speculated on the would-be princess's notable absence from the prenuptial festivities—even while her mother attended all of them. Sabrina was staying in seclusion in a remote hunting lodge. Sabrina was in hospital. Sabrina had met with an accident. And always, the whisper that Jones had run away rather than face marriage to Europe's most eligible bachelor, or, worse, that she had run off with another man.

That last possibility would have been an even greater shock to the Prince, those close to him have noted, after his mother's notorious elopement with her sons' swimming instructor in a scandal that rocked the monarchy.

Iain read the rest, every single damning word of it, then stood up, the newspaper clutched in his fist, and went for the car.

Fifteen minutes later, he was pulling to a stop above the house without any memory of having driven there, and was striding down the track and bursting through the doorway of the cottage.

Nina was standing at the kitchen sink scraping carrots, singing softly. Her voice was sweet, but that wasn't a surprise, was it? She always sounded sweet. She always looked that way. Because she was a *model.* She made her living from projecting an image.

She turned at his entrance with her wide smile. Doing it again. "Iain!" she said, as if he were her birthday present, and it was just what she'd wanted. "Hi. You startled me."

He held up the paper to show her the picture. The one that showed that matching smile, the joyful look she could apparently turn on at will. "Sorry, Nina. Or should I call you Sabrina? Is the name as much a lie as the rest of you?"

The color drained from her cheeks, and her carrot fell unheeded into the sink. "Wh-what?"

He could barely say the words. "'Runaway Bride.' This is you. That day in the airport, there was a headline like this. You left him at the altar, or near enough, didn't you? Left him guessing, left him hoping."

"I…" It was barely a stammer. Her eyes were wide, shocked. Innocent.

Well, no. Hardly that.

"You left your groom," he said. "You ran away, and you

didn't even have the courtesy to tell him you were going. Always so sweet. Always so scared. You aren't poor, and you aren't scared. You're a bloody *Milady's Boudoir* model! What is this you're doing now, a publicity stunt for your career? The rest of it wasn't enough? Now you have to find the most famous person you can scrape up and attach yourself to him? Pity it was only me, then. Pity it wasn't Nate Torrance. But oh, wait. He's not available anymore."

"Wh-what?"

He flapped the newspaper at her. "Don't pretend you don't know the captain of the All Blacks. What kind of luck was that? Your seatmate's the mum of an All Black, and as everybody knows, he's even famously single. Are you planning to sell the story, then? 'Two continents, fifteen thousand kilometers, two men? My life from princess to scullery maid to rugby WAG'?"

She was still chalk-white, but her eyes weren't confused anymore.

"Why don't you get over yourself?" Her voice might be unsteady, but it was angrier than he'd ever heard it. "I told you. I'd never *heard* of your little team. I'd barely heard of your *sport*. And why don't you wait to hear what I have to say before you start accusing me? Why don't you wait to hear my reasons?"

He dropped the paper on the table. He was, suddenly, deflated. He was done. "I don't need to hear it. I've heard it all before. I know all about cold feet. I know all about lying and being a coward. And I know all about how that bloke felt today, when he was ready to get married and you weren't there."

His granddad had come into the kitchen sometime, he realized, was standing in the doorway, cane in hand, eyes grim.

"Yeh," Iain told him, trying to speak over the hot rage that was choking him. "Ask her why, Granddad. Ask her why she left. Ask her why she lied. Ask her why any of us should care." And he turned around and walked out.

rough waters

♡

Nina picked up her carrot in shaking fingers and started scraping it again, blinking away the stupid tears.

Iain wasn't wrong. He'd been cruel, and his words had hurt, but he wasn't wrong. Her flight from the palace, the way she'd hidden ever since? It hadn't been the right way. She knew that now. She hadn't had enough guts to stand up to Matthias. She hadn't had enough to stand up to *anybody*, or even to tell the truth. It had been the only way she'd been able to manage it, but that didn't matter. She'd done what she'd done, and she had to live with it, and with everybody's judgment, too. There was no way to explain it that would sound reasonable, and Iain wouldn't believe her. She'd misjudged him, like she'd misjudged everything. She'd got it all so wrong.

But right now, she was going to make this soup. What else could she do?

When she heard Arthur's voice behind her, she jumped. She hadn't realized he was there.

"Reckon you didn't want to be a princess," he said.

She turned to see him standing at the table, the newspaper in one hand, his gaze steady on her.

"No," she said. "I didn't."

187

"Could be you had a reason for running away, too."

"Yes. I did. Or I thought I did."

He nodded. "I reckoned. Are you good with making that lunch? I'm hungry, so if you're not, tell me, and I'll finish it."

"No. I'm good with making it. Half an hour." She might be numb, but at least she could stay upright.

That was why she was still with Arthur in the kitchen, though, when they heard the clatter of shoes on the brick of the courtyard, then the scrape as the rolling door to the shed opened.

"Off to ride his bicycle," Arthur said, taking a sip of vegetable soup. "Same as always. When he's got something to work out, ever since he was a boy, he has to go off and move. He'll come back calmer, maybe, and you can have a better chat."

"A better... *chat.*" She couldn't help the angry laugh. "Yeah, right. Is that what you call that?"

"Nah. I call that lashing out because it hurts. Some people curl up when they're hurt. Some punch back. He punches back. Not always the best, but being stubborn runs in the family, eh."

She couldn't look at him, and she couldn't eat, so instead, she held her spoon up, watched the soup trickling off it, and swallowed back the tears. "I didn't mean to hurt anybody. I didn't feel like I had a choice, and I needed to get away so I could choose. So I could have time to think."

"Did it help?"

"I thought it did."

Another nod, and that was all. He was picking up his sandwich again.

Minutes passed before she asked, "Would it be all right if I made something simple for dinner tonight?"

"I told you," he said, "I don't need a minder. Or a cook."

"It's my job, though. If I don't feed you, what am I doing here?"

"Keeping me company. Keeping me from poking into the accounts of the business and driving Graeme mad. Keeping me from poking my nose into their personal business."

She had to smile, even as she felt the smile wobble. "That might not be enough to justify my existence."

"It's enough. You don't believe me, just ask Carmella."

She got up without finishing her lunch. "Right, then. I'll clean up, and then I'm going to go out for a while. I need to..." Her shoulders jerked. "I guess I need to move too."

"He doesn't know what he's doing."

She didn't turn around. She couldn't. She was scrubbing at her plate, concentrating with all her might.

"Hasn't known for months now," Arthur went on. "Just like you don't. Give it time. Least that's what Madeline would've said. She'd have—"

He stopped, though, and she forgot about her own pain for a moment. She turned around, grabbed a tea towel, then sat down again and put her still-damp hand on his. "What?"

He scowled at her. "I'm not going to cry, if that's what you're worried about. Worry about yourself." But he didn't take his hand away.

She ignored that. "What would she have said?"

"That if it's meant to be, it'll happen." His voice was gruffer than ever, the words nearly barked out. "She was usually right, so you might think about that."

"Do you believe that, though?" she asked hesitantly. "That sounds like 'fate.' I don't think I believe in fate. Not anymore."

"I didn't say it was fate. I said that she was usually right."

"You didn't know," she said, the traitorous tears lurking too close to the surface, "so you took her word for it?"

He was scowling harder now. It was easy to see where Iain got it. "Don't be stupid. I'm not talking about some rubbish like 'fate.' And of course I believed her. Why wouldn't I? People talk about love, about marriage, too, like they're magic. There's no magic. Just two people who like each other and decide they're willing to get stuck in together. If you can make your way through the bad patches, it works, and you know each other better afterwards, make a better team. If you can't, it doesn't. No secret. No magic. But you don't want to hear that, so you'd best go on and get out. That boy's out on that pushbike for the same reason you're flitting around my house like a fantail, though. You like each other, and you've hit your first bad patch. Get through this one, and there'll be another down the track. No magic to it. Just the way love works. If you don't want it, don't try. It's worth it or it's not. Your choice."

"No," she said, standing up, carrying the dishes to the sink and beginning to run the water. Flitting around, exactly like he'd said. "Both people have to try, I know that much, at least. And he doesn't want to try. You heard him. He's out there being furious with me, and training for rugby. Staying fit. There's nothing to get through, because there was never anything there."

"Never mind, then." Arthur reached for his stick and hauled himself to his feet. "Young people, eh. And they call *me* stubborn. I'm going for my walk, and then I'm going to take a rest. Don't disturb me."

♡♡♡

When she finally got out of the house, Nina hesitated. She'd read the article after Arthur had left, and now, she needed to get *away*. She didn't want to walk on the road, though. She didn't want to risk meeting Iain. She didn't want to go to the kayak office and ask for a ride up to the national park on a sea shuttle, either, even though Iain had told her yesterday that she could, and she hadn't even walked the track yet. She didn't know if Carmella and Graeme would have seen the paper, or what they would think of her afterwards, and she felt too fragile to find out. Not today. Not right now.

Right, then. Another plan. She went back into the house for a water bottle and her hat, hesitated, then wrote a note for Arthur. It was only prudent. After that, she went and got the orange kayak—what she'd thought of yesterday as *her* kayak, like she'd thought so many things here could be hers, that they could belong to her, somehow, at least for a little while, or that she could belong to them. That she could fit here.

Well, she couldn't. She'd adjust. She'd done it so far, so she'd be able to again. Just not this minute. Not today. But she wouldn't, she *wouldn't* cry. Not again. Not over Iain, anyway. Not over a man who didn't want her, who'd looked at her with that much contempt.

She got herself into the spray skirt and PFD, then began to drag the boat across the lawn and down the path. It was more work than she'd realized it would be, and she was panting by the time she reached the beach. How was she going to get it back up again?

Somehow, that was how. Somehow.

She shoved the boat out from the beach and hopped in, a little proud of herself despite everything for being able to do it, then set a good pace northward, hugging the shore. She did her best to ignore the heaviness in her chest and concentrate on the rippling sea, which was a little less gentle today. To listen to the call of the tuis in the greenery, to watch the graceful cormorants sitting, wings spread wide, on the rocks, drying their feathers before another plunge into the water.

She made an effort to notice all of it, and after a while, it worked. Her mind managed to slip away from its relentless hamster-wheel repeat of what Iain had said, what the newspaper had said, what Nina had done, what her mother would be doing, and fell into the rhythm of her paddling, the rise and fall of the waves.

It felt good to move, and better to push it. She passed Marahau Beach, nodded to a guide bringing a party back to shore, and decided to keep going. She'd be back in plenty of time to cook Arthur's dinner—and Carmella's too, she guessed. And then she'd figure out what came next. She'd call her grandparents, and one day soon, she'd call her mother. Somehow. She'd apologize for running, and she'd... close it. Close the chapter. And she *wouldn't* call Matthias. That book was already closed, just like Iain was. It was done. They were both done.

Her chest still ached, and the tears still burned behind her eyelids, but she did her best to push past them. Maybe happiness was about focusing on the things she *could* do, the things she *could* have, instead of yearning for more. She'd always set goals and worked toward them. Or had them set for her, more like, but she was trying to change that, wasn't she?

One thing she knew for sure, though. A man wasn't a goal.

Maybe Fisherman's Island was. Right across the water, barely more than fifteen minutes' strong paddle. The wind had picked up as Iain had said it did in late afternoon, making the water a little choppy, but it wasn't from the east, and the east was the bad direction. It was coming from the west, from shore, surely, so she was fine.

She'd go see the baby seals. That would make her feel better, and then she'd paddle back to Kaiteriteri. And then she'd figure out how to get on with her life.

It would have worked out fine if it hadn't been for the powerboat.

The chunky white vessel sped past her just as she reached the south side of the island. It was going faster than boats usually did here, leaving a high wake behind it. She aimed into the arriving waves, her stomach dropping with the kayak, but she was through. She saw the powerboat circling around ahead of her, then headed back toward her, but it was only when the driver edged closer and cut the motor that she realized something was off.

It was the two guys who'd accosted her on the beach, along with a couple of friends. They were plenty close enough to recognize. And for her to see the beer bottle in every hand, too.

Great. Exactly what she needed.

"Alone again?" the driver called over his idling engine.

He was the one Iain had gone after, and she had a swift debate with herself. She could ignore them, or she could respond.

Cool but pleasant, she decided. They hadn't seemed dangerous, just obnoxious. She said, "I'm fine."

The other boat's engine picked up a bit, the driver keeping pace with her as she continued to paddle. "Where's your smile?" he asked. "You'd be prettier if you smiled."

She didn't bother to answer that one, but she didn't have to. He was going on anyway. "Got to be boring, too, out by yourself. That fella wasn't with you after all, eh. That's what I thought. So you know what you should do? You should let us tow your boat and come party with us. No worries, we're going to be picking up some other girls as well. Next stop." He winked at her, a broad gesture, and she thought, *Yeah, right, buddy. I am so not getting in a boat with you.*

"Not interested," she said. Forget being pleasant. Why should she be? She wasn't feeling pleasant. Everybody else got to be a jerk? Then so did she. "Go away," she added, since he was obviously slow on the uptake.

"Well, you don't have to be a bitch about it," he said.

The other men were laughing now. "She doesn't like you, bro," one of them said. "Could be because you're ugly as fuck."

"Nah," one of the others said. "It's because he's *fat* as fuck. She's afraid they'll start doing it, and he'll squash her." That made all of them howl.

They still weren't leaving, either. The boat was barely moving, tracking her easily.

"Well, yeah," Nina told them, still paddling herself. She was getting awfully tired of men giving her their opinions of her and telling her what to do. She was getting furious about it, in fact. "I *do* have to be a bitch, actually. If I were you, I'd leave now, before I decide to share what I think about your general ugliness. Or your personalities."

That made the driver's mates hoot again, and she could see his scowl. She pressed her right foot down hard on the rudder to turn back toward shore. She was almost to the island, but too bad. She'd save the seal pups for another day.

Jerks. Why did she always attract them?

The engine noise increased, and the other boat was moving forward at last, picking up speed. Her body lost a little of its tension. They were going. Good.

Then the boat was cutting in front of her, so close she thought for a moment that it was going to ram her, and she was flinging herself backward as if that would help. Which it didn't, of course. It just destabilized her. But he wasn't trying to ram her at all. He was speeding past her on the other side. Showing off.

Asshole, she thought, way beyond *jerk* now, and tried to still her lurch of fear at how hard the boat was rocking. *Paddle across the wake. Dig in.*

It wasn't until she caught the motion out of the corner of her eye that she realized what was happening. He was driving a fast circle all the way around her. The crossing wakes rocked the kayak even harder as the powerboat fishtailed in front of her, and then it was speeding south, back toward Kaiteriteri. She had one last flash of laughing faces, a beer bottle sailed past, making her flinch, and then they were roaring away.

She barely noticed. When she'd ducked at sight of the bottle, the kayak had tilted precariously to the left. She swung herself hard to the right to counter it, and just like that, she went over.

The shock was total. She was upside-down in the water. Trapped in her boat. The panic tried to take her over, and then she heard Iain's voice during his safety lecture.

Run your hand along the edge of the skirt to the front and pull the tab.

It had felt so easy when she'd been upright and dry. But she was underwater, upside down, being yanked to left and right as the kayak bobbed in the violent wake of the powerboat. Her lungs were burning, the panic trying to take her, but she was grabbing, searching along the edge of the stretchy neoprene fabric, fumbling for the tab at the front. It took her three desperate yanks before she managed to release it, and then she was kicking her way out, falling down.

Falling *up*. Up to the light, her vest carrying her to the surface, and she was bursting through on a wheezing, whooping gasp of air.

She'd lost her paddle, and it was drifting away to the east. Five or six hard strokes, though, and she had it back.

Stay with the boat. The boat is your best flotation device. Iain again. She swam back awkwardly, one-armed, her other hand clutching the paddle. More than six strokes, because the boat was moving fast. When she finally caught up to it, she grabbed for a bungy on the side and hung on.

What now? You turned it over, and most of the water would drain out. But the waves seemed higher now. The powerboat's wake, still? She took a proper look around for the first time since she'd come up. The west wind had pushed her around the south end of the island toward the seaward side, the rougher side. And she was out of her boat.

Right, then. Get back in it. Step One would be to turn the boat over. She rode the swell, judged her moment, then heaved herself on top of the boat, lunged across it, and reached underneath for the far edge of the cockpit, somehow still holding her paddle, because you couldn't lose your paddle. She dragged on the kayak with all her might, and it worked. The boat flipped, and she went back down into the water with it.

Step One done. No, Step *Two*. She'd already found her paddle. She was finally able to shove one blade of the awkward thing under a bungy and along the side of the boat to get it out of her way, and that was better.

She was doing fine. She was scared, but she was coping.

What was next? *Back in the boat.* Iain had told her how to do that, too. You flung and wriggled yourself over the top, behind the cockpit, then slid down somehow into the hole. Which she'd have to figure out once she got there.

She heaved herself out of the water and over the boat again and again while the waves did their best to throw off her balance. On the fourth try, she made it over the top and lay over the kayak, riding the swell for thirty seconds or more while she got her breath back.

It was when she tried to swing into the cockpit, still half full of water, that it all went wrong. A wave hit her, she grabbed for the boat, and just like that, it flipped upside-down again.

She wanted to weep with frustration, but that wasn't an option. She was out here, and she was alone. She was being pulled away from the island, and she couldn't afford to be pulled any farther. And even though she wouldn't have said the water was cold, it was much cooler out here than it was in the shallows near shore, and she was starting to shiver.

Swim to where you can get back into the boat, then. A beach would have been better than the rocky shoreline of the island. She wouldn't be in this mess at all if she'd stayed near shore.

Too late for regrets now. She shoved one hand more firmly under the cord crisscrossing the side of the boat and began to kick toward the rocks that lined the edge of the island.

The kayak was heavy and cumbersome in its upside-down state, though, in a swell more than two feet high. She wondered if she should try to right the boat again, but she wasn't sure she could manage it. She was getting so tired.

Tough. Flip it.

She heaved herself up once and slipped down again. The waves lifted her, then dropped her. She lunged upwards again, and hung on. Grabbed the edge. And flipped the boat.

Now pull it. Go to the rocks.

There would be other boats out here. It was summer. But she was on the wrong side of the island, and nobody could see her unless they passed to seaward. And she was getting colder.

Then get yourself back in this boat. Swim.

She kept kicking, stroking, riding the waves, dragging the boat. She could tell she was getting closer to the island even when the trough of a wave hid her from it, because she could hear the yips of the seal pups.

You wanted to see them. Bingo. She had to stifle a bubble of hysterical laughter at the thought.

The closer she swam, the more apparent it became that it wasn't going to be easy. The seaward side of the little island was rough, with waves crashing into huge, tumbled chunks of black rock. From her spot at water level, the rough boulders might as well have been cliffs, rising two and three feet out of the water. The boat made it harder to swim, but it was her life preserver. She wasn't supposed to let go of the boat.

She swam to the south, toward the end of the island, dragging her boat, looking for a spot, for a break.

When it came, she almost missed it. She'd swum right past it, lost in a fog of effort and cold. Seconds went by before the message reached her mind.

Gap.

She had to turn around, then, and get the boat turned around, too, fighting the weight of it, the heavy swell. She judged a wave wrong, swallowed a mouthful of water, and choked. But she was still swimming.

There. A lower place, a spot where a rectangular chunk of rock sloped down into the water. She swam toward it, misjudged, banged heavily into another rock, and bounced off it, pain blooming in her shoulder. She kept kicking, though, turning, searching for the spot. And finally, she was able to get a hand onto the wet, slippery surface, to scramble with her feet to find purchase, the fingers of one hand gripping all the while to the bungy at the bow of the kayak.

An agonizingly slow climb up the shelf of rock, now, dragging the heavy boat behind her. Her bare feet were slipping, bruised by rough edges, her arm aching against the weight of the boat, her other hand grasping for any hold.

She got the boat halfway out, and that was all she could do. She couldn't go any higher, not and keep hold of the kayak. She lay sprawled on her back on the black rock, her foot wedged into a crevice between its edge and the steep face of another huge boulder, held onto her boat, and thought, *All right. All right. I'm out.*

There was no way to climb back in and relaunch the kayak, though, not on this slope of rock, not with the waves out there. She was shaking, her muscles like jelly, heaving in breath in huge gasps, clinging with all her remaining strength to the huge orange life preserver and emergency signal that was her boat.

She was out of the water, but she was also out of ideas. And the tide was rising. She hadn't seen another boat yet, and she must have been out of her kayak for twenty minutes.

Maybe nobody would come.

But if she gave up, they'd both be right. Matthias. Iain. That she couldn't do anything except run away, that she couldn't survive on her own. They'd both be right.

second thoughts

♡

Iain wasn't pedaling nearly as fast coming home as he had been when he'd set out.

He'd set a blistering pace at first along the Moutere Highway, through gently rolling Tasman hills that glowed a rich green in the summer sun, past orchards and vineyards and paddocks dotted with grazing sheep. All of it as mellow and peaceful as his mood was not.

After two hours and almost all the way to Nelson, though, he'd turned around for the ride back. That was when the doubts had begun to creep in.

A forward didn't do doubt, and Iain was nothing but a forward. He didn't do subtle. He didn't do complicated. He did flat to the boards, smash and go.

But there the doubts were all the same. And the images.

Nina, her huge eyes wide and stricken, her lips parted. The *thud* as her carrot had hit the metal sink. The tremble of her mouth.

I'd barely heard of your little team.

Why don't you wait to hear my reasons?

Nina, fainting on the pavement in front of the op shop in her ugly hat, her hideous yellow hair nothing like the shining brunette in the photo. Nina, coming out of the Arrivals hall in her baggy jersey and her track pants, not willing to look him in the eye.

Nina, taking her bags out of the back of the Toyota so she could get away from him and go to a backpackers'. So she could find a job.

Nina, who wasn't, who *couldn't* be a liar.

Oh, shit. He'd been wrong. And he'd showed her that article, hadn't given a thought to how it might affect her. Had left it with her, and left her thinking he hated her.

Still thirty kilometers to go by the time he'd thought it through, and he summoned up the strength and desire and drove his legs, drove his body, flew around the curves like a man possessed.

Because he was.

♡♡♡

He didn't bother putting the bicycle back in the garage. He just leaned it against the building and went for the cottage.

He caught himself barely in time to keep from barging in. He knocked instead, and realized for the first time that he had absolutely no clue what to say.

Never mind. He'd think of something. He could start with listening to her, maybe. That might be an idea. Couldn't work any worse.

It wasn't Nina who answered. It was his granddad. Who was frowning mightily, but no surprise. He loved Nina; that much was obvious. Probably thought Iain had been too hard on her, which was no more than the truth.

The old man cast a look at Iain's cycling shorts and jersey, but didn't stand back to let him in. "She's not with you, then?"

"No. Course not. Wait, what?"

Arthur was stumping into the kitchen, though, instead of answering, so Iain followed, for once not bothering with his shoes, the sprigs clanking on the linoleum floor. His granddad grabbed a piece of paper from the kitchen bench and thrust it at him. "Only saw this a few minutes ago, when I was wondering why she hadn't come back. Thought she might've run again, as upset as she was."

Iain barely heard him. He was reading the note written on a torn-out sheet from Nina's little notebook.

Arthur,
I've gone kayaking. I'll be back by 5.
Nina

He looked up at his grandfather. "When did she leave?"

"Dunno. I was out, wasn't I. Didn't know that was where she'd gone, either, but she hasn't come back and left again. The orange kayak's gone, right enough."

Iain looked at the clock on the wall. After six.

She's probably fine, part of his mind was trying to say. *Just stayed out longer, like you did, working it off. Working it out. Misjudged how long it'd take to come back.*

"Well?" Arthur demanded. "You just going to stand there? Do I have to go myself?"

"No," Iain said. "I'm going. I'm going now." She wouldn't have been this late to start fixing his granddad's tea. Not Nina. If she'd said she'd do something, she'd do it.

I don't take anything on unless I'm prepared to do my best.

But she wasn't a good enough kayaker. She didn't know the winds, or the tides, or the boat. She didn't know enough at all.

He changed his shoes and grabbed a jacket, and then he was running the couple blocks to the village, to the office.

When he came through the door, the fella behind the counter looked up in surprise.

Iain didn't know him. New this year, he guessed.

"Gidday," the fella said. "We've closed up shop, I'm afraid."

Iain ignored him. He was behind the counter, grabbing the keys to the water taxi.

"Oi!" the man said sharply, putting a hand out. "You can't

take those."

His mum came out of the back at the commotion. "Iain? What in the world…" But he didn't answer. He was already gone.

When he was in the boat, steering a fast course away from shore, he told himself that of course she was all right. Once he rounded the point, he'd spot her. His anxiety was all out of proportion.

But he didn't see her. He was up the coast, passing Marahau, then Split Apple Rock, cruising slowly, keeping near the shore to make sure he didn't miss her behind the rock or in a cave. On the beach, even, though she wouldn't be on the beach, not when she was already this late.

Every time he spotted an orange kayak, his heart leaped. But none of them was Nina, and his pulse was racing even as he told himself that she was fine, that nothing too bad could have happened to her in this most traveled of parks. Not with walkers crowding the track, swimmers and kayakers on every beach, and so many boats in the water. Even if she'd capsized, somebody would have seen her and helped put her right. Or she'd just have swum to a beach. She'd have stayed near shore, surely. She'd been upset, but she was timid.

She wasn't timid when she ran into a rough sea to get away from you. To get away from a man chasing her.

Nina, on a beach by herself, in her red bikini, asking for help. All it needed was one wrong person. All it would take was one.

desperate

♡

The tide crept in—ten more minutes, fifteen—while Nina shook, and shivered, and waited. The cold water covered her calves, then was over her knees. She didn't get any warmer, and nobody came.

If nobody was going to come, she had to do something else.

She had a paddle. She had a boat. She could at least *try*. She was facing the nose of the kayak, looking into the oval hole that was the cockpit. What if she straddled the boat, slid facedown toward the end, then shoved her legs into the cockpit? Then all she'd have to do was turn over. She'd do it lying down, so she didn't tip over again.

She looked at the boat and planned it out. *Hold the sides. Slide. Feet in. Turn over.* And then she did it. She couldn't stand to lie here anymore and give up.

It felt like it took about two seconds, though it must have been more. The second she leaned forward and grabbed the sides, the boat started sliding backward. She flung herself over it and scrabbled with her feet for the opening.

Whump. The boat hit the water, and she was sliding into the cockpit, clinging to the raised opening along its back, lying face-down and staring down at the boat. And then she held her breath, shifted her weight, and turned herself over.

She was in.

"Right," she said aloud, hearing her voice crack. "Right." The waves were still high, the wind was still carrying her out, but at least she was inside the boat.

Maybe she should have waited. She could have let go of the boat, climbed to the top of the island, and signaled from the top. Why hadn't she thought of that? It was late, and there wouldn't be many people out, but there'd be *somebody*.

Too late now. She was here. She'd done it. Time to get around the island into calmer waters. She couldn't worry about fastening her spray skirt back on. The boat was still half-full of water, making it sluggish and unsteady. If she didn't paddle, she'd go right over again. And she couldn't afford to get any colder.

Time to move. So she reached for the paddle with shaking hands, pulled it out from under the bungy, and dug in.

She got around the island, but the going was slow. The wind had strengthened, was trying to push her offshore, and she was so exhausted, it was all she could do to keep the kayak upright. She couldn't see how she was going to get to the beach.

When she saw the small white boat speeding straight toward her, though, she didn't raise her paddle overhead and signal it. It was those guys coming back. She had to get to shore, where there would be people. *Go. Paddle.*

When the boat cut its motor, her dread turned to panic. *No. Go. Get out.* She was turning, paddling desperately, sitting in cold water all the way over her legs, searching for another boat. Any boat.

A shout rang out from behind her, the sound cutting across the water, and she stopped paddling and turned to look back.

Too far. The kayak was rolling again, and she was swallowing a huge mouthful of seawater along the way, going down into the cold and dark.

There was nothing holding her in the boat, though, not

this time. She was kicking out, rising to the surface, coughing and choking.

He was leaning over the side, reaching out. "Over here!" he called. "Give me the paddle."

Iain. It was Iain. She was trying to tread water with legs that felt like concrete, only the paddle she still clutched and her PFD keeping her afloat. She shoved the plastic paddle toward him with what felt like the last of her strength, and he was pulling her to the side of the boat by it, then reaching down and grabbing hold of her T-shirt. He got his hand right through it, around the back strap of her bikini top, and hauled her up by it with one arm until she tumbled into the boat, fell against him, and then was falling into a bench seat, banging her shin, her forearm, and not feeling it.

"Bloody *hell,*" he said explosively, hauling her up and inspecting her. "What were you *thinking?*"

She laughed. It was hysterical, she could tell, but she was laughing anyway. He'd come for her, and now he was swearing at her.

"You could..." she said through chattering teeth. "Be nicer."

He was rummaging in a locker, tossing her a bag of clothes. "Get your clothes off," he ordered. "Fast."

She fumbled at her shirt, but she couldn't do it, and Iain was swearing again, yanking her shirt over her head, unhooking her bikini top, grabbing a navy-blue sweatshirt out of the bag, and pulling it onto her.

"Give me your hand," he said. "Come on, Nina. Help me."

She tried, but she missed, and in the end, he was the one who pulled her hands through the sleeves. Then he was wrestling off her shorts and tossing them to the floor of the boat, taking off her bikini bottoms, and pulling sweats up her legs.

She should care that he was stripping her, but she couldn't. She was too cold.

Finally, he reached for a big towel in the same locker and

put it around her shoulders. "Stay there," he told her, and she didn't bother to nod. It wasn't like she could go anywhere.

He was back in the driver's seat, maneuvering the boat over to the kayak, then pulling it close with a grappling hook and hauling it out of the water, making nothing of the weight and bulk of it. He had it out, onto a rack behind the seats in the rear of the boat, was fastening it down with bungees, shoving the paddle up beside it. And then he was back with her.

"We're going home," he said, coming forward again, past where she was still huddled in the bench seat. "Fifteen minutes."

She gave a jerk of her head, pulled her knees up in both arms, and didn't speak, because she couldn't.

Iain was back in the driver's seat, spinning the boat, heading south.

He'd come. Somehow, he'd come.

♡♡♡

Bloody *hell*. Bloody *hell*.

Iain wasn't doing any more thinking than that. He was just driving the boat. It seemed like an hour before he was jumping out into water that reached above his knees and tying the boat to the post, then going back for Nina.

"Come on," he told her, reaching his arms out. "Get over here."

She stood, staggered, and knelt on the seat. He got her under the arms, then slid his other hand under her thighs and was lifting her, carrying her out of the sea.

The thick tracksuit flapped around her, and he tried not to think about how ice-cold her body was. He'd thought it looked sculpted from ivory when he'd first seen it. Today, that was exactly how it had felt. Like bone. Like stone.

She was shaking hard, the shudders jolting straight through him, so he didn't put her down. Instead, he took her up the beach, onto the footpath, up and over the hill, and down the track to the house.

"I can... walk," she told him once.

"No," he said, suddenly so furious he could barely speak. "You can't. Be quiet."

At the cottage, he kicked the door with one bare foot, and when his granddad opened it, carried Nina straight through into the bathroom. He set her down on the lid of the toilet, then put the plug into the bath and turned on the tap.

"D-d-door," she was saying, and he looked up. His granddad was there, looking grim.

"Sorry," Iain told his granddad, closing the door in his face. "Privacy."

He was back with Nina, then, pulling the jumper over her head, yanking it over her hands, and she said, "N-n-no. Get *out.*"

"Oh. Right." She was better, then. Good. "Get in that bath."

She sat hunched over, her slim forearms crossed over her breasts as if he hadn't already seen them, and said, "No. I'm... naked."

A single tear made its way down her cheek, and it ripped something loose inside him.

"Nina," he said helplessly. What was he meant to do? Hold her? Wouldn't that make it worse, if she wanted him to leave? "Get in the bath. I'll bring you a cup of tea."

She nodded again, one more jerk of her elegant head, the yellow hair dark and matted with seawater. And he went out into the kitchen to do it, closing the door behind him.

His granddad was standing there, of course. Looking at him with a face like iron.

"Cup of tea," Iain said, and his granddad nodded and switched the jug on.

"Where was she?" the old man asked as he pulled down a mug and dropped a teabag into it.

"South end of Fisherman's Island. Being carried out to sea. And she'd been out of the boat some time, I reckon. She was wet and cold when I found her, and then she went over again." He fought back the remembered terror. When he'd been hauling her out, seeing how hypothermic she already was, and thinking about what could have happened if he hadn't come, if she'd gone in that final time and stayed in.

"You got her," Arthur said, reading his mind. "That's all. That's enough."

"Yeh." Iain waited until the tea was ready, then carried it back to the bathroom, knocked once, and went inside.

Nina was in the bath, her legs pulled up, her slim arms wrapped around her calves, and she wasn't looking at him. She'd managed to turn the tap off, and even though she was still shivering, she looked more alive.

"Here," he said, setting the mug down carefully on the edge of the tub. "Drink this. And lie down in that water, give it a chance to do the job."

"I... will," she said, her teeth still chattering, "if you'll *leave*. Don't... *look* at me."

He exhaled in frustration. "I'm not *looking* at you. I'm trying to *help* you. What were you thinking, going out on your own? And that far from shore, too? Why? How the hell did you capsize the boat?"

She shook her head, still clutching her knees, still not looking at him. "A boat... came. It went around me. In a circle. I got... I tipped over."

What? It made no sense. "Well, lie down. Drink your tea. And don't come out until you're warm. Put in more hot water. It'll take a while, so stay there until you're good. All the way good."

She looked at him at last. No flecks of gold in her eyes now. They were dark, weary pools. "I know I... owe you. Thank you for... coming. But I can't hear any more about it now. Please go away."

And he'd stuffed up again.

♡♡♡

Nina lay in the tub, surrounded by warmth, cradled the mug of tea in both hands, and shook hard enough that the hot liquid splashed into the bath water, a milky swirl of brown. And she wanted to cry, because she was spilling her tea.

She knew that wasn't really why. And she couldn't help it.

She set the tea down, lay back in the hot water, and gradually, the shaking eased and the chill began to leave her bones. She fought the tears as long as she could, but they rose anyway, as insistent as rain, until they broke through. Finally, she gave in, put her hands over her face, and cried.

Once she began, she couldn't stop. She was sobbing aloud, feeling her eyes puffing shut, knowing her face was turning blotchy and disgusting, and completely unable to care. Letting it all go into the shelter of her hands.

That she'd been so afraid. That she'd been so pitifully, excruciatingly glad to see Iain. And that even so, when he'd hauled her into the boat, when he'd pulled her wet clothes off her and dressed her again, she'd wanted so much more from him. That she'd wanted him to keep holding her, to murmur to her that it was all right, that she was safe, that she hadn't been as stupid as she knew she had been.

She hadn't told him whose carelessness and malice had tipped her over, and she wouldn't. She knew that if she did, he'd go after those guys, and he'd find them, and that that wouldn't do him any good.

She couldn't help it. She cared. And she wanted so badly for him to have cared, too. She knew it was weak to wish for it, to need it, but knowing that didn't make her feel it any less. She'd longed to be able to believe that he'd come for her, not because she was under his grandfather's roof and somehow his responsibility, but because he'd been as desperate as she had. Desperate to find her. Desperate to keep her safe.

back to church
♡

Iain went out into the kitchen, and his granddad said, "Make yourself useful, then. Lay the table for dinner."

Iain noticed the savory smell wafting from the oven for the first time. "You cooked, eh. You have enough to share?"

"Do me a favor," his granddad said in disgust. "And rattle your dags. When Nina comes out of the bath, she's going to need to eat."

"I should get her kayak out of the water taxi."

"Leave it. Get it in the morning. What's more important right now?"

He was right, so Iain got out plates and cutlery for four as his granddad pulled a pan from the oven. He spared a thought for his dad, but not much more than a thought. The stubborn old bugger wanted to stay over there, proud and silent? He could do it, then.

His mum came through the door, still in her workout gear from her exercise class, and said, "Iain, love. You over here? I'll give you a hand with dinner. Just let me get a shower." She still looked tired, and sad, too. Not defeated, but not far off.

"No need," Arthur said. "I keep telling you that I'm not helpless. I've done it. But you'll have to wait for your shower.

Nina's in the bath warming up. She's had a bit of an accident. Turned her kayak over a few times, it seems, out by herself."

"What? Why?" Carmella asked, setting down her bag. "Why would she go off on her own? I thought you were taking her out," she said to Iain.

Iain rubbed his nose, opened his mouth, shut it again, and headed for the fridge to get a salad started. Nina always wanted a salad. "Uh... we had a..." he began, but his granddad was there before him.

"Here," Arthur said, grabbing the newspaper from the bench and thrusting it at his daughter. "This is who Nina is. No surprise to anyone but Iain why she was here. That she was running, I mean. But he threw a wobbly about it and made her run again. That's why she was out there."

Iain wanted to object, but it was no more than the truth, so he set his jaw and fixed the salad, listening with one ear for the sound of the bath. If she wasn't out in five more minutes, he was checking on her, no matter what she'd said. He hadn't liked the frozen look of her one bit, and it wasn't just her temperature that was worrying him.

He heard the sound of the bathroom door opening, and his mum was headed out of the kitchen, saying, "I'll go have a wee look-in on her, then, and bring her out here. Isn't it funny?" she asked in wonder. "I'm surprised, and yet I'm not. Not a bit of it. You could see it in her. So sad, and so... I'd say, 'hunted.' I'm thinking she had her reasons."

"Get her to take a couple Nurofen, Mum," Iain said, focusing on what he could deal with, what he could do. "She banged herself up a fair amount falling into the boat."

His mother looked at him sharply, then nodded, and he had to content himself with that.

It was a quiet dinner, with his mum not talking and Nina silent as well. She was wearing nothing but a singlet, a thin sweater, and her stretchy black shorts, but she had the purple throw over her shoulders, was huddling into it despite the warmth of the day.

His granddad had done a more than creditable job on a

venison and mushroom pie, covered with puff pastry and rich with dark broth, had served it up along with a bowl of mashed potatoes, and even Nina looked up from her plate to say, "This is good, Arthur. Thank you."

"Didn't know you could cook this well," Iain said.

"What d'you imagine I've been doing on my own all this time?" Arthur snapped. "Or before that, when I was caring for your nan?"

"But you were getting so thin," Carmella said. "I didn't know..."

"Dead boring to cook for yourself, isn't it," he said. "You eat, missy," he ordered Nina. "Didn't eat your lunch, and now you're half frozen. Get that down you, every bit of it."

"I'm doing it," she protested, but she was smiling the tiniest bit, the first time Iain had seen her smile since he'd walked in on her and spoiled everything. "You really are the bossiest man in the world, you know that?"

"Nah," Arthur said. "That'd be Iain. Bet he had words for you when he found you out there."

The shutter came down over her face, her eyes going blank, and Carmella said, "*You* found her, darling? Oh. Why you took the boat. Of course."

"Yeh," he said. "Went looking for her the minute Granddad told me she hadn't come back, and I found her."

"I'm sorry," Nina said, looking down at her plate, and *not* eating. "It was a bad decision."

"Well," Carmella said quietly, "we've all made a few of those."

After that, nobody could think of much to say. When dinner was over, Carmella said, "You go on and climb into bed, Nina. I'll sleep on the couch tonight."

"No," Nina said. "I'd rather do the hammock."

"Nonsense," Carmella said, just as Iain said, "You need to be in bed."

Nina put both hands flat on the table, exactly as she'd done that first day in the restaurant in Motueka during their fairly disastrous lunch. The one where Iain had accused her of being pregnant.

"Will everyone *stop*," she said, her square jaw clenched, "treating me like a child?"

They all froze, and Nina's eyes widened a tiny bit, as if she'd surprised herself as much as she had everybody else. "Look," she finally said. "I'm grateful for your concern. I'm grateful that Iain found me. I acknowledge that I was stupid. I'm sorry that I didn't tell all of you the truth about myself, and that you had to find out the way you did. I thought I had my reasons for keeping it quiet, whether I was right or not. I appreciate everything you've done, truly I do. I appreciate dinner. And I'd like to sleep in the hammock. Please. I'll be fine tomorrow, and we can…" She shrugged, all the fight seeming to drain out of her slim shoulders. "Make a decision. About whether I stay or not."

"Of course you're staying, "Arthur growled. "Don't be stupid."

Nina sighed, put a hand on his arm, smiled only a little shakily, and said, "Arthur. Didn't I just *say* not to treat me like a child?"

"I didn't say you were a child. Said you were a woman. Heaps more aggravating."

This time, she laughed, stood up, and bent to kiss his cheek. His arm went around her waist for a moment, and he said, "Go on, then. Go lie down."

"You go too, Iain," Carmella said. "I'll wash up."

Maybe she meant for him to go look in on his dad, but he didn't do much beyond a quick word, to which his dad, watching cricket on TV, responded with a grunt. Iain shrugged, ran upstairs, had a quick shower and change to get the sea water off him, and went for a wee wander.

Nina wasn't in the hammock yet, but he already knew that. He'd checked from his window. Only one other real possibility. He headed down the track to the beach.

Maybe he was checking on her, and maybe he was doing something else. He wasn't telling.

He found her sitting in the same spot as the night before,

on the sand this time, her back against the low pohutukawa branch, her arms wrapped around her knees.

He stood in front of her and asked, "Can I join you?" At her nod, he sat down a careful ten centimeters away, one leg stretched out, his elbow resting on the other knee, and looked out at the sea.

The sun was still a full hour away from setting. Its rays fell long and low across the water, making it glow a rich, deep blue, and the evening air was warm, the earlier wind dropping down to nothing more than a soothing breeze.

They sat in silence for a couple minutes before he spoke. "She's sleeping," he said, his voice mingling with the rhythmic pulse of the surf. "But that's all she's doing. The sea's beautiful, and she's just that treacherous. You aren't the first to find that out."

She turned her head, laid her cheek on her knees, and looked at him without the hint of a smile, her eyes big, dark, and wary. "You're trying to make me feel better."

He shook his head. "Not my specialty. Tact, or whatever that'd be. I'm telling you the truth. Other places have other dangers. Wild animals, maybe. People, more likely. In En Zed, it's the sea. Easy to underestimate, and easy to pay the price."

"Thank you," she said softly. "You're a nice man."

"No. I'm not a nice man. But I try to be a reasonably decent person. I wasn't today, and I'm sorry." This time, it wasn't hard to say. It was necessary.

"Why?" Her voice was nothing but husky and sweet, and it sliced through him all the more for that. "Why didn't you give me a chance to explain? It hurt me, Iain. That you didn't even trust me that much. You don't owe me anything, and I know it, but that wasn't kind. It wasn't like you, not the you I've known."

He'd thought, when he'd first met her, that she was a girl. Naïve. Immature, even. There was nothing immature about the woman looking back at him now, her gaze steady on his face.

"No," he said. "It wasn't kind, and it wasn't fair. It pushed a button of my own, is why I said it."

The words came from someplace down deep, someplace that hurt to open, but hurt more to keep closed. Something about seeing her in the water, about the icy coldness of her body under his desperate hands, that single tear that had rolled down her cheek as she'd huddled on the toilet, her arms wrapped around her knees, hiding her nakedness—all of that had stripped the last of his defenses from him.

She didn't say anything, just kept looking at him, and he sighed and said, "And I'm about to tell you, because I need you to know. The part you'd see if you looked it up online, which you haven't. You haven't wanted to look online at all, just like I haven't. And the part you wouldn't see if you did look. I guess we both know that what you see online isn't always the whole story. Especially for people like us. Reckon you're one of the few people outside rugby who'd actually understand that."

"Tell me, then," she said. "If you want to. What wouldn't I see?"

He picked up a piece of smooth, wave-battered wood from the sand, ran it through his fingers, and stared down at it as he said, "You'd see that I was engaged myself. That I was here three months ago. When I was meant to be married. And that she—my fiancée. Sienna. That she got all the way to the altar before we... before it went pear-shaped. But you wouldn't know what happened next. Wasn't something I publicized, eh. My parents know some of it, and that was bad enough. But that 'Runaway Bride' thing?" He swallowed. "Yeh. Me too."

She sat and waited, and he finally continued. It seemed he couldn't help it. "She walked down the aisle to me, and I thought we were all good, and then she said..." He ran his palm along the stick, getting some kind of comfort from its rounded smoothness. "That we had to talk. So we walked back up the aisle, and everybody watched us go."

He'd barely noticed that at the time. The church had been

so quiet, he'd been able to hear Sienna's panting breaths. He'd known there was something bad coming, and he'd known he had to wait for it and take it. Like finishing a game you knew you'd lost, but you had to play your guts out until the whistle blew. No choice but to front up, and no solace except in not showing how much it hurt.

They'd stood in the foyer where, minutes earlier, she'd waited with her dad, and she'd dropped her bombshell.

"I can't..." she said. "I can't go on without telling you, but I think it'll be cool. I hope so. Hailey says I have to. She says it isn't fair otherwise. We were up half the night talking about it, and she just said it again. So I have to. I know I do."

This was making no sense. Tell him what?

Pregnant? The idea flashed into his mind, and he felt a momentary surge of joy. But that wasn't how this moment felt. He wasn't getting the least sense that what was coming was going to be anything he'd want to hear.

He found something to focus on, and did it. "You know," he said, "if you needed to talk something over, it would've been better if you'd talked it over with me, not Hailey. Last night, this morning, two weeks ago, whenever. Even if we'd had to do it on the phone." He was amazed that he could sound that calm, when he felt anything but. His body was taking the adrenaline and forcing it to settle, as he'd trained it to do so long ago.

"That's just it." Her nervous hands twirled her bouquet of white lilies and roses, her own adrenaline clearly nowhere close to settling. "I couldn't. You're always so sure. You don't understand what it's like to be me. But Hailey... she *gets* me. That's the point."

"*What's* the point? That you need friends? Nobody's saying you don't. I'm gone half the time. Be a pretty lonely life for you without mates, eh."

"But she's... more than that." The bouquet was spinning like a top now, and the meaning of her words sank slowly through Iain's body like a stone dropping into a pond and settling in silt. Just that hard, and just that heavy. "She's..."

"You're telling me you're... what." The words emerged, somehow, through lips that had trouble opening enough to allow them to form.

She couldn't meet his eyes, and her bouquet was still whirling. "It started at school, with Hailey, and I thought it was a phase, you know, an experiment. I like men. I mean, I like sex with them—with you. I *love* sex with you."

That was true. Nothing wrong with Sienna's sex drive, ever, or her openness to new ideas. She'd even taught him a thing or two, if the truth were known. She wasn't shy about telling him what she wanted to try, or how it was working for her. All of which he'd more than appreciated, except that she always seemed to want him to be rougher than he enjoyed.

The reason for that was right there to see. She'd already had somebody to be tender with her. That was why she'd wanted the opposite from him.

She was still talking. "I like men, and I like *you*. I *love* you, I do, but I love her too, and I can't help it. You aren't enough for me. I mean, not *you*." She was getting even more agitated now. *"One* person isn't."

"I'm not enough for you," he repeated, still trying to take it in through a mind that was doing its best to shut it out.

"But it could work," she hurried on. She must have seen the look on his face. "Hailey's willing. And if you are... maybe it could even be better. It could be everything you'd want."

"Exactly. How." His tone was still flat, but he was feeling anything but. What was coursing through his body wasn't cold anymore, and it wasn't pain. It was anger, blazing hot. "You're telling me *now* that you're bisexual, and you're saying it's all right, because you girls are willing to do a threesome? Is that it? That's going to make it up to me? If one woman's good, two are better?"

"You think she's hot, though," Sienna said urgently. "I know you do. And she thinks you are, too. I know it's unconventional, but it could be good, couldn't it? We don't have to tell anyone else. We don't have to live by anybody else's rules. I need both of you. Open up your mind, Iain. It's a new century."

His collar was choking him, but he resisted the urge to tear at it, to wrench off his tie, to betray his feelings. "Call me traditional," he said, standing absolutely still. He didn't trust himself to move. "I don't give a toss if she's hot. Heaps of women are hot. I see them every day, and they see me, too. That doesn't mean I have to shag them. I want *one* wife. *One* woman who thinks I'm the most important person in the world. And I want one woman to be the most important person in mine."

"Please, Iain." Her hand was on his sleeve, her stunning blue eyes beseeching. "It doesn't make me love you any less. I have plenty of love for *both* of you. In fact, it would make me love you even more if you could accept this. I'm trying to be honest, and it's not easy. I was up all night, talking it over with Hailey. *Thinking* it over, trying to decide. I almost didn't tell you at all, but I know I have to. So I'm here. I'm doing it, and it's... it's so hard. "

She ducked her head, then lifted her face to his again. The gossamer folds of her veil swayed, picking up a faint breeze from the open church door. "But this way could be even better. Really, it could. I know women want you. This way, you can have variety without feeling like you're cheating. And you can..." Her throat worked, her breasts heaved, and she was more beautiful than ever, but he didn't care. She didn't look beautiful to him anymore. *His bride.* "You can... you could... watch."

Maybe she could tell from his expression that that wasn't the thrill she'd assumed it would be, because she went on quickly, "We both think that'd be hot. And then... you know. You always hold back, but I'm telling you that you don't have to. Not with me, and especially not with Hailey. If your feelings about... about us give you an edge, make you lose control, well..." She shrugged. "That's what she likes best. *I* could watch that, and I'd love to. You can't honestly tell me that all of that wouldn't be a dream come true. It could *work.* "

Talking it over with Hailey. Talking about *him.* About how he did it, and how they'd like him to do it. About how they'd like him to be, what? Rough? Violent? Like *hell.* Like *hell.*

So much more than talking, too. His mind tried to go there, and balked. Of course he'd fantasized about threesomes, like just about every other man in the world. Truth be told, he'd had a few threesomes of his own when he'd been younger. When he'd been caught up in the thrill of being a sportsman, of being able to make his fantasies come true. But not now. Not with his *wife.* Or with, what? Two wives? A wife and a half? That wasn't a marriage.

There he'd been, his painfully slow mind finally informed him, lying alone all those nights after a tough match, in some hotel room in London or Paris, in Johannesburg or Buenos Aires, being faithful to her. While half his single teammates had been out on the razzle, reeling home at dawn from some pretty stranger's bed, and Sienna had been in bed with Hailey. *Up all night.*

He'd never hit a woman. He'd never come close. He didn't want to hit her now, not exactly. But he wanted—oh, how he wanted—to lash out. To strike back. And he still couldn't.

It was too abrupt a change. He'd wanted to love her. And he couldn't.

"I can't," he finally said. "Sorry I can't oblige you. Go find another bloke to watch the two of you, somebody rough enough for you. That's not me. Find someone who isn't bashing other guys all day for a living, and maybe he'll be willing to take his aggression out on you instead, play your games. I already play a game, and it's rough enough to satisfy me. I doubt you'll have trouble finding somebody who'd enjoy every bit of that, though. He may not be an All Black, but you can't have everything, eh."

"Iain... I'm sorry." She looked it, her eyes misty with tears. She was beautiful, and he didn't care.

He didn't answer her. He turned on his heel, left her there, and walked down to the altar again by himself, every eye on him, the buzz of speculation that had provided a background hum to their confrontation dying to silence. He cast one quick look at Hailey, saw her staring back at him, and that was more than enough. He looked out at the expectant congregation, willed his body and his mind into cold stillness, raised his voice to rugby pitch level, and announced, "Wedding's off. Everybody can go home. But if you're with me... feel free to come get pissed."

The hubbub started for real then. Sienna's parents rose and hurried up the aisle, Hailey with them, but Iain didn't spare a glance for them, or his own family, either. The anger and shame were both too strong for that. He needed to get *out*.

So he did. He left the church the way he'd come, through the side door into the choir room, and then straight out into the mild spring. Into all that soft, fertile promise of new life. All that lie. His best man, Hugh Latimer, followed him out and pulled the keys to Iain's car out of his own trouser pocket when he saw Iain patting the pockets he'd forgotten were empty—except for the rings. The rings, he had.

It was Hugh who led the way to the car, since Iain seemed to have forgotten where it was, Hugh who drove him back to his parents' house. There, Hugh did some texting, collected a six-pack of beer from the fridge, and headed straight out to the beach. Iain followed him, shedding his jacket, tie, shoes, and socks before taking his first beer from Hugh. The rising tide must have carried them away at some point, because he'd never seen them again.

And the rings? The rings were somewhere in the sea as well. They'd gone as far out as he could toss them, and he had a pretty fair toss. Somebody may have turned them up with a metal detector since. And maybe not. Iain didn't care.

By the time the tide had well and truly turned, he'd lost count of the beers he'd drunk. He hadn't told any of his mates why the wedding had been called off, then or since. And none of them had asked.

the right thing

♡

Nina had one hand over her mouth. This was the spot, she realized. Iain was sitting in the same place where he'd mourned the loss of his marriage, of his future. How hard must this week have been for him?

"Oh, no," she breathed. So many raw feelings today, and this one had tipped her straight over the edge. "Oh, no. Iain. I'm so sorry."

He turned his head and looked at her, his eyes so bleak, and she couldn't help it. She moved into him, put her hands around his head, pulled it down to hers, and pressed her lips to his hard mouth.

She'd only meant to comfort, or that's what she'd told herself. She'd wanted to kiss the hurt away, to do something to ease his pain. But from the minute her lips touched his, it became something else. His mouth settled over hers, and just like that, her lips were parting. He deepened the kiss as if he couldn't help it, either, as if it were rushing on him the same way it was on her. One of his hands was in her hair, wrapped around the back of her head, while the other went around her waist and pulled her in, and she heard a faint noise coming from deep inside her throat. She'd never made that sound, but she was making it now. She was whimpering.

"Oh, hell, Nina," he groaned, and he was drawing her into his lap. The thrill of it, of his solid thighs under her bare legs, of all that firm chest under her palms, tried to take her breath away. Then he was back at her mouth, taking it hard, stealing her breath for real, and her hands were on his shoulders, hanging on.

"This," he said. "Oh, yeh. I need this." His mouth moved across her cheek, over to her ear, making her shiver. His lips were at her neck now, taking sips and little nibbles at her, and she was gasping, starting to squirm, the fire licking its way down her body.

She wasn't cold anymore. She was burning up.

"You like that?" he murmured. "Want some more?"

"Yes," she sighed. "Oh, yes."

She could feel the curve of his lips against her skin as he smiled, and then his mouth was moving again, lips and tongue and teeth, teasing and taking. One hand still held her head in place, and the possessiveness of it thrilled her, however much it shouldn't. He held her like she was his, but like she was precious, too. And then she forgot to think about that. His other hand was stroking up from her waist, drifting higher, over her ribs, touching her through the thin cotton of her shirt, making her wriggle against him.

"Ticklish," she managed.

"Hmm," was all the response she got. His mouth continued its work on her neck, lighting her up, making her burn. He wasn't tickling anymore, either. His hand was sure and strong, blazing a path higher, under her sweater, tracing around the edges of the skinny-ribbed tank, until he finally settled that big palm over her breast. Not even inside her shirt, and that didn't matter. The shock, the heat of it—it was nothing but right.

"Ah," he sighed, his thumb flicking lazily over a nipple that had hardened the moment it had felt his touch. "That's nice. I'm going to touch you a little more here."

She should be doing something, she thought in some dim corner of her mind. But he had her bent back over one arm now, lying across his lap, and his fingers were outlining the neckline of the tank, brushing over her skin again and again.

"Ohh..." she said. "Oh... please."

"Please what?" It should have been amused, but it wasn't. It was deep. Almost commanding.

"Please... Iain. Touch me there. Do it again."

"Mm." He'd lifted her more upright and was kissing her, deep and slow, but nothing like gentle. And while he did, his hand was finding the bottom hem of her tank. The moment she felt that hard hand against her bare skin, over her ribs, she was trying to move closer, to feel more, to ask him to go faster. And when, at last, he was there, cupping her breast in his hand, palming the nipple for one much-too-short moment, then tracing his fingers in a maddening, slow circle around it, almost touching it, but not quite getting there, she thought she would explode.

At last, he found the sensitive point, diamond-hard by this time, trapped it between two of his fingers, and squeezed hard. At the same instant, he plunged his tongue deep into her mouth, and her hips actually bucked.

She needed him *now*. Over her. Driving into her. Right now.

"Mum!"

It was a child's voice, and the shock of it had Nina struggling up, sliding out of Iain's arms, then scrambling to her feet.

"Damn," Iain said, surprising a shaky laugh from her. He stood with her, reaching out to steady her as two kids ran by at the edge of the surf, not ten yards away. Their young mother followed behind, her gaze flickering over Iain and Nina, then back to her children. Polite. Embarrassed, maybe.

"Making out on... the beach," Nina said, hearing the unsteadiness in her voice. "Not what I'd planned."

"Fine old Kiwi tradition." Iain rubbed a hand over the back of her neck, gentle, but strong, too. Her body remembered exactly how strong and gentle those hands had felt on the rest of her, and she shivered.

"Cold?" he asked.

A puff of laughter escaped her. "No. Just... so turned on."

That one made *him* laugh. "Yeh. Me too. And fair warning. You've hit me like... like a truck. Just that hard. And that's how I think it's going to be."

"What?"

"Yeh." He wasn't smiling now. He stared down at her, his hand still on the back of her neck, and he'd never looked more fierce. She should be scared, but she wasn't.

His next words nearly sent her to her knees.

"I want to take your clothes off," he told her. "I want to put you on your back on my bed. I want to stand over you and look at you naked, see you spread out for me like that, waiting. I want to come down over you and make you forget everything but me. I want to make you lose your mind."

She was trembling, nearly panting with need, and his slow hand was still stroking the back of her neck. Now, he put his other arm around her, pulled her close, and tucked her into his body.

His arms felt exactly as sheltering as she'd always known they would. And at the same time... not safe at all. What she was feeling against her, the massive erection he was making absolutely no effort to conceal, felt nothing like safe. She was quivering with excitement and anticipation, and with apprehension, too. Like standing on a cliff edge, waiting to bungy jump. Waiting for the overwhelming thrill, and then for the shattering release of all that tension.

"Want to go up to my room and let me do it?" he asked her, his voice low and deep in her ear. "I'll make you feel so good. I promise. I'll make sure you want everything I do to you."

She had to swallow at that. "I want it," she whispered. "I do. But I can't."

"Ah." He didn't let her go, though, just kept that stroking hand moving. Down her back, now, his touch slow and strangely soothing.

He didn't ask why not, and because he didn't, she told him. "You're leaving in a couple days, and I have to leave myself. I have to start again. And it's exactly what I said last night. I like you too much. I want you too much. I don't need more... regrets. And I know," she went on, the words tumbling over each other, "that you'll say we'll regret not doing it. But I can tell that I'd be so sad. I think it might break my heart to do that and then watch you leave me. I'm not just a body. I'm a heart, too, and my heart's in this. It shouldn't be, I know, but it is. And I can't stand to let my heart get broken. I feel like it can't take one more thing. Not now. Not yet."

"I know you're a heart." His voice was almost sad. "Starting to think you're *my* heart." He laughed softly. "Stupid as that sounds. I'd never want to hurt you. And why would I tell you how you'll feel, or how you should? Why would I think I knew?"

The simplicity of the question stunned her for a moment. "Men do," she finally said.

"Not me." He stepped back from her, then, and said, "Right, then. It's no, and—Nina." He stroked a hand down her cheek. "It's all good." He smiled at her a little crookedly. "Not to say you're not killing me, but I'll live."

"Thanks," she said. "For that. Really." She had the right to say no, and she knew it. But having him say it still helped.

He nodded. "You sure you're all right in the hammock? I could trade you places, if you like."

She was missing him already. Missing his touch, his kiss. "You'd do that?"

"Not much I wouldn't do for you, it seems. Can't you tell? My stupid behavior today notwithstanding."

She could read the seriousness in his blue eyes even in the low, mellow light of late evening. She put a hand up and traced the harsh planes of his jaw, faintly abrasive with the stubble that grew so fast. "I know," she said quietly. "Thank you for coming to get me today, when I needed you. Thank you for not shouting at me any more, and for apologizing, and for telling me your story. And thank you for stopping when I asked. Thank you for..." Her eyes filled with tears despite herself, and one or two of them found their way over her brimming lids. "For... caring."

"Aw, Nina." His arms were around her again, and it didn't matter that the family was still on the beach. She was all the way wrapped up in his arms, her head against his chest, and a sob or two made their way out before she could stop herself at the pure comfort of it. "I hate it when you cry," he said, the deep timbre of his voice settling somewhere inside her. "I always want to do this. I want to make it better."

"You do." She raised a hand to swipe at her eyes. "But it's probably a pretty good anti-aphrodisiac."

"You think so?" There was amusement in his voice again, and he was stepping back and lifting her high on her toes, then dropping a soft kiss on her lips. "And here I was, wishing all over again that I could make you feel so good that there wouldn't be room for anything else."

"Hmm." She wasn't crying anymore, somehow. "I'll bet you could do it, too."

"Let's just say that I'd have a good go. But it's still no, I reckon."

"Still no." With that, she finally turned and led the way up the track to the front garden, and her hammock.

She climbed in, and he settled the duvet over her, ran a hand over her cheek, and said, "Sleep well. And bloody hell, but you're hard to leave."

He bent over her, gave her one last kiss, then turned and went back to the house. And she watched him go, her body still tingling from his touch, and thought, *But you'll leave me anyway. We have no choice. It isn't the right time. Not for either of us.*

She'd done the right thing, and she knew it. But it didn't feel that way.

step one

♡

Nina woke with the first light of dawn—impossible to do anything else, when you were sleeping in a hammock with about a million birds around—knowing what she had to do. When Iain came out to the beach dressed for his run and found her doing some gentle yoga to loosen muscles stiffened from her exertions the day before, she straightened up and asked him, "Would you be willing to lend me your phone to make a few calls? They'd be overseas, I'm afraid."

"Ah," he said. "Course. Could be I'm getting why you didn't buy a phone of your own. That it wasn't just the money."

"No, it was because I was hiding." She looked straight at him, and said it. "You're right. I thought I had to hide, whether that was true or not. But as you know, my wedding day has come and gone, and it's time to make those calls."

He nodded. "I feel like I should ask you about all that. About the prince and all. But seems I don't want to."

"Good," she said. "I'd tell you if you wanted, but it feels like a dream that's over now. A bad dream. I just want to... move on. Start over. I thought he was an escape hatch from my life, but I realize now that I was just going from one role to the other. Being pushed into it, more like. I'm tired of being pushed."

"So you're starting with making some calls."

"That'd be it."

He nodded again, headed back to the house without another word, came back, and handed her his phone.

"I'll pay you back," she said. "If it's extra."

He flicked the idea away with one big hand. "No. Let me help at least this much. Besides, I had a wee think about it last night. Considering how glad I am that you didn't get married, what was I thinking, reacting like that?"

At her startled glance, he raised that devilish black eyebrow at her and said, "In case I hadn't mentioned it."

"Oh." He stood there a moment more, and she said, "You don't shave until after you run," and then wished she could have snatched the words back. What did that have to do with anything?

He looked momentarily taken aback, then ran a hand over his dark slab of jaw and smiled, and if that smile looked a little dangerous? Well, so did Iain. "Nah. I shave in the shower, if you want the dirty details. I've got a heavy beard, need all the help I can get to soften it up. I never have figured out which way you like best, but say the word, and I'll do that. Shave, or not."

"Even though I said no."

"Even though."

"Both," she found herself saying. "I like both. I've wondered—" She broke off. She wasn't saying *that*.

"What?" he asked, taking a step closer. "What have you wondered? What it feels like? Or something else?"

"Never mind," she said hastily. "Go running."

"Not going to take your shorts off for me today?" he asked. "Not going to tease me again, kill me a little more?"

"You could tell I did that?" She was tingling again. She shouldn't be. She'd told him no the night before, and she'd meant it. But she'd had such a hard time getting to sleep, despite her exhausted, aching body. His words, the look on his face, had lingered long after she should have let them go.

She'd had a feeling that if she'd said yes, it would have been so long before he'd have let *her* go, and she'd wanted to know what that would feel like.

"Yeh," he said. "I could tell. I'd tell you to stop, but I'm not going to, no matter how much you torture me. I'm going to tell you not to stop. Just like I'd love to hear you telling me."

"Oh, God," she whispered. "Don't."

"Don't what?" He was all the way up to her now, his hand on her cheek, his thumb brushing down her jaw, and the ache had started right up again, a low, hard thrum. "Don't say it, or don't stop?"

She got both hands up between their bodies, placed her palms flat on his hard chest, and pushed him off, even though she wouldn't have had a hope of doing that if he hadn't been willing to let her. "You are a very bad man. Quit chatting me up and go running. Thanks for the phone."

He grinned. "Can't help myself, it seems."

"Practicing again," she suggested.

"Well, no. Not so much. Not too interested in practice anymore, for some reason. But," he said, shifting gears with a speed that left her wondering what was true, "it's calm on the water this morning. I'm thinking that once I'm back, we should get you into a wetsuit so you don't get so cold, then take you out there. Once I've shaved, of course. And then have you do some practice yourself. Getting back into a kayak, that is."

"Oh. Uh... I don't exactly feel like it. A little scared, to tell you the truth."

"That's why you do it," he said, not teasing a bit anymore. "Knowledge is power. Or competence is, more like. Once you know you can get back in, you won't be so scared of going over. You liked it too much to give up on it, I'm thinking. We can go or not," he added as she continued to hesitate. "Your choice, of course. But I'm offering."

"Yes, then," she said. "Please. And thank you for thinking of it. Remember what I said about nice?"

He shrugged it off. "Say ten or so, then. I'll come for you."

"And then..." She hesitated, and then asked it. "If you're going to the gym this afternoon, could I come with you? I'd like to go to the bank. And do a little shopping, maybe."

"Ah." He looked at her more closely. "You really *have* been hiding, eh. Hiding that much? Haven't wanted to get into your accounts? Is that why... the job and all? Taking this one, I mean?"

"Yes," she said. "That was why. But I'd like to look nice tonight. For your grandfather," she added hastily. "For his special night."

He didn't say any of the things she feared. Instead, he just said, "Right, then. You know I'll take you. You have to know that."

"Thanks."

He took off down the beach at last, and she shoved his phone into the pocket of her shorts, finished her yoga session, and went back into the house to cook Arthur's breakfast. And after that, she made her calls.

The first one wasn't so hard. She kept it short, told her grandparents where she was and that she was doing fine, and that she'd call again.

"Whatever you want, darling," her gran said.

"I'm thinking I'll take a break." It was the first time Nina had said it aloud. Doing some practicing of her own, maybe. "I don't know how long."

"Well, why not?" her gran said reasonably. "But come to us before you go back to LA again, won't you?"

"Yes. Of course I will. I'm going to call Mum today, too. Has she... has she called you?"

"Only every day. Not your problem, though."

"Of course it's my problem. Or it's my issue, maybe. Mine to deal with, anyway."

"Well, that's true," her gran said. "So stop chatting to me and get to it."

Just like Iain, Nina thought as she hung up. She knew a lot

of straightforward people, in fact, and she liked them all, so what was she worried about? Anybody who only wanted her when she agreed with them, when she went along with them—was that anybody whose opinion she should care about? Why didn't they just get a dog, if that was what they wanted?

That all sounded good. And then she made the second call, and was having trouble reminding herself of it.

"Mum?" she asked.

"*Nina*. Oh, my God. Nina."

"I'm sorry, Mum," she said, trying not to cry. "But I had to go."

"Why didn't you call me? I've been worried sick."

"I thought you'd tell Matthias. Or that you'd tell me I was wrong, that I should come back. I was afraid to hear it."

"Well, of course I would have," her mother said. "There I was, not knowing where you were, if you were coming back, if the wedding was on or off, and him asking me every day. What was I meant to say to him? What could I do? Did you think of that?"

"Yes," Nina was somehow able to say. "I did. And I still couldn't marry somebody I was afraid of."

"Darling." She could hear the impatient sigh right down the line. "That's ridiculous. He couldn't have been more indulgent, always. What didn't he give you? You had every woman's dream."

"Yes, well." Nina tried to will her voice into some strength. "I guess that isn't the dream I want after all."

"I don't even know what to say to you," her mother said. "I can't even begin to tell you how disappointed I am, how disappointed Matthias was. He kept me there all the way until yesterday, do you realize that? He kept hoping you'd come back. How could you do that to him?"

She had to get off this phone. "Well, I did it. It's done. I'm not sorry, but I'm sorry you were... uncomfortable. I couldn't marry somebody I didn't want, though, never mind about being afraid. Maybe that part was stupid, who knows.

But you can't have wanted me to do that."

"Uncomfortable? That would be one way to describe it. And I don't think you know what you want. You can't have. In what possible way wouldn't that life have been better?"

Nina tried to think of what to say, but she was still working on it when her mother said, "Anyway. Where are you calling from, and when are you coming back? What's done is done, I guess. All we can do is put our best spin on it, figure out your next steps. I'll call Andrea," she said, referring to Nina's agent. "We'll get the publicist in on it, have them issue a statement, and you can do a press conference. If we play this right, we can leverage it so you come out... well, not ahead, because nothing will ever make you a princess again, but as well as possible. And meanwhile, Andrea can be making her own calls."

And there the familiar juggernaut was, preparing to roll away with her. Nina felt the pull of it even as she willed herself to reject it. "No," she said. "None of the above."

Another sigh. "Of course you don't want to face up to it. Who would? But those are the consequences of your actions, darling. You didn't want to marry Matthias? I'll never pretend to understand it, but fine. Fine. Then we have to move on."

"No, Mum. That is, I do have to face up to it, but I can choose how to do it. And I'm not doing any of that now. I'm taking a break."

"Don't be ridiculous. I've told you. You may as well say, 'I've decided to kill my career.'"

"Well, maybe I have." Nina heard the words come out, and they shocked her to her toes, but they felt right, too. "Or maybe I haven't. I don't know. That's the point. All I know is that I'm taking a break. You're welcome to stay at the house—in fact, I hope you will—but I won't be back. Not for a while, at least. And after that, I don't know. I'll decide."

Nothing but silence, now. Nina wondered if it were the break that had silenced her mother, or the house. Her mother tended to forget that the house was Nina's. In her name, bought with her money. Bought, in fact, when she'd been only twenty, though her mother had been the one who'd decided to buy it and who had chosen it, too, as she'd chosen everything about Nina's career. And about her life, if she were honest.

"You wouldn't," her mother finally said. "You wouldn't throw it away."

"I might, Mum. I don't know. And I need to go. This is a friend's phone, and I've got work to do."

"Doing what? I thought you were taking a break. If you're working, you need to consult with me. You don't understand strategy, or branding, either. You never have. One wrong move—"

Time to stand up and be counted. Past time. "I'll tell you, then, but you won't like it. I'm learning how to fall out of a kayak and get back in. It's a survival skill, trust me, and it's one I need. I'm doing laundry. I'm cleaning a bathroom, I'm vacuuming, and I'm going to figure out how to iron a shirt, I think. I don't think it's anything you can help with from afar."

"You're *what?* Where *are* you? This isn't any kind of good judgment. This is mad." Her mother's Aussie accent, as always, came out more strongly when she was agitated. "You don't know enough about the world not to get yourself into trouble. You need to come back *now*. You listen to me, Sabrina Rose—"

"Mum, I'm sorry, but I have to go." The hand holding the phone was shaking, and she was sweating. She pressed the symbol to hang up the phone, and then she set it on the kitchen counter and wiped her hands on her shorts.

"Right," she said aloud. "Right. Done."

Arthur came into the kitchen. She'd thought he was still on his walk, and she jumped.

"Oh," she said. "Hi. So." She pushed herself off from the counter. "I'm going to put the wash in, make sure you've got whatever you need to wear for your big night. And then I'm going out for a while. I'll be back to fix your lunch."

He ignored all of that, recognizing it for the rambling it was. "First time you've talked to your mum since you ran?"

233

Her chin trembled, but she answered him. "Yes."

He nodded. "Good. First time's always the hardest, eh. Go on, then. Reckon you'd better get cracking."

lonesome me
♡

Iain walked over with his dad to collect the party from the cottage at seven that evening. He knocked on the door, then stepped inside to find his grandfather waiting impatiently in the kitchen, wearing dark trousers and a white shirt with a few extra creases ironed into it that made Iain smile. Nina learning again, he was guessing.

His mum was there, too, seeming nervous but defiant, looking at his dad, then away again. They hadn't been working together this weekend, Iain knew, not since they'd had their fight. His dad worked on the weekend; his mum didn't. Instead, she'd driven the other car into Nelson and had stayed gone all day.

His dad stood just behind him, wooden and silent, and Iain felt a flash of impatience. How could he do that? How? How could he be that stupid?

Then Nina walked into the kitchen, and he forgot all about his parents.

Makeup, he realized dimly. She'd been holding a couple bags when he'd collected her after the gym this afternoon, and this must have been what they'd been. Makeup, the strappy sandals with a high heel that made her legs look impossibly long, and a flowered red dress that fell to mid-calf, but was unbuttoned to well above her knee, flashing a tantalizing glimpse of silky thigh as she walked. A wrap front showed off her waist and the curve of her hips. The dress dipped low in front, revealing a hint of the cleavage he'd only seen in her bikini top. Just a hint, but a hint was too much. He was already getting lost in that shadow.

"Red," he managed.

"That all you've got to say, darling?" his mother laughed.

He looked at Nina some more, at the yellow hair that she'd parted severely at the side and slicked all the way back, revealing the shape of her skull, the devastating lines of cheekbone and jaw softened by the makeup, but cut so aristocratically fine. Her eyes looked even bigger, her lashes even longer and sooty dark, her mouth even lusher. Every inch a *Milady's Boudoir* model, but a stranger, too.

He had his voice back now, at least. "This is gorgeous," he told her. "You're beautiful, but you already know that. And somehow, I want my Nina back all the same. The one who climbs back into her kayak over and over until she gets it right. The one who's willing to show me exactly who she is. She's gorgeous as well. So you know."

Her eyes got even bigger. "Oh," she said. "Do you have to say things like that? You just… you kill me."

"No," he said, and if there were other people in the room, he'd forgotten about them. "You kill *me.*"

"Well, if you're done killing each other," his granddad said, "let's get on to the pub before they all decide I'm not coming and go home again."

Iain laughed, opened the door, and said, "Let's do that, then. We'll celebrate that you're eighty-five, and that Nina's not a princess. Both bloody good reasons, as far as I'm concerned."

His dad was silent during the short walk to the pub, and his mum wasn't, because she was making an effort. And then they arrived to a room half filled with locals, spilling over the edges of three of the long wooden tables, but with space left for all of them. Then it was all shouts, claps on the back for his granddad, beer and steaks and chat.

"Can't believe you all turned out," his granddad was saying. "Must not have anything better to do, eh."

"Nah," Nigel Witherspoon said, a laugh shaking his considerable belly. "Pure fascination that a crusty old bugger like you somehow made it to eighty-five. Like that fish you throw back, because you know it's going to be too tough and bony to bother with. Plus Iain saying it was his shout, I reckon."

Iain frowned Nigel down, but his granddad was already glaring at him. "Why would you do that?"

"Asking myself that very question, aren't I," Iain said. "I've got no judgment, apparently. It's an inherited quality, I understand."

"Watch yourself," his granddad growled, and Iain smiled.

"Going to introduce us?" Nigel asked, nodding at Nina.

Arthur said, "This is Nina. She's my cook, you could say."

"Your *cook*. That's luck, then. How you goin', Nina. A good cook's always worth meeting, eh." That was Alastair Witherspoon, Nigel's son, who really had no reason to be here that Iain could think of. Not the only single young bloke at the tables, either. All of them eyeing Nina like they wanted to eat her up, which they probably did.

"Well," Nina said composedly, "I'm not a good cook, so maybe not so much."

Alastair looked like he wanted to say something else, but the band took the stage, which fortunately limited the conversation. And even though Iain had taken care to sit beside Nina, more than a few eyes went to her, then to him. Checking, guessing. Fellas leaning over to chat, to laugh in between the band's energetic rendition of his granddad's favorite old-fashioned country favorites.

Too many eyes on Nina altogether, in fact, but she seemed unfazed. Serene, he'd call it. Armored by all her trappings, he guessed. Tonight, it was easy to see why a prince would have wanted her, easy to see her fitting into that role as if she'd been born to it. Which she very nearly had been. A child model, he'd read the day before, in the spotlight almost her entire life. The privilege, he was beginning to realize, was in being allowed to see the woman beneath the public poise.

The band's lead singer, a bloke from Nelson, finally wiped his brow and said, "We'll take a break. Back in fifteen. If the birthday boy's got any requests, or anybody else, either, now's the time. Accompanied by a big enough tip, of course."

"What d'you think, Granddad?" Iain asked. "Got any requests?"

"I do," the old man said. "I want to get Nina up there to sing to me."

"Oh, no," she said immediately. "No. I've never—"

"I know you can," Arthur said. "You don't want to give me a birthday treat, though? Then never mind."

"Blackmail," she said, frowning him down. "Pure blackmail, and you know it."

"Who's been doing yoga every day?" Arthur demanded. "Who? Me, that's who. What d'you call that? You can call it 'stretching' all you like, but I saw the book, and I wasn't born yesterday, so don't even try."

"Yoga? You?" Nigel said, as everyone enjoyed a jolly laugh.

"Yeh. Every single blessed day. Because a woman can talk a man into anything," Arthur said belligerently. "And if any of you blokes says any different, we'll just ask your missus, see what she has to say about that." He glanced around in triumph as the women smiled and the men shot them sidelong glances. "Ha. That's shut you up, eh."

"But…" Nina was still trying.

"Right, then," Arthur said. "Don't. Never mind. I didn't want a birthday anyway. Always said so."

"You are so…" she said. "So—*aggravating!*"

"Least she didn't call you an arsehole," Iain said, and Nina was opening her mouth at *him* now, unable to form any words. "Yeh. She did. Full of fire, this one. Don't let the pretty face fool you."

"I do not have a pretty face," she muttered.

"Could be true," Iain said, and she gasped again. "But you've got a beautiful one." He shot a look at Alastair, and saw him get the message.

"Iain," Nina said, intercepting that look and interpreting it without any trouble at all. "Stop."

"Sorry," he said, completely untruthfully. "Band's coming back, eh. You may want to have a word, if you're singing."

"Fine," she muttered. "Fine. I'll talk to *you* later." She murmured, "Excuse me," to Carmella, who edged out of her way, then swung out over the bench with another flash of thigh while Iain caught every eye he could manage, and walked over to where the band was coming back to the tiny wooden stage.

"You could've warned a fella," Alastair said.

"What d'you think I was doing earlier?" Iain answered. "Not my fault if you make me spell it out." He took a final swallow of beer and hoped Nina could actually sing, although all she'd have to do was stand up there, and nobody was going to complain.

When she swung around again and stepped to the microphone, the room got quiet. It was as if she'd flipped a switch, had turned on a spotlight brighter than the one that was actually lighting the band. Her reluctance to sing in public had been genuine; Iain was sure of it. And still, once she was there, under the lights? She was on.

The band started to play, an urgent beat of drums, a driving beat of guitar, and she was swinging her hips, tapping her toe. Then she opened her mouth, and his heart stopped. Just stopped.

Her husky voice, dark and low, wasn't professional, not really. It was sweet and sexy as hell, though, embracing the audience, inviting them in. She was dancing, smiling, making love to them all. Singing about how she was lonesome, and how she was looking to forget her past, to find somebody new.

"Oh, lonesome me," she sang, and every man there was wishing he could help her with that. But none of them could possibly want it more than Iain.

The band took it up a notch, and so did she. She had a hand on her skirt, was twitching the fabric and her hips back and forth, showing some gorgeous thigh. Was nodding her head, belting it out, all her personal reserve vanished. They finished it up with a swirl of guitar, and she was laughing, dropping her skirt, putting a hand up to slick back her hair, leaning down to speak low into the microphone, her eyes shining.

"That was for Arthur," she said. "And so is this one. I'm going to take it on down here, and I hope you'll come on with me, indulge me a little. This is an old one, a Patsy Cline song that my own gran always loved, and that I'll bet Madeline did, too." Her eyes were misty now, her voice so tender. "So this is for both of you," she told Arthur, with just the faintest wobble. "It's called, 'She's Got You.'"

The guitar again, slow this time, a soft, sweet drum beat, and Nina with her eyes closed, her beautiful body swaying. The words so simple, about how the one you loved was gone, and all you had left were their things. The things they'd left behind, just like you were left behind. About how it didn't matter what you had, not if you didn't have that one person, and how you couldn't get rid of those things anyway, the things that reminded you of the one you'd lost. The one you missed. The one you still loved, and always would.

She didn't do anything flash, anything special. She didn't get in the song's way. She just sang like she meant it, the music filling her body, filling the room. And when she finished, the crowd was silent for a long moment. Silent, or stunned.

"Happy birthday, Arthur," she said into her microphone. "I love you." She set the mike back in its stand, accepted the lead singer's courtly hand down the stairs, and the entire crowd was standing, applauding her.

She paid them no attention, just walked straight through the room, bent to put her arm around the old man's neck, and kissed his cheek, which was wet with tears. Iain hadn't seen him cry since his wife's funeral, but he was crying now. He had his arm around Nina's waist, and her eyes were shining as well.

"Little witch," Arthur said at last, trying to frown. "You've made me cry in front of my mates."

"Yep," she said. "Once every eighty-five years, need it or not." She kissed him once more, then stood, sighed, and said, "I'm going to fix my face. Be right back."

She walked off, and Iain sat there and tried to bring himself back under control, and failed entirely. And then she came out again, slid into her seat beside him, her arm brushing his, and he knew that nothing had changed, and everything had. She'd said no, it didn't matter how much he would've given to turn that into "yes," and it didn't seem to make any difference.

A week ago, he'd been sure he'd never love again. A day ago, he'd have said the situation was impossible. And tonight, he knew that it didn't matter how impossible it was, or how hopeless, either. He'd already started. He was already gone.

our life
♡

Graeme sat, silent as usual, and watched. He watched Nina with his father-in-law, watched Carmella, sitting kitty-corner to him instead of beside him the way she should have been, with a smile on her face that looked pained, like the way she'd smiled after their babies had been born. Like she was happy, but it hurt. He watched Iain, and thought about what his son had said earlier, in the kitchen of the cottage. About how Iain had been able to talk to a woman he'd met a week earlier, had been able to say the kind of thing to her in front of his parents and his granddad that Graeme himself had so much trouble saying, even to his wife, even when they were alone.

What was he going to do? He didn't know. But he knew he had to do something.

It wasn't long before the band was taking another break and Arthur was hauling himself to his feet, saying, "I don't care if all of you stay, but I'm going home. Not a bad birthday," he told the group. "Not bad at all."

"I'll go with you," Nina said, and Carmella stood, too.

"You stay here," Arthur told Nina. "Dance with Iain." Indeed, an intrepid few couples had eventually stood and taken the floor. They'd be doing it again, too, now that the evening was well advanced and the alcohol was flowing.

Nina laughed, her teasing gaze landing on Iain. "Somehow, I doubt he's a big dancer."

"A big one," he said, "but not a good one. But I reckon you could talk me into it."

"Nope," she said lightly. "Not safe." And left everybody there to wonder what that meant. She tucked her hand through Arthur's arm, smiled around the assembled faces, and said, "Nice to meet you all."

Iain and Graeme went with them, of course. No point in staying. Iain was hanging back, walking with Nina and Arthur, to nobody's surprise, and Graeme looked at his wife.

If Nina was beautiful tonight, so was Carmella. Still slim, still strong, her eyes still as dark and full of life as they had been the evening he'd met her. Beautiful, and as remote as a star.

"You doing all right?" he asked her.

She looked at him, and the moon shed enough light for him to see how somber her expression was. "No," she said. "Not really."

"Oh." He said it, then. "That fella. In Nelson. Is it something you do together, then? Would I ring up?"

Her face was twisting. She was looking away, and he thought, for one heart-stopping moment, that she was going to say that it was over. That she'd decided, and that the answer was, "No."

"Yes," she said quietly. "You do it together. If you do it."

"I'll ring up, then." He wanted to say more. He wanted to say how he'd felt when he'd seen Arthur tonight, had seen the tears on his cheeks. When Graeme had finally realized exactly what it would mean to lose the woman he loved, and how close he was to doing it. And that however hard it would be to do this, losing her would be worse, so he had no choice. But he didn't say it, of course.

"Yes," she said. "You need to be the one to do it. I need to know you'll make the effort. This can't be something I do, and that you go along with. Not this time. I have to... I have to take a stand here. All you have to do is say one thing, to reach out, and you make me want to come back, to say it's all right. But I can't, not unless it'll be better, not if I'm still going to wonder whether you really want me. I know you'll think this is too much to say, but I... I was dying inside."

He was so uncomfortable, all he wanted was to turn away from her, to walk away. But if he pulled himself together, he might just pull himself apart from her for good, and he knew it. "If you can't come back yet, you can't," he said instead. "I'll ring up. First thing tomorrow."

She had a hand up to her cheek, was dashing the tears away, and he wanted to hold her, but he wasn't sure what the rules were.

The hell with the rules, something from outside him seemed to shout. *They're not working.* So he put a hand on her shoulder, and when she turned to him, he pulled her into his arms.

The shock of it. So familiar, and so lost to him. He hadn't held her, really held her, for months.

She never cried, but she was crying now. He could feel the tears, hot and wet, seeping through his shirt. Surely, that meant she still cared.

She never cried, no, and he never talked, but he was talking anyway. "Don't leave me." His voice was rough, not the way it ought to be, the words ripped from some spot deep inside him. "Please. Give it a go first, at least. Let me try."

She was crying harder, and he rubbed his hand over her slender back, tightened his arms around her, and rocked from side to side with her until, at last, she was pulling back, brushing the tears away again, and saying, her voice choked, "Tell me, then. Tomorrow. When. And I'll go with you." Her eyes were searching his face now. "You'll try? You really will?"

"Don't you know," he found himself saying, "that I'd do anything for you? Don't you know that?"

"No," she whispered. "No. I don't."

"Reckon I'd better tell you, then. Come home with me. Please. Let me... let's start again."

She shook her head, her lips trembling. "No. I'm sorry, Graeme. But no. I need us to have some new... rules. Some tools. I need to know they're there to help. I feel... so battered. If we slip back, I don't think I can take it."

"You want me to win you again," he said slowly.

"That sounds like a game. It's not a game. It's our life."

"Yeh," he said. "I know it is. Just trying to understand the rules, is all. I'll ring up, then. Eight o'clock, I'll ring up, and if he doesn't answer, I'll keep on doing it until he does."

"All right," she said. They were at the track leading down to the house, and she headed down it ahead of him and, before he could say more, she was saying, "Good night," and ducking into the cottage.

He walked to the house, and he was still alone. But he wasn't hopeless. Not anymore.

Eight o'clock. He'd do it if it killed him. Because if he didn't do it... it *would* kill him.

closing the chapter

♡

Matthias's head shot up at the knock on his study door. "Enter."

Raoul came in silently, as always, and stood looking down at him. Something about his gaze was unsettling. Really, the man was almost creepy. Matthias frowned. "What?"

"I assume you still want to know," Raoul said. "We've found her."

"A bit late, aren't you? Four days ago would have been better. Not two days *after* my wedding day."

Raoul didn't answer, just stared at him. Did he never blink? "Do you want to know?"

"Of course I want to know. Where is she?"

"New Zealand. The South Island."

Matthias shook his head as if to clear it. He hadn't been drinking; that wasn't the reason. It simply made no sense. "Why?"

"She was hiding, she said."

"From what? From me?"

Raoul shrugged, the tiniest movement of his shoulders in the dark suit he seemed to sleep in, and Matthias felt another flash of irritation. "You wanted to know," his chief of staff said. "Now you know. I assume that closes the chapter."

"You assume wrong." Matthias had swung out of his chair. Now, he began to pace. "Here's what we're going to do."

try me

♡

Carmella had been afraid to believe that Graeme would actually do it. But at ten o'clock the next morning, he walked up to the bookings desk during a brief break in the action and said, "Today at five."

"*Today?*"

"Yeh. I said it was an emergency. Had a cancellation, he said."

"Oh." Now that it was here, she was terrified. "Uh... I wasn't expecting that."

Graeme looked a little sheepish. "I may also have said I'd pay double."

Now, she wasn't just surprised. She was gobsmacked. "Scotland's going to disown you," she managed to say.

She got a gruff bark of laughter for that. "No worries. He said it didn't work that way, so I wasn't put to the test. But I would've done it."

"We'll have to get somebody to cover." She was already planning. "Have to leave at four-thirty."

"Already done. You told me it was down to me," he said when she looked shocked again. "I assumed you meant it."

A young couple walked through the door then, and Graeme nodded at her, headed to the back, and Carmella pasted a smile onto her face and asked, "Can I help you?" even as she tried to calm her heart. And her hopes.

When they were in the car, though, she couldn't think of what to say. Graeme was her husband, but she felt as awkward as if it were their first date. She started with some chat about the business, and Graeme glanced across at her and said, "D'you really want to talk about that?"

"No," she admitted. "I'm nervous."

He put out a hand and gripped hers briefly before placing it back on the steering wheel. After a moment, he asked, "D'you remember when I drove you to the hospital to have Vanessa?"

"Yes. Of course."

"Never been more scared," he said.

"I didn't know that." She couldn't think what else to say.

"I put your seat back, I remember that. Trying to get you comfortable. Got you a pillow. And then I drove, and I thought—I was so afraid something would go wrong. That I'd lose you, somehow. Or that everything would change, that something would... happen." He shook his dark head, his faintly lined face still so tough and strong. "Can't even tell you what I thought."

"Oh," she said.

"And today feels exactly the same."

"It... does?"

He glanced across at her before taking a curve in the road. "You said I should talk. So I thought I'd tell you."

"Guess you'd better not have a smash on the way, then," she said, her heart beating now with something new. With hope.

"Reckon you're right."

When they were in the waiting room in a nondescript building on a quiet Nelson street, though, she could nearly feel Graeme stiffening again. Walking into the suite had felt momentous, even though, to her relief, the sign by the door didn't proclaim the word "Therapy." If it had, she suspected Graeme might have bolted. She wasn't too far off it herself.

When the door to the inner office opened, the man on the other side didn't look anything like she'd expected. She'd been thinking he'd be young, in a suit, maybe. Instead, he was their age, tall, with a bit of a belly, in khaki pants and a knit shirt, his hands as broad as his smile wasn't. He looked, in fact, like a Kiwi bloke, and she wasn't sure if that was a good thing from Graeme's point of view or not.

"Come in," he said. "And don't worry. I don't bite much."

She laughed nervously, and Graeme, to her shock, took her hand and squeezed it again.

Inside the simple office, though, set up with two comfortable chairs and a couch, Graeme looked dubious again. "Tell me I'm not lying on that," he said.

"Generally, people sit on it," Melvin said. "But do whatever you like."

They sat, and Melvin said, "You're both here. Congratulations. That's the hardest part out of the way. Whose idea to come?"

"Mine," Carmella said.

"And what did you say?" Melvin asked Graeme.

"Said no," he answered.

"Uh-huh," Melvin said. "Why?"

And it went on from there. Getting there might have been the hardest part, but the rest of it wasn't easy, either. The background information wasn't so bad, but then it got tougher. When Melvin asked Graeme, "So you met when you were twenty-four and Carmella was twenty-one, at a dance. That's a long time ago."

"Yeh," Graeme said.

"What did you think, that first night?" Melvin asked. "That first time? About her?"

Graeme looked down at his hands so long, Carmella didn't think he was going to answer.

"Thought she was beautiful," he finally said.

"Why don't you tell her?" Melvin asked.

"Uh…" Graeme looked pained. "Now?"

"Now," Melvin said. "How are you going to tell her how

you feel now if you can't tell her what you felt then? We could call it easing up to it, maybe. Or you could ask yourself if you want her back in your house."

"Yes," Graeme said instantly.

Melvin didn't answer, just looked at him, and Graeme sighed, scratched the back at his head, and glanced at Carmella. He was sitting a foot away from her. She'd sat in the middle, and he'd sat at the edge, and maybe that said too much.

"I thought you..." His mouth twisted a bit, and he was looking down at his hands, studying his nails. "That you were beautiful. Your eyes, and your smile. So... alive, somehow. More than other girls. Couldn't believe you were smiling at me. I actually checked behind me to make sure it wasn't some other bloke. I was rough as guts. Tradie," he told Melvin.

"Tell her," Melvin said quietly.

"Yeh," Graeme said, glancing at her again, while she sat and tried not to hold her breath. "I was a tradie, but you know that. Barely had my electrician's license, and you were finishing Uni and all. And then I got up my courage, asked you to dinner, and you said yes."

"Want to know why I did?" she asked him.

He nodded once, and she told him. "Because you were big and strong. And because you were gentle. Because you danced with me and didn't try to grab me. Because you looked rough, maybe, but you weren't rough. You want to know a secret?"

"Uh..." Graeme was glancing at Melvin again, and the other man raised both hands and said, "Go ahead."

"Remember how we went on those three dinners, and then I asked you to come for a picnic on the beach?" she asked. "Did you ever wonder why I did that?"

"Because you wanted to say thanks for the dinners," he said. "I remember."

"No," she said. "Because I wanted to wear my togs, and to see you in yours. I thought if I did that, you'd finally do more than kiss me goodnight. And you did."

251

Graeme was lost for words. Melvin said, "Why don't you tell Graeme why you're here today, Carmella?"

She looked at her husband sitting there, so big and so lost, and her heart ached for him. She forgot the silences and the little comments, just for a moment, and remembered the man who'd put the pillow behind her when he'd driven her to the hospital to have Vanessa, who'd held her hand through it all. And who'd cried when he'd seen his daughter born. The way he'd cradled their little girl in those big hands. The ones that could fix anything, no matter how impossibly delicate it was. Maybe even this.

If she wasn't willing to take a risk, what was the point? "I'm here," she told him, "because nothing matters more to me than you. And I don't mean, 'Nothing matters more than my marriage.' I mean, 'than *you.*' I fell in love with you for good that night, after the beach. With how strong and fierce you were with me, and how careful and tender, too. I know that man's still in there, and I want him back."

He wasn't answering at all now, and the seconds ticked by until Melvin finally said, "Graeme? Want to answer Carmella?"

"Uh…" he said. "I want her back as well."

"Tell her," Melvin reminded him.

Graeme turned, looked at her, and said, "I want you back as well."

"That's a good start," Melvin said. "And it's our time about up. But you're not in a bad spot at all, are you?"

"Not the worst you've seen, then," Graeme said, back to gruff again.

"Oh, no," Melvin said. "Not by a long chalk. Looks to me like you remember what you felt for each other at the start, and if you're here at all? You've got the desire to get it back. I know that, because this wasn't easy for you. But I'd like to see you twice a week. Knock this thing out, get you back on track, that would be the idea. If you need more after that, you can come back for a tune-up now and then."

"The business—" Graeme said.

"Ah, yes. The business." Melvin sat back and looked at him. "More important than this, or less?"

"Less."

"Well, then," Melvin said, cheerful once more, "shall we say Thursday, same time? And then next Tuesday and Thursday as well?"

"So does this mean she comes home?" Graeme demanded.

"Asking the wrong person, aren't you," Melvin said.

Graeme looked at Carmella, and she said, "No. Not yet." She saw him stiffen and said, "I don't feel ready."

"That's honest," Melvin said, "and honesty's the point, eh. Let's see. Homework. I want you both to decide on a night each week that you'll spend together. Doing whatever you please. Go for a walk, go to the pub. Doesn't matter. But you do it together, and it has absolute priority. We'll see how we do on Thursday, getting you ready to do that. And before you come back? You each make a list. Ten things you like best about each other. And five times the other did something that made you realize how much you loved them."

"What about her list where she says what she doesn't like?" Graeme said. "I know that's coming."

"Oh, I think you both already have those pretty well memorized," Melvin said. "Let's start with this instead, shall we?"

♡♡♡

"Date night, eh," Graeme said when they were in the car on the way home. Carmella was just sitting there, as drained as if she'd been running a race.

"Yeh," she said cautiously. "Sounds good, maybe?"

"Which of your clubs will you give up, then?"

She glanced across at him, but he was driving, looking straight ahead. "Do you want to know why I do things away from the house? Is that what you're asking?"

He shrugged. "Reckon I know."

She wanted to lash out, but she didn't. *Couldn't believe you were smiling at me,* he'd said. Maybe he still couldn't. Maybe he assumed she'd rather be with other people than with him.

If she wanted him to talk? She had to talk, too. She had to tell the truth, no matter how much of a risk it was.

"I do it because I'm lonely," she told him. "You started working so much at night, and it made me think you were doing that because you didn't want to be with me."

"No," he said. "I was worried I wouldn't make a go of it, of the kayaks. That I'd fail. Fail…" He stopped, then said, "You. Fail you."

"But we *have* made a go," she said.

"Maybe I got used to it. And maybe you were gone, so I thought, may as well keep on. And then Iain's wedding and all. You were doing all that. Always had some list, running off somewhere. So I thought, stay busy."

"We could hire a bookkeeper," she said. "We could sell the business, for that matter. I don't care."

He shot another glance at her. "You don't?"

"Nah. I don't. I want to make sure Dad's OK. And I want to be with you. I like working with you, doing it together, being *in* it together, so that'd be my choice."

"Oh." He was silent another minute, then he said, "Mine, too. But the bookkeeper's an idea. So when's this date night?"

"Saturday, don't you think?"

"Right." There was a smile trying to work its way out of his tough face. "Saturday." He was slowing for the limits of Kaiteriteri. "We could go for a kayak. Call it a busman's holiday. And do a picnic on the beach. So I could see you in your togs."

"You can't want to do that," she said with a little laugh.

"No?" He pulled to a stop at their carpark. "Try me."

bad dream
♡

Nina swam the last few minutes around the rocks to Kaiteriteri Beach and paused, treading water for a minute, to look around at the huge sweep of sand, fairly well populated now with holidaymakers. Children splashed in the shallows, and a few other swimmers had struck out from shore. The sea shuttle was disembarking at one end of the beach, reminding her of the walk she and Iain had taken on the northernmost part of the Abel Tasman Track this morning, before he'd headed out for yet another bike ride.

Even though she'd gone inside two nights earlier without saying more than "Goodnight" to him, he'd still taken her kayaking the next day, and hiking today. He'd walked across a narrow, swaying, heart-stoppingly high swing bridge behind her and stopped in the middle to look at the spectacular waterfall and the river rushing over the boulders far below as if it had been his first time, and had seemed to get pleasure from her enjoyment. He'd brought her down a side track to Cleopatra's Pool, a magical, secret spot tucked away behind a beach. He'd swum with her in clear, still water surrounded by smooth granite rock and fern trees that looked as if they should be hiding dinosaurs, had watched her stripping down to her bikini and toweling herself dry afterwards, and hadn't touched her. He'd looked at her, and she'd looked at him, and they hadn't done anything about it. She'd have called it "courting," if that hadn't been old-fashioned.

And it had been the sweetest, sexiest time she'd ever spent with a man. It seemed that all he had to do was look at her to make her tremble, and she could tell he loved looking. She wanted to touch him, but most of all, she wanted him to touch her. She knew how much he wanted to, how much self-control it was taking him not to, and she wanted to watch him lose that self-control. She wanted to see his eyes blaze, and to feel those powerful hands become demanding. Wanted to feel them touching her. Moving her. Turning her.

She knew he could do it. She knew he *would* do it. They'd barely done anything yet, and she already knew what kind of a lover he would be. Possessive, and demanding, and unselfish. Like nobody she'd known, and like the only man she wanted to.

Tomorrow, he was leaving for Auckland, and she was thinking that she should leave here, too, and knowing that she wouldn't. Not for a little while, anyway. Not for a few more weeks. Because of Arthur, and maybe, just maybe, because of Iain. She wasn't done with her break, and if she decided that she wanted to spend part of that break with him? If she went to Auckland for a visit? That would be nobody's business but her own, and nobody's choice but her own, either.

She still got chilled if she stopped swimming for long, though, so she turned and started back. She'd always worried about getting too muscular, which was one reason she'd confined herself to yoga. Now, she wasn't worrying. Maybe that meant something, and maybe it didn't. Another thing she didn't have to decide now.

She didn't notice the incongruity of the figure walking toward her down the beach until she'd risen to her feet and was wading out of the sea near the house. When she did notice, though, she stopped, knee-high in the water.

He stared at her across thirty feet of sand and water. Dark

suit superbly cut, and supremely out of place. Black shoes shined to a high gloss, looking as if sand would never dare to enter them.

She walked the rest of the way toward him. He had no power over her. She summoned up her best catwalk glide, and her best haughty glare, too, despite her fear.

"Raoul," she said as she approached, slicking her hair back with one hand. "What a surprise."

Not the single movement of a muscle on that ageless face. "I can't say the same," he said. "But then, I knew where you were."

She walked over for her towel, and he followed her. He seemed slightly taken aback that she'd walk away from him, or maybe that was wishful thinking. "Yes," she said, bending to pick up the towel and wrapping it around her waist. "How did you, I wonder?"

The yellow eyes flickered. "His Highness has been in contact with your mother."

"And yet I didn't tell my mother where I was." Which meant that somebody had been tracking her calls. Well, no *somebody* about it.

Raoul gave the tiniest shrug. "No matter."

"Well, yes, actually," she said. "I find that it matters a lot. I felt a little bad about running away. Now I don't. So thanks for that."

Another flicker of the eyes. "You'll have the chance to convey that message personally. That will please you."

"In what way would that be?"

"His Highness is waiting on the plane for you."

She schooled her own face into stillness with the skills she'd perfected for the camera long ago, and wished he weren't standing close enough to see the rising and falling of her chest. "Sounds boring for him. Especially having to fly back all that way without getting what he came for."

"Not attending is not an option."

"No? And yet that's exactly what it is. My option. My choice. And I choose 'no.'"

He took another step toward her, the expression not changing one iota, and it was somehow more frightening than if he'd looked furious. She couldn't help herself. She took a step back.

"What?" she asked, willing her voice not to shake. "He didn't get the message yet? It'll have to come through you, then, because I'm not going anywhere with you. Go to hell. Feel free to share that. Oh, wait. I'll say it again. One for each of you. Go to hell."

He came closer still, and she was backing again. And then he grabbed her arm, so fast she didn't have time to run.

He was holding her, squeezing tight, even as she tried to pull back, to twist away. It was her dream. They'd come for her.

And Raoul could swim.

"Nina!"

She saw Raoul's expression change, just a movement of the yellow eyes, and she twisted around.

She didn't get far. Raoul's hand was clamped around her forearm, raising it in the air. Gripping hard enough to bruise, and she was gasping.

Iain was there, then. Barefoot, but still in his cycling jersey and shorts. Huge. Furious. Fearsome.

His face looked tough at the best of times. Now, it was so far beyond that.

She couldn't say anything. Couldn't do anything but stare at him. She knew her eyes were wide, and that her legs were trembling. Somehow, her towel had fallen off. He'd be able to see how shaky she was, and so would Raoul, and she couldn't stand for Raoul to see.

"Get your hands off her," Iain said.

"This is none of your concern," Raoul said. "I am having a private conversation with this lady."

"The hell you are," Iain said. "Let her go."

Raoul's own eyes were hard. Hawk eyes. Wolf eyes. "She has an appointment. Kindly remove yourself."

One second, Iain had been standing two feet away. The

next, he was between her and Raoul, and Nina was staggering back, because Raoul had dropped her arm. He had to, in order to grasp Iain's forearm. One of Iain's huge hands was on Raoul's neck, under his chin, the other hauling him up by the lapel of his suit, bringing him to his toes.

"I said," Iain ground out, "take your hands off my *wife*."

Raoul's eyes were bulging, and he was making choking sounds, grabbing at Iain's arm until Iain finally tossed him backward as if he'd been a doll.

Raoul stumbled once, then stood up, his face not expressionless for once but blazing with fury, the mask dropped. "She is not your wife," he said. "Do you think I'm stupid?"

"I think you're dead." Iain had already thrust that deceptively fast arm out again and shoved Nina behind him. "Get off my beach."

Raoul straightened his lapels and said, "This is not over."

"Yes," Nina said. "It is. It's all over. It was over the minute I left. It should never have started."

Raoul turned and headed for the other end of the little bay, to where the steps led up to the road. His back was as straight as ever, his pace not one bit hurried, and still, Nina could tell he was running away, and that he was hating it.

She saw it in one moment, and in the next, she was running for the track to the house as if that wolf were after her. She burst through the trees, then stopped at the shout from behind her.

Iain came up to join her on the lawn and handed her the towel. She wrapped it around her body with shaking hands, rubbed absent-mindedly at her throbbing forearm, and tried to focus.

"Thanks," she said. "S-sorry."

"Was that him?" Iain still looked like he wanted to kill somebody. He still looked like he *could*. He'd picked up her hand, was running gentle fingers over the bruised skin of her forearm. "I should've hit him," he muttered. "I should've given him a good hiding, and I wouldn't have stopped."

"Of course you shouldn't have." This, she knew. "I'm sure you would've been in so much trouble if you had. He's probably got diplomatic immunity or something, and you're supposed to be a good citizen, aren't you? Isn't that part of the deal?"

"I don't give a toss about that." He wasn't looking one bit softer. "So was that him? That was the prince? How could you marry somebody like that? How could you even think of it?"

"Well, *I* give a toss. For you, I mean. For your reputation, and your record. And no, of course it wasn't. It was his chief of staff. That was Raoul. But he's here. Matthias. Waiting in the plane. In Nelson, I guess. Waiting like I'd come to him, even though I *left.*" All she'd had to do was say the words, to imagine him, and she was having to hold herself tight, held herself together and will herself not to cry. "But it's like it didn't happen. It's what it was before. Like nothing I did, nothing I said made any difference. Like I was just going to be rolled over. Erased. Married off like some kind of... Bride Barbie. It's why I ran. But there's no running that works. I can't... I can't get *away.*"

"Nina." He was pulling her in, but gently, and she went to him, because his arms were nothing but safe. She stayed wrapped up in him, her head on his broad chest and her own arms around his waist, and held on. She shook, and told herself, *He's gone. I'm safe,* and tried to believe it.

"Time for you to share all this," Iain said when his arms had convinced her in a way his words couldn't, and she was calm enough to step back. "Time to share it with more than me, I'm thinking."

"Not your... problem," she said. "And you shouldn't have said that, about being married. It was what Raoul said. Ridiculous, and he knew it."

"Was it?" He reached out and cupped her cheek in his palm as if he needed to keep touching her, as if he needed to convince himself she was there, the same way she needed to know he was. "I'm not so sure. I thought I was pretty convincing. Felt that way."

She tried to resist that hand, but it wasn't easy. "You were. But it'll just make him angrier. Matthias, I mean. It'll just make it worse."

"Well, like I said. Let's talk it out. We'll get Mum and Dad in on it as well. Granddad, too. We'll have dinner together and come up with a plan."

"I'm not getting erased again." She was still shaky, but she was sure. "It's not for you to say—any of you. It's my choice. My decision."

His hard eyes changed at that. Softened. "Yeh. It is. But there's such a thing as support. And I'd like to give it."

She nodded. How could she argue with that?

"I'll have a word with Granddad," Iain was following her to the cottage now. "I'll wait while you shower and change, then bring you both over to the big house with me. What were you doing for dinner tonight?"

"Uh... fish."

"Good. I've got more in the freezer, those couple I caught on our kayak yesterday. Veggies as well. We'll put it all on the barbecue. Easy as."

His matter-of-fact tone helped. So did the shower, and being in the big house, watching Iain lope down the stairs, his hair wet, his feet bare, after what must have been the shortest shower in history. As if he hadn't wanted to leave her and Arthur alone a moment longer than he'd had to.

Cooking with him helped, too. She made the salad, and then was setting the table again. Iain's parents came in from work, together for once. They didn't demur at eating dinner with the family, which she thought must mean something.

She was glad to see it, and all the same, those prickles tingled at the back of her neck in a way they hadn't since the Auckland airport. As if Raoul and Matthias were out there, looking through the greenery, watching her. When they'd put dinner on the table, she sat on the side next to the house, her back to the wall, and Iain took the seat beside her and didn't comment.

When they were settled, eating barbecued blue cod and summer squash along with a hastily prepared salad, Iain explained what had happened in a few sentences, and Nina looked down at her plate and tried not to remember how it had felt when Raoul had grabbed her arm. As if going with him were inevitable. As if being here, safe, in charge of her own life, had been the illusion.

"She can't stay here," Arthur said from the head of the table when Iain had finished.

Nina looked up, startled. She'd known she wasn't their responsibility, but this? "Oh," she said, her voice coming out too soft. "Oh," she said again, more strongly. "Sure. I mean, of course."

Arthur sighed in exasperation. "Don't be stupid. I mean, not with Iain leaving. They know exactly where you are. That doesn't sound safe to me."

"I don't understand, though," Carmella said. "I mean, I understand that you didn't want to be married, and that you left. We all understand that. But why would he come after you? And sending somebody else for you? That's mad. It doesn't make any sense at all."

"You're not a prince, though," Nina tried to explain. "He doesn't... do things himself. When he decided on me—decided that I was the one—in the first place, that was how it was. He decided, and other people did it. It was arranged. Like he could snap his fingers. He saw me doing a photo shoot on a beach in St. Barts. He was there on his yacht, and he just... *chose* me. It was all so fast, and I was flattered, I guess. He said the right things. He did the right things. But I still should have known."

"Pretty heady experience, I imagine," Carmella said calmly. "Like a Disney movie, eh."

"Yes," Nina said. "It was. And the rest of my life hasn't exactly been normal, either, so maybe it seemed—inevitable, I guess." She shook her head in frustration. "It's hard to explain. But when I woke up and realized that it wasn't inevitable at all, that I had options, that I didn't have to go along with what other people told me to do, it was almost too late. I told him I didn't want to get married, and it was like I hadn't even said it. I've felt all this time that I was overdramatic, the way I did it, the way I ran away, and especially the way I hid. Now, I'm not so sure. I think maybe I was right. He *did* come after me, and that *doesn't* make sense."

"That's why you were disguised," Iain said. "That's why you were so scared."

"Yes. It seems like a long time ago. But—yes."

She told them about the manure sacks, then. About the van. She told them all of it, and finished most of her dinner, not sure which part felt more like a dream. That past life, or being here.

Iain's face settled into harder lines the longer she talked, and when she finally finished, he wasn't the one who spoke. It was his father.

"And he's here all the same," Graeme said. "That's a man who doesn't hear no. That's dangerous. And this other fella? That's a wild card. I don't like that at all."

Nina didn't say anything. She'd thought that calling her mother and grandparents was the right thing. No, it *had* been the right thing. And it had put her straight back into the middle of trouble, as if she'd never have her life back again.

"So she can't stay here," Arthur said. "Reckon she'd better go with you," he told Iain.

He nodded, and Nina was opening her mouth to say, "What?" But before she could, Iain was saying, "I told him we were married. That'd be a good idea as well, I'm thinking."

"Oh, no," Nina was standing up, abandoning her dinner. "No."

At least Iain didn't grab her. He just looked at her and said, "I don't mean that you should really marry me. But I told him that, and he's going to check. I don't know what this prince is like, though I have my suspicions, but that fella? He's going to check. If we back up my story, though, I'm thinking it'll do the business."

Arthur was nodding. "You could file the notice of intent, anyway," he offered. "In Nelson. You say you mean to do it in Auckland. Then it's on record. Get the ring on her finger. Every fella checks for the ring."

"And I don't think you can search to find out whether somebody's actually been married," Carmella said. "When I was looking it up for Nan," she told her father, "remember that? Her grandparents' marriage? The site said that if the marriage was recent, it had to be your own records you were searching. You can only search the database for the older ones, for genealogy. So you file the intent tomorrow morning, before you leave, and say it's happening in a few days? Nobody's going to know whether you actually did it or not. Not if somebody in Nelson's willing to talk about you being in there getting the paperwork, and I'll bet they would."

"No," Nina said, even as Carmella was adding, "Better yet—Iain, you should have it leaked. Like you didn't want to tell because of Nina's situation, but somebody found out anyway."

The others were nodding. Nina said, "No," again, louder this time.

Iain glanced at her, grabbed her hand, and said, "Mum. Stop."

Carmella snapped her mouth shut and looked at Nina, who was standing there, her hand in Iain's, trying to hold herself together.

"Right," Iain said when silence had fallen. "All yours, Nina."

She said, "Remind me to tell you later that I like that you always say my name."

He said, "What?"

She shook her head. "Never mind. But no. Just no. Look," she went on at the Carmella's chagrined expression, "I appreciate that you all want to help. I appreciate that Iain's willing to… put himself out for me. But that's what this is all about, do you see? I didn't *want* to be married. And I don't

264

want to be married now."

"I wasn't putting myself out," Iain said. "But I'm listening," he went on hastily.

He was still holding her hand, she realized. She reclaimed it, and he let her go. "Matthias will probably leave," she said. "But in case he doesn't—yes, I think going to Auckland might be better, except that I don't really want to leave Arthur. I wanted to stay here for a while."

"We'll take him with us," Iain suggested. "If you want to, Granddad. Keep Nina company, eh. I've got good security," he told Nina. "Nobody knows where I live. The team sees to that. Got an alarm system and all that as well."

"Despite the fact that you aren't really famous," she said, somehow able to tease. "That you aren't one of the flash boys at the back."

She was rewarded with that arched eyebrow. "No accounting for taste, eh."

Nina looked at Arthur, who was frowning, as usual. "Would you be willing to come?" she asked. "I'd like it." She felt a little shy about saying it. "Just for a little while. That's all I need. Once I'm there, I could set up a press conference. I think that's my best bet. Better than any fake engagements, let alone fake marriages. You know that everybody would want to hear my story. It'll go around the world. 'Why did the royal bride run?' I won't say I'm with Iain. Nobody has to know that. But once the whole world knows, and when Matthias will be assuming I've been with Iain? Why would he want me then?"

"I don't like it," Iain said. "Doesn't seem strong enough. I'd like him to know."

"That's my point," she said. "That he'll know I really left him, that I really meant it. That I've told everybody so. If he tries to get me back then, all he'll do is humiliate himself. He won't be able to stand that idea, so that's the one thing that will work."

"No," Iain said. "I don't mean it's not a good idea. But I want him to think—to know—that you're…" He stopped.

"You won't like it, but I'll say it anyway. Protected. Mine."

The intensity in his eyes, the dark tone in his voice... She couldn't help it. In spite of everything, in spite of his family watching them, the words sent a rush of heat straight down her body. "That's... uh..." She tried again, then gave it up. "But if he knows I'm with you, that part's already done. Nobody else would have to know it. No pretend marriage. No leaks."

"It wouldn't be done, though," Iain said. "Not to somebody like that. If you're married to another man—that, he'll get. That'll get through. Especially," he added simply, "if it's me."

"You're right," Nina said, trying her best for brisk and practical. "That you'd be the best. For... size reasons, and all." Wait. They weren't going to talk about the size reasons. "I'm not willing to do it, though, so that's that. It would feel too much the same as before. Too much like I was being forced into something."

He nodded reluctantly. "Right, then. Granddad?"

"What d'you imagine?" Arthur said. "Course I'm coming. If I don't, the minute you're not around, she'll be back to those veggie things, starving herself again."

"For a while, then," Nina said. "For a few weeks, until it all dies down. I might see about getting a job."

"Thought you were meant to be looking after me," Arthur grumbled.

"That's not a job," Nina said, feeling suddenly lighter. Safer. Freer. "That's a calling."

simmer to burn

♡

Iain had to be content with that. It wasn't that he wasn't rapt about her going with him. It was just that he would've felt better with that notice filed and a ring on her finger, like his granddad had said. It wouldn't have been real. But he would've felt better.

His mother stood and said, "I'll do the washing up. Thanks for dinner, Iain. I'm going to miss you, and that's the truth."

"I'll give you a hand," Graeme said, rising with her. He was starting to pick up dishes, and both Iain and his mother were staring.

"What?" Graeme said belligerently. "A man can't change?"

"No." Carmella cleared her throat. "Of course he can. Thanks. That'd be good." And it looked to Iain that he was leaving just in time.

His parents disappeared into the house together, and he told Nina, "By the way. You're not sleeping in the hammock tonight. I'll trade places with you."

"That's probably not—" she began.

Suddenly, he was done being patient. "Yeh. It is. It's necessary. You wouldn't sleep out there alone, and I wouldn't sleep imagining you. Don't you know what having you be scared does to me?"

"Who dumped me out of my hammock and chased me into the sea?" She was *smiling*, and he was beyond impatient. He was furious. He could feel his jaw clenching, his hands fisting, and he couldn't stop it.

She saw it, stepped closer, put an urgent hand on his forearm, and said, "Iain. I'm sorry. I'm trying to laugh, I guess. Trying to make this seem real. Being here, being safe. But I'm sorry."

He exhaled, long and slow, deliberately relaxed his hands, his jaw, tried to ignore her hand on him, and said, "I'm trying to make it real, too. That's the point. I'm trying to keep you safe, and make you feel safe. But you aren't the only one with feelings."

"Right," she said. "Trading beds."

"If that's the choice."

"Where am I sleeping in your house?" Her hand was warm on him, and she was so close, he could almost feel her softness, her heat.

"Wherever you want."

She took her hand off him and said, "Good," then looked around and said, "Oh. Arthur. He must have gone back, I guess. So— I'll help him pack, and then I'll come find you?"

"Right." He fought himself back under control. "I'll get the tickets sorted."

"I can do mine," she said.

Frustration, again, that she couldn't let him do even this for her. He tried to see it from her point of view, but it wasn't easy. "You not worried about being tracked anymore?"

"Oh." She stopped and considered. "No. You're right. I forgot. Isn't that crazy? I forgot for a minute."

"Maybe it's working, then. The 'safe' thing."

She smiled, her face lighting up in the way that did things to him, and said, "Maybe so. That's something, isn't it? That's what you do for me, I guess. We could go to a bank in Nelson, maybe, tomorrow morning, if we have time before the flight. I could open a new account at a local bank and transfer money into it. An account my mother doesn't know about. Matthias already knows I'm here, so that wouldn't be any new information. We could do that, and it would help a lot. If I had my own money again."

"Ah. You think she was sharing that with him?"

She looked away, the smile gone, and he felt ashamed of his earlier frustration. "I'm sure she was."

"Right, then." He tried to imagine how it would feel not to be able to trust your own mother, and couldn't. "Then we'll go by the bank tomorrow morning so you can do that. I'll arrange the bookings so we have time."

"And once I do my press conference," she said, "I won't have to hide. Once it's out in the open, I'll be free."

And you'll have no reason to stay.

"Meanwhile," she said, "where do I find you? Since I'm kicking you out of your bed and all."

"Top of the house," he said. "You can't miss it."

♡♡♡

Nina stood at the window at the top of the big house looking out across a sky and sea that glowed faintly pink with the first glimmerings of sunset, at the distant blue line of the Marlborough hills that marked the horizon.

She heard Iain come up behind her, and saw him, too, his reflection just showing in the glass of the window.

"Beautiful," he said.

"Yes," she sighed. "I'll miss this."

She started when she felt his hands on her shoulders, and then she was being pulled back into him. His lips brushed over her temple, and he breathed the words into her ear. "I meant you."

Before she knew what she was doing, she had reached her hand back and wrapped it around his neck.

He didn't need any more invitation. He was kissing her in that tender spot just below her ear, and her back was arching. His hand was turning her head, his mouth was closing over hers, and his other hand was low on her belly, hauling her back into his body.

She gasped into him, and he was sucking her lower lip into his mouth, giving it a gentle nip that sent shock waves straight through her, then biting a little harder, making her squirm. He was deepening the kiss, still holding her in place, and she was rising up on her bare tiptoes, being pulled back even harder now.

His hand was, somehow, under the hem of her tank top, briefly circling her waist. "This," he said against her mouth. "This." Then he was kissing her again, and his hand was stroking up her rib cage.

No teasing this time. He was right there. He didn't grab, but he wasn't quite gentle, either. He was stroking her, holding her, finally flicking his thumb over the sensitive point, then holding it between two fingers, the same way he had before, squeezing and releasing hard in time with his tongue.

Her knees were shaking, and she was going under, the dark waves rising, dragging her down.

"I don't—" she gasped. "I don't—"

"What?" It was low. Fierce. Not one bit patient.

His hands were so strong, but when she unwound her arm from around his neck, he let her go. She took a shaky step forward and pressed her forehead against the cool glass of the window. "Why can't you kiss like a normal guy?" she asked plaintively into the cold surface.

"What?" he said.

She turned at last to find him staring at her. And in case she hadn't noticed enough the other day, she was all clear now. If size mattered, he was all good. "You just…" She shook her head, trying to clear it. "I mean, you're this gentleman, so careful, and then you're… not. It's like you're turned up about ten degrees hotter than a normal person. And you go straight from simmer to burn. You just… light me up."

"Ah." He sank down onto the bed, clutched the edge with

both hands, dropped his head, and heaved in a breath. "Well, yeh. Hopefully. But that's another no, then."

"My fault. It's just that you… make me burn so hard, too."

"No," he said, standing up. "Mine. I grabbed you. I'll go on downstairs, then."

"It's that same thing as before."

"Yeh. I got it." He'd grabbed a pillow and duvet from a closet and was out the door. Not waiting to have the conversation, and she couldn't blame him. They'd said it all before.

She was being smart, or she was being stupid. One or the other.

$$\heartsuit\heartsuit\heartsuit$$

She'd walked ten kilometers that day, had done yoga, and had swum twice. Her body was fully worked out, languid with fatigue. And still, she burned.

There was a cure for that, and she took it. Just as Iain had, she was sure. He'd be aching at least as much as she was, burning just as hot as she was. She closed her eyes, remembered him hauling her back against her, his lips at her ear, and she gasped into the darkness, jerked against the softness of his bed… and barely scratched the surface. But at least she slept. Eventually.

She woke to the rattle of palms, the sigh of the wind, the hiss and roar of the sea. Louder again, or just louder up here, she wasn't sure. And she was wide awake.

She rolled out of bed, finally, went to the window, and looked out. The palms waved, and the moon shone, lighting a path across the water, inviting her to step across, to escape into another world.

But she'd already done that. She'd escaped across the water. Tomorrow—today—she'd start a new chapter. *Her* chapter. She didn't need to walk anywhere. She was already there.

She'd had a wedding day that wasn't, because she'd made a choice. On that day, she'd kissed Iain for the first time. Today, she wasn't pretending to be married. She'd made a choice about that, too. She'd found her own way out.

What was she so afraid of, then? The life ahead was a series of risks, but the life she'd left behind had been just as risky. She'd risked the most important thing of all before. She'd risked herself, risked being erased. How much worse could it be to risk choosing wrong?

the lucky one
♡

It happened in an instant.

One moment, Iain had been asleep. The next, his eyes had flown open. He was disoriented for an instant at the white glow overhead, the shifting, sighing mass of palms, the pinpricks that were the stars. He sat up, and he was moving. Swaying.

Hammock.

He was tumbling out of it on the thought, then onto his feet, as fast as jumping up from a tackle and sprinting off again. Across the lawn, his lizard brain telling him that that was what had woken him. A shadow in the darkness, moving toward him. No, moving toward the hammock. Toward where Nina would be.

He was there, intent on driving his shoulder into the figure's hips, on taking him down. And there was another instantaneous, shocked recognition.

No.

He caught himself at the last moment and was twisting, falling onto one shoulder, and then his momentum was carrying both their bodies around. Nina was under him, letting out a startled, "*Oof!*" as she hit the turf and the air left her lungs.

"No." He was on an elbow, patting her down. "Nina. I'm sorry. All right?"

Her eyes were wide, her breath coming in panting gasps. "Are you all right?" he demanded again. "I thought you were—"

She laughed. *Laughed,* and he didn't know what to feel. Relief. Fury. "So does that mean you're saying no?" she asked.

Wait. She was *here.* And she was under him, like that was where she wanted to be. She was here. "No," he managed to say. "I'm not saying no."

That was all, and then he was kissing her. One hand had fisted in her hair, and she was gasping, opening up, letting him in. Grabbing his arms, running her hands over them like she wanted to feel them. Like she wanted him as much as he wanted her.

When she was pliant, moaning into his mouth, he changed it up. He was dragging his mouth over her cheek, his thumb tracing her jawline, finding the spots that made her shiver, until his mouth had to find them, too.

He feasted on her neck, her shoulders, then her mouth again, and she was pulling him closer, pulling him into her. He had an earlobe in his teeth now, was nipping, and she was shuddering. His hand was under that tiny ribbed singlet, pulling it up, then higher. And she was gasping again.

"Oh," she said. "Cold."

"*Shit.* Grass." He was rolling to one side, grabbing her hand and pulling her to her feet, going for the hammock and the duvet and spreading it onto the grass. Then he pulled her down with him, down to her knees, got hold of her shoulders, and was pushing her down onto her back, coming down over her.

"Now," he said, and he had the singlet up her body, was pulling it over her head, up her arms. He stroked a hand over the silk of her arm, then, was running it up and down, feeling her shiver. "Now," he said again. "Everything."

♡♡♡

Somehow, she was on her back, and Iain had rolled onto one elbow, his other hand stroking over her upper arm. He was kissing her there, his lips tracing the delicate skin of her inner arm. Sucking at her skin. Waking her up. *Lighting* her up.

"Iain," she gasped. "Oh…"

Not her most articulate moment, and it didn't matter. His teeth were grazing over her shoulder, then his mouth was at her neck again, biting, sucking, and she turned her head to one side and let him eat her. His hand was still gripping her upper arm, holding her down by it, but her other arm was around his back, then tugging at his T-shirt.

"Take it off," she said. "I want to feel you too."

"Later," he said, and her hand fell back again. His lips had found the spot below her collarbone, then were tracking down and along the tops of her breasts, seeking out erogenous zones she hadn't known she possessed. His other hand was stroking over her belly, higher and higher, and she sucked in a breath.

The second his hand found her breast, his mouth was at the other one. He was squeezing one achingly stimulated nipple, sucking at the other, and she cried out sharply, her hips bucking involuntarily, then clapped a hand over her mouth at the sound.

He was greedy. Possessive. So thorough. And when she was twisting, biting her own hand to stifle her cries, his hand moved again. Down to her hips, tracing the waistband of her bikinis, his fingers setting her quivering again.

"We have to go… inside," she managed to say. "No condoms out here." *Points for safety consciousness,* she thought dimly.

"Oh, no." Nothing but dark amusement in that deep voice. "We've got so much to do first." And then he was moving down her body taking hold of her underwear, dragging it down her legs, right off her. Coming over her again, a hand stroking up each calf, then each thigh, pushing them remorselessly apart.

"Oh," she said, and tried to close them, as if that would be possible, when he was holding them open. "I should... take a bath. No."

"Yes," he said. "Oh, yeh. Yes." One hand was spreading her, opening her, and the other was circling, exploring. "Ah," he sighed. "So wet. So good." He was painting her, spreading the slickness, and then one finger was pushing inside her, breaching the barrier, probing, insisting, and she was letting out another cry.

"Feel good?" He still had her spread open with the other hand, not letting her be shy. "So beautiful," he told her. "I'm going to eat this up."

"Oh, God." She was moaning, because he'd sent a second finger to join the first, was thrusting. And then he put his mouth to her, and the suction... She was going up like a firecracker, streaking into the sky. She stuffed her fist into her mouth as he worked her over with lips and tongue, as those hard fingers continued to move. On and on, as if he wanted to do nothing else. Then he shifted, found the perfect spot, and she was trying not to cry out, was biting down on her hand to keep herself quiet.

He lifted his mouth from her, his fingers stopped moving, and her hips bucked. "No," she said desperately. "No. Don't stop."

"I can't hear you." His hand had gone to her wrist, was dragging her hand from her mouth. "I need to hear you."

"I... can't. I'm too loud," she pleaded. "Somebody will hear. No."

"Yes," he said. "Yes. I need to hear you. Come on, Nina. Do it. Scream for me." Then he was back again. Dragging his face with its rasp of stubble across her tender flesh, making her squirm. His fingers inside her again, finding the spot, pressing hard. And that mouth. That *mouth*. She couldn't help it. She was crying out.

"Yes," he growled against her. "Show me how it feels. Tell me."

"Oh… no." She was moving against his mouth, his hand. "Oh, please. Help me. Help… me."

She came undone. Her back was arching right off the ground, the waves cresting and breaking, slamming through her, relentless. Like they would never stop. Like this was all there was. And he was there, drinking them in, taking her over. Taking her all the way.

♡♡♡

Iain had thought, when he'd seen her properly for the first time, that she'd been carved from ivory. Carved so perfectly. Now, she was lying under him, her legs spread, her hands flung out on either side, with her gorgeous eyes shut and her mouth open, taking in great gasps of the night air. And he wanted to be inside all that warmth. No, he *needed* to be.

He rose over her, took her mouth in a dark, deep kiss, and knew she was tasting herself. Salty as the sea, but so much warmer. So much hotter.

"Inside," he said, when he'd finally dragged his mouth from hers.

Her eyes fluttered open, and she smiled. Glorious. Huge. "Inside what?" she asked. "Inside the house, or inside me?"

"Both," he said. "Absolutely. Both."

"No," she said, and his head jerked back. Then she was sitting up in one smooth movement, both hands slamming against his chest, pushing him back. She got a leg over him, was rolling him over, and his back hit the ground.

"My turn," she said.

"No," he said. "I can't hold out much longer. I need it now." And if that was begging, color him weak.

"You don't have to hold out." She was purring the words, and she had his T-shirt in both hands, was yanking it up over his chest. "Get this off. It's your turn to take it hard."

"Uh…" He was having some trouble with his breathing. His shirt was gone, and she had his head in both hands, was lowering her mouth over his. Her tongue was there, licking into him, exploring, and he was just about too far gone.

"Two can play this game," she whispered against his mouth. And then her lips were at his ear, she was licking around its edges, and he shivered.

After that, she made him burn. Her hands, her mouth were everywhere. Stroking over his shoulders, his chest, exploring him. Licking over a nipple, taking it between her little teeth, then sucking hard for just an instant, so he jerked against her. Her hands moving down his body, firm touches that lit him up, until she was straddling him, a slim, sculpted ivory goddess, pale in the moonlight, bending over him to kiss his mouth again, then licking, kissing, biting her way down his body, pulling his shorts and briefs down his legs without one bit of hesitation. He finally had enough presence of mind to capture her breasts, at least, and it was worth it. His hands were big, but they had enough to fill them, and every bit of it was warm, and firm, and soft, and bloody fantastic.

He lost her then, though. She was sliding down farther, her hands stroking over his thighs, the rasp of hair providing delicious friction.

She didn't touch him, not at first. She kissed him instead, her lips moving over him, nibbling, and he was leaping into her. And then, at last, she was holding him. Exploring, caressing, as if it was all she wanted to do. As if she were willing to spend the night there.

"I can't... I need to go inside," he tried once more.

"You telling me you can only do it once?" She licked him, slow and thorough and not one bit shy, and he groaned. "Or that you don't want to come in my mouth? I don't believe either thing."

"Ah..." he managed. "More than... once. Nina. Please."

"Mm," she said. "Let's call this your warmup, then, shall we?"

He might have answered that, except he couldn't. He could barely breathe. She was taking him in, her hand and her mouth working hard, and he was dying.

She went on, and on, and the top of his head was about to blow off. His hips wanted to move, and he was trying to still them, trying to hold back.

She stopped, and he groaned. "No. Please. Go. Please."

"I'm going to tell you something." She'd pulled herself up, had him nestled between her breasts, was moving there, fondling him, and it was one of the best spots ever. Like the anteroom to Heaven.

And that was before she said it.

"I don't have a strong gag reflex," she told him. "And I need you to be the taste in my mouth. Please, Iain. Hold my head. Hold me hard and give me everything. Make it yours."

He was going to die. Her mouth was back again, and he had his hands wrapped around her head, was thrusting into her, trying desperately all the same not to be too much, but he was losing every battle at self-control. He was swearing softly, dark and dirty, words he'd never said to a woman.

And then she took him so deep, sucked hard, and he lost his words. He lost his mind. He lost it all. He was plummeting into darkness, spinning around and around, down and down. All the way.

♡♡♡

He hadn't actually blacked out, he realized dimly some number of minutes later, when she was lying on top of him, kissing his mouth again, her sweet body molded to his own. "So you liked that, huh?" she asked softly against his lips.

"What day is it?" he groaned. "Think I lost about a decade there."

She laughed softly and stroked a languid hand over his shoulder. "Bet I surprised you, too."

"You could say that."

"Mm." He had a hand around one firm, rounded cheek, was squeezing her there, and she rubbed her face over the sandpaper of his jaw like a kitten, squirmed against him, and said, "So does this mean we're all done? You all worn out?"

He, gripped that delicious roundness more tightly and said, "Have I mentioned that I'm a conditioned sportsman?"

"You telling me it's my lucky night?"

"Let's go inside," he said. "Get you in the shower, and we'll see who's lucky. I have a feeling it's still going to be me."

an unexpected turn

♡

There was only one tiny snag.

She'd started to search for her underwear and tank, but Iain wasn't having any. He had her by the hand and was pulling her toward the house.

"Iain." She was laughing, even as she tried to keep her voice down. "We can't leave our clothes scattered all over the lawn. What will your parents think in the morning?"

"That I finally got luckier than any man deserves. Come on." When she still hung back, he sighed and said, "I'll come out and get them myself, how's that? But in about five more seconds, I'm tossing you over my shoulder. Fair warning."

"Gosh, you're masterful." She was still laughing. She shouldn't be, because he was so damn sexy. But she was laughing anyway.

"Putting me right off my stride, aren't you." He was at the door now, yanking at the knob. And bouncing straight back again.

"Shit," he said. "You didn't happen to bring a key, did you?"

"Of course. It's right here in my pocket. Oh, wait. I'm naked. What? It's *locked?* It's never locked!"

"Course it's locked." He was standing back, his hands on

281

his hips, not even seeming to notice that he was naked, too. "The cottage is locked as well. I just punched the knobs. I'm not even sure where the deadbolt keys are. But I didn't want to risk that fella coming back and my not hearing him. Needed some warning, at least. Didn't you notice the knob when you came out?"

"Shh! Keep your voice down," she whispered. "Your dad's going to hear you. And of course I didn't notice. I was a little preoccupied." She was fighting the urge to giggle, and losing. "If you locked the doors, you must have had a plan to get back in. Tell me you did."

"Oh. Key." He was back across the dark lawn, and she was groping her way toward him. The moon was behind a cloud, and the wind had risen even more, rattling the palms, chilling her.

"Iain," she called out softly. "Where are you?"

He was back in an instant, reaching for her hand, and she said, "You dope. You weren't supposed to *leave* me."

He was the one laughing now, holding her hand and feeling his way across the patio and lawn to the hammock. "Sorry. Here we are. But I can't find it. It was in the pillowcase, but it must've fallen somehow when I grabbed the duvet. Help me look."

He was picking up the white duvet, shaking it out and tossing it back into the hammock, and she was on her hands and knees, shivering at the cold touch of the grass, patting her way around in a circle while Iain crouched under the hammock, doing the same.

She jumped at the sound of a curse. "Did you find it?" she asked.

"No. Banged my head on the tree. Ouch."

She was laughing for real now, still patting the grass with no idea of where she'd searched before.

"This is without a doubt," he said, "my least smooth moment ever. Just saying."

"James Bond, you're not," she agreed.

He burst out laughing himself at that. "Not so much. Shit.

I am not finding this key."

"We're going to have to…" She'd given up, was sitting on her heels, succumbing to a fit of helpless giggles. ". . . wake up your mom. I think we *are* sixteen. This is a total adolescent moment."

That was when they saw the beam of light and heard the sharp, "Who's there?"

"Annnnd it just got worse," Iain muttered. "Here." He picked up the duvet and threw it over Nina. It landed, of course, a half-second after the light had settled on her.

The flash took a hard jerk upward, exactly as if the owner had averted his eyes, and Graeme said, "Nina? You all right? Who's with you?"

"It's me, Dad," Iain said, sounding utterly resigned, while Nina clutched the duvet around her and slapped a hand over her mouth. Iain was standing, now, an arm across his face to shield it from the light. "We've had a wee mishap here. Hand me that torch, will you? It's in my eyes."

"Oh." The light advanced across the yard, and then Iain was taking the heavy flashlight and pointing it at the ground near his father's feet, and Nina could see Graeme. Standing barefoot in only a pair of shorts, his body nearly as broad and strong as his son's. And with a mighty frown on his face. "Sorry," Graeme said. "I heard the door, and then voices. Thought that fella had come back. I rushed out without thinking. Didn't mean to…"

"We were just… uh, talking," Nina said. Except, whoops, they were naked. "And I was about to go back upstairs, but I didn't have the key, and Iain was looking for his, but…"

Another spot of light, another male voice. "I've already rung the police. Get the hell out of here."

"Hi, Granddad," Iain said with a sigh. "I hope that's not true. It's just me."

"What are you doing, sleeping starkers in the garden?" his grandfather demanded. The light bounced erratically off Iain's nude figure as Arthur limped forward. "What about Nina? What about your mum?"

"I'm here," Nina said weakly. She thought about saying the "talking" thing again, but it seemed fairly pointless.

"Oh." The light came to rest, still on Iain, then Arthur seemed to realize what he was doing and pointed it toward the ground. "Anybody ever tell you that women like privacy?"

"I'm not the one barging in," Iain said in exasperation.

"That's gratitude," Graeme said. "Who lost his key?"

Iain's light had been sweeping over the ground, illuminating his shorts and T-shirt, which he'd collected. Now, horrifyingly, it fell on a yellow happy face, smiling out from the crotch of a pair of bikini underwear before Iain's hand closed over it and crumpled it.

The sound of a throat clearing in the darkness, and Graeme said, "Door's open now, anyway. I'm going to bed."

Arthur's own flash was lighting the way to the cottage, jerking unevenly over the ground, and he was muttering, "Can't believe it. My own grandson."

"Oh, dear." Nina had her hand over her mouth again. "What does that mean?"

Iain was beside her, pressing something into her hand. Her tank and underwear, she realized, and she was feeling for the leg holes, then saying, "Light me up, please."

He shone the light on her, and she was putting the happy face the right way up as he said, "That means, 'my own grandson, and that's the best he can do with a woman?' Can't say he's wrong, either."

She got the happy face back into its rightful spot, then got her tank turned around and pulled it on.

"Not that I don't love your undies," Iain said, lighting them up again. "Liked that face the first time I saw it, and I definitely approve now. Not saying that the sight of you putting them on isn't choice, either, because it is. But we're going in the wrong direction, aren't we? I already undressed you. Enjoyed the hell out of it, too. You were meant to stay that way."

"Yeah, right." The smile was trying to work its way out again. "I'm sure I'm going upstairs with you now, with your dad wide awake right underneath us."

"He's probably asleep again already. Sleeps like a rock."

Now, she *did* laugh. "You are a big, dirty liar." She handed him the duvet. "And you know what you've got?"

"Not you, I'm guessing."

She was still smiling when she stepped forward, put her hands around his head, and pulled it down for a kiss, and he was wrapping the duvet around her, pulling her in by it, holding her against his Incredible Hulk body, and kissing her back. She could feel his smile, and smiling while you kissed, she discovered, was a purely sweet thing.

"You've got yourself a rain check," she promised when she'd lifted his face from hers again. She rubbed her cheek over his deliciously sandpapery one before she let go of him, though, just because she could do it. "Let's talk about your house. How much space is there between your bedroom and wherever your granddad will be?"

"Heaps of space. Oceans of space. All professionally soundproofed. Practically a recording studio in there."

"It is not."

He sighed. "No. But if that's what it takes, I'll get it done."

"Nope." She shoved the duvet back into his arms again. "It's not going to take that. Maybe I just want to be sure I can be loud enough for you, you think of that? In case you do something really good. You know. Something that'll make me scream." She ran a hand over his forearm, let it linger there for a moment, then let him go. "See you tomorrow."

Then she walked off and thought, *Ha. Look who isn't a good girl anymore. What are you going to do about* that, *Iain McCormick? You've got about twelve hours to figure it out.*

all the way home

♡

One second, she was walking away from Iain, savoring her moment. The next, he was in front of her.

"Wait, how..." she began.

"That the only reason?" he demanded.

All the laughter was gone from his voice, and hers wasn't entirely steady when she asked, "Wh-what?"

He moved a step closer, put a hand under her chin, and tipped it up. "Tell me," he demanded. "Is that the only reason? That you're afraid you'll be too loud? That you don't want to do it where my dad will hear? That you're embarrassed?"

"Uh... yes," she said. "But I meant it." *Your choice,* she reminded herself. *You only do it if you want to.* The trouble was, he was still holding her chin, was staring down at her, the hungry intensity clear to see on his barbarian's face, and that was all it took. She wanted to.

"Right," he said, then dropped his hand, and she fought the disappointment. The next instant, she was squeaking, because he'd dropped into a crouch, driven his shoulder into her hips, and was lifting her, one hand secure around the back of her thighs, the other flat on her bottom, and she was spreading her hands out instinctively to brace herself against

286

his back as she was upended over his broad shoulder.

"Wait," she'd started to say, but he was already striding across the yard to the hammock, grabbing the duvet, and heading down the track to the beach. He tossed the duvet down onto the narrow strip of sand at the edge of the grass and said, "High tide. Private beach. Waves. Noise."

She was still upside-down, her hands on his broad back, feeling the muscles shift as he moved, and his hand had gone under the elastic of her underwear, was running over her bottom, his touch so dangerously thrilling.

He said, "If you don't want this, tell me now," and just like that, she was shivering.

"Uh..." She couldn't think, and it wasn't because she was upside down. "Wait. Condom."

His hand stilled. "I had a medical three months ago. Haven't slept with anyone since. And don't tell me you haven't had one, too."

"Not on... birth control," she managed to say. "I was supposed to... have a baby."

"Oh." He was still standing there, and she was still upside-down. "Do you want a baby?"

It took her breath away. "I can't—" she began. "I think— we should use one. A condom."

"Right," he said. "Right."

He turned around and was heading up the track with her, still holding her tight.

"You can't..." she hissed as he strode across the yard again and through the back door.

"Shh," he said. "Dad'll hear." He was taking the stairs two at a time, running up them as if carrying her were nothing at all, then, dizzyingly, around the spiral staircase to his room, slapping the rocker switch on the wall and letting go of her with one hand. She heard a drawer opening and closing, and then he was standing again and headed out of the room.

"Iain," she gasped. "You're crazy."

He didn't answer. The blood was rushing to her head, and she had to hold on tight to keep from banging against his back as he ran down the stairs and across the lawn. Down the track to the beach, and he was sinking onto the duvet, spilling her gently onto it, then pulling it flat around her.

The night was full of the crash and roar of the waves, the rattle of the palms. The clouds shifted in the black night overhead, the canopy of stars glittering in their gaps.

And Iain on his knees beside her.

She couldn't look away. *He's proportional, that's all,* she tried to tell herself. Not like she didn't know it. She'd had him in her hands, in her mouth. She knew exactly how big he was.

It didn't help. She was trembling with more than the night air now. With need, and with fear.

Not fear of Iain. Fear of disappointing him.

One hand brushed over her cheek, gentle now. "Hey," he said softly. "This all right?"

"Oh," she said, trying for some kind of mastery of the situation, "now you're asking me?"

"Yeh." The back of his hand was caressing her face, moving over her throat, her shoulder, down her arm, gentle as a kiss. "I'm asking you. If you don't want it, we'll stop."

What would happen after this would happen. "I want it." It was barely more than a whisper. "I do."

"Then I'm going to love you."

He had a hand under her tank, was pulling it up for the second time that night, and she arched her back and let him lift her and yank it off. He was straddling her, his hands on her upper arms again, holding them over her head. Her hands were in the sand, her arms on the cool cotton, and she wasn't cold anymore.

"Beautiful," he said. "And mine." He moved down her body, lowered himself over her, and took her mouth in a hot, sweet kiss. His hands were still on her arms, holding her gently, but firmly, too, his thumbs stroking over her tender flesh, his mouth exploring, probing, as if it were the first time. As if he couldn't get enough, and she was helpless under those hands, that mouth.

His hands slid over her, up and down, awakening every

one of her senses. Her head was full of the sound of the waves, the smell of the salt sea, the taste of Iain. When he lifted his head, she whimpered to lose him.

"Oh, yeh," he breathed. "That's my girl." Then he was rolling off her, pulling her underwear down her legs, getting rid of it, sliding a slow hand back up her calf, her thigh, separating it from its neighbor.

"This," he said, sliding down again, brushing his cheek, rough with beard, over her breasts. "I remember this."

As he sucked an aching, hardened peak into his mouth, his hand found her, was delving, swirling and exploring, and she was arching right off the duvet.

He had those fingers inside her again, was stretching her, spreading her. His mouth was at her neck now, kissing her there, speaking low into her ear.

"Think you liked me carrying you," he said. "Think you want this now."

"Oh." She was having trouble talking. Her hips were moving, as if she had no control over them. She dragged a hand down, got it in his hair. "Please."

"Please, eh." A third finger, now. "You sure?"

"Iain. Stop teasing. Come on."

He took his hand away, and she wanted him back. He was ripping the condom packet open, and she sat up herself and ran a hand over his side.

"That all for me?" she asked.

"Nobody but you," he said. "But you're meant to be lying down for it. What did I say?"

He had hold of her under the arms now, was lowering her onto her back, and she said, "That you wanted me on my back."

"I've wanted you like this for so long," he said. "And now I get it." His hand was stroking again, and then he was guiding himself inside.

He met resistance at first. She'd tensed up despite herself, and she was drawing her breath in hard. He was on his elbows, threading his fingers through hers, raising her hands high, next to her head, and that was even better. Her back was arching right off the sand. The stretch of him, the heat of it... It was almost a burn.

And then he started to move, and it *was* a burn. The good kind. The best kind.

He took it slowly at first. Smooth and even, and she'd never been filled so completely, or so well. She was panting, and the waves were pounding, the sound filling her ears as Iain filled her body. Over and over, taking his time, until it wasn't enough anymore. Until she needed more.

He still had her hands, and her legs were wrapping around his waist, trying to pull him in. Her head was thrashing from side to side, and she moaned, "Please. Please."

"Please what?"

She was trying to get closer. Trying to get more. And then he pulled out of her, and she cried out.

He rolled fast, onto his back, and was pulling her over his body, taking her hips, lowering her onto him, making her cry out again. She was on top, but he was shoving her down, then pulling her up again, driving the pace and the rhythm.

His face was urgent, straining in the moonlight. "Touch yourself," he said.

"Wh-what?" she gasped.

"You need more, and I need to watch. Do it now."

Oh, God. She put her hands on her breasts, was stroking, circling, and she could feel what it did to him.

"Yeah," he said. "Keep playing with them. Show me what you do."

He still had hold of her, was driving hard into her, and she was gasping with the force of it. She kept one hand on her breast, ran the other one down her body, and then she was doing it. Touching herself in a way she'd never dared to in front of a man, showing him how she did it. And she could tell that all it was doing was turning him on.

Iain wasn't doing all the moving anymore. She was going with him. She'd been shy at first, afraid to move in case it was wrong, in case it was awkward. Now, though, the sensation was taking her over, and she had to get him in the right place. She had to feel him.

"That's right," he said, his voice ragged, his hands gripping her hips hard. "Show me that. Arch that pretty back, Nina. Touch yourself. Ride me. Come on, baby. Do it now."

One of her hands had gone to the ground, and she was rocking on him, taking over the rhythm, timing her strokes to her frantically moving hand, letting out little mews of excitement, going higher and higher, winding tighter and tighter. He was watching, and she didn't care. She was almost there. Almost.

He *was* watching her, though, and she couldn't quite get there. So close, but drawn back from the edge every time, and she was panting with frustration, with need.

"I can't..." she said. "I can't..."

He lifted her straight off of him, and she cried out. "No," she begged. "Don't stop. Don't... It's all right. Keep going."

He had her on her back again, and this time, he had an ankle in each hand, was lifting them straight over her head, and she was squirming and saying, "Iain. No."

"Does it hurt?" he asked.

"No, but..."

"Do you trust me?" he demanded.

"Yes," she gasped. "Yes."

He was over her again, settling her legs over his shoulders. "We're going to do this harder," he said. "We're going to do it deeper. So get ready."

When he plunged into her, she screamed. The angle... the friction...

"Yeh," he said. "That's it. That's right." He was on his palms, and the position had lifted her hips straight off the ground. Then he plunged again, and again, and he was hitting that spot again, the one he'd found with his fingers. Deeper than she'd ever felt a man, harder than it had ever been. The waves were roaring in her head. It was the sea, and it was Iain. Faster and harder, more and more, every stroke hitting her just right, then sliding back along aching, stimulated nerve endings. Nothing but feeling. Nothing but being filled more completely, being touched more deeply than she'd ever been.

"Long as... it takes," he said. "Hard as . . . you need it. Forever."

It was like he'd turned the key, had unlocked the door, and there was no more frustration. No more effort. Her hands were clutching the small of his back, then rubbing over it, and he groaned.

"Oh, yeh," he said. "Do that. Touch me there."

Her fingers began to drum at the sensitive base of his tailbone, and she felt the change in him. He seemed to get even bigger inside her, and he was swearing.

"Fuck, Nina," he gasped. "Do that. Oh, yeh."

His excitement fueled hers, and she was over. She was going. Her fingers spasmed against his skin, even as her body began to spasm around him. She was crying out with every hard stroke, and he was groaning, swearing.

The waves, the wind, the darkness. She was going. Going. Gone.

♡♡♡

He barely had enough self-control left to lift her legs over his shoulders and pull out of her, then to dig a hasty hole in the sand with shaking fingers and dispose of the condom. A bad citizen, and he'd do better tomorrow. But now, he was rolling over Nina again, kissing her sweet, panting mouth.

"All right?" he asked.

She nodded, and he could feel her swallow. He said, "Nina. Sweetheart. What's wrong?"

She opened her eyes, and he could see the tears in the corners of them. "I'm sorry," she said. "I took too long, I know. I made it too hard for you. I just... I got nervous."

"Aw, baby." He laughed, and it wasn't the steadiest it had ever been. "Did it feel bad?"

"No. It was amazing. You were amazing."

"Know how it felt to me?"

She dropped her gaze. "No."

"Felt awesome, that was how. To know it wasn't easy, but that I got you there. And that thing you did with your fingers? That was the best."

"You liked that?"

He smiled at her, the tenderness almost overwhelming him. "Couldn't you tell? I liked it. I liked all of that. We're learning each other, that's all. And can I ask you a question?"

"Sure," she said, but she didn't look sure at all.

He smoothed a hand over her cheek, kissed her forehead. He wanted to wrap her up. He wanted to hold her forever. "Do you usually come with a man?" he asked her gently.

She closed her eyes and swallowed again, and he said, "You can tell me. You can say."

"No," she said. "I... I haven't. Not during intercourse, and usually not at all. I fake it. Because I... can't. That's one reason why I said no. I didn't want you to find out and be disappointed. I wanted you to think I was sexy."

He was so touched, and at the same time, so ridiculously proud. "That wasn't fake, though. I felt it."

She laughed that sweet, husky little laugh, and just like always, it killed him. "No. That was real. That was... wow. That was what they talk about."

"Do you know how good that feels to me?" he asked her. "To know I could get you there, make you forget yourself enough to let it happen? Not every woman's the same. For a man, it's easy. If you stimulate him enough, he's going to come. For a woman, though, it's trickier. So we're going to have one rule. You ready for it?"

"Yes." He could feel her trembling, and he *did* wrap her up in him then, trying to tell her with his arms whatever she couldn't hear him say.

"Right, then," he said. "No faking. I have to know what works, or we can't get you there. We find out what works for you, and we do that."

"I think you know." She was smiling now, the tiniest thing.

"I know one way. And you could say I enjoyed it. And next time?" He dropped another kiss on her sweet mouth. "We go back to school and learn some more. And I can promise that I'll enjoy every bit of that, too. If it takes longer? That's nothing but good. You know one thing I know about sex?"

"No, what?" She was relaxing now, snuggling against him, pressing a kiss to his collarbone, and bloody hell, but he was so deep in. So far gone.

He kissed her forehead again and told her. "Longer's better."

getting out
♡

He did sleep with her, in the end. They climbed the stairs together, Graeme or no Graeme, took a long, sweet shower, soaping each other up and washing each other down, all sighs and murmurs and long, slow touches. Both of them sleepy now, warm and sated. And then he went upstairs with her, crawled into his bed, and discovered what it felt like to fall asleep with his arms around her and her head on his chest.

He woke the next morning to the sound of her moving softly around the room.

"Hey." He hauled himself up in bed to find her pulling a T-shirt over her head. Unfortunately, she had a bra and shorts on already.

"I'm going back over to the cottage," she said.

He put a hand out for her. "How about coming over here a second?"

She hesitated, then came and sat beside him.

"Embarrassed?" he asked.

She shrugged and looked away. "No. Fine."

"You're rubbish at lying."

This time, she smiled and actually looked at him. "All right. A little embarrassed."

He rubbed a hand up and down her forearm. "Nah. All

good. I woke up a hell of a lot happier than when I went to sleep last night. And if you want to spend the two minutes I'll be in the bathroom getting yourself naked again and climbing back into bed, we can do a bit more of that research. I've got a few ideas."

Her shoulders had lost some of their tension, at least. "Too much to do," she said. "We're leaving at nine, and I'm betting that 'research' could take a while. Plus, I can hear your dad down there."

He sighed. "You're probably right. Never mind. Got that soundproofed room at home and all. Go on, then. You're not going to have sex with me? Then get out."

She was laughing now, and she leaned over and gave him a soft kiss on the cheek. "See you at nine."

He cooked breakfast for his dad, got a quick run, a shower, and his own breakfast, packed up his kit, and headed over there. Nina must have heard him, because she came into the kitchen with duffel in her hand.

He'd have recognized her, of course, but he wasn't sure many other people would have. She was wearing the oversized track pants again, along with the ugly hat he hadn't seen since he'd replaced it, the specs, and a navy-blue T-shirt that must have been his grandfather's.

"Well, that's horrible," he said.

She smiled. "Want to see what else?" She set down the bag and pulled up the T-shirt, and he glanced hastily into the lounge to make sure his grandfather wasn't coming in. And then he was looking properly and saying, "What the hell?"

"Elastic bandage," she said, dropping the shirt again. "I figured, disguising my face is all good, but you know, men don't always look at my face. Shocking, but there you are."

He had to acknowledge the truth of that. "That can't feel good, though."

"Nope. If you want to know the real reason I fainted that day—you try wearing this thing for about forty hours. Well, in an equally sensitive area, let's say."

"I won't, how's that. Like to have kids, wouldn't I." He'd

said it without thinking, but her eyes widened for just a moment, and he got a jolt. Of recognition, or something too much like it.

"So is that it?" he asked, picking up her bag. *Moving on. No need to send the poor girl screaming for the hills.* "And I hope you're going to tell me that all that lot's going straight into the bin as soon as we reach my house. Rubbish collection is tomorrow. I'd like it to be gone beyond recall."

"If it were your choice," she said.

"Naturally. I'll just say that it's a good disguise."

"That's the point. I need to get to Auckland without anybody seeing me, and then I can relax a little. But I still won't wear makeup or get my hair back to its normal color until I do that press conference. Fair warning."

"Told you," he said, "I like every Nina there is. I'm starting to realize how brave this one is. That's something, eh."

"Oh." It was a sigh. "I wish you'd stop smooth-talking me like that. I might forget myself."

After that, he had to put her bag down and pull her up on her toes, didn't he? And then he had to kiss her breathless. No other choice.

"Thought you already did that," he murmured when he'd finally had—well, not enough. He'd never have enough. But as much as he could get right now. "Forget yourself, that is. Can I just say again—I enjoyed the hell out of it."

"Mm." She was rubbing her face into his chest again like the kitten she was, and wasn't.

"And by the way," he said, still holding her tight, because how could he let her go? "I've been meaning to ask you, but you keep distracting me. What was that about calling you by your name?"

"Oh." She sighed and rubbed against him some more. "Just that I like that you always seem to know who I am. That I feel like a person."

"Mm. But I think I slipped a bit there last night."

"You can slip. Once in a while. When you lose control."

She lifted her head enough that he could see her smile, and he was losing control right now.

His granddad walked into the kitchen. "Geez. We going, or what?"

"We're going." Iain set Nina away from him with reluctance. "I may kiss her in the car again, though. If you don't want to see, don't peek."

"Like hanging about with a couple of teenagers," Arthur grumbled. "Her disguise isn't going to be good for much if you're holding her like that. Save it for the house."

"I'm saving it, no worries," Iain said. Nina hit him in the arm, and he laughed. He didn't know how this was going to turn out, and he wished he did, but right this minute, it was about as good as it got. And she'd lost some of that tight, pinched look, too.

Carmella was going to drive the three of them to Nelson, but Graeme had come back from the office to say goodbye. He shook hands with Iain and Arthur, but he actually put a hand on Nina's shoulder and kissed her on the cheek, then said gruffly, "Come back when you can. Anytime." Which, from his dad, was nearly a declaration of love.

They drove to Nelson, Arthur in the front seat, and Iain beside Nina in the back. Holding her hand, because hers was cold, and he knew she was nervous.

"She'll be right," he told her.

"I know," she said. "I know. But thanks."

His mum parked near a Westpac branch, and Iain said, "I don't know which bank you'd prefer, but this is as good as any, probably."

"I don't care," she said. "Fine." Sounding distracted again, and he squeezed her hand.

"We'll go get a coffee," his mum said. "Dad and me. You go with Nina, Iain. Just in case."

"You my bodyguard?" Nina asked, getting a little of her sauciness back.

"Too right," he said. "He comes for you again—either of them? They'll have to go through me."

"You say that like you mean it."

"I don't say things I don't mean," he said, and she fell silent again. He let her walk ahead of him into the bank, and stayed close behind her, like the bodyguard he fully intended to be.

He stood near the door and waited for her during the twenty minutes that followed. He didn't look at his phone, or at anything else, either. He watched the street.

He wanted them to come. He wanted to get this over with. To get them gone, however he had to do it. To get Nina free. He was itching for the confrontation the same way you did while you waited to run out of the tunnel before a match. When you were bouncing on your toes. When you couldn't wait to make that first leap for the kickoff, to get in there at the breakdown and into battle, to take your man down in that first hard tackle. When you were waiting for it to get physical, so you could help drive your team forward. For the win.

That was why you played the game. For the win. And it was how he wanted to play this one. Except that it was Nina's win he needed this time, and that made it completely different.

He waited, and watched, and wished, and by the time Nina had finally finished? They hadn't come.

"One sec," she said when she'd joined him again. She was barely looking at him, and her shoulders were tense and tight, the way they'd been since before they'd left the cottage. She was stepping to the ATM and feeding in her new card, withdrawing a stack of bills. She handed him a stack of fifties. "For the ticket," she said.

"I'm happy to pay."

"Except it's not your choice. It's mine. And I'm paying." She was already stuffing the rest of the money into the plastic bag in her tote.

He sighed and put the bills into his wallet. "Item for your shopping list, then. Purse. Or I'll take this and buy you one, how's that?"

"You won't know what I like. Never mind, I'll do it when

we get to Auckland. I can afford a fair bit of shopping, since I don't have to pay your family for a new kayak. I hope you noticed how I kept hold of it that day. It wasn't easy, either."

She was trying to joke, so he smiled at her and said, "I noticed. You did well. And I hope you noticed that I came for you, too. If we see them, we'll both do well again, that's all. And we're all good."

She didn't say anything, and he wasn't sure if he should have said that, or if he should not have mentioned Matthias. While he was still trying to figure it out, they went in search of the others, then drove the fifteen minutes to the airport, Nina stiff and watchful beside him.

"He could have people watching the airport," she said as his mum was pulling to the curb. "My disguise isn't going to stand up to that. I'll wait in the ladies' room until the flight's called, all right?"

"Nah," Iain said. "Already done. Arranged it last night." He pulled out his mobile, texted a couple words, and told his mother, "Drive on farther. Around the building. I'll tell you where to stop." They pulled up to a side door around the back, and he said, "Here."

They climbed out, and Nina said a quick good-bye to his mum, looking as if she had a target on her back all the while. As soon as that was done, Iain was hustling them as fast as his grandfather could manage to a door marked 'No Entry,' which a uniformed agent was holding open. The man led them along a passage, ending up in a tiny conference room where he checked boarding passes, took their luggage, and left them.

"Is this the VIP treatment?" Nina asked.

"Such as it is," Iain said. "They'll get us on first. We'll put you in my seat, up in the front of the plane. Nobody's going to see you."

"What do you do with your bike?" she asked, sounding distracted.

"Got two," he said. "One down here. Easier."

"Oh. Nice."

He took her hand, and it was freezing. "No worries," he told her. She didn't need to talk about purses, or kayaks, or bikes. She needed to know this. "We're almost out."

♡♡♡

Relax, Nina told herself, and she couldn't do it. *Fifteen more minutes. When the plane's gone, you're out.*

She tried not to think about how she'd had that same talk with herself when she'd boarded the plane in Geneva, and then the one to Auckland. When she'd flown to Nelson. Every time, she'd been wrong. She didn't know why she should still feel so anxious, except that she still had the black-and-blue marks of Raoul's thumb and fingers on her forearm. Her wedding day had come and gone, and still, Matthias had come after her. Why?

Things always made sense. There was always a reason, unless the person was actually insane. Matthias wasn't insane, so this made sense, however twisted that sense was. He'd come because he'd felt like he had to see her face-to-face, even though she was gone and it was over.

To do what? That was the question she couldn't answer, or the answer she didn't want to know.

Kaiteriteri had been too small, and she'd been too easy to find there. But she'd opened a bank account in Nelson; a bank account that nobody would be able to trace, because nobody else knew the details. Her mother couldn't hand over the number, because she didn't know, and Nina wasn't going to be telling her. She was getting out. She had a plan.

Her thoughts whirled, going around in the same endless loop, and by the time they were walking across the tarmac by themselves to board the plane, she was rigid again. She would have run if Arthur hadn't been in front of her. But Iain was behind her, his bulk between her and the terminal building, and at one point, when Arthur was hesitating at the bottom of the airplane steps, shifting his cane into his left hand and grasping the rail with his right, Iain leaned over, put his hand on her shoulder, and said in her ear, "All good, baby. We're almost gone. And, yeh, I called you 'baby.' Can't help it, it seems."

"It's OK," she managed to say. "I don't mind." And then, finally, she was up the stairs and inside the door, welcomed by a smiling flight attendant. Safe.

Arthur found his seat halfway down the plane, and she was heading up to the front, looking for her seat. There it was, 6A, next to the window.

When she got there, though, Iain snatched her boarding pass from her hand and was wedging himself into her seat.

"You aren't sitting there," she said. "That's impossible. You're at the front."

"Nah," he said. "You'll feel better up there. It's uncomfortable, but it's not impossible."

"Your knees are up by your ears." He looked almost comical, in fact. The seat was tight for *her*. For six foot six inches and 250 pounds, it was seven clowns in a mini car.

"I told you," he said, "fitting's in the technique. You'd be surprised at the tight spots I can get into with a bit of preparation."

She stared at him. *"What?* I'm talking about airplane seats, and you're talking about…"

"What?" His expression was totally innocent. "I never go anywhere I'm not invited, no worries. Or at least 'welcome,' we'll call it."

"You have got an incredibly dirty mind." She wasn't sure if she was amused, appalled, or, worse, aroused. "We've done it one time."

She was whispering now, and as usual, he wasn't. "Why d'you think my mind's so dirty? Because we finally did it, that's why, and now you've got me thinking. I'm guessing you could have a bit of a dirty mind yourself, in what we'll call a hospitable environment. I can't wait to find out. But right now, you'd better go sit down." He nodded across the tarmac at a straggling crocodile of passengers. "Starting to come out, aren't they."

"No," she said, hauling on his arm. "Get up there, you idiot. Nobody's going to recognize me on the actual flight."

He sighed and stood, ducking under the low ceiling. "Fine. You aren't willing to let me be a gentleman? I'm taking note of that. For tonight, eh."

"You aren't a gentleman anyway. It's all an act. *Go.*"

He edged around her, grabbing a handful of her butt along the way and squeezing, and she jumped and slapped at him.

"Nice and tight right there," he murmured in her ear, then loped on up to the front and deposited himself in his rightful seat.

She sat down herself, pulled her hat lower, and wondered what that had been about. Whether he'd just been trying to distract her from her anxiety as she dashed across this last bit of open ground before the anonymity of Auckland, or whether he'd been serious.

She had a feeling that living with Iain, even for a week or two, was going to be very, very interesting, now that the barriers were down. And she wondered why she wasn't worried about that.

I never go anywhere I'm not invited.

That was why.

let freedom ring

♡

When they landed, Iain waited until everyone had exited the plane, because Nina was waiting. He'd stood up to check on her a couple times during the flight, had seen her with her face to the window, taking no chances, and he'd wished he was back there, or that she was up here with him. She was safe, he was sure of it, but she didn't feel that way, and it killed him. She'd forgotten about it while he'd been teasing her, but it had come straight back again, he knew.

Or maybe not. When she finally edged out of her seat and he went to join her, she told him, under her voice, "I'm warning you. Don't grab my butt again. Was that to distract me, or what?"

"Could be," he said with a grin he couldn't help. "Or maybe I wanted to. Anyway, you're here. I know it may not be your first choice, but I've got to tell you, it's mine. And I'm pretty rapt about it, myself."

He was thumbing his phone while they walked together with Arthur through the domestic terminal, and she said, "I didn't even think to ask how we're getting to your house."

"Mate of mine. Waiting at the mobile phone carpark now."

"Do I have time to pick up a phone myself?"

"Ah. Of course. Let freedom ring, eh."

"That's the idea. Nice cultural reference."

"We'll let Granddad wait for the bags, then, and I'll go with you." When she hesitated, he said, "Tell me that won't make you feel better, and I'll let you go alone."

"It'll make me feel better," she said reluctantly. "Just till we're out of here."

Twenty minutes later, they were standing on the pavement outside, watching a dark SUV pull up to the curb, and the big unit that was Iain's new skipper on the Blues, Hugh Latimer, getting out from behind the wheel and coming around the car, a white grin splitting his dark, bearded face. He and Iain exchanged a man-hug complete with thumps on the back like the brothers they were, and then Hugh held out a hand and said, "You must be Nina."

She shook his huge paw and said, "And you must be a rugby player."

"I try to be," he said. "Hugh Latimer. Not too dangerous on normal occasions, no worries." He was shaking Arthur's hand, then. "Good to see you again."

"You too. Congrats on the wedding and all," Arthur said. "How's that Josie of yours? Nice girl."

"All good," Hugh said. "Got her to marry me, at least, even without this fella along to show her how much worse it could've been. It's all in the comparison, eh."

While he'd been talking, Iain had thrown the bags in the back and was opening the door for Nina. "Let's get out of here," he told Hugh. "Nina can't afford to hang about."

Hugh raised his eyebrows, but didn't comment, just waited for Arthur to climb into the front seat, while Iain and Nina got in the back. And once again, Nina was being driven off to yet another new house, in a new place, and that had to be rough. But at least this time, she didn't need to keep the disguise on. She was removing the hat and glasses before Hugh had even pulled away from the curb.

Iain took them from her. "Got a rubbish bag in here, mate?" he asked Hugh.

Hugh glanced in the rearview mirror. "Course." He asked Arthur, "Pass it back there, would you?"

When it came, Iain was stuffing the hat and glasses into it. He told Nina, "Get that other thing off, too, if you like. Declaration of independence. You won't look, eh, Hugh."

"Depends," Hugh said agreeably. He was on the motorway now. "What am I meant to not look at? I'm a married man, if that helps."

"No." Nina was laughing. "No. No way."

"Right," Iain said. "Worth a try, anyway. That's hard to look at."

"Then stop looking," she said.

"Not possible."

"Josie's going to be sorry she wasn't here," Hugh said. "She's going to ask about it, and I'm going to have missed all the, what d'you call it. Nuance. She's rehearsing today, or she'd have come along."

"Actress," Iain explained. "She'd be curious because they were both at my wedding. Hugh was meant to be my best man. He's wondering why I'm here with you, when the last time he saw me with a woman, it ended with him dragging me into the house and hauling me onto my bed, because I was too pissed to walk. Could even have been crying, though I don't exactly remember."

"Mate," Hugh said, sounding pained. "I thought *I* was clueless. Don't tell her that."

"She already knows," Iain said. "All over now anyway. Clearing the air's better. Now everybody knows, and nobody has to be careful."

"Forwards," Arthur said with a shake of his head, and Hugh laughed, the sound rich and full in the confined space of the car. A satisfied man, and you didn't need any awareness of nuance to see it.

"Granddad's suggesting that backs would be more subtle," Iain explained to Nina. "He played in the backline, once upon a time. He could be a wee bit prejudiced."

"I'm going to pretend I understand that," Nina said.

"Rugby," Hugh said. "If you don't understand it, it's always rugby. So I tell Josie you're all good, is that it?" he asked the mirror again. "Since we're putting it out there?"

"Yeh," Iain said. "I'm all good."

He wasn't, maybe. Could be Hugh was going to be pouring him into bed again one of these days. But he didn't seem to have much choice.

♡♡♡

Nina had been interested; of course she had. Interested in the gorgeous views of Waitemata Harbour from the bridge, in the sailboats tacking in the distance, bright spinnakers bellying out in the fresh breeze. Interested, once Hugh had pulled out of slow-moving traffic on a main road lined with shops and restaurants, in the big, comfortable houses both old and new on either side of the road. The North Shore, Hugh explained. Finally, he was turning uphill onto a quiet residential street, the verge grassy and lush, the trees old and stately, and then into a long driveway, past one house and stopping in front of another that was tucked behind it. The house, apparently, faced the opposite direction, where she could see nothing but more trees and greenery.

"Told you it was private," Iain said when he'd shaken Hugh's hand again and the other man had reversed and driven away with a last wave out the window.

"What's on the other side?" she asked.

"A reserve. Not a big one, but there's a stream at the base there, separating me from the public track. Peaceful, eh. And a golf course on the other side of the road," he added practically. "Half price Mondays, which comes in handy."

"Oh, dear," she said. "I've gone and hooked myself up with a golfer."

He laughed in surprise. "Don't say 'hooked up.' Granddad's going to get the wrong idea. And, yeh, you have. One thing you'll find out about sportsmen—they're always doing a sport."

"I'm nervous," she admitted. "Can you tell?"

"Aw, Nina." He put down the bags he'd been juggling, handed the house key to Arthur, and said, "Give us a sec, eh, Granddad. You remember the alarm code?"

"Not senile, am I." Arthur opened the door and went inside, and Iain turned to Nina and took her in his arms.

"You're all good," he said. "You're here. Safe."

She let the size of him comfort her, as always, and said, "Could you kiss me, do you think?"

But when he went to do it, she winced. "Sorry. Bandage."

"Right," he said, letting her go. "Let's get that off you, then. I feel like I should be carrying you over the threshold or something, but we'll go inside instead, then take a walk, and I'll show you around. That may do better."

"It's a nice house," she said lamely, when they were inside. In truth, it was pleasant enough, but a little stark. A little underfurnished. The walls were white, and there wasn't enough on them. The view was beautiful, though. That was the best part. Down a hill, over a densely wooded little park, then a golf course, it was all blue sky, green trees, and lawns. Not a golf cart to be seen, just a few people in the distance, walking the course, pulling their bags behind them. All very peaceful. Very New Zealand.

"This is the part where *I* get nervous," Iain said. "There's a bedroom up here." He opened a door to a small room at the back of the house featuring not much besides a single bed, a desk, and a view out onto the driveway. "And then there's mine. Downstairs."

She smiled at him. "Of course yours. You're the prize in my box of Cracker Jacks, aren't you?"

"Uh…" He looked befuddled.

"Sorry. Another American thing," she tried to explain. "It's sort of caramel corn, and it has a prize inside."

"Tell me you ever ate caramel corn," he said, "and I'll tell you you're lying."

She laughed, suddenly feeling so much better. "No. Of course I didn't. Not even when I was little. Too fattening, and it rots your teeth. I had very pretty teeth."

"What a surprise," he said. "But I'm glad to be the prize."

"Maybe you shouldn't be. It may be a bad metaphor. It was always a really cheap prize."

He laughed out loud. "I need to kiss you, and it's getting worse. Come on. I'll show you my bedroom. You're *my* prize, and you're not one bit cheap."

She went downstairs with him, and this was better. The bedroom led to a small patio on one side, with a bigger one on the main lawn, all edged by greenery. When he opened the glass sliders, the sound of birdsong and the trickle of running water filled the air.

"Almost like the beach," she said.

"Yeh. Beach is a couple blocks, though."

"You're kidding."

"Nah. And now," he said, stepping closer and getting his hands under her T-shirt, "tell me I get to take this off. I can't stand it anymore."

"And you aren't even the one wearing it," she said, her voice muffled by the cotton being hauled over her head.

He sucked in his breath at the sight of the bandage squashing her breasts tight, and then he was peeling off the Velcro strip and unwinding it. Around and around, finally dropping it onto the bed and looking down at what she knew were the red, corrugated wheals left in her skin.

She gasped at the relief of the pressure, the tingling pain that was almost pleasure. He sat on the bed, pulled her into his lap, and began to rub over the sore spots.

"If I see that fella again," he said, his big hand moving in circles over her breasts, her side, her back, soothing the hurt away, "I'm going to kill him. So you know."

She laid her head on his shoulder and let him rub. "Mm. You won't have to do that. I'm going to take care of it. But that feels so good. And thanks for not telling Hugh who I was."

"If you don't want to," he said, "we won't."

"Not until my press conference. I just want to... lie low

until then. Is that all right with you?"

"You can lie low," he promised. "Lie right here with me, long as it takes. You know I'm happy."

His hand was still working, and she sighed. "If you keep doing that, I'm probably going to go to sleep. You don't know how good it feels. The same way being here all this time has felt. Like relaxing, but more than that. Like... relief."

He brushed her hair back from her temple and kissed the top of her head, nothing but tenderness in his lips, his hands. "We'll just sit here, then, and I'll do it as long as you like. Because I love to make you feel good."

real life
♡

It was all very domestic, later that day, walking into downtown Devonport with Iain, past Mt. Victoria and down Victoria Street with its view of the sailboats on the Harbour. Not to mention pushing the trolley with him in New World, picking out steaks and lamb and chicken that, for the first time, she knew how to cook. Like somebody else's real life, that is. Hers had never been like this.

"I won't be doing this with you much," Iain said as if he'd read her mind. "I'll be heading to training with the boys on Monday, and from here, it's full on. I've never left it this late to get back to the squad. I usually report at the beginning of January, even though the All Blacks are entitled to the extra time off."

Getting back to my real life, he didn't need to say. While she was still hesitating and hiding. "Oh," she said. "You're not all All Blacks?"

"No. That's the international squad. The boys I was on the European tour with. The All Blacks season's only part of the year. The rest of it, we're with our regular teams."

"And Hugh's on both of them with you?"

"Yeh. My skipper on the Blues as well now. Gave me some stick about getting myself to training, though he's only just reported back himself. He was on his honeymoon. But here's when it gets serious, and I'll be leaving you on your own more. Or with Granddad, of course. We can cook dinner together, though. That'd be good."

"What, all that running and gym time and bicycling wasn't serious?" she teased, trying to keep it light.

"Rugby fit's a different story. You may have to go easy on me. I'll be blowing a bit until after that first match."

"But you love it."

"Yeh. I do. Never wanted to do anything else, really, though I'll have to sometime, of course."

"It's great that you have so much passion for it, then."

"Lucky," he agreed. He put a heavy loaf of wholemeal bread into the trolley, moved on, and picked out a dozen eggs. "What about you? What are you going to do?"

It was as if he'd picked up on her thoughts, and she shot a look at him. He didn't return her gaze. Instead, he was studying a shelf of pink coconut-studded lamingtons that she'd have bet money he was never going to buy.

"I don't know," she finally said. "Beyond that press conference." She knew that wasn't the answer he wanted, but it was the truth.

"What about the singing?" he asked. "I'm surprised you haven't tried to make a go of that. I think you could."

"Not that easy. And anyway—no. That's just for me, something I do because I love it. If I tried to make it a job, I'd lose the joy. I'd worry that I wasn't good enough. I don't want to put it out there to be judged."

He nodded. "I can see that. Something every rugby player has to come to grips with. That you love it, but you're being judged as well. That's why you need the passion. Otherwise, it'd just be pressure, and it'd be too much. But as it is, you want to do your best anyway. You want to know when you're not, so you can do better. If you aren't always trying to do better, you're in the wrong job."

"Maybe it's the difference between the pressure coming from inside or from outside," she said. "For you, the pressure might come from the outside, but the desire comes from the inside. The fire within."

He gave her that incongruously sweet smile, at such odds with his barbarian's face, and her heart gave a flutter. "You're a clever one, eh," he said. "The fire within. But you don't feel it."

"Not for modeling, really, but of course, who does love their job? Besides you, of course. I don't hate it, I just—I don't know. I've never been able to slow down enough to figure it out, I suppose."

He started walking again, pushing the trolley toward the checkout. "Good you're here, then. It'll give you a chance. You can slow down for as long as it takes."

She was hearing something in his voice, and her heart sank. Once again, she was going to disappoint somebody. She was trying not to let that matter to her so much, and what had she done? Set herself up to do it again, to the very last person she wanted to disappoint.

She did what she'd never done. Instead of scrambling around it, frantically trying to change herself to avoid it, she faced it. "Are you afraid of what I'll decide? That I'll go back to it all, and I'll be gone?"

"Yeh." Unlike her, Iain had no problem with courage. "I am."

She forced herself to tell him. "I have to do it, though. I have to sort out my own life, make my own choices. It's the first time I've done it, and it's so scary. I don't know what's selfishness, and what's—being true to myself, I guess."

He wasn't smiling. He'd stopped again, was standing at the end of one of the aisles, his big hands gripping the trolley. Paying no attention to the curious glances, the occasional double take of recognition. Not for her, for once. For him.

Finally, he said, "Granddad would probably have something to say about this, but I can't seem to think of anything."

She couldn't look at him. "He did have something," she said. "That if it was meant to be, it'd happen. But I don't know how you tell."

Saying it felt almost impossible. Almost as if the words were coming from somebody else. She'd never been remotely this honest, this open. And yet she didn't seem to have a choice, just as she hadn't all along. Or like the choice had already been made.

Just stop me, her rebellious heart said. *Just stop me.*

Iain was pushing the trolley toward the checkout, getting in the queue, beginning to set items on the belt. "We both made our choice, didn't we. I couldn't have made a different one. So let's buy this food before the meat rots. And then we'll go home, and you can get on with things." He finished unloading, pushed the trolley forward, looked at the checker, and said, "We don't have any bags."

♡♡♡

Nina didn't want to do the next thing, either, but she had to. When they got home, she took her new phone, went to sit on one of the luxurious chairs on the patio, under the shade of the umbrella, and made her first call.

Not to her mother, and not to her grandparents. Those things were going to have to wait until she was free. She'd got herself into this, and she had to get herself out of it. She called her agent.

It was past six-thirty California time, but Andrea picked up anyway. "Andrea Lawson."

"It's Sabrina Jones." Even saying her real name was a jolt.

"Sabrina. My God. Where are you? I can't get a straight answer from your mother."

"Before I answer that," Nina said, "I need to remind you of something. Your contract is with me."

"What? Of course it is."

"That means that what we discuss is confidential. Right?"

"Of course," Andrea said, sounding impatient. "But we *do* need to discuss it. The best thing, I'd say, would be for us to get on a conference call together with Trudi. She says you'll be back to work 'soon.' I need a date, and to know what you want, so I can get things moving."

"You're going too fast." Nina was sitting up poker-straight. "I'd like to talk business with you. I'd like your input. But it's confidential. That means that if you share what we discuss with my mother, that will be the end of our relationship."

"Are you saying," Andrea said slowly, "that Trudi's no longer your business manager?"

Nina was holding onto the rolled black metal edge of the table now, gripping the smooth surface for strength, and for support. "That's what I'm saying. But I haven't had a chance to have that conversation with her, and I won't for a while yet. So what I want to know is this. Are you prepared to deal directly with me, or do I need to get a new agent?"

"Of course I'll deal directly with you," Andrea said, sounding not one bit ruffled.

"Are you sure?" Nina probed. "I know you and my mother are close. You've been my agent for ten years, and I don't want to lose you, but I know you're used to dealing with her. This is a dealbreaker, though, so I need to make sure you're all right with it."

"Sabrina." Andrea let out a sigh, and Nina could nearly see her greyhound-lean form, her elegant hand resting on her desk, her perfectly manicured nails tapping out a Morse-code message as her lightning brain worked. "I'm an agent. I don't have feelings. I have interests. You say I'm dealing with you? I'll send Trudi a goodie basket and a lovely card, and I'll deal with you."

Nina sat back in her chair. "Right, then. Right. Here's what we're doing."

frustrated efforts
♡

Matthias hadn't been able to believe it when Raoul had come back to the jet without Nina.

"You've failed?" he demanded. "You didn't have the strength to bring back an underwear model? Is that what you're saying?"

His chief of staff looked as cool as ever, not a drop of sweat showing on his shaved head despite the warmth of the day outside. "No. I'm telling you what I told you at the start. That if you wanted to talk to her, you should have gone yourself."

"That isn't for you to say. Go back and get her."

"Not feasible. He saw me. The rugby player. He'll be with her tonight."

Matthias very nearly hit him. He didn't lose control, but he was close to doing it now. Too close, because of Sabrina.

He'll be with her tonight.

No.

This was who Sabrina had left him for? How? How had she even met him? He'd had her checked out so thoroughly. There had been nothing of this man. Not a whisper. If there had been, Matthias wouldn't have chosen her. He wasn't interested in a woman who'd been passed around the celebrity circuit.

Somehow, though, she'd tricked him. "You should have called and told me as soon as it happened," he told Raoul. "You should have told me you'd failed, so I *could* have gone myself."

"I did not fail." Raoul's voice was ice-cold. "I adjusted. I recommend you do the same."

Matthias wasn't letting this go. Not anymore. "Are you *rebuking* me?"

It was all as if he were seventeen again, and his father was staring at him with distaste after some teenage misdeed, then leaving the room to let Raoul spell out the message and repair the damage. After a party that had veered out of control, a girl's wild accusations, the accident on the German autobahn that had caused an injury to the idiot who had been driving so slowly that Matthias hadn't been able to help clipping him.

Raoul had changed his tune, and his tone, once Matthias's father had died and Matthias had acceded to the throne. If he hadn't, Matthias wouldn't have kept him on, no matter how efficient he was. Now, though, his tone had shifted back, and that was not acceptable.

Raoul barely blinked. "Rebuking you is not part of my brief. I'm recommending a course of action. If she stays at that house, we'll know it. But why would she? I suspect she'll leave. Eventually, she'll resurface. She'll have to, if she wants to work again, and you can have your discussion with her, if you must. Meanwhile, the rumors are out there. Her reputation isn't what it was. You've been spared a marriage to the wrong woman, and she will suffer the consequences more than you. And if you're planning more than a conversation, I feel compelled to point out that that could damage your reputation badly. She is a citizen of another nation, and we're not in Neuenstein. If we were…" He shrugged. "Then you would have more license. Here, it is another story."

"Do not tell me what to think," Matthias said through his teeth. "Do not tell me what to do. That is not your job."

The impassive yellow eyes looked steadily back at him, and

Raoul didn't answer.

"We'll stay here," Matthias said at last. "Go find somebody to watch the house, and watch the airport, too. We'll stay here until you find her. I'll talk to her, and we'll leave. That is all."

Raoul had nodded, walked off the plane again, and made his arrangements. But it had taken too long in this godforsaken, backward little country where nothing seemed to get done in a hurry. Raoul found a firm in Christchurch, but by the time they were in place at the house, Sabrina had been gone.

The man—Iain McCormick, a hulking brute of a Scot with nothing to recommend him to a woman with any taste—had left as well, it seemed. Raoul had sat near the entrance to the airport all day, with a detective eventually joining him, and nobody had sighted them. Which meant that they'd anticipated this, had gone somewhere else. When the detective had been driving from Christchurch, Sabrina had probably already left.

With the man who called himself her husband, most likely. Not true, as far as Raoul had been able to discern, which wasn't far enough. This McCormick had an agent, and the team had a publicist, and neither had been willing to share any information on his private life. He'd been engaged to another woman the previous year, and the wedding had been canceled, a piece of irony that Matthias was in no mood to appreciate.

It all took days to determine, and for all that time, Matthias was marooned in the wilderness of New Zealand, because the country was too ridiculously far from Europe—from anywhere—to allow him to have a hope of returning in time to confront Sabrina, once they found her. She wasn't with her mother, and she wasn't with her grandparents, and she hadn't reappeared in the modeling world. She almost had to be here, probably with that man, but they hadn't found him. He didn't appear to be back in training with his team. He didn't appear to be anywhere.

Finally, on Sunday, after four days of frustrating inaction, Matthias told Raoul, "We will go home. This is pointless."

"A wise decision," the older man said.

"I didn't ask you whether it was wise," Matthias said. "I told you that we're going home."

my soft side

♡

Once again, Graeme was on Melvin's couch with Carmella. Their fourth session, a week and a half since their first appointment. Carmella still wasn't home, and Graeme was fairly aching for her by this point. He saw her every day at the office, and still, it was as hard as it had been when she'd been gone over Christmas, the empty house as lonely. Or even harder and even lonelier, if he had to tell the truth, because he couldn't hold onto the anger anymore. He just missed her.

"Let's talk more about how your first date went," Melvin said. "Carmella?"

"It was good," she said, sounding almost shy. She'd sat at one end of the couch today, and Graeme had thought for a minute, then put himself next to her. That was the point, wasn't it? And she hadn't told him to go away, so that was all right.

"We kayaked," she said now, "and Graeme did the picnic. That was nice."

"Is that unusual?" Melvin asked.

"Well, yes," she said. "He normally doesn't... plan things for us. Or set things up, you know. Doesn't take initiative, you could say, in that way."

"I just ordered extra lunches," Graeme said. *Doesn't take*

320

initiative. That didn't sound good at all. "The ones the pub makes, that we give the kayakers."

"I knew that," Carmella said. "I could tell, of course. But he thought of it."

"Tell him," Melvin reminded her gently.

She turned to Graeme and said, "Of course I know. But you thought of it. You made it happen. It made me feel like maybe you might want me for more than the cooking and cleaning."

It had him so gobsmacked, it took him a moment to respond. "Of course I do. Of course."

"Oh." She didn't sound a bit like her usual confident self. "Well, I didn't know."

"But if that's what's in our way?" he said. "That you think that's all I want? I'll do more there, then. Say the word."

"Except that you never have."

"Because you let me get away with it, maybe. Or because," he found himself admitting, "I thought as long as you did that, as long as you were still willing to feed me, that was something."

"Oh, Graeme." She was getting a bit teary, and he didn't look at Melvin. He picked up her hand, and he held it.

"You want me to do more, though?" he asked. "Tell me. Washing clothes, washing up. Cleaning. Whatever. I won't do it as well as you, but I'll give it a go. New agreement, eh. New rules, like you said. If that's one of the new rules, I'm willing."

"Right, then," she said, her voice not quite steady. "I'm saying it. I've done it for thirty years, and I'm tired of it, honestly. I want you to work less, I want to spend more time with you, and I want you to share more at home."

"Didn't I already post for that bookkeeper?" he asked.

"You did." She smiled, and it was *his* smile. His girl, still, and he could hardly breathe. "Thank you," she said, and he sat there like a lump and thought, *What do I say now?*

"I suggest," Melvin said after a minute, "that you work out together how you'd like to divide things. You may be surprised, but household chores are actually one of the major sources of disagreement amongst couples. Money, sex, children, work, chores. There you go."

"Really. Wouldn't have thought that," Graeme said, because he was meant to say something, he knew. Or because the only one he'd really heard was, "Sex."

"Of course you wouldn't," Carmella retorted. "Easy not to think about them when they get done without your having to think. No magic fairies, are there. Somebody's holding that toilet scrubber."

"Ah. There you are, then," Melvin said cheerfully. "Graeme, I think you just found out what the first item on Carmella's list is going to be. Cleaning bathrooms."

"Yes," she said. "Yes."

"Right," Graeme said. "Less time at work, bathrooms, and whatever else. Date night. Got it."

"You mean all I had to do was say it?" Carmella demanded. "All this time?"

"Nah," he said with a faint smile. "Had to get my attention first, didn't you. You did that, though, right enough."

"And if you talk about chores, you don't have to talk about your feelings," Carmella said. "Easier, eh."

"Easier," he agreed, and squeezed her hand, so grateful he could at least do that. "Give me a list. I can do a list. Put it on the fridge, maybe. Give me a list, and a day."

"Saturday," she said promptly. "We do as much as we can on Saturday. Washing, cleaning, shopping. We get it done together, then we have date night, and I'm feeling happy. That'll set us up for the week, I'm thinking. You can do your blokey things on Friday nights and Sundays, I'll do my girl things then as well, and there we are. Saturday's ours. Good as gold."

"How does that feel, Graeme?" Melvin asked. "Having Carmella decide like that, and spell it out? Seems she's felt that she's too managing, and that you resent it. How did that feel just now?"

He shrugged. "Felt fine. I don't mind if she arranges things. She has good ideas. I just don't want to be—"

"What?" Carmella asked. She still had his hand, and now, *she* was the one squeezing it.

"On the edge," he said reluctantly.

"Oh," she said. "Like you aren't important. Like you aren't central."

He had to look away.

"She needs you to tell her," Melvin prompted.

"Right, then." He steeled himself, and did it. "Yeh. Like I'm not central. Like I'm hanging about at the edges of your life, of the family's life. Makes me sound like a baby, though, saying it."

"No." Her eyes were shining with the tears she hadn't shed. "Graeme, no. I feel the same way. You're my world. You always have been. You're my rock. Knowing you're there for me, loving me? That's the most important thing I have. When I thought I'd lost that..." Her voice wobbled, but she went on. "I felt like I'd lost everything. Like I'd lost *my* center. I know it should be myself, and I hope it is, but it's you, too."

Never mind Melvin. He had to say this. "No. You've never lost that. You never could. And I'm the same. You're my best thing. You're my..." He forced himself to say it. If he didn't, how would she know? "My soft side, I guess. If you think I'm strong, it's because I need to be strong for you. I need to be there for you. I need you there so I can do it."

A couple tears had escaped her eyes, and he got an arm around her and pulled her close, then stared fiercely at Melvin and said, "We'd better be done, because we're leaving."

"Don't you want your homework?" Melvin asked.

"No. I've got my homework. Got her right here."

"That's funny," Melvin said. "I was going to tell you that. Money, work, children, chores. And sex. You don't seem to have problems with money or children, and we've talked about work and chores. That must mean it's time for sex. Your homework is to spend fifteen minutes apiece, before next time, touching each other. Tonight, for preference. No pressure on either of you. Just touching. No intercourse. You're touching, and telling each other what feels good. And that's all."

"Like hell," Graeme was pulling Carmella to her feet. "Like hell."

♡♡♡

They were in the car, and Graeme was looking at her. "You want to get a takeaway?" he asked.

"Uh… sure." Her disappointment nearly choked her.

"I'll cook for you," he said. "If you'd rather. Won't be much good, but I'll do it."

"Oh. Do you mean… before the homework?" This was her husband, she reminded herself. He'd watched their babies being born. For so many years, he'd been almost more familiar with her body than she was herself. Tonight, though, he felt like a stranger.

He was already driving, pulling into a carpark beside the Indian restaurant. Inside, they sat on the chairs near the entrance and waited, then took their bag of food and got back in the car.

They didn't talk all the long way home, but when they got there, he said, "Right," and reached into the back seat for the curry. "Here's what I think. I think we both change our clothes. Make it a date, eh. Make it special. When you're ready, come over to the house. We'll have dinner. And then we'll do our homework."

"Who goes first?" she asked.

"Me," he said. "Absolutely. Me."

"Right," she said. "OK."

She went into the big house and chose her clothes, then headed back to the cottage. No dad there tonight to see her, to comment, or not to. No kids. She and Graeme were free. Just the two of them, the way it had so rarely been. Almost like starting out all over again.

She took a shower and rubbed lotion into her skin, wishing it were firmer, then brushed her teeth before doing her makeup with much more care than she usually took. Only then did she get dressed. She stepped carefully into her best, a dress she rarely wore, because it was black and a bit revealing, skimming her shoulders and dipping low in front, clinging to her waist before flaring out below the hips. An elegant dress. Too elegant for the occasion, of course, but it *was* her best, and tonight? She needed to look her best.

Her cleavage still looked pretty good, she thought with an anxious glance in the mirror. She'd done her best to care for her skin, and it wasn't too bad, but menopause had happened a few years back, and the difference it had made had been frankly appalling. She'd got more serious about exercise since then, because her naturally slim figure hadn't been "natural" at all any more, and as for her skin, and her hair... She sighed and ran a nervous hand over her waistline. The dress was tighter than it had used to be, and no mistake. And if Graeme was meant to touch her for fifteen minutes? In the light? She wasn't sure how she felt about that. Well, she *was* sure, actually. It scared her to death.

Homework, she told herself. Graeme had been so much more flexible, so much braver than she'd ever have imagined he could be. It was time for her to be brave as well. So she slipped on her shoes and headed across to the other house.

All she could be was her best. If that wasn't good enough for him, it wasn't. Time to find out.

She knocked on the door, even though it was silly to do that at her own house, and he opened it. He'd changed as well, she saw. Dark trousers, black knit shirt. As big as ever, as strong and fit, all chest, shoulder, and thigh. She'd got worse looking, no doubt about it, and she could swear he only looked better. Fifty-five, and he looked better than he had at thirty. More rugged, yes, but that was only a good thing. Not fair, but true all the same. Her heart was fluttering so wildly now, she was sure he must be able to see it.

"Hi," he said. He wasn't smiling. His blue eyes were intense. Burning bright. "You're beautiful."

"I—" she began, and couldn't go on.

"How hungry are you?" he asked. "You always told the

kids, get the homework out of the way before dinner, eh."

"Sounds good," she managed to say.

"I know it's a bit forward. On our second date. But I'd like to take you to bed."

"We could do that."

He had a hand out, was pulling her inside. She was about to kick off her heels, but he said, "Don't. Please. I'd like to undress you tonight."

He was taking her into his arms, and she was going. He had a hand on her cheek, the other one at her waist, and her own hands were around his broad shoulders. Exactly where they fit best.

When he kissed her, she gasped, because he did it with a hunger he hadn't showed for so long. His mouth changed, then, slanted over hers, took it harder, long and slow and deep. His hand was hard at her waist, and the warm tendrils were twisting down inside her, curling low.

He wasn't doing anything else, either. He was just standing there at the base of the stairs, kissing her as if he couldn't bear to stop, his hand moving over her back, almost soothingly. Almost as if he knew what she was feeling, how tentative she felt.

Just when she was relaxing, he changed it. There was coolness at her back, because he'd found her zip, and was undoing it. He was pulling it slowly down, all the way to her hips, then stepping back, pushing the black dress down her body, and watching it fall to the floor. All without a word.

He stared at her in the black strapless bra and undies she'd chosen. She'd wondered, while she'd put them on, whether he'd think they were over the top, if he'd think she was ridiculous, and now, she was more than wondering. She was terrified.

"Beautiful," he said with a sigh of satisfaction. "Step out of the dress, sweetheart."

The relief nearly made her shake. She spared not a thought for the expensive black dress, just stepped out and kicked it away with one black heel.

"You're so beautiful," he said, stroking a hand down her full breast, tracing the line of her bra, then lower, over her waist, her belly, her hip. "So perfect. And I'm the luckiest man in the world, I know it, that you gave me another chance to tell you so."

"Not perfect at all," she said. "Two kids. And I'm... getting older. I've thought you..." She shouldn't be saying it, she knew. She shouldn't be messing this up, but she couldn't help it. "That you didn't want me anymore. All the young girls coming into the shop, and I'm—when I look in the mirror, I'm so much older."

"No," he said. "No. You're gorgeous. The only woman I want, always."

She had her hands under his shirt, was pulling it over his head, running her hands down his chest.

He caught her wrists in his hands. "Oh, no. I go first. That was the deal. Come on. Upstairs. And you're walking up ahead of me."

"Graeme..." she began.

"So I can look at that ass," he said, and she gasped.

"What?" he asked. He was smiling now. Two weeks ago, he'd barely looked at her, and now, he was talking about her ass, and smiling? "You didn't know I liked it? Always have. Always will. So come on. Walk upstairs for me. Let me see you do it in those heels."

She turned around, and she did it. Walked up the stairs ahead of him, putting a swing in her step. Half of her amazed, a little embarrassed, sure he'd change his mind and say, "Nah. Awful." The other half so turned on she could barely speak.

"Now," he said when they reached their bedroom. He pulled her in from behind, right there in the middle of the room, had an arm around her waist, the other hand sliding over her belly, up to her breasts. "Now, I take all this off. And we get in the shower."

"Oh. I took one," she said. "I'm clean."

"Yeh. You smell good, too. But I want to wash you. I'm meant to touch you for fifteen minutes. That's what the man said. Thought I could do it there. Where I'll have soap, and I can reach all the best spots." He had his hand at the back of her bra, was unhooking it and tossing it to the floor. "These are good," he said. He was still standing behind her, and now, he held a breast in each hand, stroking them as if he'd never touched them before, and he was lighting her up. "Be even better if they were soapy." Then he was pulling her undies down, saying, "And here? It's already wet, I reckon. But it could be soapy as well, far as I'm concerned. That'd be good. Ease my way."

She kicked out of her heels, and Graeme was unsnapping his trousers, dropping them with his own underwear. He led her into the bath, turned on the taps of the shower, tested it with a hand, and was pulling her into it.

He was kissing her again, then. The spray pelting them, the warmth running over their bodies, and Graeme's hard mouth on hers. Demanding, and taking.

"Homework," she gasped when he lifted his mouth from hers at last. She was shivering with arousal, with the feeling of the water.

"That's managing," he said. He had the body wash in his hand now, was squeezing it out into his palm. "We discussed that, I thought. This is my time. My fifteen minutes. I get to touch you however I like. Your only job is to tell me how it feels."

"Uh…" His big hands were sliding over her breasts, caressing them, playing there, taking his time. She was back against the wall, because it felt too good, and she needed the support. "I didn't think it was… however you like. Don't remember that part."

Those clever fingers of his were still moving, and she was sighing. "No?" he said. "That's how I heard it. Made me think about that first time I saw you." His hands were headed over her abdomen now, moving on to her thighs, slicking her down with soap. "You want to know the part I didn't tell that fella?"

"Yes," she whispered, then closed her eyes. He had parted

her thighs now, and his hand was stroking, probing.

"I wanted this," he said. "I looked at you, and you were beautiful, exactly like I said. I wanted to take you out, see you smile at me like that. I wanted to hold your hand and give you a kiss. All of that. And also..." He'd moved closer again, and his hand was diving, finding its stealthy way inside her body. "I wanted to fuck you," he said into her ear. "Wanted to put you down on your back and fuck you hard. I was rough as guts, eh."

"Oh." She was sucking in deep breaths of the steamy air. Crying out. Already almost there.

"I still want to," he said. "Because I'm still rough as guts. I want to do it right now. But you're not doing your part." He was stroking now, showing her that he knew exactly how to touch her, exactly what felt best. His other hand had come around from behind, was probing, searching, and she was moaning again. "Tell me how it feels," he said. "Tell me now."

"So good," she said. "So good."

"Not enough. Tell me more. I'm doing my homework. Time for you to do yours."

"What do you... want to know?"

"I want to know what you want me to do. I want to know what you see when you look at me."

"You..." She was having trouble talking now. "You're so big. So strong. You excite me so much. When you touch me, I just want to... lie down for you. I always have."

"Not good enough," he said. "Tell me more."

She was going up higher, and his fingers were inside her, on her, almost too much. "I want you to..." she said. "To..."

"Go on," he said. "Tell me."

"Oh, Graeme," she moaned. "I've missed you so much. Please. Now. Please. Stop talking and do it. I need it."

"I'm going to do it," he said. "Going to do it now. But you're going to do it first. You're going to come, and then I'm going to fuck you. Just the way you like it."

His hands were harder. Almost rough, and she cried out.

Then she was convulsing, her back slamming against the tiled wall, the water beating over her breasts, her belly.

He growled. Actually growled, and his hands didn't stop. He worked her all the way through it, and then he had his hands around her waist, was picking her up, shoving her against the wall. His strength, as always, so thrilling. He was inside her, driving hard, and she was still coming, and crying out, over and over again.

Fast and furious, her head buried against his neck, feeling him taking her over for long minutes, driving her up and over the top again, just like that. And finally, when she was calling out, losing her grip, losing her mind—finally, he was groaning, cursing, emptying into her.

He set her down, then, and she wrapped her arms around his neck and felt him holding her close.

"Water's going to get cold," she said at last.

"Never mind," he said. "When it does, we'll get out. I'm not ready to let you go yet. Been too hard to get you here."

"Mm." She nuzzled his shoulder, loving the solidity of him. "I'm not sure you touched me for fifteen minutes, even. Guess it doesn't take me fifteen minutes, not the way you do it. We're going to get such poor marks. And we never even got to my part."

"Didn't we? I didn't notice. Felt good enough to me."

"Well, never mind," she said, back to her usual briskness. "We can do me tomorrow. We'll get in the shower again, maybe, and you can tell me how you like to be touched."

He laughed, and it sounded pretty satisfied. "No, Mrs. McCormick. You're not getting it all your own way anymore. You want me to take charge more in our life? Right. I'm doing it. I've got other plans for our next time. What I thought of tonight, and never got around to. Tomorrow, after the shower, we're going to get in bed, and I'm going to show you that I remember some other things, too. I've always loved the way you taste. Going to see if I can still make you happy that way. I'm betting I can, if I try hard enough. And you know what you always said you loved about me. That I was a hard worker. I like the idea of you telling me, too. That's going to be part of it. I touch you, and you tell me how it feels."

"Mm." She was kissing his neck, running her hands over his body, and whatever he'd said, she knew he loved it. "And I'm going to take charge enough to say one more thing, too. I *would* like to do that thing he said. Fifteen minutes touching you, and fifteen having you touch me. Not just going for the hot spots. Finding out what else feels good. Or more than fifteen. However many. Why not? I'm not going to get any younger or any better, and neither are you. So if we find things we want to do? We'd better go on and do them. Stop wasting time."

"Ah," he said. "Another reason not to work at night."

"That'd be my thought." The water *was* getting cold now, and she shivered.

He reached out and turned off the taps, then was back with the warm towels, tossing her one and starting in on himself. "Just how mad are we meant to be getting here? Could warn a fella. You been reading books or something, over there by yourself?"

"Maybe," she said. "And mad as you like, that's how mad. It's only you and me here. Neither of us is going anywhere. If we don't trust each other enough by now, when will we? Mad as you like, while we've both still got it. I'm game."

"Yeh," he said, and he was smiling. Not *almost* smiling. Smiling for real. "You are. And I just may take you up on that."

"Think you'd better," she said. "Or who knows? I may change my mind, start eyeing those young boys myself."

He laughed, gave her a smacking swat on the bottom, and said, "Pretty saucy there, Mrs. McCormick. Better watch yourself."

"Well," she said, "you can teach me a lesson, then. Drive your point home. Here I am, ready and willing to take it."

He laughed again, pulled her close, and kissed her. "I'm never losing you again," he told her. "That's a promise."

Before she could answer, he went on. "Come on, then. Rattle your dags. Let's get some clothes on and eat some of that dinner we bought. We'll take a walk on the beach, eh. Hold hands. Show everybody what thirty years looks like. And you'd better be planning on moving back in. I'm not going to sleep again until I'm holding my wife. I'm going on strike, that's what I'm doing, until I get her back."

"You've got her back." She took his beloved, craggy face in her hands, pulled it down to hers, and gave him a gentle, sweet kiss that came all the way from her soul. "You've always had her. She never left."

back in business

♡

When Iain ran out of the tunnel for the first time that season, he did it knowing that Nina wasn't there.

It wasn't that the match was important. The first preseason game, that was all, played on a Friday night against the Wellington Hurricanes in the intimate venue of North Harbour Stadium. The stadium only held 25,000, and tonight, it wasn't half full. And none of the spectators was Nina.

He'd argued with her the night before. "You can wear your hat," he'd said. "I'll change your ticket in the WAG section and get you and Granddad some in the cheap seats."

"Not yet," she'd said. "I'll go next week. I told you I will. After the press conference. Please, Iain. Try to understand."

"He doesn't know you're here, though. Matthias, or Raoul, either. Whoever. And how would he find you if he did know? So you go to a match. So what?"

"He knows I'm not a rugby fan. And he'll know who you are, that I was at your parents' house. That wouldn't have taken Raoul five minutes to put together. And if I'm seen there, at the game? I'm still news. My agent has made that more than clear. It'd be picked up, and he'd see it. And then they'll both know exactly where I am, and they'll guess who I'm staying with. I don't care how well the team guards your privacy. They'll get your address. You don't know the kind of resources they have. So *no,* Iain," she'd gone on when he would have argued some more. "No. Not yet. It's too public."

Nothing but frustrating. He was trying to understand, but it was rough. If this prince fella *did* know that Nina was with him? Well, how would that be a bad thing? So the bloke had power. Iain would like to see how much power he had when the two of them were face-to-face. For the few seconds until the mighty prince was on the ground, that is. He didn't want Matthias to come, or Raoul, either, didn't want them to scare Nina, or even bother her. Of course he didn't. And at the same time, he was dying for them to.

The press conference was set for the following Thursday, and as much as Iain dreaded what would happen after it, he couldn't wait. He hated seeing the fear in her. He hated more not being able to make it go away.

But he couldn't. His granddad was here tonight, and she wasn't. Arthur had taken to fishing from the jetty at the Naval Museum in the mornings while Nina was at yoga, and he'd made some mates there. One of them had been more than happy to use the ticket Nina had refused.

Iain was glad to have his granddad there, of course he was. But it would've been better if Nina hadn't been alone at the house. And if she'd been here instead.

Once the tape was on and he pulled on the jersey, though, she, his granddad, and everything else moved to the back of his mind. Everything shifted and settled, and he was in a different zone. The Rugby Zone.

He came out onto the pitch with the rest of the squad for the warmups, and it had already begun. He was down in the scrum, his shoulders shoving hard into the considerable, muscular backsides of a hooker and a prop, and he was feeling it already. The surge of power that was the engine room in a rugby scrum. His job. His part.

Trading bashes at the shoulder with Hugh, then, bouncing off each others' bodies in a foretaste of the contest ahead, and his heart was beating for it, his blood surging for it. His hands were itching to wrap around an opposing player's hips and bring him down, his legs practically springing from the earth with the need to jump.

A new season; a new start. And when the team ran out of the tunnel and onto the pitch behind Hugh for the first time? They were ready, and so was Iain. Ready, willing, and able.

He stood on the turf, bouncing on his toes, then settled into a crouch as he watched the Hurricanes line up for the kick that would start the match. He relaxed every muscle, and then he tensed them. Ready. Waiting.

The referee blew his whistle, the first-five sent the kick off his boot, and the ball was in the air. The Hurricanes were off after it, and so was Iain. He was running, checking angles and trajectories, his focus on the ball, not caring about who or what was coming with it. And then he was taking off, leaping high, his long arms snatching his prize out of the air.

When he came down with it, the chasing Hurricanes were there, and he welcomed the contact. He bulled his way through two tackles, his legs churning, his head lowered, until he went down in a hard tackle from the third man. Liam Mahaka, the Hurricanes' tanklike hooker.

Hugh was right there, though, standing over him, first as always to the breakdown, lending his support. Iain clung to the ball, refusing to part with it. It was his, and he wasn't letting it go until he could deliver it where it belonged.

It had started. It was on.

As always, the next ninety minutes or so passed in a flash. His chest was heaving by halftime, because the Hurricanes had pace and one hell of a tricky kicking game. By the final twenty minutes, the forwards' hands were on their hips or the tops of their heads, sure signs of fatigue. All except Hugh, who looked, as always, as strong in Minute Seventy-One as he had in Minute One. Which was one reason he was the skipper.

As for Iain—he heaved air into his burning lungs, ignored the heaviness in his legs, and pushed on. Pushed past it.

Played hard to the end, because that was what you did.

It was rough, it was bruising, and it was punishing. It was his life.

It was a win, too, albeit the narrowest of ones. Sixteen to fifteen, in the kind of mistake-ridden effort you expected the first time out. But a win was a win, ugly or pretty, and when he trotted off the field, it wasn't his aching legs he noticed. It was the grins on bruised faces, the slaps on the backs of sweat-soaked jerseys, the jubilation of another season begun, and the knowledge that the team was back, and better. Will Tawera, their new first-five recruited from Aussie, had driven the backs around the park with an assurance they'd been lacking for the past two seasons, and his boot had been on the money as well. He'd made all but one of his kicks, and that was a good sign. No, that was a *brilliant* sign.

They had the right skipper in Hugh, they had the right Number Ten in Will, and they were going to do this. They were back.

A half-hour later, he was in the sheds with the first beer cracked, sitting on a bench and having a laugh with Liam Mahaka, who'd taken him down more than that first time in the match, and been on the receiving end of a couple of Iain's own efforts.

"Next time, cuz," Mako said.

"Yeh, yeh," Iain retorted. "I'm just sitting here waiting."

The phone in the locker behind him chirped, and he turned around and picked it up.

I admit it, that worked for me. Bad to say I know. You really are a sexy beast.

Nina.

He looked at Mako and said, "One sec."

"No worries." Mako stood up and headed over to have a yarn with Hugh. The most agreeable of men, Mako—when he wasn't facing you on the pitch, that is.

Iain texted back, *Hope so.* He tried to think of something else, but he was never good at the sexting thing. It always came off sounding either lame, or too nasty. And Nina was a prize he couldn't risk.

Their "research" these past couple of weeks had been the hottest, sweetest time he'd ever spent with a woman. Her uncertainty, her surprise, her willingness to try, and then the best part. The wonderful moment when she forgot to worry about how she looked and how she was doing, abandoned all restraint, and gave in to her pleasure. And to him.

She was one hell of a hard worker. *I never take on anything unless I'm prepared to do my best,* she'd said, and it was true. Fortunately, Iain was a pretty hard worker himself.

The room around him had faded away as he thought about it, but now, he looked around again. Until there was another chirp.

Know what I did today?

No, what? he texted back. This was safe ground. One more message, and then he'd get back to the party. For a wee while, anyway. His body needed one more thing tonight, and he needed to go home so he could get it.

I went to the doctor and got a little device implanted way up high. All those fingers in there that weren't yours, though. That wasn't right, do you think?

He had a moment of brain freeze.

Oh. Birth control. Right.

He was trying to think how to answer that when he got the next message.

You're probably too tired after all that battering you did. But I've got a present for you. Got my blood test results and I'm all clean. I'm ready for you to be exactly as naked as you want to be.

This was the wrong time and place to have the reaction he was having.

And then he got another text.

I'm getting naked now.

"Right." He stood up, turned around, jammed the phone in his bag, and headed for the showers. "Right."

the conquering hero

♡

Nina sat on the edge of the bed, put her hands over her face, and breathed into them.

Why had she done it? She wasn't really a sexy person, despite all the wonderful experimentation she and Iain had done this week. No matter how patient he'd been with her, though, she wasn't anything like the women in his past, and she knew it. He always seemed to understand her hesitations and limitations, was willing to coax her gently—or not so gently—past them, but she knew he saw them for what they were.

And this? It had clearly been too far. Too awkward. Too aggressive.

It had felt so exciting to type the words. She'd always been so careful, so aware of the risks of being online for somebody in her position. She'd never even sent a suggestive text before, let alone, heaven forbid, pictures. It either happened in real time with her, or it didn't happen at all. Usually "not at all," because that was safer, too.

And what had she done? She'd tried being one of those girls, and she'd obviously scored a massive "fail." Beyond the first couple of short texts, Iain hadn't even responded, and it had been over forty-five minutes.

Maybe… maybe he'd shared it.

Her blood turned to ice at the thought. He'd been in the locker room, and she'd written *that*.

No. Of course he wouldn't do that, wouldn't be showing it around, laughing with his teammates about what he was getting tonight. Of course not. He'd just thought it was inappropriate, that was all. Or he'd been too busy, and it had been the wrong thing to do, intruding on his time after a game, whatever it was they did. Snapped towels at each others' butts, or whatever.

All right. All right. It had been a bad idea, but it wasn't the end of the world. It was that Arthur was gone, maybe, that she'd been home alone for the first time in… in forever. She'd watched Iain on TV, had drunk a glass of wine, and then another, had grown more and more warm and excited and giddy at the sight of him doing his thing. So aggressive, so powerful, so deliciously and completely male. She'd been reckless with freedom and desire, and she'd made a mistake.

He wouldn't think worse of her for this, though. He'd probably just thought it was awkward, because it was. She'd laugh it off, and they'd forget it. She didn't have to feel humiliated.

Her head went up at a noise from upstairs. Arthur coming home, of course. She heard the *beep* as the alarm was silenced.

That wasn't the sound of Arthur's cane overhead, though, his unsteady gait. It was a heavy tread, taking the stairs down at a run, two at a time. She was already backing away, fumbling for the glass sliders, falling out the door to the back.

Over the fence. Across the creek. Splash over. Run through the reserve, down the road to the dairy.

She was across the lawn on the thought, and there was a shout from behind her.

"Nina!"

It took a moment to register, and she was skidding to a stop, turning around, clutching the trunk of a tree at the edge of the yard with her heart hammering, her bare soles tingling from her flight across the patio and the grass.

"Nina!" she heard again. "Where the hell are you?"

Iain. She came out from the trees, wiping her hands on her pink cotton pajama shorts. "Oh," she said weakly. "Hi. I thought you were—I thought—"

He was standing on the patio in his Blues warmups, hands on his hips, legs planted, looking fearsome and menacing in the light spilling from the bedroom. "Thought you were naked," he said. "That's what I came home for. Get that kit off."

The breath had left her lungs. "Wh-what?"

"Send me a text like that, and then you aren't doing it?" he demanded. "Come on. Get it off."

She was still standing in the middle of the lawn. Now, she reached shaking hands to her pale-pink tank, pulled it over her head, and dropped it.

"That's it," he said. She could see his chest rising and falling in the dark-blue warmup jersey. "Now the shorts."

She had her thumbs under them, was peeling them down her legs. Slowly, now, because she'd been wrong. He'd read her message, and he'd wanted it. It had worked. And she was even more keyed up now. Still on edge, but in an entirely different way.

She took the shorts off slowly, the soft fabric a whisper down her thighs. A final wriggle, and she was stepping out of them. She was standing nude in the middle of his lawn, and he was staring at her.

"Well?" she asked. "I thought the conquering hero gets to take what he wants. You just going to stand there, or you going to do it?"

She could swear that she saw his nostrils flare. Then he was pulling the shirt over his chest, over those powerful shoulders, down his beautifully sculpted arms. Yanking his shoes and socks off, getting rid of his pants. And still, she stood there and watched. He looked... even bigger. His muscles pumped, she guessed dimly, from the workout they'd received. He was fully aroused, and awe-inspiring. The conquering hero to the life.

"You going to come over here," he growled, "or are you going to make me come get you?"

If she'd had hair to toss, she'd have tossed it. Instead, she sauntered toward him, putting all her training into it. Maybe it was the wine, or maybe it was Iain, but if he wanted to play? She was going to play. And if he were the conquering hero, she was the prize. He'd won the right to the best, and she was the best, so he was going to get her. All of her. Whatever he wanted.

He stood there, his arms by his sides, all but up on his toes, until she got there. And then he smiled. Not a friendly smile. A dangerous one. The Incredible Hulk, about to transform.

He put both hands under her bottom, lifted her straight off her feet, and took her mouth. Nothing gentle this time. He was plundering, devouring, and she was whimpering. Her arms were around his shoulders, her legs wrapping around his waist, and he had one arm under her, his other hand in her hair, pulling her head back.

He didn't say anything else. All he did was kiss her. He took her mouth, her neck, with so much ferocity, exactly like the beast she knew he wasn't. Except that he was. He was sucking at her neck, biting her there, his mouth claiming every bit of her.

She was starting to make some noise, and his hand was tightening in her hair.

"Iain," she gasped. "Iain. Please."

He was turning, now. But not taking her inside, where she needed to be. Not taking her to bed. Instead, he was letting her down, and she was sliding down the hard length of him.

He didn't hold her, though. The minute her feet touched the stone, he let her go, was moving away from her, around the table, picking up a chair, then spinning it around so it was facing out, into the yard. And then he had her around the waist and was turning her.

"Hold onto the arms of the chair," he said.

"I—"

"Do it. Now." When she still hesitated, he added, "Please. Do it. I need to do this."

She did it. The smooth metal was cold under her hands, and the position was... too vulnerable. Too exposed.

"Somebody will see," she moaned.

"Nobody will see you. I'm here." And he was. He was behind her, pressed close.

No detours this time. Both his hands were on her, one opening her, exposing her, the other stroking, touching, probing. So hard, so sure, and she was gasping.

"All those fingers in there," he said. "And they're mine."

The words, his touch, made her shiver. Made her quake.

She heard it, then. The sound of a sliding door opening, a woman's voice light on the night air.

"Gorgeous out here," she called, and Nina froze.

A man answered her, a low rumble, and Nina tried to stand, but Iain got a hand on her upper back and shoved her down again.

"They'll hear," she hissed at him.

"Quiet, then," he growled.

"I... can't be. I can't. Oh..." His hands were still moving, and she was telling herself to stand up, and she was backing into him, all at the same time.

The next moment, one of those huge hands was over her mouth, clamped tight. "Go on, then," he said, his voice low, but as commanding as always. "Go on and yell. I've got you, and you can scream now. Go on and scream for me."

Her fingers were tightening almost painfully on the arms of the chair. He'd increased the tempo, and the pressure. He was working her over, and the people next door were still talking and laughing. They'd been joined by others, too. There was a whole party over there. But she was so close. So close.

"Let it go," Iain told her. "Come on, Nina. Let me have it. Give it to me."

Her legs were shaking, her body stiffening, tightening. She couldn't resist the sweet release. She couldn't resist Iain. She was jerking against him, calling out into his hand, the sound muffled, but clearly audible. The voices were talking, talking. And she was gripping the arms of the chair, the spasms coming in hard waves, one after another, as she shook and cried out into his hand and let it go. She let him have it all.

$$\heartsuit\heartsuit\heartsuit$$

Her body slumped forward, and Iain realized he still had a hand over her mouth. *Too hard,* he thought, and let go. Then he was pulling her up from behind, bringing her to rest against his body, both his arms wrapping around her. He could feel how shaky her legs were, and he needed her so much, he thought it might kill him.

"Thought this was supposed to be... for you," she managed to say. She had her arm around his neck in the way he loved, and he'd captured a full breast, was making her moan a little more. The people next door were still chatting, and Nina was whimpering, and all that combination did was make him burn hotter.

"It was," he said. "It is. It's all for me. Come on."

He kept hold of her, was taking her into the bedroom, shutting the sliders behind them. She was going to need to make some noise, and he needed to hear it. A single lamp shed its soft glow on the bedside table near the window, and that was perfect, because he also needed to watch.

His bed was high, but not high enough for his long legs. He grabbed three pillows from the head, stacked them at the end, and sat her on top of them, then held her in place when she would have wobbled.

"Lie down," he told her. "All the way back."

She did it. Of course she did. He had hold of her ankles, and he was pulling her toward him, then shoving her knees up so her heels rested on the edge of the bed.

Her head was on the bed, her hips raised high, and just looking at her like that, her arms flung out at her sides, her gorgeous breasts uplifted, was doing him in. And best of all—

the secret heart of her, wide open for him. Waiting for him.

He entered her in one hard thrust, and she cried out, exactly as loudly as he'd known she would.

It was almost over right there. The feel of her. The heat of her, skin to skin. He had his hands on her hips, holding her in place, and he had to stop for a moment. Stop, and breathe, and wait.

She wasn't willing to wait, though. She was squirming into him, trying to make it happen.

"Please," she said "Please, Iain. Do it." And there was no resisting that.

When he started to move, he could tell that he'd got this position right. The angle, and the depth—they were working for her. Her eyes were closing, her lips parting, and she was already panting again.

She was so wet, and so warm. The need was pulling at him now, sinking its claws into him, and she was calling out again, trying to get closer. He knew what that meant. He got a hand on each knee and shoved them back until her heels rested against his shoulders, then increased his pace.

It was what she'd needed. Her back arched, and she was getting louder. "Please. *Please.*" Her favorite word, and his, too.

No hesitation this time in her voice, in her body. No anxiety. Just sweet, hot, desperate need. He closed his eyes to feel it better, and when he opened them again, he saw the reflection in the dark wall of glass. Saw himself, his hands on Nina's hips, his thumbs tight over her thighs. Her long legs drawn back, her arms flung overhead. A dark reflection of her most secret self, the one that was his, too.

"Look at the window," he managed to say. "Look at what I'm doing to you."

Confusion in her beautiful eyes, and then she was turning her head.

"That's right," he said. "Now make it better. Touch yourself. Watch yourself come. Show me."

She dragged a hand down her body, and she was doing it.

Beneath him, and in the glass. Doing it all. Her eyes huge, her breath coming in panting gasps, exactly like his. She was tipping him over the edge, past the point of no return. Too far gone to stop it.

She felt the change in him, and responded to it. Her keening cries were rising, filling the room. She began to spasm, and the waves gripped him, squeezed him tight, took him over. Her voice, her body were pulling him up higher, and higher still. Straight over the top. He tightened his hold on her, plunged deep, and lost himself in the darkness.

♡♡♡

Afterwards, when she was lying tucked under his arm in that spot that was so especially hers, he said, "Guess I didn't tell you that I liked your surprise."

He felt her soft laugh against his skin. "Can I tell you something? I thought you hated it. I thought I'd embarrassed you, or that I did it wrong. I've never sent a message like that before."

He held her closer, smoothed a hand over her shoulder, down her arm, and said, "Wrong? Never. Anytime you want to text me that you're getting naked for me? That's what we call welcome information."

"But you didn't answer me."

That stopped him flat. "Oh. It didn't occur to me. I got your message, and I was already on my way. I didn't want to type. I wanted to come home and do it."

"Mm." She rubbed her cheek against his chest. "I figured that out, eventually. That you're a man of action. Good thing your granddad didn't come home in the middle of it. Did that even occur to you?"

Now he was the one laughing. "No. Not a bit. I was pretty far gone. Good thing, you're right, or we would've had the police here. I'm going to have to see to that soundproofing after all, if you're going to make that much noise."

"Really?" He heard the sauciness again, and he loved it.

"Seems to me you had a solution for that. That was a little dominant, wasn't it, the hand over my mouth? Keeping me quiet?"

"You didn't like it?"

"I liked it." She snuggled closer, practically purring in his arms. "I liked it all."

They heard the front door open and shut, just at that opportune moment, then the sound of the alarm being shut off, and Iain groaned, rolled out of bed, and went for a pair of shorts. "I'll go check on him," he said. "You'd better be appreciating my sacrifice. Seems I told you once that you were hard to leave. I have to tell you—it just keeps getting worse."

like a princess

♡

Five days later, Nina rolled her head and stretched out first one arm, then the other. She'd been swimming in the sea every day, focusing on keeping her strokes long, slow, and controlled. She'd also been going to a power yoga class almost every morning in a boathouse by the sea. This morning, she'd taken two classes, one after the other, finishing up every time letting her body sink into her mat while the waves rolled in and out beneath the floor. Now, she inhaled and exhaled, counted her breaths, and reminded her body how that had felt. Today, she would need all her serenity.

It had taken nearly two weeks, in the end, to get the press conference set up. Enough time for journalists to fly in from overseas, for newspapers and magazines to make space for the story. She was still big news, it seemed. She hadn't been following it, but her publicist had. And as she'd suspected, the rumors hadn't been good. An affair and a major drug problem were only two of them.

She didn't look in the mirror. The stylists had done their job, and she looked perfect. When the aide said, "It's one o'clock," she nodded and walked out behind the young woman, through a blinding sea of flashbulbs, and up to the

347

table, where she sat in front of a plain dark-blue backdrop in a sleeveless dress of soft, rich pink with a high neckline and fitted bodice. Showing all of her arms, with the new tone she'd acquired. The color gave a warm glow to her skin, providing a rich contrast to her brown eyes and hair. A pair of gold hoops in her ears was her only jewelry. It was all very simple. All very classic. All very serene.

She folded her hands on the table in front of her, offered a faint smile to the room, and began the short, bland statement she'd worked out with Andrea and Heidi, the publicist, in a long phone call.

She'd decided against the wedding a week before it was to take place, had told Matthias of her decision, and had left the palace. She couldn't explain why he hadn't chosen to share that information until after the wedding day, because she didn't know. She knew that there had been a great deal of speculation about her whereabouts, all of it incorrect. In fact, she'd simply been taking some private time in New Zealand, and hadn't even been aware of the fuss until a week after she'd left.

She finished, nodded, and waited for the questions.

"What made you choose New Zealand?" a French reporter asked.

Nina leaned forward a little into the microphone and said, "There weren't any flights to Antarctica."

A little ripple of laughter, and a local reporter was asking, "You're Australian by birth. Is this your first visit across the Tasman? What do you think of the country?"

"I think it's beautiful," she said. "It's my first time, yes, but I've felt very welcome here despite my choice of birthplace."

More laughter, and an American asked, "So the rumors that you were in rehab?"

"Well, it's certainly been relaxing," Nina said. "But I suppose the beach is as much 'rehab' as I needed." One more reason for the sleeveless dress. To show that she was fit, healthy, and free of needle marks. Nothing to hide.

"What's the story on the haircut?" another American

asked.

"Time for a change, maybe? What do you think?" Nina put a light hand to the sassy, messy little cut, expertly colored back to her rich brunette.

"Very Audrey Hepburn," the reporter said. "Very *Roman Holiday.*"

"Yes," Nina said with a little smile. "That's exactly how it feels. Except that she went back to being a princess, didn't she? I'm still dancing and eating ice cream, myself." Well, no. But it sounded good.

"Do you have any message for the prince?" a British reporter asked.

Nina kept the tension out of her body, the smile on her face. "Not really. I've already given him my message."

"Are you still friends?' the American asked.

"No." Nina let the word hang in the air, but kept the Mona Lisa smile. Let him explain *that* away.

"So what's next for you?" The Aussie, this time.

"My agent is fielding offers." Fielding more after this, she hoped. "And right now, I'm enjoying New Zealand."

"And the rumors of another man?" the American asked. "Any truth to that?"

This was where it got tricky. She and Iain had discussed this as they'd sat in bed, Nina's arms wrapped around her knees, Iain's face serious. She didn't want to hide her relationship with him, and if it came out after she'd denied it? That wouldn't help anything.

He'd said, "Do what you need to do. Say what you need to say, and I'll cope." Of course he had. That was Iain. Solid as a rock, and just that strong.

She answered the reporter exactly as she'd practiced it. "Did I run away with somebody, or to somebody? No. I didn't." She leaned forward a fraction and said the words she'd rehearsed in the mirror. She said them to the room, and she said them to the world. And most of all, she said them to Matthias. "I *walked* away from my wedding because I didn't want it, and for no other reason. That relationship is over. As for any relationship I enter into now? That's an entirely separate matter, and a private one."

"You aren't on social media," another Aussie said. "Any plans to change that, to share a little more?"

"No. I don't discuss my private life. Can I tell you a secret?" She leaned forward again and spoke confidentially into the microphone. "I've barely looked at a computer in almost a month. It's been wonderful. I recommend it. The world still spins all the same, even when we're not watching."

The aide stepped forward at a prearranged signal, and Nina said, "Thank you for coming," rose with every ounce of grace she possessed, and walked away in high, nude-colored heels. Not a wobble to be seen, and nothing but confidence in her step.

She'd never felt more like a princess.

♡♡♡

It was one kind of liberation, and it felt good. The thing she did later that afternoon didn't.

She was sitting on Iain's back patio again, where she'd done all the planning for her new life. What she thought of as *her* spot, where she could hear the birds and the trickling water in the little stream and the wind in the trees. Where she could take a walk to the beach after whatever difficult decision she'd made, whatever tricky conversation she'd held, and follow it up with a swim. Where she could let all the tension flow into the endless sky, into a sea that extended all the way across the Pacific. Where she could remember how far away LA and New York and London and Neuenstein all were, and that they were just a few tiny spots in a big wide world. And that she didn't have to bounce off of everybody else's expectations, everybody else's desires, like a pinball in a machine, helpless against the levers that shoved her in one direction or another. That she could be her own steady center, wherever she was.

She had a feeling, though, that it was going to take a long

walk, and a longer swim, to put this one into perspective.

"Hi, Mum," she said when her mother picked up the phone.

"I should hang up," her mother said. "I should do it right now. Why? What did I ever do to you except my very best?"

Nina's hand was shaking. *New me. New rules.* "I'm not interested in talking about the past," she said. "You made what you thought were the best decisions for me, and I'm grateful for that."

"Too right I did. I got you to the top. I gave my life to you and your career. And now you *fire* me? Without even *telling* me? I call Andrea, and she tells me she can't talk to me, because I'm not your business manager anymore?" Her tough-minded mother was choking up, and Nina's heart twisted with guilt. "I've never been more shocked, or felt more humiliated. Why? That's what I don't understand. Why?"

"Mum," Nina said, "Wait. I'm sorry about how you found out. Really. But I knew you'd tell Matthias where I was, and I couldn't afford that. He's tried to track me down, even after the wedding day, and I don't know why. He's... he scares me."

"He has?" Her mother wasn't sounding weepy anymore, at least. "Why didn't you tell me? Not that I'm all that surprised. He gave me the boot out of that palace like I had head lice. I saw a whole different side of him."

"Really?" Nina couldn't help it. She was fascinated.

"How could I have known why you'd left," her mother demanded, "when you didn't tell me?"

"But you were so happy for me to marry him."

"Of course I was. Just like you were happy to do it. And then you weren't, and you didn't tell me why, or even that you were leaving, and I thought you were being immature and silly. I didn't have a clue, because you didn't give me one."

Nina had to sit a moment and grapple with that. "The fact remains, though," she said slowly, "that you trusted his judgment more than you trusted mine. I didn't trust mine, either. That was the problem. But at least I trusted it enough to leave. And you just assumed I was wrong."

"Of course I didn't."

It was so hard to stay strong. So hard not to give in, to please, to appease. Half of her cravenly wished that she'd waited until she'd had Iain here beside her to lend her his strength. But it wasn't his to do. It was hers.

"Yes, Mum," she said. "You did. You stayed at the palace because you assumed I was wrong to leave, and you wanted to help him get me back. That's trusting his judgment. I'll bet you shared my banking information with him so he could track me down, too."

Long seconds of silence, and then her mother said, "Well, if I did, it's because you're young, and you've always had me to look after you. And you didn't tell me, so how would I know?"

"You're right." It was here. This was the moment. "I'm telling you now, though. And yes, I *have* always had you. I'm telling you that that's changing, too. I'm turning twenty-six this week."

"I'm aware of that. I gave birth to you."

"You did. And you held on to me after my dad left. You did your best. I get that. You made good decisions for my career, and you invested my money carefully and looked after my best interests. You did all of that, and I appreciate it. But I'm older than you were when you *did* have me, and it's time for me to do all those things for myself."

"You don't know how. You don't have the first idea."

"Then I'll learn." She was shaking now, hanging onto the table the way she had during every one of the calls she'd made during these past weeks. This one was the hardest, because this was what it had all been building toward. "Whatever modeling I choose to do, I have one of the best agents in the business, and I hope I can ask you questions if I need your advice. I hope I can come to you, and that you'll still be there for me, even if it's not in the same way."

There was nothing but alarm in her mother's tone. "What

do you mean, 'Whatever modeling you choose to do?' I've told you, your time is *now*. You can't afford to throw it away."

"Yes. I can. I can afford anything I like. I have enough money invested, and enough equity in the house, for that matter, that I don't have to do anything I don't want to do."

"That's no way to think. I've told you. Living the right lifestyle costs. You have to look successful to be successful, and there's no coasting. There's success, or there's failure. If you aren't on top, you're slipping down."

Nina's fingers were white with tension now. "Maybe so. I guess I'll find out. But in any case, I'm selling the house."

"*What?*" It was almost a scream. "No. You can't. You're throwing away all our security!"

"No, Mum. I'm not. Our security is everything we've invested, and everything we can still do with our lives. I know you've invested most of what you've earned as my manager, because I've paid your living expenses."

"That is the most… ungrateful…"

"No. It's not. It's the truth. You have investments, and if you want to keep living the way you have, you could set up as a business manager to other models. More than one, which could be even better for you. You have more contacts than anyone, and you're good at it. Look how you managed my career and built me from nothing. Your security isn't me, Mum. I'm a face and a body. There are lots of us out there. How many times have you told me that? I'm not your asset. *You* are."

It had taken so many walks, so many swims to figure this out. She was the only one who believed it, apparently, because her mother said, "That's rubbish. If you do this, I won't forgive you."

There was a lead weight in Nina's chest, but for once, it wasn't guilt. It was sorrow. "I hope you will, Mum. I love you, and I appreciate you. But I need to live my life, and you need to live yours, and those two things aren't the same anymore."

"I can't talk to you," her mother said. "I'm hanging up." And she did.

new choices and second chances

♡

Iain didn't get to watch Nina's press conference until evening, and the wait wasn't fun.

He'd wanted to go with her, of course. And she'd said no.

"You have to go to training," she'd said. "And besides, I don't need any more speculation."

"I can leave for a bit," he'd argued. "For an hour, anyway. We're allowed to have lives. Things happen. I don't have to be in the room. I can wait in a side room, wherever you'll be."

"Somebody will recognize you. An aide. A reporter, when you're getting into your car afterwards. Somebody. And it'll start up everything that I'm squashing, about why I left. After this is out, Iain. Afterwards. I promise."

So instead, at five o'clock, he was sitting in the lounge, holding her hand, his granddad in the recliner beside them, watching the recording on the big screen.

The poised, confident woman on the screen, answering every question in that husky, confiding voice, telling her truth, was his Nina, and she wasn't. His Nina was sitting beside him, her long legs tucked up under her, wearing her rose-printed skirt and red T-shirt, every bit of makeup scrubbed off. Her face was naked, and vulnerable, and even more

355

beautiful. It was a strange, disturbing vision, of her being two people at once.

He watched her up on the screen, walking out like she owned the room, and asked, "How did you feel?"

"Nervous. But ready. And now?" She sighed. "All sorts of things. All mixed up. I feel great, and I feel terrible, but at least I feel done. Ready to move on."

Maybe that was good, but it didn't sound good. Not from his point of view, anyway.

"And you know what your granddad and I did after that?" she asked.

Arthur was sitting there, smiling smugly. "No idea," Iain said. "What?"

Nina got up with all the grace as she'd shown in that press conference and tugged him by the hand. "Come on. We'll show you."

It involved waiting for his granddad to get to the door with the aid of his cane, then making their slow way up the driveway to the street until Nina stopped in front of a tiny red Honda Fit and put a proprietary hand on the hood. "We went car shopping," she said. "I've got my own wheels. Pretty cool, huh?" She laughed, such a happy sound. "I've never bought a used car before. I've never bought a car at all. I've always leased. Thank goodness for Arthur. He is *tough*. You wouldn't believe what a bargainer he is."

"Nah," Arthur said. "Kiwi, is all. Cheap as."

"I would've..." Iain didn't know what to say. He was still looking at the car. "I mean, you have mine, and you're welcome to drive it all you like. I told you. I could've kept getting a lift with Hugh or Nico to training."

"No," she said. "I wanted my own. Don't you like it?"

"Nah, it's good."

"I can drive your granddad and me to the airport," she said. "For the match. My coming-out party."

Iain was leaving tomorrow for his second preseason match, this one against the Chiefs. This one was being held in Napier, another exhibition brought to Super Rugby fans. And this time, Nina was coming, because she didn't have to hide anymore. She and his granddad were flying down to Hawke's Bay, and on Sunday, his granddad was going home, because Nina didn't need him anymore. She didn't need shielding.

Her story was out there, shared with the world, and she was free. That was a good thing, even though Iain had woken in a cold sweat in the middle of the night more than once for exactly that reason. That she was free.

And she'd bought a car. That was good, he told himself. It meant she was planning on staying a while. And all the same, everything had changed today. He couldn't tell what to think. It was all spinning too fast for him to grab hold.

"But you don't like that I bought it," Nina was saying slowly. "You hate it, in fact. You hate that I've got my own transportation."

"Did I say that? No. I said it was good."

"But you didn't mean it. You *don't* mean it. You're standing there like a poker. You hate it."

"How do you know what I mean? How do you know what I think?"

"I have to guess, don't I?" she said. "Because you aren't telling me."

"I'm going back inside," Arthur said. "Get dinner started."

"Uh..." Nina made a movement to accompany him.

"You stay," Arthur said. "You and Iain take a walk. I don't need that tension in the kitchen."

He headed back toward the house, and Iain ran a hand over his jaw and looked at Nina. He should say something, but he couldn't think what.

She sighed. "He's right. Let's take a walk."

"Right." He set off down the hill with her toward the beach. He wanted to take her hand, but she had her arms crossed over her chest.

"You don't like my buying a car," she finally said.

"I didn't say that. I said it was good."

"Come on." Nina could sometimes be so tentative, but she wasn't tentative now. "You tell me to be honest? *You* be

357

honest. I can see how you feel, and I'm wanting to make it better, to change so I make you happy, and I *hate* that. I was all excited, and now I'm worried about what you think. So tell me."

"It made me feel odd, then. That what you want to hear?"

"You want me dependent on you."

"*No.*"

She looked at him, her gaze steady. "Yes. Do you know what I did today, after my press conference?"

"You bought that."

"After that. I called my mother."

He stopped where he was, beside a rope swing, heedless of the neighbor working in her garden twenty feet away. "I want you to tell me," he said. "I want to hear. But could you trust me enough to hold my hand?"

"Oh." She unwound her arms, and he took her slim hand in his own and instantly felt better.

"Now," he said, "tell me. If I disappoint you, I disappoint you. But at least give me a chance."

She did tell him, then, and he was, alternately, furious, and astonished, and proud. And then furious again.

"And then she hung up on me," she said, and he could hear the tremor in her voice. "It was the right thing to say, and the right thing to do, but it just… I just… I felt horrible. I thought this day was going to be my independence. I did all these things. They were so hard, and I wanted to tell you. And then when you said that about the car…"

"Oh, bloody hell." He turned, there on the pavement, and took her in his arms. "No."

She went stiff for a moment, and he was afraid she was going to break away from him, to tell him that he was part of it, too. Part of her problem, when all he wanted to be was her solution. He didn't know how to say that, though. So he just held her.

Three seconds. Four. And then she was relaxing against him, her arms going around his waist, her cheek against his chest. He felt the rise and fall of her breath under his palms and said, "I'm sorry about the car. That was me being stupid."

"It's not your decision."

"You're right," he said. "It's not. There you go. Got the 'sorry' and all."

She laughed shakily and pulled away, and they were walking again, across the zebra crossing and onto the beach, slipping off their shoes and stepping onto the warm sand. He was holding her hand again, and they were heading to the shoreline and along the long curve of the bay toward the green hump of North Head.

"Why didn't you tell me all this?" he asked her at last. "What you were planning to do with your mum, and about the car. Why didn't you say?"

"Because I had to do it myself." She looked up at him, her expressive face serious. "Like I had to buy my car. I'll tell *you* the truth now. I wished I'd had you sitting beside me while I talked to her."

He squeezed her hand more tightly. "I would've done it, too."

"I know you would have. But I wouldn't have been sure, then, that I could have done it by myself, and I needed to know that."

"Right. That's a lot of change, though."

"Yes." Her voice wobbled on the word. "It is. I know all those changes are right, but I'm terrified."

So am I, he thought, but he didn't say it. Right now, she needed to hear this. "Sounds like you're making good choices to me."

"My mum was right, too, though." She'd let go of his hand and had her arms wrapped around herself again. "I don't know what I'm doing, and I *will* make mistakes."

"Probably. I guess you have to ask yourself whether that's better than having her choose for you. Or than having that Matthias choose for you."

"It's better." She looked out to sea, toward the majestic cone of Rangitoto standing sentinel over the Harbour. "Of course it's better. But it's fragile, all this. When you tell me I can't buy a car, it brings it all back."

"I didn't say that."

She looked at him again. "No. But you wanted to."

"If this is going to end because I'm stupid," he said, "it's going to end for sure."

That surprised a laugh from her. "Well, I guess I just said I'd make mistakes."

"Too right. And so will I. You don't have to run away from me, and you don't have to give in. But you do have to fight."

"I have to *fight?*"

"Yeh. You do. How d'you think the shoes get worn down and scuffed?" He wasn't going to stand in her way, but he wasn't going to stand here passively, either, and let her walk away from him without trying to hold her. He was going to fight to be her other shoe. And he needed her to fight for it, too, or what was the point?

She didn't have her arms around herself anymore. She wrapped them around his waist, stepped close, and said, "You know what? You're my favorite person in New Zealand."

He put his arms around her and said, "You know what? So are you."

turn the page
♡

Matthias had already wasted months of his life on Sabrina. He didn't mean to waste any more. It was time to get this done.

He sat in his home theatre, with no company for this viewing but Raoul. It was still dark outside at seven o'clock on a dreary morning in February, and he should be conquering the steepest black *pistes* of St. Moritz or cruising the Caribbean, not stuck here the way he had been for the past two weeks since the announcement of the press conference,waiting for this.

On screen, Sabrina was gazing out at the cameras with a disdainful smile, as if she were superior to everyone there. "I walked away from my wedding," she said, "because I didn't want it, and for no other reason. That relationship is over. As for any relationship I enter into now? That's an entirely separate matter, and a private one."

Any relationship I enter into now.

"The hair is disgusting," he told Raoul. "You didn't tell me she'd cut her hair." It was one of the reasons he'd chosen her. For the elegance of it, coiled into a chignon, and the curling mass of it when he'd had his hands twisted in it, when he'd been pulling her by it. Even now, his groin tightened at the memory. He'd told her she must always leave it long, and what had she done? She'd done the opposite, as soon as she'd left. She'd cut it all off.

"I didn't think it was relevant," Raoul said.

"Everything is relevant," Matthias snapped. "We know for sure that she's in Auckland. What is being done to pick up the man?" They'd known for more than a week, actually, since the press conference had been scheduled. And *still* they had nothing.

"It's complicated," Raoul said. "They know what car he drives, but he doesn't seem to have been driving it to his practice sessions. The players come and go from behind locked gates, and he hasn't been seen. He must be driving with somebody else."

"Then they should track them all. And what of his house? Surely that could be traced."

Raoul shrugged. "The ownership is not registered in his name, apparently. He has an investment trust, perhaps. It's time to let it go. She's been on camera, worldwide, saying that she's finished with your relationship. If you appear again in her life, and she rejects you, and discusses it with the media? You'll look weak, and perhaps worse. There's nothing to be gained."

"I told you," Matthias said. "I do not require advice. Find him."

"I repeat," Raoul said, "if you break the laws of a foreign state, you put yourself in an uncomfortable position."

"I'm not breaking any laws. I want to talk to her."

"Why?"

"It's not your job to ask me why."

"And yet I am asking. Why?"

Matthias knew he shouldn't answer. He needed to put Raoul in his place once and for all. But he told him anyway, because the answer burned in him. "I need to see her face to face. I need to tell her why I shouldn't have chosen her. I need to tell her that I wouldn't have wanted her anyway, and to make her see that she was nothing. To make her *know* it. Once I do that, I can turn the page."

"It won't help."

Matthias rose to his feet. "Don't tell me what will or won't help. Find her, and find him. Enough excuses. That's what they've been, haven't they? Excuses."

"I work for the security of the principality," Raoul said. "That is my brief."

He'd known it, Matthias thought. He'd *known* it. "You've been holding out on me," he said. "Nobody could be this incompetent."

"I saw no point," Raoul said. "There is too much to lose, and nothing to gain."

Matthias still didn't lose control. *That* was where there was no point. There was only success or failure, winners or losers. "Do it now," he said, staring the other man down. "Do it, or I'll be telling you that *you* are unsuitable. I'm the one who tells you what your brief is, and it is to do what I say and nothing else."

"Your father—" Raoul began.

"My father means nothing. What he wanted means nothing. He is not the prince anymore. I am. Or is it that you expect me to have loyalty to you because my father employed you? That means nothing to me either. You were well paid for your services. If you can't get the job done, you're gone. Exactly like Sabrina."

doing the job

♡

Leaving Nina on Thursday morning wasn't one bit easy. Leaving his granddad wasn't terrific, either, not with Arthur flying back to Nelson on Sunday morning.

He said his goodbyes out on the driveway, while he was waiting for Hugh to arrive and give him a lift to the airport. And it had never been harder to do.

"You could always stay," he told his granddad one more time. "Long as you like. Company for Nina, eh."

"Got a life too, haven't I," Arthur growled. "And the fishing isn't nearly as good up here. I've got mates as well, you know. Things to do."

Iain brushed a thumb along his nose and didn't look at Nina. He knew she'd be smiling. His granddad had finally emerged from his long depression, and Iain knew exactly who to credit with that.

"I'm going inside," Arthur said. "Take care you bring Nina with you next time you come down. I see you by yourself, and we're going to have words."

This time, Iain *did* laugh. He gave his granddad a gentle hug and added a few pats on the back. The old man's gnarled hands were gripping him, too, and Iain found himself choking up a little. "Message received," he said. "Look after her this weekend, though, would you? Just in case."

"Do me a favor." Arthur had pulled back, his own eyes looking suspiciously bright. He cleared his throat. "I'm going inside. Can't hang about here all day. Hope you're on the road soon. The traffic's bound to be shocking. Another reason to go back to civilization, where people are content to stay in their own homes instead of running about all day long."

He stumped away, and Iain was left looking at Nina. She had her head up and her smile on, and she was doing things to his heart. He told her, "I can't wait to come back and celebrate your birthday with you."

"I'm celebrating the real day by watching you play," she said, "and that's a present in itself."

"Not to mention that independence and all. Pretty good way to start in on twenty-six."

"That's right." She was trying to sound confident, and he knew she didn't feel it.

Hugh's car appeared at the end of the drive, Iain heard the quick hoot of his horn, and he was taking Nina in his arms and feeling her nestling close. "Three days. And Sunday's ours. I'll text you when I get in today."

"You do that." She had her arms around him, too. "I'll be fine. You go on."

Which he did. It was his job, and if it was hard to do at times? It was still his job.

♡♡♡

Napier, Nina found on Saturday, was a picture-postcard-pretty town near the southern point of the long sweep of coastline that was Hawke's Bay. After a brief taxi ride from the airport, she walked with Arthur to his room in the Masonic Hotel, an Art Deco masterpiece on the waterfront, and asked him, "Sure you don't want to come with us?"

"What, shopping?" He snorted. "I hope I know when I'm better off. I'm having lunch, taking a walk, then having a rest before the match, and I don't need to add anything else. Mind you don't bother me until dinner."

"All right, then." Nina went to her own room, touched up her makeup, and headed to the lobby to meet Josie.

Jocelyn Pae Ata, that is. The wife of Hugh Latimer, Iain's captain and the man who'd driven them home from the airport. An actress, and an international model herself who'd called Nina the night before and invited her to spend the afternoon with her, much to Nina's surprise.

"Hugh just told me about you," Josie had said on the phone. "Seems Iain just told *him* who you actually are. I can't believe Hugh didn't know you when he met you. Men, eh. I watched your press conference, and I'd have known you straight away. Hugh does his share of the shopping, your photo's been on all those covers, and he still didn't recognize you?"

"Well," Nina had tried to explain, "I look different without makeup."

A soft laugh at that. "Don't we all. But come hang out before the match with me. I can show you about a bit."

"Well, really…" Nina had hesitated. "What I'd actually like to do is shop. I'd been lying low until after the press conference, and I'm afraid my wardrobe would shock you."

"Not me. But of course we'll shop. Shop, then have a bit of lunch and a good gossip. A perfect afternoon off."

Now, Nina walked down the staircase to the lobby and found a young Maori woman rising to meet her. Josie, unlike Nina, didn't need the camera to make her stunning. And despite her claim to be casual, the other woman looked perfectly elegant in a pale-yellow tea dress and sandals.

"Hi," Josie said, giving Nina a quick hug and a kiss on the cheek. "And welcome. I'm so happy I get to be the first to meet you. All the other girls will be jealous. They're fizzing about your story. Most exciting thing we've heard for ages."

"Oh," Nina said lamely. "Really?"

"Whoops. Too frank. Sorry. But while I'm putting my foot in it, I'll say that I was happy for Iain's sake as well. The big ones always have the softest marshmallow centers, eh. And that ends my inappropriate commentary," Josie said with a laugh. "You want to start with lunch, or shopping?"

Nina was laughing, too. She couldn't help it. She plucked at her rose-printed skirt with a rueful glance. "Shopping, please. I bought this at a secondhand store in Nelson, and I'm embarrassed to tell you how many times I've worn it. I should probably burn it."

"Nah, why?" Josie asked comfortably, heading across the lobby with decision and pushing open the brass-handled glass door. "It looks good on you, and you're in En Zed now. No need to be flash. This way," she added, heading south. "Straight to the shops."

"You say that," Nina said, keeping pace easily with this woman who was as tall and long-legged as herself, "but I notice you're pretty flash."

Josie smiled again under her giant sunglasses, looking every inch the star. "Only because I have to be. I've got a new show starting up next season, and I want people to tune in. Ask Hugh what I wear at home. You could be shocked yourself."

Unlike Josie, Nina's image didn't matter, not here and now. She wanted to look pretty for herself, though, and maybe, more than a bit, for Iain. She'd enjoyed her beauty vacation, but it was a comfort all the same to be armored behind pretty clothes, well-cut hair, and expertly applied makeup. And a different kind of comfort to know she didn't have to wear the armor unless she wanted to.

"What should I wear tonight?" she asked Josie when she was loaded down with three bags full of pants, skirts, dresses, and tops, and another two bags containing four pairs of shoes. The whirlwind trip had been nothing like a designer shopping spree, but so much more satisfying. Just for fun, and just for her. "I was thinking the brown-and-white polka dots." Not because she thought it was necessarily rugby-appropriate, but because the full-skirted, light-as-air pleated chiffon with its vintage cut and print matched so perfectly with the town around her, and made Nina feel so pretty.

Josie laughed, but it didn't sound unkind. "You'd freeze, and you'd be heaps too flash for Napier. Wear the skinny jeans and the sweater that slips off your shoulder. That'll be perfect. But right now, I'm starved. What would you say to lunch?"

When they were eating salads in a sidewalk café with a view of the sea, resting their weary feet after their labors, Josie said, "I'll tell you the truth, it's a treat to eat lunch with somebody who isn't always telling me to have more. Hugh tries to watch it, but he slips. And my mum?" She shook her elegant head. "Hopeless. The body pays the bills, eh."

"*Yes,*" Nina said. "Why don't they get it? It's the job. Maybe you shouldn't have to be so thin, but you do."

"Specially if you model undies," Josie said with a teasing light in her brown eyes.

Nina looked sharply at her, and Josie laughed. "No worries. The booking that got me my house, a year or two ago? Nothing on me in those shots but a few strategically placed leaves and the occasional horse."

"I confess," Nina found herself saying, "I'm wondering if there's another option. I'm not ashamed of what I've done," she hurried to add, "but I'd rather do it on my own terms. The kind of bookings I want, on the schedule I want."

"Too right," Josie said. "You want my advice?"

"Yes, please." Why was it so easy to tell Josie what she'd had a hard time articulating even to her own mother? Because Josie got it, that was why.

"Tell your agent what you want to do," Josie said. "If she—he?"

"She."

"If she won't help you, or if she digs in her heels? Heaps more agents out there, and you're a hot ticket. You're in the power seat just now, and you need to recognize it. All that publicity, and the way you handled the press conference? You made it sound like that prince wasn't all he's made out to be."

"He wasn't."

Nina didn't want to say more, and Josie didn't press her. Instead, she said, "So tell your agent what you want. Want to do something more high-end, show less of the body? Use the 'princess' leverage to get it."

"I didn't turn out to be a princess, though," Nina pointed out.

"People don't follow things as closely as we think," Josie said. "To the public, you're close enough. Got glamour now, haven't you. If you want to use it—go for it. If you don't dare to say what you want, who's going to know? All they can say is no."

♡♡♡

All that was good, and so was dinner with Arthur and an entire group of rugby WAGS—wives and girlfriends—who turned out to be a lot more down-to-earth than Nina had feared. The rest of them walked to the stadium, but she and Arthur took a taxi, in deference to Arthur's hip. Walking into the grounds, then up the concrete steps to their seats turned out to be exercise enough, and she knew the hard plastic would be uncomfortable for him, though he'd never complain.

She hadn't been to a live sporting event since one or two football games in high school, but to her surprise, the atmosphere tonight felt much the same. A festive, small-town environment, all families and laughter and chat from the half-capacity crowd.

"Preseason," Arthur said when she commented. "Wait until you see the All Blacks at Eden Park. Fifty thousand, and every seat filled. This is a warmup, is all."

For all that, he applauded as loudly as anyone when the teams ran onto the field to the accompaniment of a surge of music from the loudspeakers.

"Captaincy's sitting well on Hugh," Arthur said to Josie, nodding to where the big, bearded figure had run out in front of his men, holding the ball.

"Yes," she said proudly. "He'll be up to the job, no worries."

Nina barely heard them. She was watching Iain. The tallest man on his team, he was at the sideline now, stripping off his warmups with the others until he was dressed only in a skintight blue jersey and short shorts. He was bouncing on his toes, swinging his enormous arms, rolling his head. So clearly ready to engage, jumping out of his skin with the need to get physical, and she got a frisson of pure desire from the sight.

A muscular, handsome Maori whom she recognized from the televised match the week before kicked the ball for the Blues, and from there, Nina was lost. One team had the ball, then the other. There were some boring minutes where half the team formed up in what Arthur called "the scrum" and shoved at half the other team, then did it again and again because the referee kept blowing his whistle.

Mostly, though, it was fast. There were a few juking breakout runs, and a few moments here and there where the ball was passed backward from hand to hand at a full run with a skill that made her heart pound, the players seeming to know instinctively, without looking, where another set of hands would be. Otherwise, it was all hard hits, churning heaps of bodies, and ferocity.

And Iain in the thick of it. *Not one of the flash boys at the back,* he'd said, and now, Nina realized what he'd meant. The week before, on TV, she'd barely seen him, since the cameras had mostly been on the ball carrier, and that was rarely Iain. Now, she was able to focus her attention on him, whatever else was going on.

As she'd seen the week before, he touched the ball only occasionally, carrying it in short, grinding runs that mainly seemed aimed at drawing tacklers, since it took two or three of them to bring him down. Otherwise, he spent most of his time tackling opposing players and doing some sort of support thing. At least, when there was a heap of bodies on the field, pushing and shoving, he was usually in it.

And then, late in the second half, with the Blues behind by six points and Nina's eyes having honestly glazed over a little, something actually happened that she could understand.

An opposition player had the ball down near his own line, and Iain was among three players charging at him. The Chiefs player was kicking it away, trying to get his team out of trouble. The ball was off his foot, arcing up. And Iain was leaping, jumping impossibly high, his long arms stretching, his big mitt of a hand slapping the ball down. Another roar from the crowd as the ball took a crazy bounce off the turf and Iain reached for it and, somehow, came up with it.

Just like that, he was off with a burst of acceleration astonishing in a man of his size. The player who'd kicked the ball was lunging for him, grabbing at him, but Iain had his head and shoulders down and was plowing through him, sending him bouncing back like a pool ball hit by a cue.

Iain had the ball cradled in two hands now, his powerful legs churning, showing the effects of that time in the gym, all that running and bicycling, all that sweat and dedication. He was going through a second tackler, then outpacing another who came in at a diagonal to intercept him. He was flying. Across the white strip at the end of the field and diving for the turf, his arms outstretched, still gripping the precious ball.

Nina didn't know she was on her feet until she found herself jumping, together with half the crowd. She turned a laughing face to Arthur, and found him still sitting, a huge smile on his face.

She sat down again, hugged him, and kissed his cheek. "Touchdown!"

"Nah," he said, but he was grinning. "Try."

"Oh, right." She laughed happily. "I forgot. But we're still behind."

"Quiet," Arthur said. "We're kicking now."

"Oh." Nina looked, and he was right. The Blues kicker, who'd been running as fast as everybody else only a minute earlier, was lined up behind the ball, studying its position on the tee, then lifting his head to look at the vertical bars that marked his target. The crowd was quiet, the seconds stretched out, and then he took three running steps, his leg going forward, his arms counterbalancing, all in one smooth, coordinated movement. The ball sailed through the posts, the scoreboard changed again, and the Blues were ahead by one. And one turned out to be enough.

Whatever Arthur muttered about "preseason," a win had to be better, and the looks on the Blues players' faces told Nina she was right. They raised their hands, clapped to the crowd, and ran back into the tunnel. And she stood with Arthur and prepared to leave the stadium.

She wanted to see Iain afterwards. Of course she did. And she knew she couldn't.

"I'll be with the squad," he'd explained. "See you at home tomorrow, though."

She texted him again anyway.

I'm naked, she wrote, *but you don't care. Good job with the swatting thing.*

She could almost see his grin when he texted back, *I care. I'll show you tomorrow. The swatting was fun. Happy birthday, gorgeous girl.*

She had to be content with that.

♡♡♡

In the morning, though, she wasn't thinking about Iain. She was focused on Arthur.

The moment of truth came in Napier Airport, which was barely larger than the terminal at Nelson. Arthur was headed home via Wellington, and his plane left first. That was better, of course. It meant she could see him off. But it tore at her heart all the same.

She waited in the plastic chairs with him for his flight to be called. Ten minutes to go, then five. He gathered his cane, and she couldn't help the tears that sprang to her eyes.

"I wish you weren't going," she said.

"Nah," he said, pulling the boarding pass from his pocket.

"It's time. You need to get back to work yourself, don't you?"

It rocked her. He'd never said a word about it. "I... haven't decided."

His shrewd brown eyes studied her. "Starting your life up again," he said. "Finding out what it'll be. Time for that, I'd say. It won't all be here, I reckon. Exactly how much will be, that's the question, eh."

"I don't want to... " She had to gather herself in order to go on. "I don't want to lose it, though."

She didn't say what *it* was. She didn't have to. "Could be you need to have some faith," Arthur said. "You going to stop loving him?"

She couldn't answer for a long moment. "No," she finally said. "But I don't know if he's willing to... keep going. Not if I'm not here. He hasn't said he is. He hasn't said anything."

"Because he's scared to. Sometimes a woman has to be the brave one. If you want it, do it. Tell him you're his to hold, and that it's his job to do it. After that?" Arthur shrugged his bony shoulders. "If he doesn't hold on? That's on him. His choice."

"What you said, you mean." She was having a hard time with her voice. "No magic. You either want it, or you don't. And making your way through the bad patches."

"I may have been wrong, I've been thinking," he said. "Could be there's a bit of magic in there as well. Or something close enough."

"Finding your other shoe."

"Ah. Iain told you that."

"Yes. He did. It was beautiful. It's what I want."

The loudspeaker crackled into life, a voice was announcing the flight to Wellington, and Arthur hauled himself to his feet.

"Why d'you reckon he told you that?" he asked her. "He's found his shoe, maybe, but he's scared to believe it. Somebody has to go first. Could be you're the strong one after all."

She was biting her lip to control herself as she stood with

him, put her arms gently around him, and felt his hand patting her back. So much comfort. So much love.

"Thank you," she told him. "Thank you for everything. I hope all the fish are big."

He gave his short, dry bark of laughter. "Too right. See you soon, missy." He stumped his way off, and he was gone.

island time

♡

She kept tearing up on the short flight home. Having Arthur leave felt like the end of an era. Or maybe that was her birthday. In any case, something had shifted this weekend. Watching Iain do the job he was so clearly meant for, maybe. Meeting Josie, who had taken her future in both hands. Only Nina herself, it seemed, was still teetering on the edge, uncommitted.

If you want it, do it, Arthur had said.

An hour after she'd landed, she was sitting at the arrivals gate and watching Iain walk out with the mass of rugby muscle that was his team, all of them moving a little stiffly on this morning-after, and having another off-kilter moment.

He was the same funny, exasperating, exhilarating man who'd chased her into the sea and carried her out of it, who'd painted his parents' shed and made love to her under the stars, and he was so much else, too. A celebrity, yes, a performer under the big lights, but more than that. A teammate. A team *man.*

Now, though, he was coming toward her, his grin huge, dropping his duffel, lifting her off her feet, and twirling her around.

"Happy birthday, sweetheart." He gave her a kiss that

threatened to steal her breath. "Let's go celebrate."

He'd told her he had a whole day planned for her on the island of Waiheke, and she couldn't wait. First, though, they stopped at the house to drop their bags, eat lunch, and change.

"Do I get to be pretty?" she asked, poking her head into the bathroom where he was standing, dressed only in a pair of low-slung rugby shorts, every hard slab and bulge of muscle—and every shocking red bruise—on display, with shaving cream covering his square jaw. "And—mmm, can I say?" she added, leaning against the door jamb. "You're very sexy."

He finished stroking the razor over his thick neck, then grinned at her in the mirror as he rinsed the razor in the sink. "Careful. You keep smiling at me like that, and you aren't going to get out of the house. But, yeh. Pretty as you like. Shoes you can walk around town in, that's all."

"Not going to make me take a hike?" she teased. "Or put me in a boat and make me wear a PFD?"

He laughed. "I've exercised enough. This is where I get to take you out and show you off for the first time, and spoil you a bit as well."

"Well, when you put it like that," she said, "how can I refuse?"

"That's what I'm wondering," he said, and she went back out and put on the brown and white polka dots and ballet flats.

Maybe she'd be too flash for Waiheke, too. But she'd be pretty.

When Iain came out, though, he took her by the hand, twirled her as if they were on the dance floor, and said, "Oh, yeh. That's what I'm talking about. That's my girl," which was good enough for her.

It was all sweet, after that. A thirty-minute ride on the ferry across the Harbour to the bucolic island that had become an unlikely glamour destination for the rich and famous, and felt so adventurous for her right now, so much farther afield than she'd ventured during her lying-low period. A twenty-minute walk in the sunshine from the ferry terminal into town, and she was strolling down a sidewalk lined with shops and restaurants, with the blue sea beyond and the scent of salt in the mild summer air, holding hands with Iain. No baseball cap, no cockatoo hair, and no oversized clothes.

"First stop," he said when they got to the gelato stand. "I've been waiting to do this almost since I met you."

"What? Eat ice cream?" She laughed. "I don't do that."

"No worries." He gave his order to the woman behind the counter. Three scoops. "I already decided that having you eat mine works."

When he was sitting at a sidewalk table, holding the spoon to her lips, and watching her lick it off, she may have had a weak moment in more ways than one.

"That's it," he said, and there was so much heat in his eyes. "That's the picture I had. Looks just as good as I imagined."

She smiled slowly at him and said, "Feed me a little more, then," just to watch him heat up. And this time, she may have put some more effort into it. Into closing her eyes, sucking the rich chocolate off the spoon, licking her lips, and then slowly opening her eyes again to see him staring at her.

"Killing me," he said under his breath.

"Well," she said sweetly, "it *is* my birthday. I get to do whatever I want. Even if it's naughty. Know what I want to do next?"

"No, what?" He wasn't quite managing "normal," and she smiled again.

"I want to do a little more shopping," she said. "Try on a few dresses, maybe even some lingerie. What do you think? I've been a lingerie model, you know. I'm good at putting on filmy little things. And taking them off, too."

"I've heard." He finished the gelato in three bites and tossed the rubbish.

"And you didn't look for yourself?"

"I may have had a wee peek."

She had a wee peek herself up at him from under her lashes, then stood, twitching the hem of her floaty dress. "Did you have a favorite? Just for reference."

He cleared his throat and stood up with her. "Could be."

"Care to share?"

"Uh…" He was looking a little hunted. "There may have been some undies. High-cut in behind, I guess you'd call that. A shot of you in them, if I'm forced to confess. I can barely remember it now, but I seem to recall."

"Ah," she said. "Would that be the one of me on my knees on the seat of an armchair, holding onto the back of it and looking over my shoulder at the camera? They put me on a full spread once."

"A full… spread."

She widened her eyes at him, then tucked her hand into the crook of his elbow and snuggled up close. "A catalog spread. Why, what did you think I meant?"

"Ah… never mind."

"And you already got that, remember?" she asked him.

He was clearing his throat now. "Well, not exactly that. Close. But not exactly. I could stand to see it again, let's say."

She kept him waiting for a good forty minutes in the first shop, sitting on a husband-chair in a corner while she tried on clothes, occasionally prancing out and twirling for him. He looked patient and resigned, mostly, until she came out of the fitting room in a short, clingy little hot-pink slip dress that had unfortunately failed to accommodate her bra.

"How about this one?" she asked.

"Uh…" There was that hunted look again. "Is it a nightie?"

"Nope. It's a dress." She turned around, cocked a hip, and peeked back over her shoulder at him, exactly as she had in the shot he'd remembered so clearly. She didn't have the curtain of luxuriant, shining hair half-hiding her cheek, but he didn't seem to mind. Besides, the hair would also have hidden the fact that the dress was cut all the way down to the small of her back.

"No?" she asked, because his face was set into some pretty hard lines.

"No." His deep voice was absolutely firm.

"Why not? Not pretty?"

"Because no."

A few other women were sneaking curious looks at the two of them, and a husband a few seats down from Iain was fairly gawking, but Nina ignored him.

"I thought you weren't one of those guys who told his girlfriend what to wear," she said.

"Changed my mind." Iain's blue eyes dared her to disagree. "Want it for your birthday? I'll buy it for you. You can wear it tomorrow night. At home. Because, yeh, it's too pretty, and so are you. Stop teasing."

That got a sigh from a woman browsing nearby. "Lucky," she muttered.

"I'll take it for a birthday present, then," Nina said. "And thank you. I'll buy the caramel one I tried on for myself."

"What was the caramel one?" Iain asked.

"Brown."

"Oh. That was all right," he said, and she laughed.

"So," she said when they were out on the sidewalk, her hand gripping Iain's bicep again. "You up for lingerie shopping, or are you all worn out?"

"No modeling," he said. "I'm meant to be a good citizen, you know. Part of the job. And that doesn't include dragging my saucy girlfriend into an alley and having her against the wall."

"So disappointing," she sighed, and got another stern look for her trouble that made her bite her lip to keep from laughing.

They were in front of the store now, and he seemed to be particularly taken by a tempting bra and thong set made of rich black lace. No surprise there. Iain was a black lace guy all the way.

"I'll buy you anything you like in here," he said. "I'll buy out the store. You can give me a private showing at home, and it'll be happy birthday to me."

She kept it simple all the same. Two sets and a couple of nightgowns, the kind that she wouldn't manage to keep on for long once Iain saw them. She did let him buy her the black set, though.

When they came out of the shop, he got serious. "This is my bit," he said. "This is why we're here." He was taking her hand, then, leading her down the road and into a goldsmith's shop, where individual pieces sat displayed in proud array under glass on pedestal mounts or wooden cases ranged along the walls.

She caught a glimpse of a few price tags and winced. Iain didn't make as much money as she did, she was fairly sure. And all the same, he was stopping in front of a central display stand showing off a necklace of flat, intertwined, shaped pieces of hammered gold. A little barbaric, and a lot bold.

"That," he said. "Try that one on."

"Hmm. This one's nice, too." She pointed to a necklace beneath it, a simpler gold chain with an asymmetrical hammered-gold pendant made up of three triangular pieces. She didn't have to look at the price tag to know that the other one would be incredibly expensive.

"Nah," he said. "Give me pleasure. Let me buy this one for you, if you like it."

The saleswoman, Nina noticed with amusement, cast a dubious eye over Iain's battered barbarian's face, seeming especially concerned by the huge red mark of a bruise on his forehead, one Nina had already pressed gentle lips to today. The woman opened the case, but kept a watchful eye on Iain as he took the necklace from her, turned Nina by the shoulder, and fastened the clasp behind her neck.

He stood behind her, his hands on her bare shoulders, and looked into the mirror with her, and she fought to suppress her shiver of pleasure at the feel of him there, and the deeper emotion that was something dangerously more than pleasure.

"Yes," he said. "That's it. Isn't it?"

She smiled at him in the mirror, picked up his hand from

her shoulder and kissed it, then rubbed it over her cheek. "Yes."

♡♡♡

It hadn't been an exciting day, not compared to the night before, and yet it had been such a good one. Nina teasing, Nina laughing, Nina feeling free and easy and saucy and sweet. And that moment in the mirror, when she'd looked at him with so much softness in her face, and his heart had squeezed so tight, it was almost painful.

He wasn't done yet, though. He took her for an early dinner, and they sat on a restaurant balcony overlooking green hills, golden sand, blue sea, and scudding white sails. Nina ate fish and sipped at a glass of chilled Sauvignon Blanc, looking slim and serene in her filmy dress, the heavy links of hammered gold around her neck giving him an almost visceral jolt of pleasure every time he looked at them. Meanwhile, he did his best to eat his way through the menu, touched her hand from time to time, talked to her about the match the night before, about his granddad, about anything and nothing, and noticed almost nothing but the light in her eyes, the lingering caress of her fingers when she put her own hand lightly onto his wrist to make a point, and then kept it there.

It was her birthday, but so far, it had been all for him.

The sun wasn't yet touching the horizon when he was walking up the street beside her toward the cinema, her hand tucked through his arm again. They could walk like that everywhere, as far as he was concerned.

"Last bit," he said. "For our first date. Ice cream, dinner, and a movie, right? And then home. Isn't that how it's done?"

She laughed softly. "First date? Is that what this is?"

"Well, yeh, I'd say, wouldn't you?"

She considered. "I suppose so. But you're tired, I know. We don't have to do the movie."

"The next ferry's not for well over an hour," he said

practically. "And this film's meant to be a good one. Got a bit of steam in it, I hear, which is never a bad thing."

"Body Heat," she read from the program taped to the door. "Sounds steamy, all right. You need inspiration?"

"We'll call that a 'no.' Besides, Granddad's gone home. That has its compensations, and some inspiration all its own. And I may have another birthday surprise for you along those lines."

"Oh? Am I going to like it?" She was still going for breezy, but it wasn't working quite as well now.

"I'm hoping," he said, "that you're going to love it. But we'll see."

He took her into the cinema, which was little more than an overlarge room with broad risers built in, and a concession table in one corner. The seats, though, weren't seats at all, but twenty or thirty mismatched couches.

"When somebody in Waiheke has an old couch to get rid of," he told her, "they bring it here. Island tradition. Want to sit on a couch with me, drink another glass of wine, and watch a naughty movie? Like being eighteen again, eh."

"Not how eighteen was for me," she said. "Better late than never, I guess. But that'd be two glasses."

"It would," he said. "It's also your birthday. Come on, bad thing. Let's drink wine and sit in the back row."

♡♡♡

Nina couldn't get her breath. They couldn't have been a half hour into the movie, and the wine had already gone down smooth and easy, making her feel relaxed and warm, tucked in close beside Iain on the highest riser in the back corner of the cinema.

The movie went on, though, and there was nothing smooth and absolutely nothing easy about what she was watching on screen. Or about the tension she could feel in Iain. He was holding her hand, and that was all, but it was as if he were touching her, his fingers on her, inside her. She was watching the woman on screen looking out her window into a dark tropical night, and seeing herself on that last night in Kaiteriteri, gripping the edge of the window frame while Iain hauled her in from behind and kissed her neck. It was the man on the screen, but it was Iain, too, who was pulling her onto the floor, yanking up her dress, and taking her hard.

And then it got worse.

On the screen, the palms were swaying, the wind rattling through their fronds, the wind chimes dancing frantically in the dark night. A view through a window, into a bedroom. A woman's hand twisting frantically at white sheets, her cheek pressed into the mattress, her mouth open, panting, gasping. Her body slamming forward, again and again, taken over by the darkest, deepest pleasure.

Nina couldn't look away.

Iain's hand moved. Still holding hers, but on her thigh, where she'd left the last few buttons of her dress undone. His fingers were inching up, drawing a slow path up the smooth surface of her inner thigh. Higher and higher.

Her gaze flew to his face, but he wasn't looking at her. He was watching the screen, seemingly intent on the action, which was back to the suspense plot now. But his hand was all the way up her thigh, her skirt barely covering her. He was stroking, touching, every brush of his fingers a jolt straight up to her core, and it was all she could do not to squirm.

Finally, she couldn't help it. She shivered. A quick turn of his head, and he was glancing at her, then away again, his attention going back to the film. He let go of her, and she tried not to be disappointed, tried to still the throbbing arousal that had left her trembling and weak. They couldn't make out in the back of a movie theater, darkness or no, couches or no. It would be completely inappropriate, and somebody would see them and recognize them. Both of them.

When Iain put his arm around her, she jumped. And when his hand started stroking her upper arm, she bit her lip. His thumb was reaching around to the sensitive flesh of her inner arm, exactly the way he'd stroked her that first night on the beach. When he'd been holding her there, and he'd been over her. Before he'd pulled off her clothes and devoured her.

The theater was air-conditioned, but she was burning up. She put a hand on Iain's muscular thigh, below the hem of his own shorts. Her fingers traced the edge of the fabric, a delicate whisper over hair-roughened male skin.

He was hot, too. Hot, and hard with bunched muscle. He was holding himself rigid, the same way she was. He wasn't one bit relaxed, however lazy his stroking fingers were on her arm.

On screen, the man and woman were talking, planning, scheming. The movie was getting darker, going deeper, the undercurrents swirling. On the couch, Nina sent her fingers tunneling slowly up under the leg of Iain's shorts, lingered there for a tantalizing minute, then let go of him and caressed the side of his neck before pulling his head down toward hers.

She breathed into his ear, "Do you want some of that?"

It had barely been a whisper, but he'd heard it. His hand stilled on her arm, and his entire body seemed to vibrate. But he didn't move his head.

Nina took his earlobe between her teeth and gave it a hard nip that made him jump. Then she was whispering again. "I think you should take me home."

♡♡♡

The fever had started for him with the first scene. By half an hour in, he was practically panting. He'd felt Nina's tension beside him, and he hadn't known whether she could possibly be as turned on as he was, or if it were something else. It could be shock. He didn't know what she read, what she watched. So often, she seemed surprised by what they did. It thrilled him, and at the same time, he kept waiting for her to ask him to back off.

By the time that scene appeared, though, he wasn't

worrying about Nina. He was going up in flames. The silk sheet twisting under the woman's desperate grip, her face contorting with strain and desire, the hoarse muttering of the man behind her...

He had to touch Nina. He had to. And when his fingers brushed her thigh, he could swear he felt her legs parting for him.

The next minutes were exquisite torture. Her sweet, soft skin under his fingers, and him not daring to do more. He wanted to take her by the hand and pull her out of there, but this was her birthday outing, and it was a good film. He could tell that, even though he couldn't have told you what was happening anymore.

Then she said that.

He was standing, grabbing her purchases, pulling her by the hand along the back aisle, opening the heavy door and shutting it hastily behind them, then taking his phone out of his pocket to check the time.

"Thirteen minutes until the next ferry," he said. "We may be able to get it if we run."

"Then," she said, "let's run."

"You first," he said. "So I don't go too fast for you."

They were going to miss the boat, he thought after two blocks. He could've made it easily, but she wasn't a big runner. He was going to be stuck here with her for the next hour, drinking another glass of wine, watching her have second thoughts, losing the moment.

He saw the taxi at the curb, was grabbing Nina's hand, jogging over, and leaning in to ask the driver, "Take us to the ferry terminal?"

"Hop in, mate," the man said, and Iain had the door, was ushering Nina into it. When the driver stopped in front of the wharf five minutes later, Iain was tossing a twenty at him, saying, "Keep the change," and pulling Nina out again by the hand.

"Iain," she said with her husky laugh, "we're in time."

"Just in case," he said. 'Run."

They had five minutes, in the end. Five minutes to find a spot at the farthest table on the bottom deck. Nina sat against the window, facing the back wall, and Iain sat beside her. They kept their heads down, and nobody recognized them, and nobody came to join them at their table for six. If they had, he'd have paid them to leave.

At last, the big boat was pulling away from the wharf, and he asked her, "Would you like a glass of wine?"

"That would be three today."

Her hair was a little messy from the run, her eyes bright, her cheeks tinged with pink. "Mm," he said. "You're right. That'd be pretty naughty of you. We could share, if you like. We're half an hour's sail from Auckland, though, and then we still have to get to Devonport."

A saucy smile was trying to escape her pretty mouth. "Somebody wasn't planning ahead quite well enough about my birthday outing."

"Somebody's kicking himself, no worries."

"Maybe it's just as well. Give you time to talk dirty to me. What do you think? Think you can fill up half an hour?"

"Uh… wine," he reminded her. "If you get me started on that line of chat, I'm not going to be in a position to get you a drink."

"Then yes, please," she said demurely.

"Sharing?" he asked.

"Oh, I think I can handle it all," she said.

He slid out, not quite able to feel his feet, and said, "Right. We'll hope you can."

♡♡♡

She should probably feel embarrassed. But she didn't. She just ached for him. When he left her, her body missed him. And when he slid in beside her again five minutes later and set down two glasses of Chardonnay, she waited for the touch of his side against hers, for his thigh brushing her own, and sighed to get it.

He lifted his glass, and she raised her own. "Happy birthday, sweetheart," he said, touching his glass gently to hers and smiling into her eyes. "You're even more beautiful at twenty-six."

Her own smile was a slow, secret, seductive thing. It was the kind of smile she'd used for the cameras, but she'd never meant it the way she did tonight. She touched her lips to the glass and took a swallow, letting the cool liquid run down her dry throat. "So," she said, "either that was a really good choice of movie, or a really bad one, because we're never going to know how it turns out."

"We could rent it." His hand was under the table and on her thigh again. Hard hand on bare skin, his fingers caressing.

"I'm still not... sure." She took another sip of wine just for something to do, and tried not to shiver at the sensations his hand was evoking. "That I'd make it to the end."

"That's some sexy stuff," he said. "Particularly that one bit."

"You mean when you started groping me?"

"That would be the one. Though the parts before it weren't too bad either."

"Can I say..." She hesitated.

"Oh, baby," he said, "you can say."

"That part." She swallowed, realized she was running her fingers up and down the stem of her wineglass, saw him watching her do it, and stopped. "Uh... where he was over her, and she was... face-down. It sure looked like they were suggesting..."

"Yeh." His hand was still on her thigh, and he wasn't drinking his wine. He was looking at her. "That's what they were suggesting. You liked that, eh."

She closed her eyes. "Yeah," she whispered. "But I couldn't tell if it hurt."

"You've never done it."

"You know I haven't." He'd touched her, sometimes, in the shower, a sneaky, soapy finger, a straying thumb. It had made her gasp, had excited her, and had made her nervous, too. "I can't see how it wouldn't hurt. But I'm…"

"It turns you on," he guessed. His fingers were all the way up her inner thigh now, so close to their goal. She longed for him to touch her, was burning for it, but she was afraid of what she would do if he did. She wasn't nearly cool enough. She'd betray herself for sure, even here at the back of the boat.

"Turns me on, too," he said. "If we were talking dirty here?" The noise of the ferry's engines was all around them, a low, deep rumble, and Iain's voice slid under the edges of it, along her nerve endings, making her quiver. "If I were telling you the truth? I'd tell you that taking your ass would be the best birthday present I could ever imagine."

She took another sip of wine, because her mouth was dry. "It's *my* birthday, though," she managed.

"It is. So I'd have to make it good, wouldn't I? I'd have to make it the best you'd ever had. I bought you a present along those lines. I already know I'll make you happy. I've got a plan. And as for me… I'll be happy either way, no worries."

"We could…" She was trying to stay in control of this, but it wasn't easy. "It *is* my birthday. Maybe you could give me a… present. Maybe you could give me a surprise. And I could tell you if I liked it."

"Maybe I could." He'd shifted closer, and one long finger was brushing across damp silk, beginning a lazy circle. "Maybe I could."

win the girl
♡

The ride was endless. Iain's stealthy fingers remained on her though all of it, never getting her close enough, keeping her at the burning edge of arousal. She drank her wine and tried to hold still, doing her utmost not to react to what he was doing, to betray what she was feeling. It was torture, it was much too risky, and it was absolutely irresistible.

But even the longest ferry ride had to end sometime, and finally, the boat was slowing, the huge horse-shaped cranes of the busy freight terminal coming into view, lit brightly even on Sunday night. The ferry turned and backed into the wharf, and Iain took his hand away, turned his body toward her, and made an adjustment under the table himself while she pulled down her skirt and tried to still the pounding of her heart.

He muttered, "Could've thought this out better," then shifted away, put his hands flat on the table, and took some deep breaths of his own.

"Yes," she said, getting some of her sassiness back. "I'd say this is one person's fault, and that person is you."

"You wait," he said, his blue eyes burning right through her. "You wait."

"Wait" was what they did, too. Ten minutes on the wharf, then another ten backtracking across the Harbour to

Devonport, during which they sat in an open row of seats, held hands, and didn't talk, maybe because neither of them could think of anything to say that wouldn't set them off again. Then, finally, this ferry was docking as well, and Iain was picking up her bags and leading the way up the ramp and along the wharf to the carpark.

When they reached the car, he opened her door, handed her the bags, and shut the door again, and got in on his side. And then he put both hands on the steering wheel and laid his head on it.

"Bloody hell," he said, "that was the longest journey of my life."

She laughed, and he turned his head, glared at her, and said, "And that laugh of yours doesn't help. Your voice could turn me on in church."

"Really?" She leaned across the car and kissed his neck, then let her lips linger there, tracing down the thick column, minus its usual bristle of evening shadow, because he'd shaved for her. "Maybe you need me to relieve the pressure a little," she murmured in his ear. "You know when my voice sounds really good? When you're hearing it from all the way down in your lap."

He was turning the key, pulling out of the carpark. "Not that that isn't one of the most brilliant suggestions I've heard all day, but seems to me you made another one first. I'm a stickler for getting things done in order. And it's your birthday, eh. The birthday girl receives."

That one shut her up until he was pulling the car into his garage. He turned the key, and she half-expected him to kiss her, but he didn't. Instead, he was climbing out, closing the garage door, and heading for the front door, as usual. But when they were inside, he said, "Right. You. Downstairs. In five minutes, I'm going to be coming down and getting in the shower, and you're going to be in it. With the necklace on."

"Uh…"

He dropped her bags in the entryway. "Nina. My self-control's this close to snapping. If you want some privacy first, I'm giving it to you. But that's it. Five minutes. Clothes off. Necklace on. Shower. Go."

She went.

She could swear it wasn't five minutes. She'd barely managed to get her teeth brushed, had just finished stripping off her clothes and tossing them into the hamper when he was in the bathroom, closing the door behind him.

"I said in the shower." He was The Hulk again, the slow, merciless teasing of the ferry a thing of the past.

"Sue me," she said with a toss of her head. "I'm late."

He didn't smile. Instead, he reached beyond her, turned the tap to full, and pulled her straight into the huge tiled space. She was gasping at the freezing shock of the cold water, but he was already turning so he took the force of it onto his back. She was shivering, calling out, and he was paying no attention at all. He had her shoved back against the tiled wall, and finally, he was kissing her. His hands around her head, his mouth lowered onto hers as the water warmed around them, and his tongue was plunging into her mouth, going deep, taking it all.

He kissed her until she was liquid, until she was whimpering, and then he let go of her, picked up the bar of passionfruit-scented soap that was her favorite, and said, "Turn around."

When she didn't move fast enough, he had a hand on her shoulder, was spinning her. "Hands on the wall."

One part of her said that she could still tell him no, and that he'd listen. The other part, the primitive back of her brain that seemed to be calling the shots tonight, wanted to know that he could do anything to her. That he could take her body and use it in any way he wanted, because it was his.

"Bend over," he said. "And hold still."

He'd directed the showerhead straight onto her lower back, and the hard spray was hitting her there, running down her bottom, the backs of her thighs, an assault and a caress. And then his soapy hands had joined in. One big forearm came around her breasts, his hand capturing one of them,

391

playing hard. The crown of her head was resting against the backs of her hands now, and she was letting him do it. His other hand slid down her back, lingering on her lower back, the base of her spine, and she was pressing back against him, wanting more.

He took his hand away, and she wanted it back. Then it was there again, his fingers sliding down, slick and soapy and insistent. He knew how she liked to be touched, and he was doing it.

"Oh." She was backing into him, calling out. "Yes. Please."

His hand had left her breast, was moving down the front of her body, replacing the first one and taking up its work. His right hand had shifted, was behind her, soapy again, parting her, circling, exploring.

She started to stand up again, and his other hand was at the back of her neck, pressing the plates of chilly gold against her skin and her head into the wall. "Hold still," he said. "So it doesn't hurt." He kept his hand there, holding her down, and she should be objecting to that. She should. But his other hand…

He'd touched her like this before, yes. But never like this. Never with her bent over. Never with him holding her down.

It should scare her. He had a second finger there now, was pushing it slowly inside. It burned, and it thrilled. Alien, and so exciting. She was panting, gasping, and when she moved again, he shoved her back.

"Hold still," he said again. "I need to make sure I don't hurt you, and you need to hold still, or I might."

Gradually, her muscles relaxed, and the stinging had turned to something so much warmer. So much hotter. Her knees were quaking, but she wasn't trying to move anymore. She wasn't sure she could.

When he let her go at last, it took her a moment to react. He took her wrists in his hands, pulled her up, turned her around, and kissed her, dark and deep, while the water pelted them.

"Open your eyes, Nina," he said gently. "Open your eyes and tell me how you feel."

"Uh…" she managed. She dragged her eyes open and stared up at him, barely able to focus. "I… can't. So… strong. So good."

"Ah." He sighed. "Do you want this? Do you trust me not to hurt you?"

"Yes," she whispered. "Yes."

He had the water off, was pulling her out of the shower, wrapping her in a towel and then patting himself impatiently dry before dropping the towel to the floor and picking her up, carrying her into the bedroom, and setting her on the bed.

"It's going to be a little different for you tonight," he said. "And I need you to tell me. If you want to stop, if it's too much, if you change your mind, you tell me. Right? Just like always."

She was barely able to swallow. "Right."

He dropped the towel, now, and was pulling two pillows off the head of the bed and setting them in the middle of it, then pushing her gently down over them so she was resting on her elbows, her hips propped high. He switched on the bedside lamp, went to the door, and turned off the overhead light.

"If there's any better sight than that," he said, "I don't know what it could possibly be."

She had her head turned, was watching him, tinglingly aware of the way she was raised high in the air, of the slabs of gold around her neck adorning her. Bold, and barbaric. "I could ask you what you're going to do," she managed to say, "but I've got a pretty fair idea."

He smiled, and it wasn't her sweet Iain now. Not a bit of it. And he knew what she was really saying. That she wanted to hear the words. So he gave them to her.

"I'm going to take your ass," he said. "The only part of you I haven't had, and tonight, it's mine. Just a bit of it, or all of it, deep and hard. Your choice."

She couldn't even answer. She was shivering, watching

him open the drawer of his bedside table and pull out a tube of something—not something. She knew exactly what it was. It was lube. And an oddly shaped gadget, patterned in... leopard print?

"But first," he said, "we're going to warm you up. This is your surprise, sweetheart. Happy birthday." He pressed a button on the leopard thing, and it began to buzz. "I think it's going to be a good one."

He was behind her now, straddling her, setting the vibrator in place, and she was jumping as if she'd been hit with a live wire. Because she had.

Suction. Just like his mouth on her, and it was... incredible.

"Feel good?" he asked in her ear. He was on an elbow, his big body covering her, one hand holding the instrument to her.

She couldn't answer. She was humming, squirming, shaking. And then he did something else. The suction increased, and just like that, she was spiking up. Up, and over.

The arousal that had been building ever since the movie had begun, that had simmered under Iain's torturing fingers during that entire long ferry ride, that had spiked while he'd invaded her body in the shower—it was all here now. It was this. It was everything. It slammed into her, and it rolled her hard.

Her hips were rocking, and she was calling out, loud and incoherent. Iain had grabbed her hand, was shoving it underneath her, placing it on the vibrator, and saying, "Hold it there. The button controls the intensity. Lower or higher. You choose."

She wanted to tell him that she couldn't, that she couldn't stand it, but she didn't, because he was holding her hips and sliding inside her. Not what she'd anticipated, or half-dreaded, whichever it was. But she was so aroused, so wet and ready, and the angle, the friction, were almost enough right there. The size of him, the way he moved, combined with the suction... as soon as he started, she was climbing again.

He wasn't being careful, wasn't being gentle, and neither was the incessant little machine. They were both insistent, relentless, taking her over, making her theirs, and she was nearly screaming as the second orgasm hit her harder than the first. She was climbing the wave, crashing over the other side, spinning down and down. She was soaking wet, and she knew Iain could feel it, that he was loving it.

He was pulling out of her, then, and she moaned, "No." She still had the vibrator pressed to her. How could she let it go? But she needed him, too. She needed him now. She needed it again.

In a moment, he was back. His finger, wet and cold and slippery, entering her again, but in that new, thrilling spot, where she was so tight. Working its way inside her, and then that second one coming to join it, and she was moaning, biting the hand that was still under her face, her fingers grasping the duvet, twisting it hard.

Three fingers, stretching her, gently spreading her, and she was rising into him.

"Do you trust me?" he said again, his voice a dark caress. "Believe that I'll stop if you tell me it hurts? You ready to tell me so?"

"Yes," she gasped. "Yes."

At first, it *did* hurt, and she didn't tell him. She was biting her hand for all she was worth, because it was too much. Too strong. A stinging pain, and the intense pleasure from the device that was, somehow, pulling her up yet again. Both of them together, the sensation incredible, overwhelming. And then he was all the way inside, wet and warm and hard, doing nothing but holding still.

"Oh, God," he groaned. "Oh, God. I can't... I can't... Too tight. Too good."

She couldn't help it. She was backing into him. "Do it. Iain. Do it. Make me feel it."

A long groan. A dark curse. And he was moving. Still slowly at first, nothing but gentle. And all the same, it was too much. Over the top. She was climbing more slowly this time, the very intensity of her pleasure somehow slowing her down. Her hand was clenching, grabbing a fistful of the duvet under her head. She was shoving off into it, pushing against him, and he was moving faster.

More. Deeper. Harder.

This time, the orgasm came in like a monster tide. The ripples gathering from afar, coalescing, arriving. Closer and closer. One wave merging into another, then another, until they became a tsunami headed straight for her, and she was held there, powerless to resist. Iain over her, one hand just below the back of her neck, holding her head down, his other palm flat beside her as he pushed off, then plunged, again and again. Taking all of her.

Her thumb accidentally hit the switch on the vibrator again, and just like that, the force of it overpowered her. She was calling out, and then she was wailing, loud and long, and Iain was swearing behind her, groaning, thrusting.

They tumbled, and they rolled, and they fell. They lost it all.

♡♡♡

Iain moved first, in the end. He went to the bathroom and washed up, then brought back a warm cloth and washed Nina. Gently, and tenderly, and so slowly, while she sighed and smiled and let him do it. He watched her roll over, saw her eyelids flutter open, looked at the slabs of hammered gold around her graceful neck, and thought, *Bloody hell, girl. I love you.*

"I figured something out," she told him drowsily, reaching up to pull him down with her. "You've played two games so far, and both times . . . look what's come home to me. Are you telling me that's what you get when you win the game?"

"Nah." He had his hand running up and down her back, feeling the silk of her skin, and he couldn't have stopped smiling if you'd paid him. "That's what I get when I win the girl."

"Hmm." She nuzzled his neck. "You were too sexy, that's why."

He laughed. His body was still aching from the night before, and she was probably sore, too, despite all his care. But if she were anything like him, her body was humming with satisfaction all the same. "When?" he asked. "On the paddock, or just now?"

"Both," she said. "Both. My sexy beast."

erased

♡

It had been one hell of a night, and, Iain thought, a pretty good week, too. The best part was that he and Nina didn't have to hide anymore. They could stay in at night and make dinner together, or they could go out.

Which was why, on Thursday, they were eating dinner at Manuka, sitting in the corner all the same for both their sakes. Despite Nina's makeup and her pretty new hair, Iain still got recognized heaps more than she did, which suited him fine. Sooner or later, the press was going to report that they were together, but it hadn't happened yet.

"I've got something to tell you," she said, cutting a dainty bite of seared scallops and asparagus. She was eating delicate lady things, and as usual, he was eating everything but the menu.

"Tell away," he said.

She chewed her bite, took a sip of water, and said, "I'm taking a trip to California late next week, and I'll be going to Australia after that. That's the first thing. I'll be gone a couple of weeks."

"Oh." He tried to ignore the sinking feeling in his gut. "I'll be gone after that myself, though. Didn't I mention that I've got a road trip to Perth and then over to Jo-burg? You couldn't put it off until I leave?"

She wasn't smiling now. "I already have. I need to meet with my agent, and to see my mother, too. That's the biggest one. I need to meet with a real estate agent about my house, and after that, I need to see my grandparents. I should have gone already."

"Right, then." He told himself to calm down. She'd be coming back, and nobody knew better than he did that schedules didn't always mesh. And all the same, he wanted to think of her in his house while he was gone. In his bed at night. Safe, and *there*.

"There's another thing," she said. She'd set her fork down, even though her dinner was half-eaten. "Something I'm excited about. Which I hope is preparing you to give the reaction I'm hoping for," she added with a smile that didn't look entirely genuine.

"What's that?" His muscles were bunching, the adrenaline surging.

"I signed a lease on a new place today." She still wasn't eating, but she was clutching the handle of her fork all the same.

The blood was draining from his head. "What?"

"I'm getting my own place. Furnished," she added, as if that made it better, when it actually made it worse, because what it meant was "temporary."

Fight or flight, his body was saying, which was always a simple choice for him. Except now. "Why," he said, keeping his voice completely level.

She had her hands in her lap now, and he could tell she was shredding her paper napkin. "It's time."

"What d'you mean, 'it's time?'" He wasn't doing quite as well on the level voice anymore.

Her chin shot up. "Don't bully me."

"I am not bullying you! I'm asking you for an explanation. I've got a house. I'm in it barely half the time, except a couple months in the summer. It's a big house. Want your own room? You've got it. Want..." He cast his mind about.

"Some new curtains, or something? A new couch? Something changed? You've got that as well. Why would you want to move?"

"Because it's not mine." She was sitting rigid, her face white, but she was still looking straight at him. "Because I've never had my own place, and I've never made my own decisions."

"You own a house in California. You told me so. Probably bigger than mine."

"Twice the size," she agreed. "Not to mention the pool and the pool house and the guest quarters over the garage. And my mother chose it. She bought it, and she furnished it, and she ran it. Just like you chose your house, and you're in charge of it. It wasn't my choice, and I need to make my own choices."

"How does living with me keep you from making your own choices? You just told me you were going away, and I'm not happy, but I didn't say, 'Don't go,' did I? It's your choice. I know it's your choice."

"You didn't do anything wrong," she said. "It's not you. It's me. It's that if I'm in *your* space, *your* life, I can't be sure I can do it myself. I can't be sure of my reasons." She shook her head. "I know I'm right, but I can't say it right."

"Don't tell me, 'It's not you, it's me.' Do not tell me that. If you're leaving me, it's me."

"I am not leaving you!" Her voice had risen, and a couple at the next table looked around. Nina said more quietly, "I'm not leaving you. I'm moving out of your house, I'm taking a trip, and then I'm coming back to New Zealand, and to you. Don't you get that?"

"Temporarily. To a used car, and a furnished—what? Flat?"

"Cottage," she said. "In a back garden. It's tiny, but it'll be mine. I've never lived alone. Ever. I need to make sure I can."

"Because you don't want me to take care of you even that much. Because you don't want me to have anything to say about what you do, or even to know it, maybe. Maybe even about who you spend time with." *Who you sleep with,* he didn't say, because he wasn't quite that out of control yet.

"Iain." She put a hand on his forearm, and he looked down at slim fingers resting on bunched, knotted muscles. "I have a lot of money," she said gently. "I'm guessing I have more than you do. I don't need you to take care of me."

He shoved his chair back, the sound shocking in the quiet restaurant, and her hand fell from his arm. "You think that's what I'm talking about," he said. "How much money you have."

"Yes." She didn't move from where she sat. Her voice was trembling a bit now, but she went on. "I think you're afraid that if I have power, my *own* power, my own life, I won't choose you. That I'll leave you. Why would I leave you, when I'm in love with you? Why do you think I'm coming back from the States?"

His head went up at that, and he'd opened his mouth, but she was still talking. "But that's what could hurt me, too, if it keeps me stuck in the same spot. If I'm making all my decisions based on what *you* want, on *your* feelings. If I lose myself. If you only want me when I'm weak, what does that say? I need you to want me strong, or this isn't going to work. I need you to trust that I'll come back, and that we can work our way toward whatever we'll have together. That you don't have to hang on to me so tightly to keep me."

He shook his head, trying to clear it. "No. This isn't how it works. If I were going to decide something big now? Whether to move to another franchise, to shift house? I'd talk to you. Even though we haven't been together that long, I'd talk it over. I'd want to know what you thought. Seems to me that you don't want me to have anything to say at all about... about anything. Like we're some kind of hookup, like I'm somebody you're having sex with for now, in between your real life. That's not what I want."

"But don't you see," she said, "that you're so different from me? You can talk it over with me, because you *know* you're making your own choices. You *know* the final decision

401

is yours. With me—it's so new. I can lose it so fast. You're so strong, and so sure, and you've been deciding for yourself forever, in charge of your life, and I haven't. I can't... I can't afford to fade. I can't afford to get swallowed up in you and get erased. I need to know it's *my* choice. *My* house. I need to be on my own before I can be with anybody else. Even somebody I want as much as you. Even somebody..." Another deep breath. "Somebody I love as much as you."

He was standing, because he couldn't sit anymore. Going to the register, paying the bill, leaving her to follow behind.

Fight or flight, his raging body was shouting at him. He'd always chosen "fight." But how could he fight when he couldn't stand to hurt her? When all he wanted to do was hold her and protect her, and she didn't want it?

When he turned around, she was gone, and he had a dark moment before he saw her on the pavement outside the restaurant.

He went out to join her, she looked at him, and he said, "Let's go home."

"I'm moving into my new place tomorrow."

"So we can't even discuss this."

"I already decided."

He reached into his pocket, pulled out his car key, and said, "Take the car home. I'll be there in an hour."

"Iain—"

"I'll be there in an hour," he repeated. "I need to run."

"Fine," she said. "I'll see you."

♡♡♡

When he got home, his knit shirt soaked with sweat, his chest heaving from two final sprints up and down Mt. Victoria, then a hard push back to the house at his fastest pace, the house was dark.

He went downstairs calling Nina's name, but she didn't answer. He went into the back garden and called her again, but the musical buzz of the cicadas was his only response.

Bloody *hell*. Had she gone for a walk of her own? His neighborhood was safe, but his skin still crawled at the thought of it. It was dark out there.

He opened the closet to see if she'd changed, and the cold doused his body as if he'd dived into a freezing lake.

Hangers.

He pulled open one drawer after another in her side of the dresser.

Empty.

He sat on the bed and tried to pull together the thoughts, the feelings that were whirling out of control, and failed. He went upstairs again, thinking... something. Thinking nothing. And found a note on the kitchen bench.

Iain,

I decided it was better if I moved out tonight. It's too hard for me to hear you right now, and it feels like you can't hear me either. All I want to say is "yes," to agree with you, to do what you want so I won't lose you, and I can't do it.

Remember when we were saying how your pressure came from inside, and I said, "the fire within"? You have so much pressure on you, and I know it. You don't always get to choose how things turn out for you. I know that. You could get injured. Somebody else could be better no matter how hard you work, and they'd be picked and you wouldn't. I get that. I do. But you know you're the one pushing to get what you want. You're pushing yourself to be the best so you achieve those things, if they're possible. You're pushing yourself to do your very best, but it's for yourself. It's not for your parents, and it's not for your coach, and it's not for the fans. It's so you know you did your best.

I've never done that, and I need to. I need to be the one pushing. I can't let myself be erased again.

I know you don't get it. You can't, because it's so far from how you feel. Which is what makes you so incredible. I need you to trust that I know how I feel, though. I need you to want me to be as strong as you.

Remember how you said that I needed to fight? This is me fighting. It's so hard, and it feels so horrible, but I'm fighting. I'm fighting for me, and I'm fighting for us. The shoes are supposed to be together, but they're equal, aren't they? The right one isn't better than the left, and they're both walking forward. One foot isn't dragging the other one along.

I know, I already said all that. You didn't understand me, I know. I guess I keep wanting to try to explain, because I want so much for you to understand. More than anybody.

I'll talk to you after your game. Maybe we can have lunch on Sunday, if you still want to. Maybe we can try again.
Nina

At the bottom, something else had been written, then crossed out. He turned the paper over, trying to read the impression of what was under the strikethroughs. And then he saw it.

I love you.

He read the letter once, then set it down and walked around the kitchen, into the lounge, and stared out the windows into darkness. Then he came back in and read it again.

That was when he realized that he hadn't asked Nina where her new place was. That he had no idea where she'd gone. That she'd run again, and this time, she'd run from him.

He pulled out his phone and rang her up. Voicemail.

"I didn't mean for you to leave," he said. "We should talk. How d'you expect to work it out if you leave?"

He rang off, then stood and looked at the phone.

Wait.

That had sounded pretty narky, he had a feeling.

He rang her back. Voicemail again.

"Uh, erase that last one," he said. "I mean, I'd like to talk. I don't get it. I won't pretend I do. But you can't just leave without even trying. Call me back."

He rang off and stared at the phone some more. Silent. He texted her.

Left you 2 voicemails. Call me.

He sat on the couch, turned the telly on, and flipped

channels. Soccer in the UK. *Click*. A squeaky-voiced pink cartoon pony. *Click*. A couple blokes he knew, looking like their ties were too tight, chatting in a studio about rugby. *Click*. Somebody's house in the UK, knee-deep in clutter, and a gloved hand lifting a rat-chewed purse. That one got a *click* so fast, he practically wore a hole in the remote, to a channel where a terrier was yapping frantically and running in circles.

He pushed the *Off* button and checked his phone in case it was on silent. Nothing.

A shower. If she came back to talk, he should be cool, not standing here sweating. He took the phone into the bathroom with him, though, just in case.

He heard the *ding* of a text while he was still in the shower cubicle toweling off. He stubbed his toe on the tiled edge lunging for it, but he barely noticed.

I'll talk to you Sunday, if you want to talk, he read. *Right now, you're angry and I'm sad. Let's wait.*

He started to text back, but his hands were wet, and it wouldn't work. He scrubbed them impatiently on the towel and typed back, *Talk to me now.*

A long wait, then the answer. *I already told you how I felt. You didn't like it. I don't hear you saying you've changed your mind. I think you just want to change mine.*

He texted back, *Of course I want to change yours,* then thought, *Wait.* He was going to erase it, but his thumb somehow hit the wrong button, and it went through.

He was texting back, *Wait,* when her message came through.

I'll text you Sunday. Not until then. I'm going to bed.

He'd stuffed up again, or she was still being stubborn, or both. And he still didn't know where she was.

my other shoe

♡

It wasn't a comfortable night, and Iain was glad when morning came and it was time to go to training. A short one today, the Captain's Run always held on the day before the game, when the coaches went to the sidelines and the skipper ran the show. When you thought and talked and worked together the way you would the next night on the pitch, because when those eighty minutes began, the coaches wouldn't be on the paddock playing the game.

You'd be out there all alone then, so it had to be inside you, and inside the team, or it wouldn't be there at all. The job you had to do, and the awareness of what was happening around you. The game plan, the actual game, and the difference. The adjustments you made, because being able to see clearly, and to adjust to what you were seeing, meant the difference between winning and losing.

He set it all aside—Nina, her letter, his empty house—and focused, working all the strain and indecision and anger out of his body along with the sweat, and for a few hours, he was free.

Back in the sheds again afterwards, he'd showered and was at his cubicle getting dressed when Hugh came and sat on the bench beside him.

"Josie wants to know if you and Nina would want to come for a barbecue Sunday night," his skipper said. "We could have a few of the boys over with their families, give her a chance to get to know them. Bring Arthur as well, of course, if he's still here."

Just like that, it was all back. "He's gone home," Iain said. "And Nina's gone as well." He pulled his shorts on to give himself a second.

"Oh," Hugh said. "Huh."

He was still sitting there, though, and Iain looked at him and said, "What?"

Hugh shrugged a big shoulder. "Josie'll be surprised, that's all. Unless it was you."

"It was me. Some, anyway. Not that I wanted her to go."

"Stuffed up, eh," Hugh said.

"Say that it wasn't working out the way I thought it should, and that I got pretty narky about it. I'm trying to sort out what to do, but I'm coming up against a bit of a wall."

"Ha," Hugh said. "I could pretend I don't know about that, but I'd be lying. At the time I met Josie—nothing that happened was anything like I'd planned, and I was always about three steps behind. There my future was, tapping me on the shoulder, and me looking the other way."

Iain didn't answer, because he couldn't think of what to say, and Hugh got to his feet and said, "Never mind, then. See you tomorrow. We're going well, anyway. Got everybody on the same page at last."

"The boys are fizzing," Iain agreed. "You may want to work on your speech in the sheds, though," he added, trying to joke. Trying to pretend that he didn't want to go sit on the beach with Hugh and a few six-packs and let his skipper pour him into bed again. Not an option on the day before a match, so it was time to harden up and get past it. "Get Josie to help you. Maybe she can come up with something besides, 'Get out there and do the business, and no mucking about.' That one's not going to win you any Sporting Personality of the Year awards."

The white grin split Hugh's tough, bearded face, making him look more like a pirate than ever. "We won, didn't we?" He dropped a hand on Iain's shoulder, gripped it for a brief instant, and said, "See you."

Iain finished dressing, dragging it out because he didn't want to go home, and the room slowly emptied around him. The equipment manager, a veteran named Wally who'd seen it all in his twenty-eight years with the team, was collecting kit in a corner, and Iain was still sitting there.

Wally came over to pick up some discarded mouthguards and said, "It'll be all right on the night. You can always tell at the Captain's Run, once it's not down to the coaches anymore. You can see plain as day if the squad has it or not then. If they've got it inside them."

Exactly what Iain had been thinking, and he was trying to figure out how to tell Wally that that wasn't what he was worried about, then giving it up as impossible. But while he was still working it out, the older man gave a decisive bob of his short-cropped gray head and headed off again.

If they've got it inside, Iain thought. *The fire within.*

He had it. He'd always had it. The hard burn.

Nina did, too, no matter what she thought. He hadn't been able to understand her doubts the night before. They'd seemed so unreasonable.

Did that mean they weren't real, though?

Maybe all that noise from her mum, from that bastard prince, and whoever else had told her what to do—even, maybe, from Iain himself—maybe it had drowned out her own voice. Maybe it was there, but it was only a whisper. Maybe she needed quiet in order to hear it. Maybe the coals from her fire had burned so low, she wasn't even aware of their heat.

There my future was, tapping me on the shoulder, and me looking the other way.

The sheds were quiet now. Wally, the lone remaining figure, walked out pushing a cart of equipment, and still Iain sat. Finally, with a sigh, he pulled Nina's letter from his gym bag.

He'd felt weak when he'd tossed it in there this morning after reading it ten—twenty—times the night before. At first with anger, arguing every point. Then with a sort of hollow futility. And finally, with something too much like despair. Now, though, he read the words again, and he was feeling something else.

He set the letter down and picked up his phone.

He didn't like to text. His thumbs were too big to make it anything but awkward. But he did it now.

Hi.

Been thinking about you ever since. I did it again, and I know it. I didn't listen, just like when I found out you weren't a princess.

You wrote me a letter, though, and it helped, because I could read it over again and listen. I'm going to write you one and hope you'll listen too. Not sure I can do it as well as you, but I'm going to try.

You said I'm strong, but you're stronger than me. You said you loved me, not knowing if I'd say it back, and I didn't say it back. Then you told me again anyway.

I got scared because I thought I was losing you. I hurt you because I didn't have the guts to tell you how I felt.

His fingers hovered over the keys. "Get out there and do the business," he muttered aloud. "No mucking about."

He started typing again as fast as he could go, flinging the words onto the screen.

There's something a rugby player knows, though. You can't look past this week. You can't live in the future, because it could all be gone by then. You can break a leg in training that will end your career. And looking past next week loses games and series and championships, so you don't do that either. You look at this week. You live in the now. You do everything you can, and once you have, you take what comes and cope with it.

He rested his weary thumbs on the phone for a second,

then plowed on.

I can't see past next week with you, and it scares me. But I want next week. So I'm going to do everything I can to make this week good. And then the week after that. And then the one after that. I'm going to take what comes, and I'm going to cope. I'm going to keep walking toward it, whatever it is. I'll hop if I have to, if I don't have my other shoe. Or if that other shoe's busy giving me a swift kick up the arse. But I'll hop to get to her, because I need my other shoe. So if you're willing to walk with me, even if I'm a piss-poor excuse for a shoe, then please. Talk to me. I need you. I love you.

He thought another minute, then typed, *I'll be home in an hour. Then all the way till tomorrow morning. If you want to try again, come to the house, or ring me and I'll come to you. Either thing. Anything.*

He didn't read it over. He didn't stop to think. He pressed *Send*, and then he waited.

The minutes passed, and Wally came into the room again. "Still here, mate? They'll lock you in if you're not careful."

"Yeh, nah." Iain stood up, collected his bag, and headed for the door, feeling like every step was through sand.

He told himself that she wasn't necessarily sitting at home—wherever home was—waiting for him to come to his stupid senses. That she was swimming or walking or making business plans instead. Or shopping for groceries for her new place. Living her life. And that she'd read it. That she'd listen.

But it was so hard to make himself believe.

surprise
♡

Nina stepped into the shower in her minuscule cottage, shivering despite the heat of the day. She was still chilled, even though she'd changed out of her swimsuit. Too long a swim, but she'd needed it.

Fifteen minutes under the warm spray, and she finally felt warm enough to dry off and dress in shorts and a T-shirt. The enthusiasm for anything prettier, or for makeup, seemed to be beyond her. Who was going to see her?

That's no way to think, she told herself. *You're going to see.* It didn't help much, though.

Cup of tea. She took the five steps between "bedroom" and "kitchen" and switched the jug on. Her phone was sitting next to it, and she hesitated, then picked it up.

She saw the notification on the screen and almost set the phone down again. *Sunday,* she tried to tell herself, but of course it didn't work. She was swiping, and reading.

The jug boiled and shut itself off, and she didn't notice. She had a hand out, was gripping the counter for support, and then she was swiping back up to the beginning and reading again. After that, was pulling her sandals on, grabbing her purse and shoving her phone into it, and running for her car.

It was only five or six kilometers, but the traffic was as horrible as always on Lake Road. She inched her way along, fretting as another light changed from yellow to red two cars ahead of her.

He'll wait, she told herself. *No rush.* But it didn't feel that way.

Finally, she was turning, then turning again, was up the hill to Iain's street, finding a parking place behind an unfamiliar—and enormous—black car, and running down the long drive, almost skidding in her sandals, her footsteps unnaturally loud on the concrete.

She had her key in the door, was pushing it open, calling Iain's name. She felt the touch on her shoulder and whirled, the smile already beginning.

It began, and it died.

Matthias was crowding through the door after her, slamming it shut behind him, and flipping the deadbolt.

"What…" she asked. "What are you doing here?"

"Sabrina." He sighed. "How can you ask? I told you that we were going to be married. And what did you do?"

"I *left,*" she said. "I left."

Beep. Beep. Beep.

The burglar alarm, waiting for the code. Matthias's pale-blue eyes tracked the sound. "Switch it off."

"No."

His hand shot out, closed around her wrist, and raised it to the keypad. "Switch it *off.*"

His fingers were pressing tight against the fragile bones, finding a nerve, and she cried out in pain. "Do it now," he said. "Or you'll be sorry."

She punched in the code, her breath coming in sobbing gasps, and the beeping stopped. He relaxed his grip, but he didn't let go of her. "See how easy it is," he said, "when you follow instructions?"

"I won't marry you," she said. "I'll never marry you. You can do anything you want to me, and I still won't do it."

"I have no desire to marry you," he said. "Why would I

want a lying little slut like you?"

"Then why are you here?" She was trembling with shock and fear now, trying to focus, to plan.

"I'm here to win. Why else?" He put a hand on the top of her head and tightened his grip on her wrist again. He began to push down, and her knees were buckling.

"There was only one thing you were really good for," he told her through his teeth. She was going down, dropping, with his hand twisted in her hair, his grip hard and painful. "You're going to do it. And then I'm going to put you in the car, drive up some back road in this godforsaken wasteland of a country, and make you do everything else I can think of. I might give my bodyguards a turn before we toss you out again. You can see if he wants you then, once we're all done with you, when you're sore and bruised and half-broken. See if he wants that."

He had her on her knees, and she was panting, gasping at the searing pain as her hair was pulled nearly out of her scalp.

He let go of her wrist, was fumbling with his belt, his grip slackening on her hair in his haste, and it was her chance. She drove the crown of her head forward with everything she had. Straight through the pain. Straight into his groin.

His breath left his lungs in a *whoosh*, and he'd let go of her and was doubling over. The second he did, she stumbled to her feet, and she was running. Down the stairs, slamming open the lock on the sliding door.

Over the fence. Across the creek. Splash over. Run through the reserve, down the road.

She was sprinting, her mouth wide open, pulling in great gulps of air. She was plummeting down the paved track of the reserve, then looking behind her and stumbling.

Running feet behind her. Around the corner.

She was going faster, somehow. A lightning decision, and she was heading to the sea.

He hates to swim.

She didn't dare look back, but there were cars here. People on the golf course, pedestrians up ahead. If he caught her, she'd struggle. She'd scream. She'd fight. And somebody would come. It was New Zealand.

She was halfway across the zebra crossing to the beach and running fast. A car screeched to a stop in front of her, the driver laying on the horn. Her hand went out to push off its hood, and she was running again.

She was almost to the sand. Almost.

A hard hand was grabbing her above the elbow, swinging her around, and she was kicking at Matthias's knees and swinging her other arm. The heel of her hand caught him on the bridge of his nose, a lucky blow that sent him back again. Then she was across the beach, running into the sea, splashing through the water. Plunging in. Starting to swim.

She almost made it.

not fast enough
♡

Iain drove home cursing the traffic. On the Harbour Bridge, through Takapuna, all the way down the peninsula. It wasn't even three. Where was everybody going?

There hadn't been a sound from his phone, and all the same, he was being pulled on as urgently as if Nina were calling him. And not getting there fast enough.

He saw her car as soon as he turned into the street, that bright flash of red, and his heart was suddenly beating twice as fast. He was down the driveway, not bothering with the garage, out of the car and inside the house.

"Nina!" he was calling as soon as he got in, not even waiting to shut the door behind him.

No answer. And something was wrong with the air.

His hand went out to the alarm box out of habit, and it took him a second to realize that it was turned off.

He'd set it that morning.

He heard the sound of the door opening behind him and whirled to see a man walking through. The man from the beach in Kaiteriteri, with two others following him in, crowding into the entryway. Two hulks without necks.

Nina's car was there.

It all clicked, and Iain was down the stairs. The sliders

were open down there. That had been the other thing wrong with the air. The breeze coming up through the house, and the sound of the birds. He hit the outside at a dead run, hearing the sound of feet on the stairs behind him and not caring. They weren't going to catch him.

Down through the trees. One hand on top of the fence, and he was vaulting it and down the bank, splashing through the stream, down the track.

He got to the pavement across from the golf course, looked left and right, and saw something. Another figure incongruously clad in a black suit in the summer heat, running hard to Iain's left, more than a block away. Running toward the beach.

Iain took off after him, and by the time he'd crossed the first street, he'd made up almost half the distance. He could see Nina, now, in front of the man, running as if her life depended on it. And not fast enough.

He put his head down. He ran as if he were going, not for the try, but to save the try. Harder than that. Harder than he ever had.

Ten or fifteen schoolkids in their uniforms were crowding the zebra crossing, and Iain was dodging around them, losing precious seconds. The man in the black suit was on the beach, and Nina was running into the water.

The man didn't stop. He ran straight into the sea after her, suit and all, shoes and all. He was wading out after Nina, who had struck out swimming, only a couple meters ahead of him now.

Iain took two precious seconds to get his shoes off, and then he was in. Covering meters with every stride, putting all his muscle into fighting the drag of the water. The instant he got deep enough, he was swimming. Powerful strokes, eating up the sea, closing the gap. Then switching to a breaststroke to find them.

That was why he saw it. When the man in the black suit, the water all the way past his shoulders, got hold of Nina's ankle, pulled her back by it, then took hold of the other ankle and held them both up. When Nina's head went under, and stayed there.

Iain didn't stop. Didn't think. He was swimming, and he was there. He'd stood in the chest-deep water and was throwing an arm around the other man's throat from behind. Hauling him back by it, his other hand chopping at one of the man's arms, hard enough that he heard the crack of bone. Nina's own arms were thrashing, her feet kicking against the restraining hands, her face still underwater. The man let out a strangled gasp, and then he'd released her, was twisting, turning, losing his footing, and going down. Going into the sea.

Iain gave him a shove out, and that was all. Nina had come up, and she was coughing. Choking. Swimming the wrong way, swimming out toward Rangitoto. Iain swam to her fast, got her under the arms, and was hauling her back into shallower water.

She was struggling, though. Trying to twist away, trying to fight.

"It's me," he said. "It's Iain. I've got you. Let me get you out."

She didn't seem to hear him, and he said it again, said it until it sank in. She was still coughing, still bringing up water, and he hugged her to him and dragged her out, all the way up the sloping beach.

A dogwalker had come over, was asking, "What's happened? All right?"

"No," Iain said, still holding Nina against him. "Ring 111. Tell them to send the police. Call it attempted murder." His own phone was still in his pocket, he realized. Dead, now. As dead as Nina would have been in another few minutes.

That made him look out to sea again. What had happened to the man? *The prince,* his sluggish brain told him. That had to be who he was.

He realized that there were more black suits in the sea. The two no-necks were standing in water up to their waists, and the man from the beach was farther out. Diving under.

"Tell them to send the ambulance as well," Iain told the dogwalker.

real
♡

Nina was dry, and she was at Iain's house again, because Iain had insisted.

"As soon as we get a statement," the cop in charge had said.

"As soon as she's warm," Iain had answered. "I'm taking her home. If you want to stop me doing that, you'll have to arrest me. Or you lot can come with us. Your choice."

He'd refused a lift in the police car, too. "If they put us in there," he'd told a shivering Nina, "who knows where they'll take us? We're going home. If you need me to carry you, tell me."

She hadn't needed him to. She'd walked. She'd looked inside the ambulance as they'd passed it and seen Matthias being lifted inside on a stretcher, an oxygen mask on his face and a paramedic already hauling out equipment. Raoul was climbing in beside him along with another cop, and the two bodyguards looked like they wanted to be in there as well. It appeared, though, that the uniformed men around them had other ideas.

Now, Nina was sitting on the couch in Iain's lounge in dry clothes, with a blanket around her and Iain's arm providing some additional support. They'd been separated during the questioning, while she'd gone over the story again and again, and all she'd wanted was to have him with her.

"How is he?" she finally asked. "Matthias?" She didn't know if she wanted him to be dead, or if she wanted him not to be. She just wanted him to be *gone*.

"Don't know," the senior police officer said. "Unconscious when they pulled him from the water, they said."

"You'll tell us when you know," Iain said, and it wasn't a question.

"We'll tell you. If he's charged, you'll both need to give evidence, eventually. Assuming he recovers, of course."

"And if you can hold onto him," Nina said. "He's the head of his country, in case I didn't make that clear. They'll make a push to get him back."

"Not now, he isn't," the man said. "Now, he's suspected of a serious offence on New Zealand soil, and he'll be in hospital with a guard on the door."

"What about Raoul—the other man in the ambulance?" Nina asked. "What about the bodyguards?"

"Being questioned," the officer said. "I'm guessing that somebody will be watching them going wheels-up and on their way out of the country before much longer." He put his pad back into his pocket and stood up, along with his partner. "I'll be back later with a statement for you to sign. You'll be here?"

Nina looked at Iain, and he opened his mouth, started to say something, then gave a faint, lopsided grin and said, "Reckon you'd better answer that."

"Yes," Nina said. "I'll be here."

It took a few minutes after the police had left for the two of them to get to the point of talking. It seemed Nina had to cry first, to rest her head against Iain's chest and finally let it go. The pain, and the fear. The effort, and the panic. When she'd been running, and struggling, and drowning. The overwhelming relief when she'd realized whose arms she was in, when she'd realized she was safe. She cried all of it out, and he held her tight and didn't say anything. He didn't have to. He'd been there.

She sat back at last, her eyes and nose streaming, and took a couple ineffectual swipes at them. "Help," she said weakly.

He got up and brought back a box of tissues, and she mopped up, laughed a little, and managed to say, "Some class, huh?"

"No," he said. "Some guts." Which may have set her off again.

"Thanks for coming," she was finally able to say. "Thanks for saving me."

"Anytime," he said. "And I mean that."

She gave him a watery smile, rested against him again, and tucked her legs up under her, and he put his arm around her and pulled her in closer.

"You wrote me a letter, too," she said after a minute.

His arm tightened around her shoulder. "Well, a text."

"A letter," she said firmly. "A beautiful letter. If I try to tell you how it made me feel, I'll cry again."

"If I try to tell you how *I* feel," he said, "I'll probably cry myself. So that's two of us."

She smiled at him again, not caring that her eyes were sure to be red and swollen, her face sure to be blotchy. Not caring how she looked. That didn't matter to Iain right now. He saw all of her, and he loved her anyway. She could never be ugly to him, just like he could never be ugly to her.

Because they were Real.

epilogue

♡

It was October, Iain had two weeks off before he left for the European tour, and this time, Nina *had* made absolutely sure she'd be available to spend them with him. Starting with visiting his family. She hadn't managed much more than a few dinners with his mum and dad when they'd all traveled to see Iain play, and another short stay by his granddad. When she'd been in New Zealand, that is.

It had been more than frightening to put her requirements in front of her agent during that February meeting, to believe that she could do more than accept the bookings she was given. But she'd done it anyway, and after a month or so, Andrea had come back with a contract Nina could definitely live with. For the next two years, she would be the face of the cosmetics line for one of the most prestigious French brands on the planet. No lingerie, and no swimsuits. Nothing but elegance. Evening gowns, manicured nails, and most of all, her soulful face. That was what they'd wanted. Not just her body. Her image.

She'd sold the California house within a few months and had been glad to see it go. Her mum had organized the whole thing, and Nina had paid her a commission for her efforts and been happy to do it.

Things had stayed frosty between them all the same until Nina had arranged for her mum to fly to Australia to visit her parents in September, when New Zealand's All Blacks had played Australia's Wallabies in the first of the matches that would decide the Bledisloe Cup. Nina had sat and cheered Iain on in the company of her mum and grandparents, and even though her granddad had worn his yellow Wallabies jersey and waved his flag, he'd taken the All Blacks' win with philosophical grace. And best of all, when Nina's mum had met Iain over breakfast on the morning of the match, the frost had gone some way toward thawing.

"I'm not saying he's a prince," she'd told Nina over a coffee the next day. "But then, princes aren't necessarily all they're cracked up to be."

"No," Nina had said. "They're not, are they?"

Matthias had never fully recovered from his adventure in the sea. The water he'd inhaled and Iain's energetic efforts had resulted in pneumonia and a broken arm, but he'd recovered from those. The mild brain damage he'd suffered from his near-drowning, on the other hand, not to mention the criminal conviction—those hadn't worked out so well for him. After an emergency session of the Privy Council, Matthias had been given his own wing of the palace, and Raoul was serving a new prince. Prince Andreas of Neuenstein. Reportedly a much finer human being.

"And Iain," Nina's mum had continued. "Iain's— something. I'll say that for him. He's something."

Nina's satisfied, secret smile had curved around the rim of her cup. "The Incredible Hulk, that's what I thought when I met him. It's what I still think. He's a pretty irresistible combination of everything I like best, even when I didn't know it *was* what I liked. And I know it upsets you, Mum," she'd gone on, taking her mother's hand across the little table. "I know it isn't the future you had mapped out for me. But I couldn't leave him if I tried, and he couldn't let me go. I never believed in 'meant to be,' but maybe I do now. He's my other half. He's so different from me, and he's my perfect match. And I'm happy in a way I've never been." The tears had stood in her eyes, and she'd squeezed her mother's hand and said, "I want you to be happy, too. But I have to take this chance. I have to take my life in my own hands."

"Whoever said you shouldn't?" Her mother had sounded cross, but her own eyes hadn't been quite dry, either. "If I'd had somebody like that, I'd have taken him, too, no worries. And I'm on track to do better without you than I did with you, so you know. Got three girls I'm working with, and one of them's going straight to the top."

"That's great, Mum. Long as you'll still love me best."

"Well, of course I will. You're the only one who's my daughter."

Nina had come around the table, crouched down, and put her arms around her mother, and her mum's arms had gone out and pulled her in, fierce and hard.

"And you're the only one who's my mother," Nina had said, her cheek pressed to her mum's carefully made-up one. Thank you for taking me back."

"I never let you go. I couldn't. I'm your mum. I just told you. Now sit down and drink your coffee. We need to go shopping. I don't like that sweater of yours one bit."

Nina had laughed, had drunk her coffee and gone shopping, had asked her mum's advice on her clothes and listened to her opinions, and then had kissed her goodbye and gone home. Back to her own life.

Today, she and Iain were flying down to Nelson. She was beside him this time in the bulkhead seats, he was pointing out the graceful, razor-thin curve of Farewell Spit far below, and she had her hand tucked into his elbow. Then the plane was descending, and they were arriving. Back to one of her favorite places on earth, and beside her favorite person.

♡♡♡

The first day Iain had planned to spend with his family was almost over, and it had been a good one. He'd taken Nina kayaking, and when they'd pulled up onto a beach, she'd gone into the sea as far as her knees and come out shivering. She wasn't much heavier than she'd been the day he'd met her. A few kg's had made some difference, and she didn't look quite so fragile and transparent now, but she still wasn't much chop in cold water.

The past seven months hadn't been without their ups and downs, but he still had her, even if she wasn't in his house, and it felt solid. It felt right. Especially when she was in his granddad's cottage, going around to touch the vase of flowers on the kitchen table, the yellow-flowered placemats.

"You're using Madeline's special things," she told Arthur. "I'll bet she'd have loved that. But you've cleaned out some, too. Her shoes aren't by the door anymore. That must have been hard."

The old man shrugged. "I don't need her shoes to remind me. That's not where her memory is."

Nina gave him a gentle hug and kissed his cheek. "Love lasts best inside, I think."

Arthur didn't answer that except for a clearing of his throat. "We going over there? That fish I caught won't keep, and I'm hungry."

Nina laughed. "We are. That's why we're here. To get you."

They went to the big house, and Nina made the salad while Iain roasted the potatoes, then turned on the barbecue and cooked the fish. The parts you did with heat. And when his parents came home, they all sat on the patio together and ate it. It was a bit chilly out there, but they rugged up and did it anyway, because the wisteria was in springtime bloom, and it was beautiful.

Afterwards, with the sun sinking toward the horizon, Iain asked, "You all right doing the washing up, Mum? I want to take Nina for a wee wander."

"You go on, darling," she said. "Your dad and I will do it together."

Iain's dad, in fact, had his arm around his wife, and was

looking like life could offer him nothing finer than doing the washing up with her. Yet another piece of Iain's life fallen back into place, or more than that. Surely it was better than before. His parents looked like newlyweds, contentment showing so clearly on both their faces.

"And I'm going home," Arthur said, pushing his chair back to stand. "You coming out fishing with me tomorrow morning, mate?" he asked Iain.

"Yeh," Iain said. "I'll be there." But just now, he was standing, taking Nina's hand, and pulling her to her feet. "Probably not as early as you'd like, though."

"Fish won't be biting, then," Arthur grumbled.

Iain laughed. "Hard lines. I've only got two weeks with this one, and I'm going to make the most of them."

After that, he walked with Nina down the track and onto the beach. The tide was low, the water calm, but they didn't walk far. Iain went to their tree and said, "Sit with me a moment, will you?"

She dropped to the sand beside him, resting her back against the low horizontal trunk, and looked out to the murmuring sea. They were quiet for a minute, and then she said, "I love seeing your parents like that. So happy. Amazing, isn't it?"

"Yeh. Because he tried."

"He told you?"

"He did. While I was giving him a hand in the maintenance shed today. Said they'd been to talk to somebody. A counselor. Could've knocked me over with a feather. Last thing I'd have thought my dad would do, or to tell me about if he had. But he said that he wanted me to know, in case I ever needed the information."

"Hmm." She had her long, jeans-clad legs pulled up, her cheek resting on her folded hands.

"He said," Iain told her, "that if it's worth it, it's worth taking a risk to keep it. Hardest thing he'd ever done, he said, and the best."

"Have you ever had a conversation like that with him?"

He had to smile at that. "No. And it wasn't so much of a conversation. What I've just told you was about the size of it."

"A man of few words, your dad. But I suppose what you do counts most, doesn't it?"

"It does. And I've got something to do myself. But I've got something to say as well. It may take a few more words than that."

She was lifting her head off her folded hands, sitting up straight. "OK. Shoot."

It was like waiting in the tunnels to run out before the match. When you couldn't wait to get stuck in, even though you couldn't see the outcome. When you knew that you could be walking back in there after eighty minutes gutted, or you could walk back elated, and the only way to find out which it would be was to play the game.

He filled his lungs with sea air, then took the box out of his pocket. He opened the square black-velvet box, and she looked at what was inside and didn't say anything.

Game on.

"This thing," he said. "It's more than it seems. I had it made by the same jeweler who made the necklace I bought you that day on Waiheke, when I loved you so much it hurt. I wanted a reminder of the day when I realized everything I felt about you. But I wanted it to be special for you, too. *More* special. So I did some other things as well. Granddad gave me Nan's ring, and I asked your own Gran, too. She gave me the one that had belonged to her mother. Her..." He may have had to stop for a moment. "Their engagement rings. They're both in here. The gold's melted down, part of the band, and the...the wedding band that goes with it as well. And these two diamonds?" He pointed out the small stones on either side of the huge round stone in the center. "These are from those rings. The big one, though—it's us. Surrounded by family, and the two of us in the center, solid, just like this. That's what I tried to do. That's what I hope this is. So— Nina. Sweetheart." He hauled in another breath and did it.

He planted a knee in the sand and took her hand in his. "I love you. Will you marry me?"

That was everything he'd practiced. Everything he had. She had one hand over her mouth, her eyes shining with tears above her shaking fingertips. Now, she dropped the hand and said, "I can't believe you did that. I can't believe you thought of it."

"Not an answer." He thought it was a "yes," but he had to know. He had to know *now*.

Her sweet face was so serious. "I want to say yes," she said. "So much. All I want to say is yes."

He swallowed hard and thought he was going to be sick.

Finally, when he thought she never would, she went on. "But I have to know. You want me, you want this, even though you know you'll get grumpy when I won't do what you want? Even though I'll cry, or I'll get mad, and you'll have to say you're sorry, and you'll hate it? Even though you'll have to forgive me sometimes, too, when I hurt *your* feelings? Even though you'll want a baby, and I'll say it isn't time yet, and I'll go off to the States or the UK and you'll miss me, and you'll be gone and I'll miss *you*? Even with all of that?"

"Oh, sweetheart." He was having some trouble with his voice, but he went ahead anyway. "Even with all of that. You're right, I'll want a baby. I'll want as many as you'll give me, and I'll probably want them sooner than you're ready, and I could grumble a bit about that, even though I'll try not to. I'll want you with me, and I'll get grumpy when you're gone too long, because I'll miss you. But none of that is what matters most. Mostly, I want you. You're my other shoe. We're not exactly a matched pair, I know. You're something so beautiful, and I'm more of a... gumboot. But we go together all the same. It's what you said. Walking together toward whatever it is, through everything that comes. One of us won't be dragging the other, no, but maybe that'll happen sometimes, too. Maybe sometimes, one will be doing more of the walking, holding the other one up. But that's all right, too.

I'm guessing that sometimes, it'll be you doing the holding."

She was crying for real now, and there may have been some tears in his own eyes. Sometimes, that was all right. Sometimes, it had to happen.

"Yes," she said. "That's what I want. *You're* what I want. So could you please put that ring on me? I want to wear it. I'm saying yes."

He took her hand in his and slid the ring onto her finger. The big stone shone bright and bold as love, and the smaller ones beside it nestled close, winking out their steady support.

"That's it, then," he told her. He looked at their joined hands, then into her eyes, as the clouds turned pink, the water turned that vibrant shade of sunset-blue, and the peace of this most special spot held them in its gentle embrace. "That's us started."

"No," she said. Not one bit tentative. Not one bit weak. Strong, and sure, and real. Shining as bright as the diamond on her finger. "We've already started. We're already on the road. We can't see what's ahead, but it doesn't matter. Whatever's around the corner, we're going to walk right through it. We're going to do it together."

a kiwi glossary

♡

A few notes about Maori pronunciation:
- The accent is normally on the first syllable.
- All vowels are pronounced separately.
- All vowels except u have a short vowel sound.
- "wh" is pronounced "f."
- "ng" is pronounced as in "singer," not as in "anger."

ABs: All Blacks
across the Ditch: in Australia (across the Tasman Sea). Or, if you're in Australia, in New Zealand!
advert: commercial
agro: aggravation
air con: air conditioning
All Blacks: National rugby team. Members are selected for every series from amongst the five NZ Super 15 teams. The All Blacks play similarly selected teams from other nations.
ambo: paramedic
Aotearoa: New Zealand (the other official name, meaning "The Land of the Long White Cloud" in Maori)
arvo, this arvo: afternoon

Aussie, Oz: Australia. (An Australian is also an Aussie. Pronounced "Ozzie.")

bach: holiday home (pronounced like "bachelor")

backs: rugby players who aren't in the scrum and do more running, kicking, and ball-carrying—though all players do all jobs and play both offense and defense. Backs tend to be faster and leaner than forwards.

bangers and mash: sausages and potatoes

barrack for: cheer for

bench: counter (kitchen bench)

berko: berserk

Big Smoke: the big city (usually Auckland)

bikkies: cookies

billy-o, like billy-o: like crazy. "I paddled like billy-o and just barely made it through that rapid."

bin, rubbish bin: trash can

binned: thrown in the trash

bit of a dag: a comedian, a funny guy

bits and bobs: stuff ("be sure you get all your bits and bobs")

blood bin: players leaving field for injury

Blues: Auckland's Super 15 team

bollocks: rubbish, nonsense

boofhead: fool, jerk

booking: reservation

boots and all: full tilt, no holding back

bot, the bot: flu, a bug

Boxing Day: December 26—a holiday

brekkie: breakfast

brilliant: fantastic

bub: baby, small child

buggered: messed up, exhausted

bull's roar: close. "They never came within a bull's roar of winning."

bunk off: duck out, skip (bunk off school)

bust a gut: do your utmost, make a supreme effort

Cake Tin: Wellington's rugby stadium (not the official name, but it looks exactly like a springform pan)

caravan: travel trailer
cardie: a cardigan sweater
chat up: flirt with
chilly bin: ice chest
chips: French fries. (potato chips are "crisps")
chocolate bits: chocolate chips
chocolate fish: pink or white marshmallow coated with milk
    chocolate, in the shape of a fish. A common treat/reward for
    kids (and for adults. You often get a chocolate fish on the
    saucer when you order a mochaccino—a mocha).
choice: fantastic
chokka: full
chooks: chickens
Chrissy: Christmas
chuck out: throw away
chuffed: pleased
collywobbles: nervous tummy, upset stomach
come a greaser: take a bad fall
costume, cossie: swimsuit (female only)
cot: crib (for a baby)
crook: ill
cuddle: hug (give a cuddle)
cuppa: a cup of tea (the universal remedy)
CV: resumé
cyclone: hurricane (Southern Hemisphere)
dairy: corner shop (not just for milk!)
dead: very; e.g., "dead sexy."
dill: fool
do your block: lose your temper
dob in: turn in; report to authorities. Frowned upon.
doco: documentary
doddle: easy. "That'll be a doddle."
dodgy: suspect, low-quality
dogbox: The doghouse—in trouble
dole: unemployment.
dole bludger: somebody who doesn't try to get work and lives
    off unemployment (which doesn't have a time limit in NZ)

Domain: a good-sized park; often the "official" park of the town.

dressing gown: bathrobe

drongo: fool (Australian, but used sometimes in NZ as well)

drop your gear: take off your clothes

duvet: comforter

earbashing: talking-to, one-sided chat

electric jug: electric teakettle to heat water. Every Kiwi kitchen has one.

En Zed: Pronunciation of NZ. ("Z" is pronounced "Zed.")

ensuite: master bath (a bath in the bedroom).

eye fillet: premium steak (filet mignon)

fair go: a fair chance. Kiwi ideology: everyone deserves a fair go.

fair wound me up: Got me very upset

fantail: small, friendly native bird

farewelled, he'll be farewelled: funeral; he'll have his funeral.

feed, have a feed: meal

first five, first five-eighth: rugby back—does most of the big kicking jobs and is the main director of the backs. Also called the No. 10.

fixtures: playing schedule

fizz, fizzie: soft drink

fizzing: fired up

flaked out: tired

flash: fancy

flat to the boards: at top speed

flat white: most popular NZ coffee. An espresso with milk but no foam.

flattie: roommate

flicks: movies

flying fox: zipline

footpath: sidewalk

footy, football: rugby

forwards: rugby players who make up the scrum and do the most physical battling for position. Tend to be bigger and more heavily muscled than backs.

fossick about: hunt around for something

front up: face the music, show your mettle

garden: yard

get on the piss: get drunk

get stuck in: commit to something

give way: yield

giving him stick, give him some stick about it: teasing, needling

glowworms: larvae of a fly found only in NZ. They shine a light
to attract insects. Found in caves or other dark, moist places.

go crook, be crook: go wrong, be ill

go on the turps: get drunk

gobsmacked: astounded

good hiding: beating ("They gave us a good hiding in Dunedin.")

grotty: grungy, badly done up

ground floor: what we call the first floor. The "first floor" is one
floor up.

gumboots, gummies: knee-high rubber boots. It rains a lot in
New Zealand.

gutted: thoroughly upset

Haast's Eagle: (extinct). Huge native NZ eagle. Ate moa.

haere mai: Maori greeting

haka: ceremonial Maori challenge—done before every All Blacks
game

halfback: rugby back (No. 9). With the first-five, directs the
game. Also feeds the scrum and generally collects the ball
from the ball carrier at the breakdown and distributes it.

hang on a tick: wait a minute

hard man: the tough guy, the enforcer

hard yakka: hard work (from Australian)

harden up: toughen up. Standard NZ (male) response to (male)
complaints: "Harden the f*** up!"

have a bit on: I have placed a bet on [whatever]. Sports gambling
and prostitution are both legal in New Zealand.

have a go: try

Have a nosy for… : look around for

head: principal (headmaster)

head down: or head down, bum up. Put your head down. Work
hard.

heaps: lots. "Give it heaps."

hei toki: pendant (Maori)

holiday: vacation

honesty box: a small stand put up just off the road with bags of fruit and vegetables and a cash box. Very common in New Zealand.

hooker: rugby position (forward)

hooning around: driving fast, wannabe tough-guy behavior (typically young men)

hoovering: vacuuming (after the brand of vacuum cleaner)

ice block: popsicle

I'll see you right: I'll help you out

in form: performing well (athletically)

it's not on: It's not all right

iwi: tribe (Maori)

jabs: immunizations, shots

jandals: flip-flops. (This word is only used in New Zealand. Jandals and gumboots are the iconic Kiwi footwear.)

jersey: a rugby shirt, or a pullover sweater

joker: a guy. "A good Kiwi joker": a regular guy; a good guy.

journo: journalist

jumper: a heavy pullover sweater

ka pai: going smoothly (Maori).

kapa haka: school singing group (Maori songs/performances. Any student can join, not just Maori.)

karanga: Maori song of welcome (done by a woman)

keeping his/your head down: working hard

kia ora: welcome (Maori, but used commonly)

kilojoules: like calories—measure of food energy

kindy: kindergarten (this is 3- and 4-year-olds)

kit, get your kit off: clothes, take off your clothes

Kiwi: New Zealander OR the bird. If the person, it's capitalized. Not the fruit.

kiwifruit: the fruit. (Never called simply a "kiwi.")

knackered: exhausted

knockout rounds: playoff rounds (quarterfinals, semifinals, final)

koru: ubiquitous spiral Maori symbol of new beginnings, hope kumara: Maori sweet potato.

ladder: standings (rugby)

littlies: young kids

lock: rugby position (forward)

lollies: candy

lolly: candy or money

lounge: living room

mad as a meat axe: crazy

maintenance: child support

major: "a major." A big deal, a big event

mana: prestige, earned respect, spiritual power

Maori: native people of NZ—though even they arrived relatively recently from elsewhere in Polynesia

marae: Maori meeting house

Marmite: Savory Kiwi yeast-based spread for toast. An acquired taste. (Kiwis swear it tastes different from Vegemite, the Aussie version.)

mate: friend. And yes, fathers call their sons "mate."

metal road: gravel road

Milo: cocoa substitute; hot drink mix

mince: ground beef

mind: take care of, babysit

moa: (extinct) Any of several species of huge flightless NZ birds. All eaten by the Maori before Europeans arrived.

moko: Maori tattoo

mokopuna: grandchildren

motorway: freeway

mozzie: mosquito; OR a Maori Australian (Maori + Aussie = Mozzie)

muesli: like granola, but unbaked

munted: broken

naff: stupid, unsuitable. "Did you get any naff Chrissy pressies this year?"

nappy: diaper

narked, narky: annoyed

netball: Down-Under version of basketball for women. Played like basketball, but the hoop is a bit narrower, the players wear skirts, and they don't dribble and can't contact each other. It can look fairly tame to an American eye. There are professional netball teams, and it's televised and taken quite seriously.

new caps: new All Blacks—those named to the side for the first time

New World: One of the two major NZ supermarket chains

nibbles: snacks

nick, in good nick: doing well

niggle, niggly: small injury, ache or soreness

no worries: no problem. The Kiwi mantra.

No. 8: rugby position. A forward

not very flash: not feeling well

Nurofen: brand of ibuprofen

nutted out: worked out

OE: Overseas Experience—young people taking a year or two overseas, before or after University.

offload: pass (rugby)

oldies: older people. (or for the elderly, "wrinklies!")

on the front foot: Having the advantage. Vs. on the back foot— at a disadvantage. From rugby.

Op Shop: charity shop, secondhand shop

out on the razzle: out drinking too much, getting crazy

paddock: field (often used for rugby—"out on the paddock")

Pakeha: European-ancestry people (as opposed to Polynesians)

Panadol: over-the-counter painkiller

partner: romantic partner, married or not

patu: Maori club

paua, paua shell: NZ abalone

pavlova (pav): Classic Kiwi Christmas (summer) dessert. Meringue, fresh fruit (often kiwifruit and strawberries) and whipped cream.

pavement: sidewalk (generally on wider city streets)

pear-shaped, going pear-shaped: messed up, when it all goes to Hell

penny dropped: light dawned (figured it out)

people mover: minivan

perve: stare sexually
phone's engaged: phone's busy
piece of piss: easy
pike out: give up, wimp out
piss awful: very bad
piss up: drinking (noun) a piss-up
pissed: drunk
pissed as a fart: very drunk. And yes, this is an actual expression.
play up: act up
playing out of his skin: playing very well
plunger: French Press coffeemaker
PMT: PMS
pohutukawa: native tree; called the "New Zealand Christmas
 Tree" for its beautiful red blossoms at Christmastime (high
 summer)
poi: balls of flax on strings that are swung around the head,
 often to the accompaniment of singing and/or dancing by
 women. They make rhythmic patterns in the air, and it's very
 beautiful.
Pom, Pommie: English person
pong: bad smell
pop: pop over, pop back, pop into the oven, pop out, pop in
possie: position (rugby)
postie: mail carrier
pot plants: potted plants (not what you thought, huh?)
pounamu: greenstone (jade)
prang: accident (with the car)
pressie: present
puckaroo: broken (from Maori)
pudding: dessert
pull your head in: calm down, quit being rowdy
Pumas: Argentina's national rugby team
pushchair: baby stroller
put your hand up: volunteer
put your head down: work hard
rapt: thrilled
rattle your dags: hurry up. From the sound that dried excrement

on a sheep's backside makes, when the sheep is running!

red card: penalty for highly dangerous play. The player is sent off for the rest of the game, and the team plays with 14 men.

rellies: relatives

riding the pine: sitting on the bench (as a substitute in a match)

rimu: a New Zealand tree. The wood used to be used for building and flooring, but like all native NZ trees, it was over-logged. Older houses, though, often have rimu floors, and they're beautiful.

Rippa: junior rugby

root: have sex (you DON'T root for a team!)

ropeable: very angry

ropey: off, damaged ("a bit ropey")

rort: ripoff

rough as guts: uncouth

rubbish bin: garbage can

rugby boots: rugby shoes with spikes (sprigs)

Rugby Championship: Contest played each year in the Southern Hemisphere by the national teams of NZ, Australia, South Africa, and Argentina

Rugby World Cup, RWC: World championship, played every four years amongst the top 20 teams in the world

rugged up: dressed warmly

ruru: native owl

Safa: South Africa. Abbreviation only used in NZ.

sammie: sandwich

scoff, scoffing: eating, like "snarfing"

selectors: team of 3 (the head coach is one) who choose players for the All Blacks squad, for every series

serviette: napkin

shag: have sex with. A little rude, but not too bad.

shattered: exhausted

sheds: locker room (rugby)

she'll be right: See "no worries." Everything will work out. The other Kiwi mantra.

shift house: move (house)

shonky: shady (person). "a bit shonky"

shout, your shout, my shout, shout somebody a coffee: buy a
   round, treat somebody
sickie, throw a sickie: call in sick
sin bin: players sitting out 10-minute penalty in rugby (or, in the
   case of a red card, the rest of the game)
sink the boot in: kick you when you're down
skint: broke (poor)
skipper: (team) captain. Also called "the Skip."
slag off: speak disparagingly of; disrespect
smack: spank. Smacking kids is illegal in NZ.
smoko: coffee break
snog: kiss; make out with
sorted: taken care of
spa, spa pool: hot tub
sparrow fart: the crack of dawn
speedo: Not the swimsuit! Speedometer. (the swimsuit is called a
   budgie smuggler—a budgie is a parakeet, LOL.)
spew: vomit
spit the dummy: have a tantrum. (A dummy is a pacifier)
sportsman: athlete
sporty: liking sports
spot on: absolutely correct. "That's spot on. You're spot on."
Springboks, Boks: South African national rugby team
squiz: look. "I was just having a squiz round." "Giz a squiz":
   Give me a look at that.
stickybeak: nosy person, busybody
stonkered: drunk—a bit stonkered—or exhausted
stoush: bar fight, fight
straight away: right away
strength of it: the truth, the facts. "What's the strength of that?"
   = "What's the true story on that?"
stroppy: prickly, taking offense easily
stuffed up: messed up
Super 15: Top rugby competition: five teams each from NZ,
   Australia, South Africa. The New Zealand Super 15 teams
   are, from north to south: Blues (Auckland), Chiefs
   (Waikato/Hamilton), Hurricanes (Wellington), Crusaders

(Canterbury/Christchurch), Highlanders (Otago/Dunedin).

supporter: fan (Do NOT say "root for." "To root" is to have (rude) sex!)

suss out: figure out

sweet: dessert

sweet as: great. (also: choice as, angry as, lame as ... Meaning "very" whatever. "Mum was angry as that we ate up all the pudding before tea with Nana.")

takahe: ground-dwelling native bird. Like a giant parrot.

takeaway: takeout (food)

tall poppy: arrogant person who puts himself forward or sets himself above others. It is every Kiwi's duty to cut down tall poppies, a job they undertake enthusiastically.

Tangata Whenua: Maori (people of the land)

tapu: sacred (Maori)

Te Papa: the National Museum, in Wellington

tea: dinner (casual meal at home)

tea towel: dishtowel

test match: international rugby match (e.g., an All Blacks game)

throw a wobbly: have a tantrum

tick off: cross off (tick off a list)

ticker: heart. "The boys showed a lot of ticker out there today."

togs: swimsuit (male or female)

torch: flashlight

touch wood: knock on wood (for luck)

track: trail

trainers: athletic shoes

tramping: hiking

transtasman: Australia/New Zealand (the Bledisloe Cup is a transtasman rivalry)

trolley: shopping cart

tucker: food

tui: Native bird

turn to custard: go south, deteriorate

turps, go on the turps: get drunk

Uni: University—or school uniform

up the duff: pregnant. A bit vulgar (like "knocked up")

ute: pickup or SUV

vet: check out

waiata: Maori song

wairua: spirit, soul (Maori). Very important concept.

waka: canoe (Maori)

Wallabies: Australian national rugby team

Warrant of Fitness: certificate of a car's fitness to drive

wedding tackle: the family jewels; a man's genitals

Weet-Bix: ubiquitous breakfast cereal

whaddarya?: I am dubious about your masculinity (meaning
    "Whaddarya ... pussy?")

whakapapa: genealogy (Maori). A critical concept.

whanau: family (Maori). Big whanau: extended family. Small
    whanau: nuclear family.

wheelie bin: rubbish bin (garbage can) with wheels.

whinge: whine. Contemptuous! Kiwis dislike whingeing. Harden
    up!

White Ribbon: campaign against domestic violence

wind up: upset (perhaps purposefully). "Their comments were
    bound to wind him up."

wing: rugby position (back)

wobbly; threw a wobbly: a tantrum; had a tantrum

Yank: American. Not pejorative.

yellow card: A penalty for dangerous play that sends a player off
    for 10 minutes to the sin bin. The team plays with 14 men
    during that time—or even 13, if two are sinbinned.

yonks: ages. "It's been going on for yonks."

about the author
♡

Rosalind James, a publishing industry veteran and former marketing executive, is an author of Contemporary Romance and Romantic Suspense novels published both independently and through Montlake Romance. She and her husband live in Berkeley, California with a Labrador Retriever named Charlie. Rosalind attributes her surprising success to the fact that "lots of people would like to escape to New Zealand! I know I did!"